A MAGNIFICENT
DISTURBANCE

Praise for Lee Lynch

"Lee Lynch has been writing lesbian fiction since the 1960s, and is an important influence in modern lesbian literature."—*RVA Magazine*

Sweet Creek

"Like Chaucer's pilgrims, Lynch's characters tell stories throughout the novel. The novel wanders through stories of the characters' past lives and present events at a leisurely pace. Chick, Donny, Jeep, and the women who comprise their closest circle of friends are compelling characters, and readers will want to know more about their motivations, fears, and dreams. Lynch has to be commended for tackling a novel of such grand scope. From characters who lived their early years deeply closeted to characters who have benefited from the pioneering work of those women who were brave enough to break away and blaze the trail to places like Waterfall Falls. These women—warts and all—show the reader that this pilgrimage is still underway."—*Story Circle Book Review*

Beggar of Love

"Lynch is the master of creating the 'everydyke,' championing the underdog and providing a protagonist with whom garden variety lesbians can relate."—*Lambda Literary Review*

"The highest recommendation I can give Lee Lynch's writing is that you will not mistake it for anyone else's. Her voice and imagination are uniquely her own. Lynch has been out and proudly writing about it for longer than many of us have been alive. In her new novel, *Beggar of Love*, she creates a protagonist, Jefferson (known by her surname), so fully realised that the story seems to distill the last several decades of lesbian life. Lee Lynch finds the words."
—*Lesbians of North London Reviews*

Lambda Literary Award Finalist
An American Queer: The Amazon Trail

"Thirty years ago, Lynch moved from the East Coast to the West Coast and started her amazing journey depicted throughout almost 400 'Amazon Trail' columns. Editor Ruth Sternglantz has distilled these through the selection of 73 Trails, providing the author's half-century perspective of lesbian life as lesbians have moved from invisibility to public life and even marriage—for most LGBT people in the United States...*An American Queer* follows the tradition of 'the personal is political' in an accessible quick read, both heartfelt and gentle, that stays in the reader's thoughts. It is recommended for all public and academic libraries."—*GLBT Reviews: ALA's Gay Lesbian Bisexual Transgender Round Table*

"This very fine collection of columns by Lee Lynch, spanning the period from the 1980s to 2010, is required reading for those who want to remember and for those who are hazy or inadequately informed about LGBT history. *An American Queer: The Amazon Trail* is not a stiff academic text. Lynch is a passionate advocate with a quiet humor, and her columns are an entertaining yet informative read."—*Carol Rosenfeld*

"Lynch, whose novels, such as *Old Dyke Tales* and *Sweet Creek*, have won numerous awards, deserves to be in the pantheon of legendary lesbian journalists since her columns straddle the literary and the journalistic, always contemporary in their look at queer women's culture and beyond."—*The Advocate*

"Some stories crawl under your skin, diving deeper until you can't separate yourself from them. Reading that kind of book is like throwing down a time marker, because who you were before is not who you are when you've finished it. And even when you try to explain to someone why it's so important to you, you may not be able to access the right words because you're trying to describe an experience, which is so much more than a plot or set of characters. And yet, try you must because all you want is for someone else to love the book as much as you do."—*Curve Magazine*

Rainbow Gap

"Sometimes it is hard to write a review because you can't find the words, in this case it's hard to find words big enough to describe such an epic tale...This is both a coming out and growing up story, but also a timeless work of literary fiction, with classic writing that draws you into its world. *Rainbow Gap* will win awards across the board, and deservedly so. It is simple in plot, but complex in emotion. It is a genuine classic telling of nothing more or less than real life. More than anything it's a story of the birth of our community and the fight to be openly who we are."—*Windy City Times*

"*Rainbow Gap* by Lee Lynch is a book so exquisite that I just want everyone to go read it. Like, seriously, stop reading this review, buy it and read it right now...*Rainbow Gap* is not only a wonderful, moving book, it's also an important book that should be required reading...it reminds us that we've been here before and we can do this again. I cannot recommend it highly enough."—*The Lesbian Review*

"[T]his book covers a broad period of lesbian history, seen through the eyes of two relatively ordinary women...A real feel-good novel: I can see I need to catch up with this author's back catalogue."—*The Good, the Bad, and the Unread*

Previous Books by the Author

Bold Strokes Books

Defiant Hearts

Accidental Desperados:
Book 2 of the Rainbow Gap Lesbian Family Saga

Rainbow Gap:
Book 1 of the Rainbow Gap Lesbian Family Saga

An American Queer: The Amazon Trail

The Raid

Beggar of Love

Sweet Creek

Naiad Press

Cactus Love	Dusty's Queen of Hearts Diner
Morton River Valley	Home in Your Hands
That Old Studebaker	The Swashbuckler
Sue Slate, Private Eye	Old Dyke Tales
The Amazon Trail	Toothpick House

Flashpoint Publications

Our Happy Hours, LGBT Voices from the Gay Bars,
Curated With S. Renee Bess

TRB Books

The Butch Cook Book, Edited with Sue Hardesty and Nel Ward

New Victoria Publishers

Rafferty Street

Off the Rag: Women Write About Menopause,
Edited with Akia Woods

Visit us at www.boldstrokesbooks.com

A MAGNIFICENT DISTURBANCE

by

Lee Lynch

2025

A MAGNIFICENT DISTURBANCE

ISBN 13: 978-1-63679-031-2

This Trade Paperback Original Is Published By
Bold Strokes Books, Inc.
P.O. Box 249
Valley Falls, NY 12185

First Edition: June 2025

CREDITS
EDITOR: RUTH STERNGLANTZ
PRODUCTION DESIGN: STACIA SEAMAN
COVER DESIGN BY ANN MCMAN

Acknowledgments

I have worked with many talented and caring people in the queer literary community. I have a special appreciation and the highest respect for Bold Strokes Books Publisher Len Barot. From the first time I contacted "Rad" at the urging of Connie Ward and author Shelley Thrasher, I knew I was working with a real dyke who was committed enough to lesbian literature not only to enlarge the field with her own stories, but, with her business acumen and foresight, to publish books for the whole queer community. I can't thank Rad enough for being the upstanding visionary trailblazer she is.

I am grateful as well to my exemplary editor, Ruth Sternglantz.

It is an honor to know my work is supported by the devoted professionals who keep the wheels turning at Bold Strokes Books: Sandy Lowe, Cindy Cresap, Stacia Seaman, Lee Ligon, and the proofreaders, among others.

Close to my heart are Lori Lake, Marianne K. Martin, Ellen Hart, KG MacGregor, Connie Ward, Cate Culpepper, and my Florida cousin Carol.

Mike Miller has been a terrific source of for information and inspiration at https://www.florida-backroads-travel.com/

This book is for Lainie Lynch, my inspiration, my unimaginably devoted wife, who has all my respect for her patience, acceptance, bright mind, love of literature, history, family and friends, quick sense of humor, free-flowing laughter, and all she teaches me. As Taylor Swift sings, "I'm so in love that I might stop breathing."

And to my valued friend Lori Lake, who has given and given and given to the lesbian writing community and to me.

CHARACTER LIST

Allison Millar: mayor of Four Lakes. Cullie's partner
Anika: MJ's elderly dog
Batson Vicker (Bat): Jaudon's older brother
Benedict Lam: Gran's gentleman caller
Berry Garland: Jaudon's partner, RN, MSW
Bo Beaudry: MJ's father
Cal: Jaudon's cousin and employee
Christina Obrenger: MJ's first girlfriend
Cullie Culpepper: sheriff's deputy, Allison's partner, Jaudon's longtime friend
Doug Obrenger: Christine's son
Duval Lanamore: Pansy Lanamore's son
Eddie Dill: Gran's late live-in boyfriend
Emil: Vonnie's coworker
Emma Jean: Christina's daughter
Emmett Ponder: attorney, Olive Ponder's son
Grady Lowe: Vonnie and Vaughn's father
Grammy (Lutie) and Gramps Garland: Berry and Opal's paternal grandparents
Gramps Binyon: Berry and Opal's maternal grandfather
Gran (Ida Tommie Binyon): Berry and Opal's maternal grandmother
Jaudon Vicker: Berry's partner, Beverage Bay owner
Jimmy Neal Skaggs: RN, Rigo's partner
John Lau: Bat Batson's Army buddy, business partner
Josiah Howell: troubled teen son of Opal and Klem Howell

Judy Fish: friend
June Binyon: Berry's mother, Gran's daughter
Kajen: Berry and Jaudon's cat
Klem Howell: Opal's husband
Laura Bathgate: Berry's coworker, Olive Ponder's sister
Leslie Gardner: Gran's caregiver, health center admin
Lollie Lowe: Momma's sister, Vonnie's mother
Mercie Lewis: women's group member, RN, partner of Judy Fish
Michelle: Shady's niece
Miki Vicker: Jaudon's niece
MJ Beaudry (Emma Jean): co-owner VONCO, Vonnie's partner
Momma Vicker: Jaudon and Bat's mother, Beverage Bay founder
Mrs. Obrenger: Christine's mother
Nisa Larbi Lowe: Vaughn's wife
Officer Friendly (Jeff Maple): sheriff's deputy
Olive Ponder: manager at Beverage Bays, Jaudon's best work friend
Opal Howell: Berry's sister, wife of Klem
Pansy Lanamore (Mrs. Lanamore): owner Pansy's Café, MJ's champion
Patsy Beaudry: MJ's niece
Penny Slumkey: wife of Rich Slumkey
Perfecta Maldonado: women's group member, friend
Pops Vicker: Jaudon and Bat's father
Puddin: Jaudon, Berry, and Gran's dog
Rich Slumkey: attorney
Rigoberto Patate (Rigo): Jaudon's best friend from college
Rouie Waver: accountant, Jaudon's mentor
Roy Jack: Jaudon's cousin
Samantha O'Connor: women's group member
Shady: Tad's buddy, MJ's mentor
Stacey A. Ponder: Emmett Ponder's wife
Tad Lanamore: Pansy's son, Duval's brother
Tanice: Pansy Lanamore's restaurant dishwasher
Vaughn Lowe: co-owner VONCO, Vonnie's twin
Vergie Redfern: Vonnie Lowe's boss
Vivian Gainer: docent
Vonnie Lowe: social worker, MJ's partner, Vaughn's twin
Yan: health center supporter

CHAPTER ONE

MJ Beaudry

It was the thirteenth of June 1994 in Rainbow Gap, Florida.

MJ Beaudry, one foot on her tallest ladder, the other balanced in the air, stretched to a roof truss. She was replacing a metal joist hanger in Jaudon and Berry's prewar pole barn. It was so hot that the sun faded the sky to the lightest azure blue. She was damp and smelly from this Florida humidity, and the mosquitos ignored her bug spray. Were humans in fact meant to live in this wacko subtropical state where the concrete of overdevelopment covered lush and languid old Florida? She had a love/hate relationship with the heat, the state. The mosquitos she thoroughly detested.

A staccato siren on Eulalia Road was the least of her worries until an ambulance turned onto and bumped along potholed Pineapple Trail. Disturbed, a dark-winged fish hawk shot up from the pond to its roost. White egrets and pink roseate spoonbills lifted in a graceful silent retreat to their high perches. Nature's fantastic creatures took her breath away daily.

She'd made no progress persuading Jaudon to let her send a road guy to fill the potholes. Jaudon Vicker was close with a dollar when it came to work on her family homestead, despite the fact that she spent freely to maintain and upgrade her remaining five drive-through convenience stores, the Beverage Bays.

MJ continued working, her schedule tight. A new project started tomorrow, her biggest yet, converting a condemned hotel to modest, safe senior apartments, and she was jazzed. After that, she'd make good on her promise to take Vonnie, her life partner, to see the Beaudry hometown in Washington State, loath as she was to go there. Vonnie was having fun researching the place at the library, looking for signs of MJ's wackadoodle birth family.

The emergency must be at the one house between Jaudon and Berry's land and the four-acre natural pond, which the haughty snowbirds who lived there persuaded the county to officially name Rainbow Lake. Jaudon had laughed—silly to call it a lake when it was pond pines that thrived there, even though they also grew by lakes, in swamps, bogs, and savannas. Might as well call it Rainbow Swamp.

But no, the siren stopped too close. Was there a more plaintive sound in the world? It was like the doves who mourned incessantly in the tall oak behind the building.

Who was hurt? She half dangled as her airborne leg searched for a ladder rung. Once found, she scrambled down.

It had to be Gran. Dismay like lightning streaked through her. Berry's grandmother. Everyone's Gran. Eighty-one-year-old Gran was home alone.

Lithe and thin, MJ ran flat out to the house. A pair of EMTs trotted to the back of their rig, removed a gurney, and left it at the rescue truck. Her elderly dog, Anika, barked from the foldable pen MJ carried to jobs.

An EMT asked MJ, "You called 9-1-1?"

She found she was panting, but she wasn't winded, she was scared. "No, but Gran must be in trouble."

She led the two men to the focal points of Gran's life: the kitchen, her bedroom. Gran wasn't in the house. They ran out the kitchen door, to the kitchen garden. There sat Gran, leaning on the clothesline pole in her faded pink capris and capacious white T-shirt, short home-cut hair gray going white, clear-framed glasses askew.

Gran tried to speak through her newly lopsided mouth.

The electric-meter reader stooped beside her, his vehicle on Pineapple Trail, door open.

"I found her on the ground and hollered. No one came. I radioed dispatch to call 9-1-1."

She wrung her hands, felt the wetness of her black VONCO polo shirt under her arms, across the width of her back, and in the crotch of her black denim shorts. Despite the strap holding her big black-framed glasses, they repeatedly slid down her nose.

Gran can't die.

She thanked the meter reader and turned to the paramedics, who were securing Gran on a gurney.

One asked, "Is she used to this kind of heat?"

"Only all her life."

Gran told everyone she was born with a tan. Over eighty years, the lauded yet merciless Florida sun darkened her further. She had shortened with age and grown rounder. The furrows on her face might have started as wounds of hardship, but her smile wrinkles balanced them out. Hers was the face of a woman who'd seen it all and come through, as Gran would say, happier than ol' Blue layin' on the porch chewin' on a big ol' catfish head.

It was time for the call she was dreading. No way she wanted to be the one to break the news to Berry. She went inside and watched the medics as she took a couple of long breaths before dialing the Buffalo Street Beverage Bay store, where Jaudon kept what passed for her office behind the walk-in coolers. "Jaw-dun, pick up," she shouted at the phone.

As soon as MJ explained, Jaudon, in her raspy voice, said, "I'll track down Berry," and broke their connection. Gran had raised Berry from the age of eight, shaped her into an empathetic, upstanding woman. Gran ran their household.

In a flurry of activity, the men wheeled Gran to the rescue van.

Gran made feeble mewling noises before the EMTs affixed an oxygen mask to her face.

"Where to?" asked MJ.

"Lecoats Memorial."

"Berry will meet you at the hospital, Gran," she shouted, then puffed out her cheeks in embarrassment for assuming Gran didn't hear her. Gran grimaced, a pained smile in her eyes. She knew Gran had her number from day one and had always seen right through her insolent runaway posturing. It wasn't something she broadcasted to one and all, but Gran had held and rocked her more than once over the years. Sometimes she needed to talk with a grandmother figure.

MJ led Anika into the house and made sure the doors were locked. She took off, squeezed her trusty red GMC Jimmy through yellow lights, avoided main roads, and entered the hospital in under ten minutes, despite the perpetual lack of parking spots.

Crazily, Berry was already at the ER and in with Gran. Jaudon paced the waiting room in her cargo shorts, cotton Hawaiian shirt, and a red vest embroidered with the name of her business. She was Berry's life partner of twenty-one years.

Jaudon looked dazed, was unable to form words, and finally

blurted to MJ, "Cullie left not two minutes ago." Jaudon's best friend Cullie Culpepper was a sheriff's deputy and lovers with Allison Millar, the mayor of Four Lakes. "Cullie heard our address on her radio and gave the ambulance an escort. Berry was already here at a training session."

Laura Bathgate, Berry's close work friend, came in, breathing hard. "Is Berry's Gran okay? What can I do?"

Through an ache that nearly paralyzed her, MJ said, "We don't have any answers. Yet."

Laura dropped her oversized pocketbook on a seat and walked over to Jaudon, pressing her close, rocking her. "One of the docs at work said it brought to mind stroke symptoms. He said there's a respectable partial to full recovery rate from stroke."

CHAPTER TWO

Berry Garland

Early fall 1994

Nineteen ninety-four was not the best of years for Berry Garland. She sat on the wraparound porch under a metal roof overhang at the Vicker house, her home since childhood, in a newly repainted white rocker, mulling things over, something she seldom had time to do.

It was already fall and President Clinton was expected to start the country moving in the right direction, and it was, economically. Socially, he got it wrong in his effort to protect gay people—no one could do that. Not in Florida, anyway, where Johnny-come-lately sun-seekers with their traditional values were closing minds.

The president kept the country out of wars, too. But his and Hillary Clinton's health care reform efforts failed, and Berry had counted on them to help the Center succeed.

Her friend and coworker, Larry Riyanto, died of a bacterial infection in his lungs after losing his life partner Gregory to AIDS a year earlier. Two young, excellent physicians, gifts to the human race, dead and gone, from one tragic needle stick. She and Jaudon worried about their closest male friends, Rigo Patate and Jimmy Neal Skaggs, but curly, copper-headed, husky Rigo, after many youthful indiscretions, had pledged fidelity to big Jimmy Neal lest he lose the love of his life— his *manatee man*. That decision, and Jimmy Neal's insistence on it, may have saved their lives.

She was encouraged that Jaudon's stores, now legally called the Beverage Bay and Bakery, had slowly taken on new, more profitable lives with the addition of drive-through sweet tea, hot and iced coffee, high markup impulse buys at the register, and a line of baked goods featuring Caribbean-style specialties: coco bread, cassava pone, and fry bake made by the Lanamore brothers, friends who, with their mother, owned Pansy's Pastries.

Convincing Jaudon to accept a coffee maker and microwave oven was a job in itself.

"Put radiation in my stores?" Jaudon had protested. "Not on your life. I read up on them, and they leak."

Mrs. Lanamore chided her. "Not that kind of radiation. A microwave won't harm you one iota. I don't know anymore what I'd do at the restaurant without mine."

Once she gave in, Jaudon quickly learned how to operate the coffee maker but approached the microwave as if entering a den of lions. On the first day she used it, Jaudon shoved in spicy beef patties. When she opened the door, steam spewed pepper in her face. Fortunately, Olive Ponder—her manager, close friend, and the first person she ever hired against Momma's wishes—was a veteran of civil- and voter-rights demonstrations. She hastily steered the coughing, spluttering Jaudon into the employee bathroom to irrigate her eyes, out of sight of their customers.

Berry's careers were fulfilling, but demanding. As an RN, she'd worked at an ob-gyn practice for the past twenty-two years, since college graduation. Evenings, as a licensed mental health counselor, she met with private clients. On Saturdays, she and her friend Laura Bathgate, the receptionist at work, unattached and available to volunteer, operated a free women's health clinic out of Gran's old camper van, which she, Laura, and Jaudon had giddily refurbished with a tiny reception counter, curtained exam room, a major supply of pink sponges, a sterilizer and examining table, the essential medical instruments, children's books, and educational handouts. Berry and Laura envisioned the clinic, and the doctors at the practice made it legal by donating space in their parking lot, and supplying electricity, water, a phone line, supplies, and supervisory time.

She was worn slap out.

And thoroughly caught off guard by Gran's stroke.

Gran Binyon had taken her in after Berry's parents went west on their motorcycle, not to be seen nor heard from to this day. Berry continued to pine for them but, at age forty-three, had mostly gotten past thinking she'd driven them away with some childish misbehavior. No one but Jaudon and Gran knew the deep hurt Berry carried. To this day, she sometimes woke, her cheeks wet with tears, to find Jaudon tenderly holding her.

When Gran lost everything except the acreage she inherited on Stinky Lane to a large sinkhole—including Eddie Dill, her roughshod, live-in man friend—Pops, Jaudon's father, offered her and Berry shelter at the Vicker home down the road, which had started as a so-called cracker house, expanded and updated little by little over generations of the Vicker family. The sinkhole spared Gran's twenty-foot travel trailer, so Pops Vicker, in his pickup truck, pulled it over the railroad tracks, across Eulalia Road, and onto his property.

Initially, Gran lived in the trailer. In the house, Pops and Momma had the main bedroom, and Jaudon and Berry bunked together in Jaudon's room. Bat Vicker, Jaudon's older brother, kept claim to the third bedroom until his Army stint in Vietnam ended and he relocated out West. Gran prettied up his room and moved in.

Eventually, Momma and Pops Vicker moved into an upscale brick house in an established and moneyed neighborhood that reflected what Momma considered was her status in the county. She had, after all, started with a roadside stand and grew it into a chain of seven stores. Once the dementia hit Momma, Pops moved them to a more reasonable house in the supersized fifty-five-plus development of Sun City Center, just south of Tampa. Pops assured Jaudon—who took over the business—if she never made another dime in profit, he and Momma would be okay.

Berry, Jaudon, and Gran lived simply in the old Vicker homestead on Pineapple Trail, content as companions. How could they not be, surrounded as they were by flowers, trees, and shrubs that bloomed purple, yellow, peach, orange, red, pink, white—and the slews of butterflies and birds they drew.

A couple of pawpaw trees, heavy with green fruit in season, grew under great big oaks. The raccoons, possums, and birds were welcome to the custardy banana-papaya-mango-tasting fruits no one in the house other than Gran found palatable. Uninvited, sabal palms and southern magnolias had grown without interference or special care. Birds loved the tall pignut hickory, and the wide southern sugar maples. A red-berried wild coffee hedge gave the household privacy from the increasing traffic along Eulalia Road.

❖

Berry expected she never would overcome the shock of the split second Jaudon exploded through the hospital conference room door, beckoning her with frenzied hand gestures. She knew immediately that something had happened to Gran, her sole living blood family, as far as she knew.

"The meter reader found Gran on the ground under the rotary wash line, a basket of wet clothes by her side, clothespins everywhere. Why won't she use our perfectly functional dryer?"

"She likes the smell of the outdoors on her clothes," Berry answered as they ran from her meeting to the emergency room.

"It's an ischemic stroke," the ER doctor told them, explaining needlessly to Berry that a blood vessel to the brain was blocked by a clot.

"Can Gran speak?"

"She initially reported experiencing headache and loss of balance, so she hasn't lost every communication skill."

"Brain swelling?"

"No. She's beginning to use her extremities, and her lethargy is dissipating already."

"May we see her? We're her granddaughters. I'm an RN, and we three live together."

Jaudon was often taken for a man with her barely tamable facial hair, short, straw-straight, straw-blond hair, roughhewn eyebrows, and a semipermanent cowlick. She'd occasionally tell someone that before Momma had her, Mother Nature put her in a tumbler, bleached her, and fabricated a hash of would-bes and could-bes. Throughout her childhood, she carried herself with self-protectively forward flexed shoulders. The position became permanent and served the welcome added purpose of camouflaging her breasts, which Jaudon complained were cumbersome and embarrassing. Berry believed her love and the longevity of their bond helped sustain Jaudon's self-worth.

The doctor's glance took in Jaudon, and he became snippy. "I require peace and quiet for my patients."

Berry sniped, "Yes, Doctor. And they're normally hospitalized up to a week if there are no complications. A care team will evaluate her and come up with a rehab plan. Now, I want to see her."

Berry took vacation time to stay at Gran's side in the hospital until five days later, when she, Jaudon, and Gran met with Berry's old friend, Mercie Lewis, who was now a discharge planning nurse.

"No more bedpans for you, Nursie Mercie?" Jaudon teased.

Mercie slid her glasses down her nose and gave Jaudon a severe Whoopi Goldberg look. "Your sidekick hasn't changed, has she?"

Berry, laughing, said, "I hope she never will."

Slowly, Gran managed to say through her half smile, "Never will. Guaran-teed."

Mercie laughed out loud. "I see you haven't lost your sense of humor either, Mrs. Binyon. I almost didn't recognize you on the paperwork since I never knew you as anyone but Gran."

Berry had started right away to induce Gran to talk. In short spurts, she read her snippets from the local papers and Gran's beloved supermarket checkout stand tabloids. Gran's comments went from barely decipherable to distorted to today's labored slurring.

"I understand you're going home and not to a rehab center. The care team has you scheduled for outpatient physical and speech therapy. They bragged that your progress is remarkable."

"Butter's not slipping off *my* biscuit yet," Gran said.

Berry said, "You're also covered for some sessions with my favorite person, Judy Fish. You remember Judy, Gran? She's made a point of doing your respiratory therapy whenever she was available."

"Crazy women's meetings in our living room. Stirred up trouble, didn't you?" slurred Gran.

"And elected Allison mayor as a result."

Berry asked, "Has it been twenty years already?"

"It has." Mercie turned a photograph of Judy to face them.

Jaudon and Berry grinned at each other.

"Oh, I know you two think you were matchmaking in those days, but we would have figured it out. After we got together, Judy went to school and studied respiratory therapy. This picture was taken when she was promoted to head up the department."

Berry clapped her hands together. "You married well."

"So did Judy," said Jaudon.

"You got that right, girl. Let's do some initial scheduling for you, Gran. You have someone to take you to appointments, help you do your home exercises? I know these girls are as workaholic as you can get."

"Benedict," suggested Jaudon. Benedict Lam was Gran's gentleman caller. She had stayed over with him in his comfortable home occasionally, but his son and daughters shamed him from continuing that and badgered him until he moved into an assisted living apartment.

Berry chastised herself for thinking it but suspected they were worried about Gran claiming their inheritance. "We'll interview a private home health aide tomorrow," she told Mercie.

"You have our list of certified aides?" Mercie asked.

"Allison printed the county list for us. You remember Allison from our group."

"'Course she does," Jaudon said. "Allison Millar posters were everywhere when she ran for mayor of Four Lakes and won. She and Berry never stopped being tight as two thieves."

Mercie was nodding, repeating, "Uh-huh, uh-huh. That Allison was a firebrand from day one. Judy and I went house to house for her campaign. We get together once in a while. Allison's put on considerable weight since her radical feminist days. Cullie calls her porky, and I ask, what does that make me—zaftig? We spend most of our working days at a desk or a boardroom table. I admire Allison for struggling to change the system from within."

Jaudon's gruff voice was proud. "Cullie clowns around, but I'll be dog if she hasn't taken on an air of authority."

"Will wonders never cease," said Mercie, smiling and shaking her head. "Your gran's gone slightly pasty."

"You're not k-k-keeping me here. Doc said home today." Her eyes were locked on Mercie.

Mercie raised her palms. "Best if you stay calm, Gran, or you'll be in more trouble. I only need a couple of signatures and I'll wheel you to your car myself."

Jaudon quickly stood. "I'll bring the car around on the double, Nurse Lewis, ma'am." She saluted.

"Our silly Jaudon," Berry boasted.

"Our Jaudon keeps me laughing," Gran said.

"Then keep her around, right, Gran? She's healthy for Berry and you."

Gran had difficulty signing her name but went slowly and finished with a flourish. Berry saw Mercie's encouraged look and gave her a hug.

Mercie kissed Berry and Gran on the cheeks. "You'll be right as rain soon."

Jaudon was outside the front entrance and gave a formal bow before she helped Gran into the front seat. Berry buckled Gran's seat belt with care. She raised crossed fingers to Mercie.

CHAPTER THREE

Berry Garland

Berry had gotten home from work not ten minutes earlier when she heard a knock and the screen door opened. MJ entered with her customary fleetness, followed by a new applicant.

"Quick intro," MJ said. "This is Leslie Gardner, the super caregiver I told you I met when Vaughn and I rehabbed a house for that lady with a disability. Leslie, this is Berry Garland, Gran's grandchild, and that's her partner, Jaudon Vicker. You're okay on directions home?"

"Don't worry," said Leslie with an elfin smile on her not-quite-white, not-quite-dark face. She gestured to a compact yellowish Toyota pickup with a shell. "The Canary and I will manage."

"Git along, then," Jaudon said to MJ. "We know you have more construction projects than Carter has liver pills."

"Come on to the kitchen, Leslie." On the way, Berry ejected her Barbra Streisand cassette tape from their compact stereo system. References or not, she was encouraged by Leslie's promptness and manner. Would the old Vicker house, with its high humidity, lack of air-conditioning—they kept the windows open and let the sun in to fight mold—and its cooked-in odors—currently deep-fried hush puppy oil—put her off?

Berry said, "Gran is watching her soaps right now. She's addicted."

"I'm used to that," said Leslie. "My own mother can't miss an episode of *Guiding Light*."

"Did she carry on when that character died last year?"

"She was mad enough to write a complaint to CBS."

For the first time, Berry and Leslie laughed together.

Leslie was a short and slender composed woman, heavy-browed with wavy brown hair tumbling down her shoulders, hoop earrings the circumference of curtain rings peeping through. She was dressed in white pants and a coral V-neck T-shirt under a lace-collared denim jacket. Around her neck, much the same as a flashing neon sign to Berry, was a dainty silver disc necklace depicting entwined woman symbols.

"A stroke," Leslie said. "MJ told me."

"When I first saw Gran in the hospital, I watched her light flicker."

"I know. You're like, helpless. Is that what she likes to be called—Gran?"

"You can ask her. Ida Tommie Binyon is her actual name."

"Seminole?"

"How'd you know?"

"I went to school with a Robert Tommie."

"Come sit awhile."

Jaudon silently supplied glasses of sweet tea. Berry smiled her thanks for the help.

They chatted about Leslie's experience in caregiving and Gran's circumstances.

Jaudon was at the counter, fixing a new pitcher of tea. "Do you have a nursing degree?"

Leslie started to speak, hesitated, pushed her hair from her face. Her earrings glinted. "My parents were college grads and passed on their love of reading and learning. I was a wild child, restless and impulsive. I believe I've outgrown that." She looked up. "If you value experience as much as a degree, I'd love to take care of your grandmother—providing she likes me and you approve. MJ said she's a gutsy, fun lady."

Jaudon snorted. "Knowing MJ, she gave you every fact she knows about Gran and threw in a short history of the Seminoles. She knows everything."

"Gran's gutsy, alright," Berry said, pretty sure Leslie, wild child or not, was right for Gran. It didn't have to be forever—the doctor said Gran would improve. "Wouldn't you know, our jobs are most demanding when Gran needs us most. Jaudon and I can't spare the time. Are you free for live-in care? Gran's put her foot down to care facilities."

"I have a cottage rental between gigs, but with business so decent, I'm considering giving it up."

Jaudon said, "Berry works a paid job, and she's halfway to opening a health center for low-income women."

"Don't be bragging on me."

"We need your dream," said Jaudon. "I'll brag about it on billboards, on TV, with a thousand flyers."

Leslie nodded vigorously. "Can you pull off that kind of revolution? Health care is nowhere near the level we need, and what's there is too often inaccessible or inadequate."

Jaudon slapped her thighs. "Jumping Jehoshaphat. You're a believer too."

"I've seen too much abuse. In high school I worked at convalescent homes to save up for college. I discovered big companies want the patients' fees but scrimp on care. Sometimes helpless people are left to lie in their own waste or snooze in wheelchairs for hours between meals. I tried to change that at Southdale Nursing Center, but one suggestion after the other, I was turned down. Which is why I work on my own for private clients who find me by word of mouth." She laid her certifications and a list of references on the table.

Jaudon reviewed them while Berry said, "Tell me who you are, what you like—whatever you're willing to share to introduce yourself."

Leslie was originally from their area. Her mother and father worked in property management. "The work wasn't always steady, but it kept us in books and newspapers. My mother was massively smart. My brother and I deserved graduate degrees after growing up with her. I was supposed to finish college but fell in love with a musician, and we bummed around women's music festivals and any other performance spaces we scoped out."

"And you're settled here?"

"I'm not sure *settled* is the best word. Our last stop together was in Tampa. She took up with a band and went on tour, never to return."

"Oh, poor baby," Berry said. "That was out-and-out rotten."

"I should have known no idyll lasts forever. I was eighteen, she was twenty-four. She was going places with her music, and well, she was more passionate about music than about me. We had a lot of fun together."

"Were you a hippie? Did you take drugs?" Jaudon asked. Her eyes shone with fascination. Berry anticipated she would ask more off-the-topic questions than on.

"Hippies were not my generation, but my inner Good Samaritan clamored to show her face. I saw a lot of sisterhood on the road, but I saw a lot I didn't care for too. After I faced the fact that my ex was gone, I took a job in another nursing home—it was the only way I knew to support myself. I kept at it, rented a cottage, planted a vegetable garden, and discovered a crying need for private in-home care helpers."

"I'm impressed. For someone so young, you've done a lot," Jaudon said.

"Not that young. I'm twenty-nine."

"Oh, honey," said Berry. "You took charge of your life and forged a career out of thin air. You're a reader too. Would you read to Gran? She's partial to Florida anything, but especially Florida history."

"As long as history doesn't put your gran to sleep."

"Jiminy," Jaudon said. "Sleep's smack dab what the doctor ordered."

Berry touched Jaudon's hand. "The discharge nurse encouraged lots of rest, but Gran's resisting, complaining we make her go to bed with the chickens."

"She loves to be outdoors," said Jaudon. "The call of a pileated woodpecker or a tree full of sparrows makes her day."

Leslie's laughter was quiet and genuine. "Oh, count me in on bird listening. I think I'd like your grandmother scads. As a matter of fact, I was pleasantly shocked to see a big-headed shrike on my way in, patiently sitting on a branch, watching for prey the way they do, for hours."

"They have a nest in some thorny shrubbery behind the house. For myself, I love the catbird's song," said Berry. "There's something sweet about it."

They discussed wages. Leslie wanted everything done legally to be eligible for Social Security. She commanded a higher rate than most nurse assistants because of her supplemental training in stroke care, medication administration, balance issues, pain management, and elder financial management. Her own health insurance would be unaffordable if she charged less.

"I might be able to put you on the store's plan and cover part of your premium if it would be cheaper than what you're paying," Jaudon said. "You're freeing me up to work, and that makes you an employee in my eyes."

"Anything is cheaper than what I've got now. Insurance is a racket."

Jaudon said, "Something is out of kilter up in Washington, D.C., and those big insurers, seems to me they're the ones calling the shots too much of the time. Thanks to whatever games they play, insurance has become too dear for regular folks."

"They've squirmed their way between the patients and their medical providers. I have some ugly stories about big business and politicians."

Watching Leslie and Jaudon talk made up her mind. She was ready to hire this intelligent and, she hoped, grounded twenty-nine-year-old if her references held up.

Before she said another word, Gran needed to meet Leslie. It took a lot for Gran to disapprove of anyone, but her dead-on intuition was uncanny. It was four o'clock on the flower-shaped kitchen clock, the end of Gran's last soap opera.

She told Leslie, "Gran lost some vision in one eye, but we see signs of improvement. She lives to cook and garden and is real motivated to regain full function of her limbs, as well as her mind and speech. The physical therapist says she's too weak to navigate around the house, so you'd need to help with mobility too, when neither of us is here." She hesitated, worried this would be too much to ask. "Your days off might fluctuate if I'm stuck at work and Jaudon's called in to cover at one of the stores. Are you able to finagle that?"

"I'm flexible most of the time."

Berry exhaled with relief.

Jaudon barked a laugh. "Flexible? I'll hire you to work at the Bays."

Leslie laughed too. "My only commitments are yoga class twice a week and the meditation group I lead, all in the evenings."

"I wish the Women's Health Center was up and running right now. You have a lot to offer."

Berry led the way to Gran's room. Sunshine pried through the slots of the blinds, casting bars of light across Gran in her recliner. Kajen the cat huddled on her lap, bony in her declining years, but a feline healer. Berry turned off Gran's TV and reverently stroked her hand. Gran's head bobbed up, eyes blinking.

"Fell 'sheep," said Gran. She struggled to hide the damage to her speech.

It hurt like crazy to see her weakened.

Berry made introductions, striving to disguise how optimistic she was about Leslie.

"You're going to try and take me on? Be my babysitter? You

think you can handle me?" cracked Gran. "I'll be r-r-right as rain soon 'nough, and you'll be out of a job."

Leslie's laugh was self-assured. "Are you that rambunctious you need a handler?"

She liked that Leslie straightaway made Gran laugh and left them to get acquainted while she and Jaudon consulted in the living room.

"I'll talk to Rouie Waver about the ins and outs of putting Leslie on our payroll." Rouie was the Beverage Bays' longtime accountant, retired except for Jaudon's stores. "She'd be covered by worker's comp that way."

"Do you think Leslie's the one?"

"It's as if she's kin already, whatever the references turn out to say."

Berry lowered her head and opened herself to the Great Spirit of Gran's—and her own—ancestors. Gran taught her what had been passed down by Gran's grandmother. Young as she had been, Berry straight off knew to honor her connection to their ancestors by giving up meat at an early age. The Seminoles apologized to the animals they killed for food with a ritual of sweating and bathing after the hunt. They believed in the Great Spirit, and Berry learned to hear it inside herself. She sensed not a rumble of disfavor about Leslie Gardner.

Laughter came from Gran's room off and on for over a half hour before Leslie pushed Gran's wheelchair cautiously through the living room.

"Watch the braided rug, y'heah? It'll bog us down for a month of Sundays. And see to the kitchen corner. Jaudon likes to tear up the l-l-..."

"Linoleum?"

"I bet you'll help my crosswords."

She heard Gran's expectation as acceptance.

Gran huffed the words, "You h-h-hire Leslie. She's a sweetie."

CHAPTER FOUR

MJ Beaudry

May 1995

MJ didn't consider herself the nervous type. She'd made her way across the country on her own, supported herself while earning her bachelor's and master's degrees in finance, built a thriving business with Vonnie's brother, and was mostly accumulating money in a mix of tech and blue-chip stocks and bonds.

However, she'd never flown before. She didn't know the ropes and didn't want to come off as a rookie. Vonnie occasionally flew to work conferences and trainings, so she followed her lead, well aware of Vonnie's silent sensitivity—MJ was touchy about appearing naive. Onboard, a stewardess asked for her order. Vonnie saw her started look and swiftly covered for her, making an order for both of them. She found herself looking at a plastic-encased assemblage of fruit cup, granola, yogurt. The yogurt was a possibility, but for some reason, a tooth that had nagged her off and on erupted into a rip-roaring toothache as they ascended today.

The trip was certainly not her idea. For their fourteen years of life together Vonnie was bound and determined to see where and how her lover grew up. MJ had a vague fondness for her rural roots in Washington State but was leery of running into someone from her dismissive family. Her father claimed she wasn't his; her mother had scarce tolerance for the kid who'd made it necessary to marry.

Who needed them? She missed Anika a lot more than any of them. Anika, almost sixteen, had been diagnosed with malignant neoplasia a few months ago. At first the vet thought it was anemia. Anika soon developed a lump on her leg, then another near her neck. She started losing weight and lost control of her bowels. Always active Anika lay motionless most of the time, aside from her eyes, which were closed or watching MJ. When staying upright became too much for Anika, Vonnie had gone to the vet's office with MJ. They'd cried together.

Growing up, she'd never traveled west of White Salmon, Washington. One look from above at the area around the Portland airport and the overpopulation was obvious.

At a shop in the airport, they plucked a postcard from a rack to mail to Gran. Vonnie bought a green Oregon hoodie with a duck on it, not realizing it represented a football team. They stood in a lengthy line for a rental car, drove out of the lot, and became so entangled in highways and bridges, they found themselves in downtown Portland.

It was decidedly rush hour. The roads out of the metropolitan area were dizzying. If the people were packed like sardines on the plane, driving the unfamiliar roads made her think of crowds of salmon wrestling their way upstream.

Nevertheless, with Vonnie's help, they crossed over the Columbia River to SR 14 in Washington. Her toothache had returned as their plane landed. It had since receded, but her gum was sore to the touch.

"I've never seen you so tense," said Vonnie once they were away from the heavy traffic.

The road had MJ's total attention.

"Squirrel, it's me. The woman you trust and open up to. Are you that tense you can't talk to me?"

She couldn't deny that Vonnie was a truly compassionate woman. She owed it to her to be honest.

"I'm not tense—I'm scared out of my wits."

"That makes sense to me. Can I help?"

"Ignore me."

"That's my lover, always neglecting herself, forging ahead. Should you be driving?"

"Driving may help ease me into Depot Landing. I'd rather be a tour guide than shake in my shoes."

"You'll be extra cautious, though? An accident here would be pretty inconvenient."

"Have I ever had an accident?"

"I've never seen you this frightened."

MJ's fear of seeing her family was only compounded by that devilish toothache. She needed to distract herself.

"SR 14 is the continuation of the Lewis and Clark National Historic Trail," she said. "America the beautiful, right? If it wasn't for the Latinos and a sprinkling of American Indians out here, it's white enough to blind you."

Vonnie swung the flyaway ringlets of her long, dark hair. "Like this is new to me?"

"'Course not." It always worked and was something she loved about the woman. Whenever MJ wanted to change the subject, she'd mention a historical fact, if she had one handy, and Vonnie would be off and running to an encyclopedia or a library.

The Columbia River was exactly as she remembered it, not that any human had the capacity to grasp its actual breadth and strength as it poured toward the Pacific Ocean.

Beside her, Vonnie's mouth was open, as if she experienced the force of nature surrounding them with every sense attuned to it, taste included.

MJ's emotions pitched and yawed as the miles went by. Vonnie extolled the river-sculpted cliffs and wide lively waters, the unexpected grassy mounds of hillsides. She laughed aloud as Vonnie whooped out the window and listened to her echoes while they drove through the stone tunnels.

"Nothing I've seen before beats what you had here," said Vonnie. "It's out of this world."

The road was not protected from the river, and at times MJ fought winds as she drove, but she had to agree, after living far away, she'd grown up in exquisite country.

She knew restaurants used to be scarce, so they stopped at a tavern in White Salmon and read the chalkboard menu: salmon burgers, salmon and chips, salmon chowder, and a smoked salmon salad.

"This is delicious," Vonnie said. They'd both ordered chowder and salad.

"As a kid, we only had salmon at salmon bake fundraisers or if a neighbor caught too many. Never heard of these other dishes, but then, we had no restaurants where I lived."

"No restaurants at all?"

"A bar called The Canteen made some sandwiches, heated up food from their grocery shelves: Vienna sausages, bowls of Chef Boyardee, chow mein—no salmon except packaged smoked. Everyone from the

Landing and their sister drank there, depended on it for essentials, or worked there. Best toasted cheese sandwich in Washington State. There was a room with bait, tackle, beer, milk, soda, cereal, bread, canned goods. And my father wasn't big on sitting around in a boat with a fishing rod, waiting for dinner to take his hook. Frankly, I think he was afraid of water. Something happened during his Army days, according to my mother. Embittered him."

"I lucked out family-wise compared to you."

They paid the bill and set off again for Depot Landing.

"Man, oh man," Vonnie said. "If ever a place was windswept, this is it."

"It's the wetter, cool air around Portland meeting the dry air and heat east of here. That merges with the pressure and makes for this pretty constant wind."

"Those brown cliffs look designed—are they castles? Or fortresses?"

"Basalt. That's the work of the Missoula floods at the end of the Ice Age. Look over your shoulder. You can see Mt. Hood. And ahead of you upstream is Haystack Butte, a landmark around here."

"There's so much space. It looks as if wildflowers are growing in every crevice and patch of earth. The air is honeyed with them. Aren't you drawn here? The geography of our childhoods is embedded in us. It shapes us. You with your renovations and salvage—did you ever observe that you may be tearing down and rebuilding your formative years?"

A gong vibrated inside MJ. The reverberations washed through to her fingertips. "You may have something there."

She pulled to the side of SR 14 and stretched to the rear seat for her flat cap, which she pulled low to the top of her sunglasses, trying for incognito. "Here we are."

"Depot Landing?"

"All 1.8 square miles of it. The population doesn't change much, around three hundred and twenty-five plus or minus." She wrung her hands, a telltale nervous habit.

"You seem to be shrinking. Will you be okay?"

MJ's first instinct was always to flee, but she held on. "I'm trying not to think about what you said. My whole life instantly fizzled. If you're right, I haven't overcome my childhood, I've reacted to it. I'm not a successful contractor or builder—I'm managing a salvage yard littered with bits of me, trying to put them to constructive use."

"I wasn't criticizing—"

"No, you weren't. You're naturally insightful. I thank my lucky stars for you and for our family in Rainbow Gap. For your love and theirs. For taking care of one another no matter how we're damaged. The warmth in Rainbow Gap, human and climate—I'll pretend I'm a tourist in this cruddy town. We'll go see the trains first."

"Wait, do you know what any of these wildflowers are?"

"Sure. See the tall purple flowers? Those are some sort of lupine. We'll come across meadows of them up higher. Same with that dazzling yellow batch—Oregon sunflower. It's usually found at higher altitudes, but I suppose anything can wash down and take hold."

"What about those hairy plants over there? Do the orangey blooms jump out of the fat green pods?"

"Probably. It's unusual vegetation. I'll bet livestock transplanted these down here with their hooves. It's tarweed fiddleneck, toxic to cattle."

There was a diminutive parking area for commuters who took the passenger train that stopped in Depot Landing. They walked to the tracks over the river.

MJ said, "Freight trains run through here day and night. I was fascinated as a kid. There's the roundhouse to our left, where trains were switched in and out, locomotives got serviced and exchanged or staged for later trains. Crews might be swapped out. They used to have a pen for livestock by the freight yard, but I see that's gone now."

They watched for a while and listened to the boom, clang, of a train coupling. She closed her eyes to breathe in the so familiar smells of an early wildflower mixed with creosote on the railroad ties, hot metal and oil from the tracks, and the musky, slight fishiness of the river, which seemed to create its own breezes. She was awash in the sensual experiences of her childhood, so much stronger than memories of her family.

"I'll bet it makes you nostalgic, doesn't it?" Vonnie said.

She was quiet for a beat, returning to the present. "It's a jolt. For a place too undersized to be a real town, there are a lot of changes. The Canteen is gone. I can't tell if that shabby old bar in its place is operational or not. My father could step out of it any second now. Nostalgic? Sometimes. I couldn't live here now, but we carry home in some yearning corner of our hearts, don't we?"

There wasn't much more to show Vonnie. They went to the car. MJ was embarrassed the town came off so scuzzy. "This used to be a cool spot. Same as everywhere else, I suppose drugs got hold of it." She made a quick turn up a steep hill. "I lived up this road. Can you imagine the exhilaration of biking down it?"

"Don't scare me. My mother never would have allowed it."

"No one cared what I did. It gave me a freedom I took advantage of." She pointed west. "There's the school we went to, from first grade on up. It was my job to herd the younger kids in the family to and from school—which didn't please them as they got older. I learned how to be stern. We didn't have a library, but we had the bookmobile lady. She stopped at our house every week because I tore through books faster than she replaced them."

The hill leveled off partway to the top. MJ turned right and braked so hard Vonnie braced her hands on the dashboard.

"What do you know. Someone clear cut across this ridge and slapped down a streetful of houses. See that old brown place at the top of the bluff? That's where I lived."

"Do you think any of your family lives there now?"

"We're not staying long enough to find out."

She cruised along the new street, shaking her head when she saw a limp Confederate flag drooping in front of a house. She continued onto a rutted gravel street where, farther down the road, an abandoned building had been spray-painted with a giant swastika. "The houses are new, but the residents aren't. I remember the cars up on blocks, one-wheeled strollers, rusted bicycles, torn-up couches, moss on the roofs, moldy siding. Depot Landing is no longer much of a railroad town—these are rural slums."

They went farther uphill until the land flattened into farms and horse ranches. MJ tooled around for a while, pointed out a meadowlark, a white-tailed deer, a bald eagle on a high pine branch. Buzzards rode air currents. She pointed at plants that stood out: golden currant, tubular salvias, pink rhododendrons everywhere. She wished Anika was with them to gambol through these unforgotten woods and meadows.

"My friend Christina Obrenger's family had that farm."

"The girl you were caught with?"

Sadness made her sigh. "I always wonder if Christina dared to come out. I picture her and a hardy woman in the hills in a white house, a half porch out front, enough acreage to grow what they need, and flowers, every kind of flower. She loved the wildflowers up in our meadow."

"That mailbox says *Obrenger*. Pretty, how they alternated the petunias with the impatiens."

"I guess Christina's mom and dad farm to this day. She had no siblings."

"Or she inherited the place and works it with that hardy woman. Let's ring the bell and see."

"Her mother wouldn't want me on the property. Her dad had a deer rifle."

"What if it's only Christina?"

They idled in front of the white farmhouse. From around the side came a chunky teen on a riding mower. MJ let her foot off the brake, but Vonnie insisted, "Stay put. Roll down your window." She leaned across MJ and yelled over the mower's roar, "Does Christina still live here?"

The boy was polite enough to turn off the machine. "That's my mom. She's down the back forty. You want to talk to them?"

"We'll drive around that way, see if we can catch up. What's your name?"

"Doug, same as Mom's dad. He's on the porch, but since our grandma died, he's not very with it, if you know what I mean."

She stared directly ahead while Vonnie questioned the boy. Vonnie's warmhearted geniality was a skill that came naturally. People opened up to her as if they'd known her for years.

"You have brothers and sisters?"

"My sister Emma Jean. She's at college."

MJ whipped her head toward the child and stared, speechless. Her own birth name was Emma Jean.

Vonnie said, "We'll let you work. Nice to meet you, Doug."

"Same here. Hope you spot them."

Vonnie told MJ to go, go.

But she was unable to move. "She named her daughter after me."

"You want to see her now, don't you?"

She reflected for a long minute. "No. I want to remember her as she was. It's a consolation that I meant that much to her then. Besides, we have reservations for a hotel and dinner across the Columbia in Hood River."

"Don't you think she'd want to see you?"

"Why disenchant her? We had lots of sweet moments together. Would she want her kid named for me if she saw me now?"

"If it were me, I'd be thrilled."

"But I hurt her."

"That's your guilt talking. She knew about your family and would have helped you run off."

"I never told anyone about my family. Why bring them into it? We were two very young women floating inside our first bubble of love. Our families didn't matter one whit."

She followed the road slowly, searching. "Look how the sun shows off at those larkspurs. The phlox are practically flinging themselves over that old cinder block wall."

"MJ. I think you carry…not a torch, but one of those trick birthday candles you can't extinguish. It has Christina's name on it."

"Don't be ridiculous."

"And the pain is yours, not Christina's. You don't name a kid after someone who left—you name her for someone you admired and cared about."

"I wanted to call or go tell her I was leaving. I was banned from their house, from Christina."

"You were a freaked-out fourteen-year-old. Forgive yourself."

She swallowed hard and put her thoughts on hold while she swung around to find her father's survivalist compound. To see if it remained there.

As soon as she made her three-point turn, out of the blue it seemed, there was Christina, high atop a piece of farm machinery dragging a two-row planter. Her face was sweaty and dusty, beneath a funny-looking straw hat atop home-cut blond hair. Her ample proportions hadn't changed, but the bewitching girliness had been replaced by a disheveled grownup in faded denim overalls and a graying white T-shirt. She wore a gathering apron, and her former languorousness had given way to a woman frowning with purpose. Nubby gloves protected the slight, pretty fingers whose tentative touch had once thrilled her.

Vonnie gave her shoulder a push, and she succumbed, stepping out of the rental car, immediately smelling tractor diesel and dusty soil. She called, and Christina squinted into the sun to make her out. MJ walked around the car, took her cap off, and waved it. Christina shut off her engine and climbed down.

Shimmery hummingbirds buzzed by—dragonflies and darners skipped on the hot afternoon air. Nearby, a bullfrog croaked loud and deep, as if something disturbed its sleep. She heard the distant hum of the lawn mower. Christina was a backlit blur. Light blue camas dotted this end of her land, and salmon-red columbine hung from the sheds.

"Hi, Christina," she called. "It's Emma Jean Beaudry."

"The sun's so bright today, I was sure you were a mirage, Emma Jean."

"I go by MJ now, if you don't mind."

Christina mopped her face with a red bandanna she pulled from behind her bib. "When we heard you left home, my mom signed me up for enough church work to fill my days and consciousness."

"Come inside the air-conditioned car for a minute. We have some soda in our cooler."

"Well, for a minute or two. I need to finish my planting before Luke comes home. He has the rural postal route. Here, a taste of home." Christina pulled a plastic bag of miner's lettuce from her bib pocket.

"I saw a big patch of it in the shade of your shed."

They sat in the rear seat, Christina upright against her door. MJ gave Vonnie a portion of the bright green leaves. "I grew up on this stuff—try it."

Vonnie held out a cold pop to Christina.

"This is my partner, Vonnie Lowe."

"Pleased to meet you." Christina started to offer her hand, wiped it on her overalls, and extended it again. "I admire your name."

Vonnie grinned and offered to go for a walk, but Christina repeated that she needed to plant the seeds in the ground, pronto, and didn't encourage them to stay. She never stopped twisting, bunching up, then smoothing against her thigh the wet red bandanna.

MJ asked after Christina's kids and listened to her affectionate descriptions of Doug and MJ's namesake.

"What about MJ's family?" asked Vonnie. "Do you ever hear anything about them?"

"Well. It's not my place to tell you, but anyone in town will, so better me than them."

MJ was mortified. She would never have asked about them. She crossed her hands over her heart and looked at Vonnie. That twitchy nerve in her face started up. The toothache was prepared to strike again.

Vonnie touched her knee to ground her. "It's okay, Squirrel. I'm here with you."

Christina wove her bandanna around her fingers.

"Well, I don't know what they drank or smoked out at that

survivalist camp your people moved to, but rumors circulated about bringing the kids up by the rod and enjoying one another's wives and manufacturing illegal guns and forbidding the women birth control and not believing in doctors and other gossip people only half believed, if that."

"It's always the women and children who suffer," Vonnie said.

"Well, that may be so, but they had the choice not to follow their men. By the time your siblings disappeared, they passed for mountain men and cult Christian women in long cape dresses and white kapps."

MJ had forgotten what a chatterbox Christina was, and it dawned on her that feminism may have passed Christina and Depot Landing by. "Have they moved?"

"Well, that's the thing, they disappeared. The way you did. The whole gang of them." She shook out her bandanna.

Vonnie asked, "What do you mean by disappeared? Into thin air? Taken away by aliens?"

"They sure didn't take off to find me in Florida," MJ said.

"Well, they wanted somewhere warm." Christina cracked her knuckles. "I heard that from another mom at a youth football game. Our Dougie is a quarterback," she boasted.

Vonnie's lips were drawn. "But why would they run?"

"Because they built on the reservation."

"Those dopes," exclaimed MJ. "They ignored me when I told them they'd better check the maps."

Christina looked taken aback at MJ's emotion. "Well, the federal people who look after Indian rights found out. It was a mess there for a while. The survivalists built about a dozen houses and a community building. It was practically a town. And they were not pleased that the government tried to shut them down. Shots were fired, arrests were made, and word is, they ignited the fires that burned the compound down."

"Were they hurt?"

"Well, it was planned, so no one was supposed to, but the authorities found the bodies of two grade school kids. It was heartbreaking." Christina tied the damp bandanna around a wrist and tried to knot it one-handed. "My bet is they started over in crazy Idaho, though it's only hot part of the year. That's an easy state to be lost in. The community and the animals were already on their way when timed explosives went off in every building.

"But that was a long time ago," Christina continued. "Eventually your youngest sister fell for the son of one of the founders. They were both disenchanted with prepper living, married and made their way to their roots. The boy managed to hire on with the railroad. Well, they had three kids, but the youngest, showing off for his friends, slid into the river from a rock and never came up. Now tell me about you?"

By this time, MJ had thoroughly steeled herself, clamped down on her emotions as tightly as she had as a child, but managed to say, "That's tragic—his parents must be the soundest of that whole agglomeration of crackpots." She supposed she ought to care, but she didn't.

"To answer your question in a nutshell, I made it across the country, got more education, and now run my own business." She wanted to stop Christina's fidgety hands from their constant motion, the superficial gabbing that obscured what unnerved her.

"It's uncanny how much you resemble…I can't put my finger on who."

"Not my mother or father?"

"Well, not your dad. Your mom, kinda-sorta. Why? Do you think you were a foundling?" Christina allowed herself a smile.

"All my years here, my father said I wasn't his. Have you heard that sort of talk?"

"When my mom and dad were so mad at you? Yes, they said that and, worse, said you were exactly what your mother deserved."

MJ flinched.

"It makes sense why your mom and maybe-dad treated you so poorly. As if it was your fault she got taken advantage of and had to find some boy to marry her."

"Is that what your parents said?"

Christina's voice was sorrowful. "I don't know that any of it was true or if they were just bad-mouthing your family. Anyway, after hearing that kind of thing, I understood why you had to take off. Where did you go?"

"I don't want word of where I am getting out. I ended up in the Southeast."

"Key West? That was your dream."

"You remember? Not quite that far."

As she had those thoughts, Christina opened the door with her bandanna. "Well, I'm so glad it turned out for the best for both of us. You know where I am—keep in touch."

Christina stumbled in her hurry to cross the street.

MJ moved to the front seat. "She's scared of me. Why is she so scared of me? Does she think I'd expose her to the whole town of Depot Landing?"

"I suspect she's scared of something you triggered in her. As if church work could erase the way you must have touched her heart and her body. If she's the same as me, that spark kindled at the sight of you. It's a big deal, naming her child after you."

"Chances are she liked the name." She tossed her cap over her shoulder and said, "No more sneaking around. My family, the worst of them are mostly gone, Von, and apparently, I don't resemble them enough to be recognized."

"We can walk holding hands down Main Street. If only there was a Main Street."

"I wouldn't go that far. Not all the crazies left for Idaho. Remember the Confederate flag we passed on the way. And the horrible swastikas on those abandoned buildings."

Vonnie visibly shuddered. "Never expected to see those out here. To tell the truth, I'd rather we stayed far away from survivalist camps."

"Agreed, since what Christina described was insanely messed up. I have to assume her husband treats her well."

"It's probable he doesn't know about you, and jittery as she was, she doesn't want him to find out. It's so easy to threaten men's egos. But their son seemed mellow and had impressive manners. How did Christina seem to you, other than the scared rabbit demeanor?"

She took Vonnie's hand, held it to her heart. "All I can say is, I am seriously relieved I waited for you."

CHAPTER FIVE

MJ Beaudry

Fall 1995

That monumental fall of 1995, Pansy Lanamore turned her restaurant door sign to its *Closed* side and locked up. "Come through with me, the four of you."

MJ and her business partner Vaughn Lowe, Vonnie's twin brother, stepped behind Berry, who jounced on her feet in anticipation. Mayor Allison Millar was there because the Women's Health Center would be a countywide service, including Four Lakes, and she'd helped make this day happen.

Mrs. Pansy Lanamore, who smelled as though she wore hot-coffee perfume, moved laboriously through her eight-table restaurant and counter, joints about worn out. No wonder, MJ thought. For decades, Mrs. Lanamore cooked and served residents of Rainbow Gap and neighboring towns, not to mention truckers who drove across Central Florida, from the Gulf of Mexico to the Atlantic coast, or went out of their way for her homestyle cooking.

She noticed Berry watching the older woman's side-to-side shifting gait and increased weight.

Pansy's Home Cooking was an unpretentious breakfast and lunch eatery on the ground floor of a brick former factory building that faced Laudre Flats Boulevard. After years of renting, Mrs. Lanamore was able to buy the entire building thanks to the counsel of the local Small Business Administration, which referred her to a minority business fund—she was Afro-Caribbean—and another for women entrepreneurs. They walked through the café's stinging scent of freshly mopped floor in the adjacent Pansy's Pastries and Breads, a bakery operated by her two sons. Earlier in the day their ovens had pumped out the molasses, ginger, and nutmeg aromas of bulla cake, and now Mrs. Lanamore invited her guests to tear off chunks of the round, flat loaves.

Mrs. Lanamore said, "My businesses take up two-thirds of the floor space and face the boulevard. You can fit your health center in the L space that faces Bess Street. It's shadier under those live oaks, and the renters keep up old homes." She came to a stop at a heavy metal door and turned the key over to Berry.

Berry had a heart-shaped face full of faded freckles. Her eyes were wide-set, her short hair bouncy with natural curls, and her ears showcased a pair of delicate mermaid earrings. A licensed mental health counselor with a popular private practice, and an advanced practice registered nurse who continued to work part-time at the ob-gyn office where she started her career, there wasn't a kinder, more agreeable, or more level-headed person in the world. As her counselor, she'd led teenage MJ through some major growth, particularly around working through and controlling her anger.

Berry held the key against her lips, about-faced to the door, went to insert it in the lock, but dropped it.

Mrs. Lanamore tended to make a beak of her lips before she spoke, pecking out her words. "Now, that's a bad sign, young woman. You have to hold on as strong to the key as you've hung on to your ambition for this women's health center you've talked about since I met you years and years ago."

"I'm overexcited," Berry said as Vaughn, especially gallant on Berry's big day, bent for the key and pressed it into Berry's palm.

Berry closed her fingers around the key and held her hand to her chest. She had a child's look of awed wonder that this was happening.

"Uh-huh," said Mrs. Lanamore. "I remember the upheaval of my heart when I moved the café here after feeding friends and friends of friends on the porch of my rental house, seven evenings a week, for donations. If there was another way to raise Tad and Duval on my own, I don't know what it is." Mrs. Lanamore laughed. "The best? We ate free. My porch customers built the restaurant around me when I rented the space, taught my boys how to hammer and nail, and I fed them all. You'll see, when you do right, you light up others."

Berry worked the key in the lock.

MJ said, "I had a thought." She saw her friends brace themselves for the velocity of her thoughts. "This space would mean Berry's health center can qualify for grants, pull in donors, bill insurers, Medicaid, Medicare, none of which she can do from the Saturday Women's Health trailer. We'll fundraise rent—"

"A dollar a month is what I'll charge her," said Mrs. Lanamore, with the quick nods of a bird, "so she can bring health to poor women. You give and you get—you get and you give. That's the way it works."

Allison took Berry's hand.

"You can't mean that," Berry said.

MJ was grateful Allison knew how to ground Berry.

Mrs. Lanamore said, "Don't worry, my reward's waiting for me in heaven—and some free health care on earth."

Berry's mouth seemed stuck open.

"Go on in. I'm not done cleaning the kitchen yet."

Berry's eyes were glassy with tears. "I don't know how to thank you, Mrs. Lanamore. I never dreamed of this kind of help."

Rusted, the door stuck. Vaughn reached past her to yank it hard, and it gave way with a screech of metal on concrete. Before her was a tremendous empty, mute chamber. Musty air, greasy settled dust, and the odor of industrial lubricants were a shock after the bakery's sweet smells.

The two-story roof served as a ceiling; the walls were bare red brick. Large ducting hung suspended, some of it separated and dangling. Fist-sized bolts secured the iron plates that studded a cracked cement floor where machines and assembly stations must once have stood. She tripped on an exposed rebar end and almost went ass over teakettle. Tall, hazy, multipaned windows, set only three feet off the floor, lined the front walls.

Berry's mouth fell open again. "This is enormous. I never imagined…"

"You better start to imagine, yeah, because we need you. I plan to be your first patient."

"I expected to take months to bring it to this point."

"Enjoy your head start. Three months it took Tad and Duval. Weekends, evenings after work. They cleaned, hauled out trash, painted every square inch that light, light gray you wanted." Mrs. Lanamore gestured to her apartment above the restaurant. "They'd come upstairs, hair full of cobwebs—and Tad, he's as scared of spiders as he was the first time he met one."

Berry's eyes were loving. "We'll thank you and your sons somehow. Take care of their babies down the line?"

Mrs. Lanamore clicked her tongue. "I'm losing hope of grandchildren from those two ninnies."

"Did MJ mention," asked Vaughn, "that our crew volunteered to help convert this space for use as a women's health center?"

Berry looked flabbergasted. MJ hadn't told anyone outside work about her offer of free labor.

"They love that you're doing this," MJ said. "They want to be associated with such a historic breakthrough."

Allison's business facade faded as she looked MJ up and down. Nobody smoldered as well as Allison, although she'd curtailed her wild woman ways long ago. She once told MJ, in her slow, upscale Southern accent, "Renouncing nonmonogamy is the same as quitting cigarettes—we tend to become moralistic and judgmental of people who haven't." MJ remembered wanting to jump Allison on the spot.

"If bringing our crew to work here is alright with you, Mrs. L," said MJ. "Every day may be different—it may be all of us or one of us."

"You do what you need to. It surely started with you, a scrawny Western gal who showed up at my café hungry and scared after days alone on the road."

MJ, essentially unparented and thoroughly emotionally neglected, ran away at age fifteen from her family in Washington State. The man she called her father often questioned her origins; her mother called her a thorn in their marriage. MJ ended up with a glut of guilt and rage. Not that she was conscious of the source of her guilt. That came from working with newly licensed counselor Berry Garland. But that was later. First, she'd found refuge at Pansy's Café after a trucker who'd given her a ride attempted to abuse her.

Mrs. Lanamore pulled MJ to herself and told Berry, Vaughn, and Allison, "She was so hungry, I was waiting for her to lick the plate, but she was too polite to accommodate me."

That, thought MJ, was before she learned to survive as a burglar. A burglar with scruples—she only stole from the well off. She also worked for Jaudon under the table, put herself through college, and earned a master's degree in record time. Soon thereafter she started work with talented young Vaughn Lowe, seven days a week, buying, refurbishing, and either selling or turning properties into vacation rentals. She'd come across a saying: When she had no direction, a turn onto a wrong road would lead her to the right road.

Mrs. Lanamore kept MJ close. "Look at her now. You and Vaughn better hurry that conversion, youngster. I haven't seen a doctor in a month of Sundays."

MJ and Vaughn dutifully nodded and grinned at each other.

Berry asked them, "You've only done residential work. Is VONCO ready for this?"

"I certainly am," Vaughn said. "You're doing us a favor to let us cut our teeth on commercial."

MJ concurred in her own way. "Don't stomp on our passion."

Mrs. Lanamore nodded at the determination in MJ's voice. It was only then that MJ accepted the Center as a done deal.

❖

"Can you visualize a health center in this space?" asked Berry.

MJ was gazing through the big windows at a showroom of clouds, some radiant, others a threatening gray. Now, she turned around to jump in and counted on her fingers. "A waiting room, exam rooms, a couple of offices, a meeting room, bathrooms—will you need one for men too? Let's see, you wanted a day care space, that's, what, eight rooms plus storage space. We'd want to use the thickest Sheetrock and insulation. Put in an industrial grade heating and air conditioning unit and extra-large air purifiers and hot water heaters. Are you up for starting the drawings, Vaughn?"

MJ had worked with Vaughn for fifteen years now, starting not long after she and Vonnie got together. Vaughn was more freckled than his sister, though lighter skinned and slightly taller, which put him near six feet. He wore his hair in a precise Caesar-style cut.

"Not before I take a closer look," said Vaughn. "See if we can tweak the plumbing for the health center's needs, and whether the electrical line will carry the added loads. You'll want a washer and dryer somewhere."

"Berry can make keys for you and MJ," said Mrs. Lanamore. "Sooner you start, the better. Could be a store around here might donate the big appliances. You'll need a fridge."

Berry seemed mesmerized by the factory. "I see ghosts of machines."

Mrs. Lanamore glanced around. "Near fifteen hundred square feet on the ground floor alone, with parking and a bus stop. That's a lot of healing. From what I read in the county records, the company here before us manufactured fishing equipment. Nets, rope, twine, float lines, lures."

When she was thinking, Allison steepled her hands so her fingertips met at the bridge of her nose and her thumbs rested on her jaw. Her fingers were dimpled, as was her face. Unless she was angry, a slight smile stayed on her lips, but her wrath at injustice was something to behold. "Weapons for sport killing. I picture a line of poor white and dark-skinned women bent over long tables, sweltering over piecework sixty hours a week for pennies."

MJ stopped sketching preliminary ideas in her head. "We know you're determined to right the wrongs of the world, but no one can fix history, Allison. No one can undo the wrongs committed in this space any more than we can undo the Oklahoma City bombing or the slavery that went on in this country. We can only do better. And this health center is better. Berry Garland, you're a hero in my book."

"Those poor souls in Oklahoma. One hundred sixty-eight," said Mrs. Lanamore.

Berry said, "And survivors suffering the rest of their lives from injuries or grief."

The others went silent until Mrs. Lanamore spoke. "Don't forget that big space in the open storage loft next to my apartment."

Berry blinked twice and asked, "How would we access supplies up there?"

"My son Duval suggested a conveyor belt or a hydraulic lift. There's a wide door to the outside up there."

Vaughn shook his head. "You don't plan to convey your workers up a belt, do you? You need an elevator."

The door scraped open.

Berry's partner Jaudon stepped inside. "Sorry I'm late for the tour. How are your cookies crumbling, Mrs. Lanamore?"

"No crumbs in my bakery." Mrs. Lanamore pantomimed a broom and swept invisible crumbs toward Jaudon. Selling Pansy's Pastries at Jaudon's stores had made them both a good amount of money.

Allison cleared her throat, something she did frequently because of her various allergies to the weeds, grasses, and molds of Florida, compounded by the years when she shouted and led chants at rallies and protests. "I'm going to take some *before* pictures of the space. Let's get one of the whole bunch of you first."

"Hey, Boss," MJ said after the shoot, "what do you think? Enough space here for a health center?"

Jaudon smoothed her cowlick as she did a three-sixty. "For now. You wait and see. Berry will outgrow this office lickety-split and need an extension in a year or two."

She passed her notes over for Jaudon to see.

"You're pretty savvy for a kid."

"Kid? I'm no kid anymore."

Jaudon patted her on the shoulder. "Sure, you are. You and Vonnie, you're our next generation."

"I don't think ten years' difference is a generation."

Jaudon leaned in close. "In lesbian years it is." They bumped fists.

Mrs. Lanamore spread her arms. "I own the land ninety feet behind," she said. "The concrete is already poured. The owners before me had big plans, got their permissions. Tad says there are electric and plumbing hookups. When you want to build out that way, yeah, come see me."

MJ reattached her notes to her clipboard, then returned it to the canvas messenger bag she called her office.

Vaughn looked at her with raised eyebrows.

"Are you thinking what I'm thinking?" she asked.

"I am," Vaughn said. "An extension. Two stories. I don't think it's zoned for more."

"And that elevator Vaughn mentioned," Mrs. Lanamore said forcefully.

"We'll connect a new building to the old one—there's the solution to your loft storage problem." MJ nibbled at a stick ballpoint. "You've said VONCO needs a physical presence other than a room at home, so customers know you're on the up and up. Until the Center needs the space, why not rent it?"

Vaughn prodded the air with both hands in fists, thumbs up. "We'll do it sometime after the Center is finished, between moneymaking gigs."

Mrs. Lanamore narrowed her eyes. "Who exactly plans to pay for this? I'm not handing out all my land for free."

MJ said, "You're more than generous. If you're game, we can work that out."

"I don't know. You pickneys might be biting off more than you can chew."

MJ was accustomed to Mrs. Lanamore's occasional return to Jamaican patois and how she often called anyone younger than herself a pickney—a child. "I might be able to help some," she ventured.

"Let me look into small-business tax credits and loans, zero interest loans. See if we fit into any rural development programs. You know the renovation—with permits, inspections, some volunteer help—will take a couple of years, start to finish."

"But we're finally on our way," said Berry.

Vaughn scratched at his cheek. He was determined to grow a beard. "It would be our first commercial building, but the old fellow who trained me, he's done plenty of them and I know he'd be glad of something to occupy his time. He'd do it solely to sport the title Consultant."

"Speaking of going commercial," said Jaudon, "you might qualify as a start-up if you branch out. I was eligible when we added the bakery section to the Bays."

Berry made it her business to take care of everyone. At the ob-gyn practice, she never made the decisions, but she excelled at patient relations. With a visage of intense but kind interest, she was expert at drawing facts from patients. From Gran, she'd acquired her unique perspective to problems, treating them as puzzle pieces that required examination from various angles before fitting each into the exact right place. She became the go-to gal who unraveled tangles and overcame obstacles. She said, "Let's not put the cart before the horse. If you install an elevator, though, is there a chance of locating it so Mrs. Lanamore wouldn't have to use those steep, narrow stairs from the restaurant to her apartment?"

"A two-door," Vaughn said. "One side to the Center's storage, the other to the bakery downstairs and your apartment upstairs."

Mrs. Lanamore pressed prayerful hands together. "Jesus loves you."

Vaughn looked aside. At age thirty-three he still hid the bashful grin he'd never outgrown.

CHAPTER SIX

Vonnie Lowe

Winter 1997

Sunday morning at their home in Causeway, about thirty minutes from Rainbow Gap, started as an easygoing day with an unusually cool temperature. Vonnie and MJ dallied as long as possible over breakfast in bed, enjoying the hot candied scent of Vonnie's apple-cinnamon pancakes.

Vonnie, in a faded college T-shirt and tights, stretched and rolled her body to MJ's. "What will you do while I'm in DC meetings, bored silly?"

MJ ran fingertips the length of her back, kissed her neck. "Think about you."

Vonnie shivered at the teasing touch. She teased back. "What'll you be thinking?"

"I'll remember how we met. You were a favorite at New York Pizza, where the gays hung out. I wasn't in the market for a girlfriend, and anyway, Christina and I never went far, so I had no idea what to do.

"Besides, I was too busy clawing my way through college, selling illicit alcohol for Jaudon, working at her aboveboard stores for under-the-table wages, and accumulating ample proceeds as I relieved the well-to-do of their excesses. I built a stash that would support me through my master's and help me support myself lawfully. I admit the redistribution of wealth was entirely gratifying."

"If you'd been caught?" Vonnie said. "I might never have met you. The chances you took don't bear thinking about."

"You were such a feisty nymph then, you got me to show you the house I rebuilt around me despite the fact I was humiliated because I lived in this wreck with holes in the walls, leaks in the roof, mold, and critters. But you didn't care."

"I knew we were meant to be."

"And you knew how to make us happen."

Hand in hand, they lay together and listened to the clattering of wood stork bills snapping together in courtship rituals. A colony of them lived high in nearby trees. When the chicks arrived, the braying racket woke Vonnie every morning.

With a nostalgic half smile and reminiscence in her eyes, MJ went on. "Sometimes I think about donning my gloves to stay in practice for a day the market crashes and the building business slumps. I remember the lives of empty houses—clocks ticked, the refrigerator, freezer, air conditioner cycled. I jumped at the tick of a stove. Was it cooling off, or would the owner return soon to tend to something in the oven? What's more frightening or more stimulating to a burglar than evidence of habitation?"

"Every now and again I wonder about you, MJ, how you simply don't capisce that it was morally wrong for you to steal people's money and property."

Frown lines deepened on MJ's brow, and her eyes narrowed. She lashed out. "Isn't it you who's always talking about the unequal distribution of wealth? I did my part. I never said it was right. It was necessary."

"I'm only trying to understand you."

"Sarcasm doesn't become you. When was the last time you faced survival on your own or were denied work cleaning gutters in the street? I had no legal recourse that wouldn't send me to my parents in their crazy survivalist colony."

"But how can you speak fondly of theft?"

"I've made up for it, haven't I? I've grown the stolen money in order to pass it on where it's needed. I've trained dozens of young people, so they can make decent wages. I discount jobs for people who can't afford to pay. You know how much we donate to the food bank and environmental organizations. I thought this was settled between us and you understood. I swear your job makes you hostile and suspicious outside of the Housing Authority."

"Because I try to understand my lover of eighteen years, I'm suddenly hostile?"

"Von, it's built up, don't you see? There are times you act like you've fallen out of love with me and you'd be happier if I got out of your life."

"How? How have I given off that message? What have I said?"

"Like just now. You argue about what's over and done. You question picky little things—why haven't I repaired the sink yet. Last week, you said it's unhealthy to have no interest in reconnecting with my family. You were very worked up over that. Yesterday, you stopped by my worksite all bent out of shape that I was on the roof while the rest of the crew did less risky work. Where is my supportive Vonnie?"

She did find it hard to be with anyone at all when she got off work and was out of sorts. It was true, too, that she was critical of MJ if she worked late. *Am I fighting with MJ on purpose?* Conceivably she was taking her own work disgruntlement out on MJ. The new maintenance director at the Housing Authority was a good old boy who doubted her role and her purpose. If she was let go, she knew how difficult it was to find a job, based on her clients' experiences in the job hunt program. "You scared me. I didn't want you to fall and do damage to yourself."

MJ said, "I know when something's bugging you. Are you tired of me?"

"How could you think that?"

"I don't know what to think or what's changed to make you this insecure."

Vonnie's hand danced on her collarbone. "Maybe it is my job as well as worrying about something happening to you. I can't think of a life without you. Other than my family, you're the most stable, the most reasonable person I know. You're honest now. You never lie. You give your all to your clients and employees. What is it inside you that enabled you to stoop so low and allows you to laugh about your crimes to this day? Tell me what I need to be aware of, what might blast out of you if you're trapped in a corner again?"

"You're worried I'll revert to a terrified fourteen-year-old?"

"Now and then—"

"Alright, alright, the line between right and wrong was always crooked for me. Lies came so easily—they were my defense because I didn't fit in and thought I had to cover that up." MJ took her glasses off and fiddled with them. "Ever since I clued in on my automatic lying, I listen for and censure every false word that pops into my head. I know I'm not perfect. I bite your head off every now and then when something irritates me: slow traffic, not meeting a deadline because someone doesn't show for work, monthly cramps."

Vonnie wanted to do more for residents in the housing projects. The agency, by its very nature, blocked her. It made more sense for her insecurity to come from her frustrating job than from the woman she loved. "Is honesty something Berry helped you with, in counseling?"

"I knew nothing about myself before Berry. What insight she has. Every time I'd glom on to accusations of how the world had done me wrong, she'd halt my session, bring me a cup of water, lead me in breathing. When we talked again, we'd identify my triggers, and gradually, I came to recognize them myself, defused my own anger."

Vonnie had never been troubled like MJ. She was born happy and fully energized. She had no tools to combat her current demoralization or to aim her frustration at the right target, in the right way. She didn't recognize this new condition in her life—she needed help and reassurance. She didn't want therapy.

"Von, remember that hurricane when you were in college? How you got a ride into the storm because you were desperate to be with me when I was in danger? That's what you can expect if I or we are threatened again. I survive. You will survive. I'll lie and steal as much as I need to, and morals be damned."

She'd have to accept that whatever was getting under her skin, it wasn't MJ. "I'm sorry. It may well be the job, and I'll do my best to give you a rest from my aggravations. You are one of a kind, my handsome enigma, my bastion."

"Yer dern tootin', Missy. We need to hustle if you want to make that flight."

She pressed herself into MJ's arms. "I can tell my boss the flight was overbooked."

"All the more reason to get cracking, because flights usually are, from what I read."

MJ drove her to Tampa International for the 2:30 flight to DC. Vonnie, as the coordinator of the Family Self-Sufficiency Program with the Lecoats County Housing Authority, was required to attend training. She'd been with the LCHA since interning there in her senior year of college, and now, with President Clinton in his second term, she hoped it would be given more funds.

They pulled over short of the airport. The palm trees that lined the access road were motionless, a positive sign for flying, she thought. Whitney Houston sang on the car radio, and they kissed, the long warm kiss of women continuously surprised to have found a perfect home in each other.

"I know you hurt without Anika," said Vonnie. "She's running in a sunny, green grass meadow, rolling over a very stinky dead worm, wishing you were with her. I'll be happy with any four-legged friend you want to bring home."

Vonnie watched MJ's jaw muscles tighten. At times she thought MJ would always have trouble feeling her feelings. It was a relief of sorts to watch her try to bury her grief; it meant those emotions were in there, seeking the light of day.

MJ's words were choked. "Not yet."

She held MJ's hands in her own, firmly squeezing them. "I'm sorry I took my stress out on you. Don't overdo while I'm away. We've learned that's when you hurt yourself."

"Says the woman whose briefcase is full of too much work and who is prepared to trust herself to an aluminum barrel at thirty-odd thousand feet." She pressed Vonnie's hands to her heart. "Too soon is not a problem. If you bump into a critter that needs to be saved, save it, understand?"

"Of course," she said, hesitant to impose such a change on MJ.

"You stay on the ground if there's bad weather in D.C. and come home to me in one gorgeous piece."

"Promise."

Vonnie stepped out of the car at Departures.

Following her, MJ said, "God, I love you in a skirt. You set my imagination on fire."

Vonnie held her close before MJ handed over a garment bag and large backpack from her Jimmy truck. She'd chosen the vehicle for its conversion crew seating and cargo space.

"Don't let me hear you're not wearing your hard hat," Vonnie said. "I'll get Vaughn to tattle."

MJ Beaudry

She watched with proud amusement as Vonnie grandstanded away. Her Vonnie had grown from a skinny, sunshiny seventeen-year-old filled with determination and naively insisting the world honor liberty and equality for all, to a polished, articulate, accomplished woman whose determination had not diminished despite the hard lessons she learned, when she hit the workplace, that *all* was never meant to include people of color. Or women. Or gays. Or old people. With the ferocity of discovery, she brought home stories of discrimination embedded in the Lecoats agency on up to the heavy hitters in DC.

MJ drove to the Women's Health Center to work on the reception area, which, to date, consisted of the wooden teacher's desk and a rolling office chair Vaughn picked up at a school district auction. Berry scored a dented six-drawer lateral file cabinet that was replaced at her job. MJ planned to knock together a base for the countertop today. This work was seriously satisfying. She'd already sanded a nice piece of Corian she bargained down at a surplus outlet. Vonnie's top-notch grant writing skills got them some medical equipment, which was on order, but each step took so long. The grand opening wasn't yet on the horizon.

When she arrived, she saw with a shock that she wouldn't come to grips with the counter today. Instead of *Women's Health Center*, the temporary sign that hung over the doorway was spray-painted to read *Lesbo Baby Killers*. Volcanic with a fitting anger, she didn't read the graffiti on the walls but drove directly to the Vicker house. Berry was loading the clothes dryer and keeping an eye on Gran. Benedict was due any minute with Popeyes fried chicken, Cajun rice, and coleslaw for his Sunday visit. Olive Ponder had stopped by after church to jaw with Gran.

MJ described what she'd seen as they waited. Berry seemed to swallow her devastation while she told Gran she needed to go out for a while. As soon as Benedict arrived, they told him and assigned him to Gran-watch. MJ and Berry sped along Eulalia Road in her powerful Jimmy.

Berry's determination never seemed to falter, but there was an unaccustomed tremor in her voice today. "I only want to help women and children, not hurt them."

"This is Florida," said MJ. "The South. Did you genuinely think there was a chance the white gloved ladies would roll over and play dead? They fired up some men to deface the building the way they push voters to pass Bible-based laws."

Berry beat her fists against her knees and her voice hardened. "Why do they assume we perform abortions here?"

MJ pulled up to the front of the Center. As she cut the engine, the Jimmy gave a shudder, a replay of her own at first sight of the graffiti. Berry got out and stood by the car to scrutinize the scene.

MJ put her nose right up to the yellow block-and-brick wall, rubbed at the substance with a finger, and tasted it. Berry came beside her.

"Nothing exotic," MJ told her. "Spray paint is acrylic, which is a plastic akin to what you use on a house. But you can spray layers and layers because it dries in no time. Our next problem is the concrete—it's porous, and the pressurized application does a number on it."

She remembered the time she had of it in her teens, when she cleaned off a defaced Beverage Bay sign—and that was an easier surface.

"Baby killers? Hippie vermin?" It was Mrs. Lanamore, who grumbled toward them and put an arm around Berry. "Law', they can have their opinions, but not on my property, not next to my businesses."

Berry kissed her cheek. "I don't know why anyone would do this. We provide the same services as regular practitioners," Berry said, her face truly puzzled. "If asked about abortion, we refer to Planned Parenthood, but that's far from our main purpose. Our volunteer doctors write scrips for birth control. Goodness knows we need that. And lesbos? How would they know?"

Disgusted and ready for battle, MJ said, "It's a typical bottom-of-the-barrel smear tactic to call women dykes."

Mrs. Lanamore spoke dismissively. "They don't give two hoots about abortions. It's the word *woman* that sets them off. I've heard comments. These invaders go right up to patient cars and scream in the windows, *Where's our men's health center?*"

Not much got MJ's dander up more than misogyny, except racism and cruelty to animals. "Give me a break. The whole of medicine is about men's health." She assessed the extent of the spray paint. "Let's obliterate these vile words. We have to be careful not to use a chemical that'll eat away at the brick or concrete. I use TSP for concrete, but we can also use oven cleaner or Goof Off. We'll need a hose, a pressure washer, and wire brushes for everyone we can round up to help."

Mrs. Lanamore said, "We better make this go away quick quick. There'll be hell to pay for these vandals. I'll see to that myself. Duval, Tad, you went to school with half the neighborhood. Usher some volunteers this way to help us. Enough of them have said they're behind the Center. Looks as if we're in for a fight about the Center like we are for everything else."

"Bright idea, Mrs. Lanamore." Her next thoughts poured out with authority. "With enough volunteers, we'll be rid of most of it tonight. We'll need to be gentler for the brick, though, use a softer brush, rags, and leave on the dissolver—I believe thirty seconds will do it."

MJ turned away from the building. Mrs. Lanamore and Berry stared at her, as if stunned by her rush of words. MJ realized she spoke in the manner of the boss she was at work: brisk, brief, authoritative.

As MJ waved Berry into the truck and struck off to the hardware store to collect what they needed, Mrs. Lanamore remained on the sidewalk, clicking her tongue at the affront to her property.

CHAPTER SEVEN

Jaudon Vicker

December 1997

Jaudon rarely booked off work, but she did that day, after she cajoled two of her part-timers and her cousin Cal to go help with the cleanup. Olive's industrious daughter-in-law, Stacey A. Ponder, covered the store.

Pops Vicker, who'd hung around the Beverage Bay that afternoon, lonesome and in the way, was fit to be tied. Today was his respite afternoon as Momma's caregiver. Momma all too much enjoyed ordering around the poor home health aide, as was her way.

Pops followed Jaudon to the Center and sounded off to anyone whose ear he caught about the years of Berry's hard work and savings, the permits and licenses, the fees and rental deals that fell through—and she was rewarded with this? Jaudon handed him a wire brush and pointed him to a defaced telephone pole. The man who'd operated an amphibious Water Buffalo personnel carrier in World War II and worked in phosphorus mining, until it near to disappeared, dutifully followed his daughter's order.

MJ and Berry rejoined the volunteers with more supplies, and MJ took command and made assignments. Tad and Duval brought their friend Shady, who worked the lower walls from his wheelchair alongside his grandniece, both of them eager to right this wrong. Mrs. Lanamore drafted Tanice, her dishwasher, to assist.

The damage was extensive if cosmetic. Jaudon knew Berry believed in the positive, healing properties of harmonious design. She must be torn up about this visual assault.

Kids from the subdivision behind the Lanamore property watched; some helped as long as their attention spans lasted. Jaudon listened as a girl told Tad she saw from her window who did the damage, but it had been dark, and she described them as white dudes in muddy trucks.

A very young boy asked no one in particular what they were going to do with the dead babies.

Berry dropped to a knee and looked him in the eyes. "No dead babies, mister. That's the last thing we want. We'll take care of mothers and sisters and grandmothers so they can raise healthy children."

"I live with Great Auntie Celia," the boy replied. "She's old."

"All the aunties are welcome. You can tell her that if she's ever sick or wants a checkup, to come see us once we're open. Will you tell her that?"

"She knows. That's her, across the street on her red kitchen step stool."

Berry saw her on a porch up the street, waved and smiled. The great-aunt waved too and beckoned the boy. He ran across the now animated street to her side.

Duval had names on a sign-up sheet and made a night watch schedule through the next weekend.

A sheriff's deputy interviewed Mrs. Lanamore and said he'd request extra patrols.

"Bad timing, with Cullie at firearm training and Vonnie in DC," Jaudon commented within hearing of the deputy.

"Excuse me," said the officer, "I couldn't help but overhear. Is that Deputy Culpepper you mentioned?"

"Yes, sir," Jaudon said. He looked familiar, but she'd had a negative encounter with the sheriff's department at one time and lost the hearing in one ear as a consequence. She'd been cautiously respectful since.

"Are she and her partner involved with this?"

Jaudon said, "Why?"

"This is right up their alley. Mayor Millar's got game."

Now recognizing him, Jaudon offered him a hand. He was older and had filled out some, but he was the policeman they'd long ago called Officer Friendly. He was the one who'd warned her, way back when, that she was about to be raided for selling liquor from local stills. She'd taken to that desperate measure temporarily to keep the family business afloat. MJ, a minor then, had been at risk, too, but needed employment, was smart, and fit perfectly in an underground business.

Jaudon asked, "Will the police go after whoever did this if we catch them at it again?"

"Tell you what. Call it in—on the non-emergency line. Let me know what they say." He wrote a number on his business card and pointed to a black slab of a phone on his passenger seat. "You can contact me anywhere on that brick. I'll light a fire under someone."

She thanked him and stepped into the street to admire the nearly graffiti-free Center. MJ and Shady spooled red extension wire away from the floodlights they'd worked with since dusk. MJ's cleaning formulas were a success.

Berry appeared by her side, and Jaudon touched her fleetingly. No one saw, but Berry was distraught and eased her closer.

Jaudon said, "Apparently somebody threw a clod in this churn, didn't they, my poor Berry. I better go tell Duval to have any sightings reported to me." She bragged, "Remember Officer Friendly? He gave me his direct phone number to turn in these clowns if they repeat their mistake."

"I doubt that will end it. I don't know why I assumed we already won this fight. It's 1997, Ellen DeGeneres dared come out on TV, and it might as well be 1973, right after *Roe v. Wade*. Murders, assaults, bombs, fires set throughout the country. Will people never accept women have the right to make our own choices about our lives?"

Jaudon wound her onyx pinkie ring round and round her finger. Rigo had given it to her to keep her strong and self-confident. "What do they have against healthy women?"

"I doubt they care about our health—they care about control. They're irate that women aid and support other women rather than depend on men."

"And who is *they*?" But she already knew one answer—people like her brother, Bat.

It made her sad to think about her cracker brother. Once her champion, he was now retired from the Army and established in the Christmas tree–growing business out in Washington State with his buddy John Lau. While she was named after one side of Momma's family, Bat, short for Batson, got Momma's maiden name. He had become one of those so-called patriots who hated the government. She wouldn't put it past him to harass a clinic like this or incite others to do so. Pops cared a lot about his distant veteran son and let him have a fair share of Beverage Bay earnings, but she was relieved Bat left Florida.

She was proud to be called a cracker, because that's what she was. Her ancestors never enslaved people, but they were as backward about people of color, Momma's side especially. It was the Vickers who had a change of heart sometime around the Great Depression. As the story went, one family helped another out—she'd forgotten which did what. From that time on, the Vickers swore off judging others based on where they came from and taught their children right thinking.

Berry played with one of the blue sea-glass earrings Jaudon had given her as a thirtieth birthday gift and answered the question. *"They* would be the medical establishment, people who believe life begins at conception, religions invested in maintaining a patriarchal society, mentally unbalanced individuals who need a cause to fixate on. For starters."

Jaudon walked to Berry's Subaru wagon with her. "I'd add politicians who need a target to pull in votes, the way they used us when Anita Bryant was all the rage. Mercifully, that's over."

"I swear you haven't changed since you were eight years old and trusting as a newborn puppy."

"What? What did I say?"

Berry was oddly curt with her. "How many times have you told me gay people will always end up with the short end of any stick available? There is exactly one law in Florida that protects us, and it's for city employees in Palm Beach County, not here. Republicans in Congress tried to destroy the actual Civil Rights Act with a Civil Rights Act of 1997, which made equal rights appear discriminatory, but their bill failed. And remember what today's graffiti called us. They assume we're lesbians because we care about women."

Jaudon let her shoulders slump. "We should have called the papers, let them take pictures, talk to you, expose them."

"Oh, sweetheart, let's keep this low-key and very local. Newspapers love conflict and might blow this up. That would bring the crowds."

"Aggressive advertising?"

"Oh, sure. Look what the media did for Princess Diana. Do you want to put up a *Sponsored by Beverage Bay* sign?"

For an instant she did, if it helped Berry—and sales. She remembered how successful the three years of orange juice boycotts had been. Retail food didn't have a large profit margin. "I don't want to come off like a yaller dog, but I can't afford to be boycotted. If Publix or Target signed on, they'd make a difference, but my stores are piddlee'o outfits, compared."

"Don't, my Southern knight. Now you go take care of whatever business needs you at the stores, and I'll skedaddle home to relieve our Leslie. She was able to send Benedict home."

"It's so late. I forgot about Leslie. She's got some snap in her garters, freeing us to fix the Center."

Jaudon watched Berry drive away, happy she'd broken down and bought a new, reliable car. But her sharpness, so unlike Berry—that was worrisome.

No one was there yet to guard the Center, but she guessed the neighborhood would be vigilant tonight. She watched MJ, her polo wet with sweat, sleeves rolled tight at her upper arms, pack gear in her truck with Tad's help.

Jaudon pitched in too.

"So, what do you think?" asked MJ after Tad went upstairs to the apartment he shared with Mrs. Lanamore and his brother.

"Think?" Jaudon said. "All I have are questions. Why do we have to fight tooth and nail for everything we need?"

MJ went quiet, briefly shut her eyes, as if she listened for future tidings. "Once word gets around how much the Center will help women, life will calm down. We've survived before."

Jaudon jutted out her jaw. "Jiminy. After so many centuries, we ought to do better than survive. You'd think we invented women's health to spite them."

CHAPTER EIGHT

Jaudon Vicker

May 1998

"We got 'em," called Cullie Culpepper one pleasant May evening as she, true to form, let the screen door on Jaudon and Berry's front porch bang shut. "It took us six months, but they're in lockup."

Berry stood to greet her, Jaudon right behind. "Gracious light, you caught the Center vandals?" Berry asked.

Cullie made a show of sniffing the air. "Hey, Gran, this house isn't the same without you in charge of the kitchen. No homey smell of red-eye gravy, ham, and grits. Did y'all switch to frozen dinners too?"

Gran sat in her new power recliner, mending a vest pocket for Jaudon. "Makes me sad. Women are taught right off the bat that we're useless after going barren. It may be true—certain efforts my body won't take on again. But cook? It won't be long before I'm in the kitchen. Leslie will help me fill this house with those smells you long for. Ask Leslie for her favorite childhood foods, and she's likely to tell you phoo or that raw sushi stuff."

Cullie said, "If you mean phở, I've heard it said *fuh*."

"Except for special occasions," Berry admitted. "I don't have time to cook a decent meal on my own. And Jaudon…"

Cullie placed her hands on her hips. "I know, I know, unless Gran or Berry looks over her shoulder, Jaudon can't cook Jiffy Pop without burning the bottom kernels."

Gran said, "I know you girls are busier than springtime birds building nests."

"Did we or did we not catch the bad boys, Gran?"

"You surely did."

Cullie patted herself on the head. "A bunch of rowdies impatient for mud race rallies to start."

"No one put them up to it?" asked Jaudon.

"Not sure. Detectives might look into that. Florida Right to Life told Sheriff they monitor new health organizations, whatever that entails. Said they never approve of vandals, though they can't speak for all their members."

Jaudon said, "Those detectives better attend a sermon or two, watch them rile up the crowds. Besides, isn't there a law to protect—"

Berry answered, "*Reproductive health care providers and their patients*—and that's a quote. Allison and I reviewed that 1994 Freedom of Access to Clinic Entrances Act. We think we're covered because we offer that kind of care, but we're a general women's health clinic. Florida opposed the law up to the Supreme Court, which declined to hear its challenge. Covered or not, the Act won't protect us unless it's enforced, which is not going to happen in this neck of the woods. It takes money to force the issue."

Looking over her glasses, Gran asked, "The boys—"

"Want to stir up trouble. The detectives suspect this uptick in attacks around the state—you're not the only ones—is organized by new groups of fanatics or right-wing politicians or the megachurches—or all of the above. I saw more fish stickers and church decals on those trucks than you can shake a stick at. As if Jesus would act like them."

"If only they'd act like him," Berry said. "Who turned them in?"

"No one. We keep our eyes out. Officer Friendly came across three trucks idling outside the Center. The men never had a chance to do any damage, so we had no cause to arrest them for that, but one of them took a swing at me. We got him for assault on a peace officer and issued a citation to another on the county noise ordinance—no muffler on his truck. There was one lunkhead with an expired license and no insurance. We hassled them enough I don't think we'll see them again soon."

Jaudon tapped a closed fist against her chin. "They're taking this up a notch if they continue to attack deputies."

Cullie rubbed her upper arm, swollen and red where her uniform short sleeve ended. "Only my arm, when I blocked the punch from that big bruiser."

"Let me see that." Berry studied the injury. "Put ice on it before it starts to look like I don't know what."

"I'll bring you some," said Jaudon.

Cullie lifted a flat hand to decline. "I'll do it later. Need to hit the mean streets."

"It'll take but a minute," Berry declared. "Bring her one of those gel ice packs, would you, angel? And a Co-Flex bandage from the bathroom. You don't want that swelling up till it's tender enough to interfere with your job, but if it does or shows red streaks, you come to the practice and tell Laura on reception I want to treat you."

Cullie rolled her eyes at Jaudon. "Your girl is getting tender on me."

Berry knew Jaudon admired the heck out of her pal Cullie. The three of them had gone through school together. Most of the time she and Jaudon had packed extra lunch food to share with ill-fed Cullie and often invited her for suppertimes. Cullie was a thorn in the Culpepper marriage for some silly grownup reason. Gran suspected Cullie's folks had to marry because of Cullie, and husband and wife found themselves incompatible soon after their daughter was born. As Catholic Charismatics, they were forbidden to divorce. Home became an uncomfortable place for Cullie as she matured. She moved in with an older girlfriend as soon as she was hired, underage, as a pool boy— the first girl in the county to be hired for that job.

Allison was clearly brighter than her partner, Cullie, but they couldn't keep their hands off each other. It was the pool boy state of mind, Allison had once confided. Cullie was a playful foil to Allison's passionate intensity on bleeding-heart issues far and wide. Cullie and Allison had been a couple almost as long as Jaudon and Berry. Cullie had worked her way out of poverty, and Allison's family came from money, but they saw the world through similar lenses.

Berry invited Cullie and Allison for a home-cooked dinner that Sunday to thank Cullie, thinking it would serve the dual purpose of forcing themselves to cook a decent meal. "And pass the invitation to Officer Friendly."

"He always declines invites," Cullie told them. "I've known him for years and have yet to know if he goes for men or women, both or neither."

"Doesn't matter to us one bit," Gran said.

Cullie said, "He endlessly rushes home to feed his cats. He has about a dozen of them. If he doesn't arrive immediately at the established feeding hour, his cats act like it's a sign of global end-times. When he's home early, they think it's the miraculous beginning of a new age."

Berry applauded, gleeful.

"Our kind of people," Jaudon said.

"How about I bring my Frank Sinatra albums along. We can mourn him together. You heard he died?"

Berry said, "Gran saw it on the TV and had a peachy good cry for herself. What Elvis and rock 'n' roll was to us, Frank and the big bands were to her."

❖

That Sunday, Sinatra serenaded them as Berry and Jaudon sat around the table with Olive, Cullie, Allison, Gran, Leslie Gardner, and Officer Friendly, whose actual name was Jeff Maple, when the *Pink Panther* doorbell went off. Kajen the cat crept for cover, but Puddin wasn't there to howl. They'd lost her to old age at seventeen, and Gran, though she loved her dogs, wasn't ready to handle a new one.

"You mended the doorbell." Berry gave Jaudon a peck on the cheek. "Thank you."

Jaudon pushed away from the table. "Too corroded. I replaced it."

"Too bad nobody uses it."

"I hate to break it to you," Cullie said, "but as of today, somebody does."

With clear reluctance, Jaudon left her tomato pie, grilled chicken, corn on the cob, and green salad to answer it.

Berry followed Jaudon with her eyes and was shocked. It seemed like overnight Jaudon put on weight. Would she have a belly like Pops as they aged, or widen at the hips like Momma? From now on, she'd make sure they ate Gran's heart diet along with her. What could she do about Jaudon's eating habits at work? Her stores were packed with processed foods and tempting sweets, easy means to stifle hunger. She knew for a fact Jaudon sometimes ate only a pint of strawberry ice cream for lunch. Olive Ponder had squealed on her boss.

Jaudon's voice was at growl level at the visitor. She feared the Center's enemies were at the door. Over the Sinatra tune, she heard an accent from somewhere deep in Georgia. Berry had spoken with that same muddy drawl when she came to live with Gran Binyon. Jaudon had coaxed most of Berry's telltale accent away, but she'd know it anywhere.

CHAPTER NINE

Berry Garland

The woman who followed Jaudon into their house looked like deep South Georgia. Unlike Berry's, her straight brown hair was thin and lifeless. She seemed to force a pale-lipped smile as she surveyed the diners. Her full cheeks pressed up and narrowed her wide-set eyes. Their blue was the darkest Berry had ever seen, which, combined with sharply angled eyebrows, gave her a menacing demeanor that marred a pale prettiness.

"Hello," Berry said to this mystery woman in a below-the-knee skirt and plain short-sleeved blouse. Hesitantly, she rose to greet her, all of a sudden lightheaded, aware her smile faltered.

Jaudon shook an official-looking document, her brow furrowed with skepticism. "This lady says she's your sister. Her birth certificate calls her Opal Garland."

"My sister? But that would mean Ma and Pa—"

The woman raised one hand as if in warning. "No, there was a terrible accident. They—oh, bless me, you never knew? Gramps said Grammy wrote to your Florida grandmother to tell her—"

Gran said, "I never saw any such letter."

"—our parents didn't survive."

Gran gasped. Leslie took her hand, brushed soothing circles on her shoulders.

Berry dropped into her seat. She tried to read the document, saw it was for a baby named Opal Pauleen Garland. Ma had loved opals, and Pa had given her an opal for their engagement. Gramps Garland's name was Paul. Her eyes blurred with tears, she made out the date of birth, less than a year after Ma and Pa went away. She chewed on her lower lip, a habit she tried to tame.

She studied Opal, saw the resemblance to Ma, Pa, and herself. "If they died, how did you—"

"It was a couple of weeks before my due date. Somewhere east of San Francisco, a tractor trailer driver fell asleep at the wheel, ran over their motorcycle."

The woman had a habit of interrupting, an irksome trait passed down from Grammy Garland.

Berry heard Gran suck in a breath.

"By the time they got our parents out from under the truck, our father was dead. The emergency workers saw our mother was hugely pregnant and, once they were sure she hadn't survived, performed a cesarean right then and there."

Jaudon drew Berry tight to her side, and Berry pulled Gran to her. She felt Gran tense so hard she shrank inside the haven that was Berry. Gran shuddered over and over, silent, leaning into Berry, who was frozen with shock.

Opal said, "I only know this because our parents stayed the night before with friends who sent a newspaper clipping to the Georgia address on our father's driver's license. Grammy never showed me the accident write-up, but I came across it after she and Gramps passed, when the uncles and aunts helped me clean out the house. It's yellow from age, but here, I made you a copy." Opal handed it over. "You can thank the good Lord, they didn't have you with them."

In her mind's eye, she saw her eight-year-old self watch them cut out her sister while Pa lay nearby, smashed to smithereens. Ma was only twenty-seven, Pa was twenty-eight.

Berry was thoroughly afraid, though what of, she couldn't begin to say. Her heart raced, her mind straight away melted her memories, emotions, and what this woman said into a clump. It exhausted her, trying to extract a simple thought or word. Normally hospitable, she wanted this woman to leave without delay, before she got up and knocked her to kingdom come.

Now that the mystery was solved, she'd do anything to change the outcome.

Gran straightened, pulled Berry's hand into her own, and held it tightly. She found her voice pretty quickly. "Your Grammy and Gramps Garland took you in?"

"Drove way out to California and back for me."

"I'll bet that lousy Eddie Dill got ahold of the letter and burnt it up rather than feed another kid," Gran said. "I would have taken a second granddaughter in a twinkling."

"Grammy didn't think so since she never heard from you. She told me you lived rough in a trailer camp with a man you weren't married to and didn't see that as a fit way to raise a girl child."

"She didn't have it in her to pick up the telephone?"

"Gramps wasn't happy about paying for long-distance calls."

Through the fog of her shock, Berry noted more than a hint of Grammy Garland's sharp tongue in Opal. Unsettling memories assailed her. The Garlands lived up in the town of Anthea, Georgia, a crossroad full of empty except for the Anthea Community Church and some railroad tracks. Pin-thin Grammy was devoted to her strict church. A few times a pastor wasn't available, and she gave sermons to make your hair stand straight up. During Ma and Pa's stretched-out stays in Anthea, Grammy taught her how to make arrangements for the altar, play simple hymns on the piano, and imitate an itty-bitty church lady.

She prized the times Pa was laid off a job in Georgia, and they once again crowded into the freedom of Gran Binyon's single-wide trailer home in Florida.

Poor Gran. Berry turned to her now. In the space of a minute, Gran found then lost her only child and discovered a granddaughter.

They held each other. Jaudon moved behind them, hands on their shoulders. Which was worse: loss of a daughter or loss of a mother?

Gran blotted tears from her face as Sinatra sang "That's Life" in the background. She blew her nose and looked at Opal. "Where's my manners? Opal, you're my brand spanking new second granddaughter. Have a seat. I'll find you a plate, and you help yourself."

Officer Friendly was already on his feet. "Thank y'all for dinner," he said. "It's best I leave you to your rather magnificent disturbance."

Olive, who hadn't yet removed her Beverage Bay vest, left the table with him, giving Jaudon a long, troubled gaze and signaling her to call. It wasn't often their schedules allowed them social time with each other.

Allison, who'd been director of the Lecoats County Public Health Department before she went on to become mayor, steepled her hands as she studied the birth certificate, nodded that it appeared authentic, and stood to hug Jeff and Olive. "Thanks for joining us."

"Don't be a stranger," Jaudon called.

Olive said, "I don't see that happening anytime soon."

Berry, emotions now sparking and flaring, listened to her internal counselor repeat *That's life.*

Her vulnerable, abandoned self gradually took in the finality of this loss of Ma and Pa. She was unable to comprehend a full-grown sister of her own, one who knew about her yet had never before contacted her. Why had she come now?

And Gran on the mend from a stroke, brave but trembling beside her. It was a wonder she wasn't hit with a full-on heart attack given this staggering revelation. Berry held tight to her hand.

Cullie was at the tape deck, and Jaudon nodded agreement that music might not be the ideal fit right now. Cullie switched it off.

"Come on in, Opal Garland," Gran ordered. "There's a seat at this table for you."

Opal claimed Jeff's seat and kept talking. "Except for our irresponsible parents, I'd be an October baby, the right month for opals. Grammy was told I was born pale as a white opal, so the name stayed." Now her skin was overtanned. As soon as Cullie shut the front door behind Jeff, she commented, "I didn't mean to chase off anyone's... friend."

It was clear to Berry that Opal wanted to know who belonged to the lone male in evidence, but no one responded. Gran retreated into the kitchen with Leslie to make up a plate for their new guest. The two lesbian couples were left at the table with Opal. If Opal was as much a carbon copy to Grammy Garland as she seemed, she was about to work out some unwelcome news herself.

Cullie's police radio went live, and a dispatcher summoned her for a multivehicle traffic accident. Jeff's siren whooped once, and they heard his cruiser roar to a start. Cullie was up and out in a flash with a wave to them all. Allison stayed for a while to monitor the two very different sisters in case friction arose. Berry might be the professional counselor, but Mayor Allison was an experienced negotiator.

Talk was tiring for Gran. She returned to the table, increasingly wan and confused. Leslie unfolded her walker, but Gran straightened on her own, headed for her room, stumbled, almost fell, and kicked the magazine rack that tripped her. She sent the door to her room flying shut and howled her daughter's name. "June!"

With no notion that Opal would ever leave, Allison finally took her leave. Opal remained another two hours, jabbering on about her idyllic childhood with the Garland grandparents. Her husband, Klem

Howell, was from Abilene, Texas. She said he worked as a temporary civilian maintenance technician for the Air Force. Why he was moved from Moody Air Force Base in Georgia to MacDill in Tampa was not explained. They rented a house in a Port Tampa City development. Opal, at the tail end of her thirties, had a troubled eighteen-year-old daughter and five sons aged eight to seventeen, enrolled in the church school.

Leslie entered the room. "I'm on my way home. Gran looks as if she cried herself to sleep. I got her nightgown on her, she took her pills, but that's all she'd allow. You might want to keep a close eye on her."

"You know it," Jaudon said.

Under the table, Jaudon placed a hand on Berry's thigh, squeezing it. Berry covered the hand with her own and tried to stay attentive. Once in a while, Opal asked a question about Berry's life, quickly cutting her off with comments that returned the spotlight to herself.

A vehicle honked in front of the house. Their visitor stood so fast something might have burned her bottom.

"That's my husband," she said, all aflutter, jamming photographs, lip balm, tissues, and a handful of other items into her purse. She threw a kiss at Berry and was out the door in a jiff. From the window, Berry watched her new sister hasten to a white van. She tried to make out the words on its side. Opal barely closed the door as the male driver hightailed it, firing pebbles in his wake.

Days later, Gran would ask, "Now, wouldn't you think he'd come in and introduce himself?"

CHAPTER TEN

Jaudon Vicker

They turned in early that night, drained by the events of the day. She lay there imagining what Berry might have been like if raised by her Garland grandparents. She could have taken longer to grow into her warmhearted self, but following Berry's Pa, Jaudon guessed she'd rebel rather than let her guardians mold her in their emotionally stingy images.

Jaudon was well aware of the sister's opinion about the decidedly masculine woman at Berry's side. Berry allowed Opal the ask-me-no-questions-and-I'll-tell-you-no-lies route, but surely, she noticed Jaudon wasn't a powder puff. She was robust as a field hand, from her rugged, unshaven, ever banged-up legs, to her overlong arms muscled by a lifetime of stacking and unstacking cases of cheap wine, kegs of beer, crates of dairy, and weighty cartons of canned goods.

In August, Jaudon would turn forty-seven if, as she was inclined to say, she stayed out of trouble. She was a scrapper who learned early on to define and defend what was hers—and some of the vendors she dealt with made hornets look cuddly. If she wasn't able to josh her way out of a situation, she glowered, curled up her hands, and turned on the secret font of cusswords she never used in front of her more discerning true love.

In her day, bigger- and meaner-than-life Momma, founder of the Beverage Bays, would have keened in horror at the way she managed the business. The idea tickled her.

The stores were her joy. She'd loved them since the first, a card table at the end of Pineapple Trail. The second iteration was a tin hut with an icebox for refrigeration. When Momma bought the bare plot of land on Buffalo Street for a song, and the Vicker and Batson men constructed a metal drive-through building that was the image of an airplane hangar, she came close to throwing up from excitement.

Clear-sighted Berry insisted she stay in high school rather than drop out and be a store clerk forever. She was glad for the business classes now, which taught her how honest businesses worked, the plumbing of it as Rouie Waver liked to say. Rouie helped her start again after Momma got them so deep in the hole they faced bankruptcy. Jaudon was forced to sacrifice two low-earning stores but proud that she kept five thriving.

The day Jaudon qualified for her CPA license was one of the proudest of her life.

At the Beverage Bays she always played a country-western radio station. As the customers drove through, her regulars, the old fellas who came by for coffee, a pastry, a paper called her the dancing grocer and asked to two-step with her. Some of the women asked too—the ones who assumed she was a guy. When they worked together, Olive laughed and clapped at her antics.

She danced with her hand truck as she wheeled stock around the store, sang in the cooler and stacked milk cartons. On special occasions—like Halloween—she might wear her lace-up roller skates and swing around the counter to tap dance her fingers on the cash register. She always had a smile on her face at her stores, and most customers left with smiles of their own. Others, mean or disturbed in their heads, never stifled their objections to her appearance. What did they think, that she chose to be hairier than most women? That she wanted her arms to be disproportionately long or her legs bowed?

She rolled onto her side and tugged the white sheet to her ear, aware it wouldn't remotely protect her, but this was how they liked their bedclothes, cotton and worn thin to make the lightest of covers.

"You can't sleep either?" whispered Berry.

Whenever the house went quiet, they became sensitive to out of the ordinary pings, whirring, ticking, and movement, intensely alert to Gran's needs. Leslie had declared she was ready to have a social life again about the time Gran consistently managed safe bathroom trips through the night, so they were Gran's sole night caregivers. They didn't want to miss a fall. Despite Gran's despondence at her daughter's death, they'd made her laugh earlier, chatting about Opal's weirdness while they played with Jaudon's old sets of tiddlywinks, pick-up sticks, and jacks. The games were valuable occupational therapy.

"Seems I forgot how to sleep," Jaudon answered.

"What did you think?"

"I don't know, Berr. There's something plumb peculiar about her."

"That's my take, and I can't quite put my finger on what's wrong."

"Not to mention appearing all of a sudden in our neck of the woods, never a word over those years."

"Grammy Garland didn't care much for Ma. Or Floridians in general. She warned Opal away from Gran and me, I'm certain."

"And you the kindest, smartest, most stick-to-it person in the world. Except for the stores, I have never wanted anything more than to make you happy. If Grammy Garland was alive now and kept in touch, she'd be proud of your accomplishments."

"I have to take that blame—I never told her."

She caught Berry's hand under the covers. Berry entwined their fingers. "You would have had to tell her about me. Or she heard you'd taken up with me. Anyway, Grammy Garland's the one who stopped sending you birthday and Christmas cards. You didn't quit sending cards until your Georgia cousin's wife took pity on you and wrote you that card about Grammy Garland dying."

"I can't believe I have a sister, no matter her oddities."

"I was surprised you didn't run and throw your arms around her. And then I wasn't."

"There's a—what would your *Star Trek* people call it—a force field around her. A forbidding force field."

"Uh-huh. Like flies around a privy."

Berry gave a chirp of a laugh and pushed at her. "It wasn't that bad."

Jaudon grabbed Berry's wrists and straddled her. Berry pulled Jaudon all the way down and nipped at her lips. "Oof. Have you resolved to catch up with Mercie and Allison in the weight department?"

Nevertheless, when Jaudon backed down the bed and pressed a breast between her legs, Berry gyrated against it. Shortly, the way Berry sometimes liked it, Jaudon commanded, "Come."

As they fell asleep, she pictured Opal in her homely ensemble. Those white anklets and spotless white sneakers took the cake.

She thought, yes it was. It was that bad.

CHAPTER ELEVEN

MJ Beaudry

January 1999

MJ wrote fast as Vonnie came up with idea after idea about the Center.

They were at home in Causeway that Friday night. Both were on a high—the Gators won thirty-one to ten against Syracuse, during the last game ever played at the Orange Bowl.

"We'll install wheels on anything heavy to avoid injuries."

MJ reminded her that the slow renovation of the old factory depleted funds as fast as they came in. "There's not enough to purchase a pencil, much less build in flood precautions, or computerize like we're doing at VONCO."

She jotted their ideas in her field notebook between listings of unfamiliar birds, places they wanted to visit, construction drawings, permit and supplier contacts, and birthday/anniversary reminders. She gave Vonnie flowers monthly, on the thirteenth, their anniversary date.

Vonnie said, "Hospitals and medical practices are always upgrading. They might donate older waiting room chairs, examination tables, sterilizers, blood pressure monitors, scales, cabinets, wheelchairs."

MJ followed Vonnie to the bedroom and showered off the day's sawdust while Vonnie performed her ablutions in the other bathroom.

Vonnie's energy and smarts were big attractions for her, and neither had lessened in these...was it seriously twenty years since they got together? Since she ended her life of crime? Her friends in the underworld, Tad and Shady, had called her a cash magnet, and it was true; she'd had an uncanny ability to reason out where money was hidden in particular homes. She had awesome luck, doubtless used up a lifetime of it, but she learned to be very thorough, especially in her research of burglary victims.

Today, she researched construction manuals for fun. It slowly became clear how to use her college finance coursework. The state of Florida allowed contractors to rapidly cover agricultural land with concrete, a business she wouldn't touch, though it was currently a gold mine. The poor birds scrounged food in wetlands behind big-box store parking lots. The orange orchards, the old homes with porches and thick canopies of trees, were supplanted by rafts of development, usually homeowner associations, and too often bankrupted developers who overbuilt time and again. They ripped up habitat and left concrete roads, plumbing and electrical setups, cables that protruded from sand, and model houses to tempt buyers to pay for another build.

But they couldn't destroy the sky. Only nature turned night clouds purple after a hurricane blew. Only nature designed rainbow clouds. Only something in cahoots with science cleared the sky over Tampa Bay so the white moon, at its fullest, illuminated the water. From their very deck the Milky Way poured toward them. Nature won out over greed when seed-bearing breezes brought rugged weeds to tangle up the abandoned lots, to recolor them green.

She'd pledged never to break new land. As soon as she accumulated enough money, she bought a wreck of a lakeside cottage at a Lecoats County auction and spent months restoring it as a vacation rental, with skills she'd acquired as she watched her father and his survivalist friends.

From the first, she avoided cutting down trees. She made it a point to scrounge for free reclaimed boards and fixtures and relied on hardware store clerks and the library for new know-how. On the proceeds of her first vacation rental, she acquired another property. By the time Vonnie graduated from college, in 1985, MJ and Vaughn Lowe were making a success of VONCO, their green construction company. They also built the unique hurricane-resistant dwelling where MJ now lived with Vonnie, a prototype VONCO had replicated twice so far for other at-risk homes.

As she dried off, she asked, "Where will Berry procure this many people to trick-or-treat for her fundraising? Especially while our pro-choice, apparently too charming president endures an impeachment hearing, and a professional wrestler was sworn in as governor of Minnesota. I'm honestly disgusted."

"She's so well-liked, it'd be hard for most acquaintances to turn her down. We can try tapping into some of the volunteers who promised to help if Allison runs for the state senate. They're hardened after doing battle in the mayoral campaigns with detractors who exposed her activist past."

"Let's at least alert them," MJ said. "Women like that, they might offer once they know what's up."

"How about Berry's grandmother and Leslie?" Vonnie whispered. "They're both chatterboxes."

"Has Gran's speech improved enough? It might lift her spirits. What a sad discovery, that your one child, missing for decades, was buried in her in-laws' plot, over the Georgia border. We can urge her to recruit her gentleman friend. He's involved with an Asian American professional group. Maybe he'd help spread the word that we exist, or will exist."

"Surely Leslie has friends who might help. She does have friends, right?"

"I think she's actually found someone."

"We'll rope her someone into this too."

"I'll ask your brother if he can round up a friend or two to make calls."

"See?" said Vonnie. "We have resources. I can adapt a script from the Family Self-Sufficiency Program's fundraisers."

"Hey, the school district. They have nurses' offices and a stake in this."

"I already asked," Vonnie said. "Anything they ditch has to be sold at a county auction, but keep thinking. You watch the auctions anyway, so that's your job."

"Yes, ma'am," said MJ with a salute. "I'll look for state auctions too."

Vonnie's hand went to her throat. "I'm so sorry. I manage people at least five days a week. I need to leave that part of me at work." She stroked her collarbone as her eyes searched MJ's.

MJ kissed Vonnie's head. Vonnie smelled of citrus shampoo. Last month it was mint. "I know what you're saying. I'm sure I do the same."

Vonnie raised MJ's black polo shirt, embroidered with the company name, ran her hands up her flat belly and defined ribs, and laid her lips on one teardrop breast. "What a great body."

MJ kneaded Vonnie's shoulders and nuzzled the top of her head. "What's up with you? I mean, honestly, Von, you must have as much paperwork here as you do at work."

Without moving her lips, Vonnie said, "The director wants to use my Family Self-Sufficiency funds elsewhere."

"What the hey? Did I hear you correctly? You were right to be insecure when he was hired."

Vonnie let the polo shirt fall into place. "The Housing Authority has a shortfall in its maintenance budget and wants to use my social service funds to make up for it. Understand, I was told this secondhand, but I trust the source."

She sat. "Who? The little janitor with a crush on you?"

"Who else but Emil? He doesn't see eye to eye with the new head honcho, and skittered up to me the way he does, kind of sideways, a push broom to lean on."

"How can the maintenance boss compete with you for the same pot of money? That must cross some line."

"My monthly meeting with the director is next week. Fingers crossed it's not too late. Most districts across the country haven't taken advantage of Self-Sufficiency. Maintenance will use those statistics as an argument that my whole program is unnecessary and the money can be put to better use. Any financial decrease will gut my services."

"That makes no sense."

"Nor do the budget shortfalls in maintenance. Vergie isn't allocated adequate funding either—I don't know. He drives a new car, brags about the swimming pool and lanai he added to his house, and complains about the cost of putting three kids through college. Emil said Vergie gets kickbacks."

"And no one's reported this?"

Vonnie lowered her head, shaking her curls. "Believe it or not, that's a mere fraction of what goes on. Public housing is chronically underfunded, and the bureaucracy is an obstacle course worse than any *Super Mario* game. For a long time, domineering men have privatized, monetized, skimmed what they can from public programs across the board. The wait for a Section 8 voucher can take years—if a landlord can be persuaded to accept one. Renters can end up in neighborhoods like the ones they tried to leave. There are never enough Section 8 inspectors—they're overwhelmed and sometimes crooked enough to look the other way."

She'd do anything in her power to protect this woman, but Vonnie's job was out of her hands. She'd settle, as Vonnie said long ago, for being her bastion. She'd given her all to be that kind of reliable partner, to become trustworthy and honest.

Vonnie raised her gaze. "This is why the process is pathetically slow. It's senseless. HUD covers most of the Self-Sufficiency costs, and the program benefits the Housing Authority as much as it does Section 8 residents."

"Because…?"

"Residents are prepared for the labor market, which translates into paying their rent regularly, which means turnover is lower, which decreases work hours in the maintenance department. We teach housekeeping and budgeting skills as well as healthy childcare practices to improve the client's chances to be self-sufficient and not depend on us."

"Do you want to look for another job?"

"And do no more to solve housing problems?"

"Then go in there tomorrow and demand that your needs take priority?"

"Demanding is your style, not mine. I know I need to work on that."

"Meaning you femme, me butch?"

Vonnie's throaty laugh never failed to remind MJ why she fell for her.

"Femmes can be as chesty as you. I need to follow protocols to keep my job. And I don't want to cause trouble for Emil."

"I don't want this underhanded maintenance director making your life miserable. What's his name?"

"Vergie. Vergie Redfern." She stuck out her tongue. "He's crass. The women in the outer office call him Goose because he can't keep his hands to himself."

"We can ask Allison to pull strings and cook this goose."

"MJ, you do appreciate HUD isn't a dinky city program?"

"How about Cullie? There must be a law she can use to pull him over and hassle him. Does he wear a seat belt?"

Vonnie moved her fingers along her collarbone, something she did when nervous. "Vergie's a heavy drinker. The entire office knows what girlie club he drives home from." She propped up her chin with a thumb and scowled at MJ. "But I don't want the mayor's partner made to look like a harassing cop."

"Come on, then. We'll think of something. I'll load the dishwasher, you put away the food the way you like it. We'll walk down to the beach for the sunset. Saturday, I'll give our list of needs to Berry."

❖

MJ originally bought the bungalow on this odd-shaped lot to spiff up and turn over, but she and Vonnie liked the locale so much she kept it. A storm surge handily dismantled it for her, at notable risk to their lives. In danger, they'd taken shelter that night, along with Anika, in a neighbor's round home on stilts. When she found her own bungalow demolished, she vowed to build a home like the one that saved them.

The house was in Causeway, a quiet, faintly shabby city west of Rainbow Gap. Eight- and nine-hundred-square-foot mid-century homes lined engineered canals off the bay. Homeowners built docks outside their back doors to tie up boats.

MJ and Vonnie's home sat to the rear of the canal-front houses on a plot that looked like a jigsaw puzzle piece. The neighborhood was well-established and, despite hurricanes and tropical storms, retained mature trees that cast large patches of shade. Curtains of mosses afforded privacy between the scatter of residences farther back from the canals. Storm surges had taken down branches but not whole trees; much that had been lost grew back. More than the hullabaloo of the hurricane, she remembered the poststorm silence. The buzz-crazed mosquitos blew away. She heard no birds, who left for the duration and began to return when the winds died.

After nearly losing their lives, her first impulse was to persuade Vonnie to move far from Florida, but the thing about the state, it was offbeat in ways that appealed to a part of her. Shapes never stood out with sharp clarity, as if heat melted the edges of trees and telephone poles and the patient, watchful wading birds. In a stormy sky, hanging balloon clouds were so active, the earth seemed to rotate around them. Sunsets were regularly orange and gray or orange with a range of blues and, some evenings, hosted a march of dark empty clouds across the blazing horizon.

Their first house dismantled to broken sticks, her car bent and submerged—seawater had lifted it and floated it into another canal—MJ spent considerable time in the public library researching the house she planned to build. She borrowed a book of her favorite models.

"You want a rondavel," Vonnie had explained, "traditional housing in some parts of Africa. Round, the way you want to build, or oval. Here's another photo, a Western adaptation of the rondavel, on stilts."

"So that's why I didn't find what I needed—there it was in Africa all along."

Vonnie stuck her nose in the air.

"I know, I know. It's my racism revealed again. Unlearning it never ends. Tell me architecture began in Africa."

"Naturally. Seventy-five thousand years ago." Vonnie crooked her finger. "Come on, we'll miss the sunset."

MJ continued to talk as they descended the stairway with its anti-slip treads and wall-mounted, baluster-supported banisters. She wasn't about to take any chances around safety. "This supersized hut shape is perfect for us and the elements. And you were so right about living on one story—the stilts make us climb enough."

It was breezy enough on the docks that halyards tapped at flagpoles, motorboats bobbed on shallow swells. Low tide was pungent with plant matter and decaying algae, a sulfury stench at certain times. Tonight, the wind wafted it back into the bay.

They made their way past their flowery tropical plantings: coral-colored jasmine, large yellow and orange daisies, blue salvia blossoms, elephant ear plants, feathery ferns.

"We need one of those stair elevators," said Vonnie. "Not for us, but to carry our groceries."

"I've speculated about that. Remember dumbwaiters? Why not build a simple outdoor dumbwaiter?"

"Count on you or my brother to come up with a rope pull device."

"You're right. Not electric—I know how expensive my closest electrician crony, Ro, can be. Wait—were rope pulls invented in Africa?"

"I don't know, but I'll bet rope was," said Vonnie, skipping ahead of MJ to hurry her to the beach.

But MJ strolled backward to admire their elevated home. "I do like our screened deck."

"Bug free suits me."

"Very funny. Vaughn warned it was risky to build out a partial roof here near the water. He worried we might lose it in a big storm, but we anchored the heck out of it."

Customers clamored and VONCO's profits had suffered, but they'd moved into the finished house within a year. Two adequate offices, a large bedroom, a combined living room and kitchen, two bathrooms, and a snug space between the bathrooms for a washer and dryer, countertop, and cubbyholes. Their windows were made of tempered glass. They installed hurricane impact doors and used the strongest fiber cement siding in a light gray-green to blend with the trees. Bamboo decking was new to the market, but, on top of MJ's contractor's discount, they received a substantial rebate to take the risk. The loan that enabled them to storm proof their 1,500 square foot hut was almost paid off—they'd never dipped into her investments at all.

"Come at us, wind and water," she challenged. "We're ready." Hurricane Andrew tried its best in 1992 but brought a windy sigh of relief and welcome rainwater to Causeway. The weather had for the most part behaved since then and left their quirky dream home intact, for now.

She jogged to catch up to Vonnie. "I mean honestly. I needed this break and some exercise."

Vonnie didn't hesitate to race her the length of the dead-end road to the beach. Once there, pink herringbone clouds paused over the water while long-legged Vonnie danced barefoot along the lip of the lapping waves and softly sang Mariah Carey's "Vision of Love."

How many times in the past eleven years had they walked this lane to their crescent of snow-white sand? She was astonished at her unreserved, desire-infused contentment.

Where had her belligerent, reckless girl-self gone? With the attacks on Berry's health center, she might want to resurrect that self again, and soon.

CHAPTER TWELVE

Berry Garland

September 1999

"Oh, for pity's sake."

Berry, on her hands and knees at the Center, snaked a computer cable behind a desk where Leslie, jean jacket for once chucked to the side, short and slim enough to wedge herself where the older women couldn't, waited to make a connection. Vonnie sat on the desk, legs crossed, and read instructions aloud. Sweaty, thirsty, but immediately before she buckled in frustration, Berry spotted the loose end of a wire and matched it to an empty slot. She cheered for the team and pointed at what she'd done. Leslie tapped the power button, and Berry watched the computer come to life.

She'd planned to use a computer for scheduling and billing and had worried excessively about the looming necessity to buy and launch electronics. It helped that they bought at back-to-school prices. MJ and Vaughn had successfully done it for VONCO, though, and MJ, ever the dashing hero, had planned to lead the install today. Berry awakened that morning to a call from MJ—half of her crew was down with a new strain of flu. She canceled but encouraged Berry to proceed without her and to phone when completely baffled.

Berry wasn't the sort to bother anyone at work, and now, she thought with pride, she didn't need to.

Excitement spilled from Leslie's normally composed voice. "Why convert paper to digital? Let's put everything on these computers from the get-go."

That idea triggered another bout of alarm. "Medical records and government forms too? Is that safe? What about patient privacy?"

"Isn't that what your office is doing?"

Berry said, "The practice can afford the best security. I worry our attackers will come in here and steal confidential information."

"They can do that with paper records," noted Vonnie. "Or burn them. At least it's possible to back up computers. Take the floppy disks home at night or keep them here in a safe."

Leslie rose and delicately brushed grit from her hands and skirt. "They're password protected. I'm enrolled in advanced classes in Windows 95 and might be able to find more ways to secure the information."

Berry tried to keep her enthusiasm from her question. "Is it possible to make a program for a unique medical office like this one?"

Leslie had a bashfulness that never allowed her to toot her own horn. "I can try. It would be rudimentary, but I have a friend who I can ask for help."

Vonnie rubbed her collarbone. "HUD sends me to enough regional computer seminars that I'm good with Windows. There must be some program out there that's ready-made, adaptable, and affordable. We need to enter symptoms, prescriptions, billing, diagnoses, appointments. Is simple possible in a medical environment?"

"MJ will know, or find out for us. She is way ahead of me when it comes to computers." Berry had been MJ's counselor in her private practice off and on for years. The poor kid grew up with minimal useful guidance and no one to talk to except a bookmobile lady. She flinched at the memory of the extraordinary amount of pent-up rage that had the potential to turn MJ into someone like the Columbine shooters.

Over time, MJ learned to redirect that ire into two focused ambitions: learning how to make enough money to live securely, and devising ways to share it. At a counseling session a few years back, MJ boasted to Berry that her initial non–real estate investments included new technology stocks. The other day, though, MJ told her she was uneasy about the boom in tech stocks and divested herself of all but the two that seemed most solid. She used a fraction of her returns to purchase VONCO's first computers. Now she taught Word and Excel to Berry and Jaudon. Berry focused on the expedience of computers while Jaudon had already created her own basic inventory management program. Jaudon also bought a gaming device and was endlessly captivated by *Sonic the Hedgehog.*

With their first computer ready to use, Berry propelled her friends to the waiting area to indulge in a break. Leslie and Vonnie collapsed in donated orange molded chairs while Berry wheeled the new padded receptionist's swivel chair out from behind the counter.

Berry stretched her arms high to shake off her tension and enjoyed another charge of pride at the way the Center had come together. She wanted this time of accomplishment and comradery to last forever.

"We need massages. Daily," said Leslie. She slipped into the denim jacket she wore at the merest air-conditioned chill, and out of caution that there might be a chill, like a true Floridian.

Vonnie tapped the sheet of instructions. "We should wait and let MJ finish up here before we run into as many problems as we have so far."

Leslie pressed her fingertips together and pressed them to her lips. "What will the Center do when MJ's not available?"

With a laugh, Vonnie said, "We'll depend on you."

"What if I'm not around? Wouldn't you rather know how to use your own tools?"

"Not around?" Leslie had become part of their family so quickly it wasn't possible to imagine their lives without her. "I don't like to think about the possibility, but you're right as rain," answered Berry. "Have I bitten off more than I can chew? The red tape to carry mifepristone has convinced me not to offer it on-site. I simply want to bring improved health care to women who can't afford much of it, not run a business."

"These days," Leslie said, "everything's a business, thanks to insurance companies and government regulations."

Vonnie said, "When you put it that way, I have to agree. If we're taking health care into our own hands, we'd better understand the technology it runs on."

"This last computer isn't much different from the other two. It'll be a snap. You'll see." Leslie's confidence was convincing. She announced she was off to Pansy's for cold drinks and took orders.

"That woman is a gem," Vonnie said once Leslie left with her habitual skip.

"Leslie's bright as a new penny. She's rehabbed Gran so thoroughly, we don't need her anymore at night. She has a business of her own to run, but I don't want to let her go. She's with Gran weekdays for appointments, cooking, gardening. She changes her bed linens and launders them—the chores Gran once insisted she do herself, but no longer has the stamina or inclination."

Vonnie asked, "Is Leslie with anyone? I mean, is she likely to stick around, or will she fall for another wandering minstrel?"

"There was someone, but I didn't ask for the status. Dollars to doughnuts she's here to stay."

"I'd love to hire her for the new program at the Housing Authority— it's too much for one person to run alone, but with my future assets under attack, I'll be lucky to pay for one part-time person."

"She says she wants to work for herself, or I'd ask her to take on the front desk position here: reception, scheduling, bookkeeping, computers, supervising the aides. She'd learn medical records and coding. Leslie could plain keep us in business."

Leslie stepped in through the doorway with a cardboard beverage tray. "That's quite a job description."

"Oh, good, you heard what we want to do," Berry said. "If we can dredge up the money. I'm determined to hire a woman like you who's both skilled and compassionate."

Leslie waved the drinks to encompass the Center. "I wouldn't mind working for you, for this. Gran hardly needs me at this point except as a friend. I could find a part-time gig as a caregiver and schedule around what you need."

Berry silently thanked the Great Spirit—and MJ—for bringing this woman into her life.

Leslie's face was glowing. "What a day. This, plus I got a pretty good look at a Carolina wren a minute ago in the stand of trees out back."

"How do you find these birds?" asked Vonnie. "I'm happy to catch sight of a mockingbird or to hear a cardinal. I love them all, but spotting and putting names to them—I guess I'm always too busy to take the time."

"I heard it. *Teakettle, teakettle.* That's its song. They're so cute, cocking their tails when they hunt."

"You're practically an encyclopedia of birds."

"Studying nature is a comfort when your heart's broken in as many pieces as mine."

"Your day will come, out of nowhere, when you're not looking," Vonnie said and let out a satisfied sigh at her first sip of tea. She turned to Berry. "Did you ever think about your sister Opal working with you?"

There was silence but for the HVAC guys grappling with sheet metal down the hall. Talk of her sister never failed to renew the unfathomable shock of Opal's news, the repellant image of her sister as she was violently removed from her dying mother, the abysmal reverberations of loss.

When Berry answered, her voice was thick with swallowed tears. "I am thankful I landed in Gran's tried-and-true hands. My father's mother meant well. You know how they do, grandparents—they judge the in-law, find them lacking, grab what control of the grandchild they can because they're certain they know best. Whenever I was at Gran Garland's in Georgia, it was like I was twisted to the breaking point. Ma's easy laughing ways, Grammy Garland's dogged stringency."

"So, Opal is a pill?" Vonnie asked.

"It's too bad. I try to like her. A sister of my own—I ought to be overjoyed. Jaudon tells me I'm a dumb cluck to worry this half to death, and maybe I am. It's not right, how cool I am to my own flesh and blood. Ma would want us to feel a rapport. Let me tell you, Opal's a thorn in my side."

Leslie set her cup on the counter. "If you don't mind my two cents, I've been unimpressed when I've seen her at your house. She patronizes Gran—and me—and avoids the obliging Jaudon like she's an infectious disease." Leslie turned to Vonnie. "Opal stares at Berry as if she'd like to dissect her mind."

"My sister wants to know what makes me tick. It shames me to say I don't much care for her."

Vonnie tut-tutted her. "That so-called church your sister belongs to is riddled with do-gooders who won't help a soul unless you accept their religion. Before they hand you a meal, you have to bow your head and repeat after the server, *Thank you, Jesus*, whether you're an atheist, Buddhist, Muslim, or Jewish. They'll feed gays but won't offer us temporary shelter because they believe we proselytize homosexuality as much as they do Christianity. Like anyone approaches their aggressive level."

"I don't understand that. What kind of God doesn't love us all?" Leslie looked at her wild Swatch watch with its third eye. "Can we finish that last computer?"

"Wherever did you come from, Leslie Gardner?" asked Berry. "I thank my lucky stars that you're able to keep us on task. Did your folks raise you to be a leader?"

Leslie skirted the question. "I'm no leader, but I'd like us to go home sometime tonight."

Cullie walked in, stopped, and listened.

"Don't be a spoilsport, Leslie," said Vonnie. "I want to order in a pizza and pull an all-nighter."

Cullie said, "You'd leave your gorgeous hunk of woman to her own devices?"

"MJ can take care of herself on her own once in a while."

Leslie was laughing. "That's exactly what I'd be afraid of."

"Is that why you're not with anyone? You don't want to be burned again?" Vonnie asked.

Leslie fiddled with the computer mouse. "I'm not exactly not with anyone."

Vonnie exchanged a glance with Berry. "Do tell."

Leslie obviously tried to hide a smile. "She's a regular person, nothing glamorous. Works at the airport, in the tower."

"Air traffic controller?" Cullie guessed.

"And the stress got to her."

"How do you fix that?" Berry asked.

"She posted for other types of jobs. And she lifts weights." Leslie was petite but lifted an invisible weight in the air, puffed out her cheeks and lips under the fantasy strain. "She is beyond strong."

Berry rubbed a thumbnail across her bottom lip and contemplated the inconceivable loss of Leslie. "She applied for jobs away from here?"

"I hope not."

Vonnie read the now familiar instructions aloud as they returned to the office. This setup did go smoothly. They congratulated one another, and Cullie broke up the computer boxes.

"We can do that," protested Berry.

"Three fetching femmes? You'll break your pretty nails."

Vonnie tossed a piece of packing Styrofoam at Cullie. "Watch that butch chauvinism."

Cullie fended off the Styrofoam with a forearm. "I just came off shift and finished a pile-up of reports. Allison's at a council meeting. If anything needs to be done here, let me do it, okay?" She took the handcart Berry kept by the door.

"You? Help?" Leslie looked at the others. "Isn't this the woman who keeps us in such stitches we can't accomplish the teensiest task?"

They waited with silent curiosity. Cullie grunted and cursed before she backed into the office with a water dispenser and five-gallon jug on the dolly.

Leslie hopped up and helped her steady the items.

"Do you want it? One of the district stations put in an electric water cooler that chills the water, and I nabbed this sucker before it disappeared into county storage. You'll have to pay for water and paper cups."

Berry clasped her hands with zeal. "Of course we want it. Under staff control. If we leave it here, kids will turn reception into an aquarium. Go ahead and bring it behind the counter for now."

Cullie maneuvered it into place and swiveled the dolly from under it. "Thanky, thanky, for relieving me of my watery burden." She wiped sweat from her face with her uniform shirttail.

"Who in the county supplies water for this at an affordable price?"

"Boy howdy, let me think while you lovely lasses tackle whatever it is you're tackling."

"Lovely lasses?" Vonnie repeated. "One more macho cop remark from you and I swear, Cullie…"

"No swearing," said Cullie. "Berry's a lady and doesn't 'preciate cuss words. She cured Jaudon of it, and I guess by and by she'll teach the rest of us."

Berry clapped a hand to her head and made a long-suffering face. "You were right, Leslie. She's an honest-to-gosh comedian. But we'll forgive you if you come up with a water company."

Cullie twirled an index finger until it stood upright by her head. "I've got it. Citrus Source Water Suppliers. That's the one we use at work."

Berry knitted her brow. "Isn't that a company started by Opal's outfit—Intracoastal Ministries—to employ their followers? They have sales and delivery routes in Florida, Alabama, and Georgia."

"It's a small world," said Vonnie. "Too small sometimes."

Cullie turned serious. "Now that I think of it, I've seen the trucks. That Jesus fish symbol stands out, sure as can be."

Fear stabbed through Berry.

"Why do they act like an endangered cult with their secret symbol?" asked Leslie, tapping her chin with a knuckle. "Christians are the majority religion in this country."

Berry knew she needed to hold her tongue, but she was mad. "To pretend they're victims, targets of liberal plots. That whips up fear in their congregations and unifies them. It brings in more money when they claim a cause. Control of women's bodies is the favorite. They've gotten away with it for so long."

Vonnie said, "Your newfound sister has the fish sticker on her car."

"I never noticed." Berry massaged her forehead. She pined for… she wasn't sure what. Had she experienced serenity so far in her life? There had been times, with Jaudon in particular, and likely before Ma and Pa left, certainly while in the garden or at the edge of the pond, riveted by the rummaging, whinnying, laughing moorhens. A nonnative big-footed purple swamp hen stalking across water hyacinth and lotus rendered her euphoric. But peace? Something always got in its way.

She asked Cullie, "You're around town. Can you find us a more sympathetic source?"

"At your service, amigo, and I'll do you one more. I'll donate the first year of water."

Berry got up and hugged Cullie. "You can't afford that on a cop's salary."

"Can't afford not to. I'll be going now. It's my night to cook, and I need to stop at Publix to buy a couple of chicken, mashed potato, and peas frozen dinners."

Vonnie cocked an eyebrow at Cullie. "You call that cooking? What's for dessert, Fluffernutters?"

"Heck, yeah, forget the TV dinners, I'll make Fluffernutters plus cook up a poke sallet on the side, for our health."

They laughed. "Allison will love that," Berry said.

"There are many deep secrets you don't know about your pal Allison. She wants me to cook fried okra. Her family turned up its noses at okra. As Allison often quotes, culture is more powerful than political systems."

Vonnie moved behind Cullie and massaged her shoulders. "Be respectful of your mayor. Where would we be without Allison Millar to lead the way?"

"I'd be single and scrubbing algae slime off pools for a living."

The mailperson poked her head inside the office. She placed one envelope on the counter.

"Uh-oh," said Cullie as she backed toward the door.

Tight-lipped, Berry picked it up. The return address was the county Code Enforcement Department. She met Cullie's eyes.

Cullie said, "You and Jaud come around our place and show that to Allison anytime, you hear?"

CHAPTER THIRTEEN

Berry Garland

October 1999

The obstacles they had to overcome and the final preparations to open the Women's Health Center dragged on and on. One slightly chilly October day, to end her little sister's importuning and to take an afternoon off from her job at the ob-gyn practice, as well as Center battles, Berry drove to Opal's home near MacDill Air Force Base. The house backed up to the formidable smell and noise of an auto body shop.

One room after the next was painted a shiny white. The windows were hung with semisheer white curtains doing a poor job of barring the sun. Surely someone raised in Georgia knew to block the sunniest sides of a house throughout the day, thought Berry.

Opal wore a white top with a droopy calf-length white skirt, white crew socks, and her polished white sneakers. She announced that the air-conditioning was broken.

The color scheme might have worked in one room, but Berry squinched her eyes against the ongoing visual shock of blank walls and wiped sweat from her face with an old tissue she found in her pocket. The powerful lemony scent of an air freshener didn't help. Opal's six children lived at home—how was the white furniture this pristine?

Opal opened the door to a sizable den, saying, "Quite the trophy hunter, isn't he?"

Taxidermied animals were mounted on the walls. She was sickened and turned away. Opal knowingly married a murderer of innocent creatures. What right did he have to deprive them of life? This semi-industrial strip they lived behind was no more than the spoils of humanity's war on nature. It replaced animal homes and feeding grounds with housing for people who assumed they were earth's highest priority and entitled to take whatever enriched and empowered them. Before she gagged on her fury, she pointed toward the laughing and yelling coming from the pool.

"This pool has been a godsend," Opal said, drifting away from the cruel room. "Once church school is done for the day, they pile out here, and I can relax before I start dinner. Weekends too, after Saturday Bible school or church." She opened the lanai door to reveal an inground swimming pool. "There's a lot of work to one of these. I have to test the water, add chemicals, clean a mile of tile."

The children had gone silent and watched their mother with startled eyes.

"Here's Aunt Berry come to visit." As one, the youngsters, who ranged from toddler to teen, moved their eyes to Berry. A boy about eight years old cleared his throat and led her nephews in chorus.

"Pleased to meet you, Aunt Berry."

Before she responded to this quick *Sound of Music* style performance with anything other than a startled smile, their mother slid the door closed and marshaled Berry along the glossy white hall into the glossy white kitchen.

She needed to slip away from the unsettling house and its strange children. She motioned to the large window. "It's such a lovely day, let's walk while we talk."

Opal narrowed her eyes and folded her arms. Two lines deepened between her eyebrows. "We agreed on tea. I made sandwiches and baked my special lemon pound cake for you."

Prickly, she thought, and sat where her sister pointed in the breakfast nook. How did she feed six children and a husband in such a dinky space? Doubtless there was a trough somewhere, she reflected a bit viciously. That room of murdered animals stuck like an earworm in her thoughts. She looked out the window at a chain-link fence and the house next door, a twin to the one she was in but for a vibrant lawn. Here was a whole different Florida, miles from the Vicker homestead in way of life as well as distance. She wished herself at tonight's softball game. The Beverage Bays and a local soft drink distributing company cosponsored the Rainbow Ragers.

Opal removed a large dish from the refrigerator and fussed with plastic wrap. She brought a tray with a pitcher of tea and two glasses to the table, followed by the platter of tiny sandwiches.

"I'm sure you'll like Grammy's special recipe for deviled ham," said Opal.

She knew she'd told her sister she was vegetarian and met her eyes, flummoxed. "I didn't know there was a meatless deviled ham."

"Meatless? No, it's pork."

"I'm sorry. I'm vegetarian. Would you mind if I stick with pound cake and tea?"

Opal looked at the sandwiches. "Do you think these will keep two days? I may bring them to the ladies' Bible group."

"Won't the kids like them?"

"If the ladies don't sneak them out in napkins for their husbands. If they do, I'll stir up a pot of whatever for the goobers later. As long as I leave a loaf of bread on the table with soup, they fill themselves up. What can you eat?"

"Anything but meat, fish, and poultry. I do eat eggs and dairy products."

"Egg salad sandwiches would work?"

"I love them."

"I can make you a fried egg sandwich right now."

"No, no, I'm fine with tea and cake."

She watched as her sister swathed the sandwiches in plastic, fetched the cake, cut and served it.

Opal wiped crumbs from her hands on her apron. "Now. I want you to tell me about my parents."

She expected this question about their one commonality and was prepared. "Ma and Pa were fun-loving kids themselves, and they were high on playing with and showing off their cute kid. They married because of me. I remember motorcycle rides up to Grammy and Grandpa Garland's in Georgia, me on Ma's lap behind Pa, Ma's arms around Pa. I had my own helmet. Sometimes we lived here, sometimes there."

"Until you were eight, when they left you too."

"I was supposed to fly to California when Pa had a job and money for my plane fare."

"Are you sure about that?"

"At first, yes, but when we never heard from them again, I was afraid I'd been bad and drove them away."

"Or they didn't want the burden of a kid anymore."

"How can you say that when you have six?"

Opal's eyes revealed a frantic anger. "Grammy Garland said our parents wanted to abort me. She gave them hail Columbia. They made me, she said, it was plain sinful to turn their backs on me."

"I wish they never told you."

"She also warned them they had no call to run off and motorcycle across the whole country with a child inside her. A million mishaps happen in the middle of nowhere. She made them swear on the family Bible they would treat me like another precious gift from the Lord. They never did keep that promise," Opal said with a derisive laugh.

Though the pound cake was perfectly fine, it became more and more difficult to swallow. "I had no idea."

"'Course you didn't. Poor left-behind eight-year-old. You weren't a plaything to show off anymore once you started school and made friends your own age. It's hard on children when their roots are yanked up and they're tossed from one school to another. I know my kids aren't fond of their father's roving career, but they've got the two of us doing our best for them. You and me, we weren't blessed that way."

"But they planned to send for me."

"They wanted to be hippies more than they wanted to be parents."

Tremors rippled through her body. She massaged her forehead with the tips of her fingers. She refused to allow those uncertainties into her life again.

"That is not true," she said. "Why do you make them out to be ogres? They were young, joyful, living their lives. Pa taught me to swim. Ma schooled me on the natural world. They helped me with my lessons, made learning fun. I was flying to California before my ninth birthday."

"Do you have any idea what it's like to know you were so unwanted your parents planned to kill you?"

"You don't know that."

"Grammy—"

"Those were cruel words if she, in truth, said them." She wished Ma and Pa had been saved, instead of her sister, and automatically reprimanded herself for the thought. Could be Grammy, for her own reasons, made up other facts. Had Ma really died before they delivered Opal? Why not save her instead of this aberration?

When she opened her eyes, sunlight on a white wall made her squint again. "Is that why you have six children?"

"I can't imagine a one of them not walking this earth."

It took every drop of graciousness inside her to say, "Tell me about them."

And Opal did, in detail, from their births to the youngest's church school report cards. "It's my job to bring my husband's children into this world and teach them the Lord's word."

Later, the children filed past the kitchen door, wet towels draped over their shoulders, their rubber flip-flops slapping the floor. The eight-year-old boy stopped the procession, announced that they were going to do homework, and led them upstairs.

Berry took the opportunity to stand and wish her sister a happy weekend. She offered a light hug, which was more lightly returned.

At Opal's front door, Berry said, "Next time, why don't you visit at our house? Gran would like that."

Opal hesitated, looked away.

Berry didn't know her well, but she knew the signs of someone ready to fib.

Motioning to the second floor, Opal said, "I've got my kids."

"Some morning, then? While they're in school? I can take a morning off."

Opal pulled the front door open. "Those are working hours. I go over to the church to help out. It reduces their tuitions. This is my free time."

Berry shrugged her shoulders in defeat and went to her car. The paint fumes from the auto body shop stung her nostrils and blocked them. Opal's kids needed to wear industrial masks outdoors.

From between the mock columns at the front door, Opal called, "Y'all come back, you hear?"

Sure enough, she thought, but why in the world didn't her own sister want to visit her mother's mother?

As Berry pulled out of the driveway into Opal's street of copycat houses, she shook her head, sad to see the Howells' yellowed lawn and weeds killed off by lingering summer heat—and probably shop toxins. Opal wasn't wasting water on her yard. The landscapes we create, she thought, reflect who we are. What did that say about her and her own catch-as-catch-can gardening?

CHAPTER FOURTEEN

Jaudon Vicker

January 2000

Jaudon and MJ were alone at the Center to replace a window cracked by vandals the night before. MJ, from a ladder, lifted the sash, swung out the bottom, and began the real work. Jaudon handed and retrieved MJ's tools: screwdrivers, caulking gun, cordless drill, putty knife, level.

MJ wore safety goggles and gloves as she unscrewed the frame and removed broken glass. Splinters fell to the ground. "Has there been any movement on the zoning complaint?"

"The Center's up and running the best it can with that hanging over it."

She emptied a dustpan filled with glass pieces into a paper grocery bag, straightened and gave MJ a utility knife, bent to brush more glass into the pan, and came up declaring, "I'm ready to go to the sheriff myself and raise Cain about it. Why they let some ignoramus hog-tie Berry's boon to the community I don't know—except the county never has paid no nevermind to what goes on in this part of town."

"It shows."

"Poor Berry is itching to have a grand opening, maybe get some good publicity and draw in donations, but zoning won't give her any information except the property is set aside for commercial use, not for a nonprofit. They'll fine us if we don't close shop. They let the shopping centers, cinemas, and luxury retirement communities swallow whole orchards and farmland, historic homes, and the mom-and-pop businesses. Can you believe some county boneheads are siding with the complainer to protect big businesses against us do-gooders?"

"You have no idea who lodged the complaint?" MJ asked.

"Some man Cullie says must be new in town or live out of state because she can't find a record of him. He's a lady-killer, she heard, and not in an admirable way."

MJ crooked her neck. "There's never an admirable way." She gave a careful tug to the last large piece of glass stuck in the frame. "Could be the big bad supermarket across the street is afraid more nonprofits will open and compete with them. As if. Or the county doesn't want so-called undesirables to congregate along a state route."

"You mean they're being small-minded about poor people."

"Isn't that always the bottom line?"

"But here at this end of Laudre Flats Boulevard?" She picked up a box cutter to help loosen the window's original caulk and envisioned other actions she'd take with a cutter if she found out who complained. "Berry's scared spitless they'll give Mrs. Lanamore trouble for having an apartment in a nonresidential zone."

"Did Cullie tell you the guy's name?"

"Never heard of him. Howser? Howland?" Jaudon laughed. "Probably Howlin'. Allison's trying to make out what stake the mystery man has in stopping the Center, if any."

MJ puffed out her cheeks and slowly discharged a breath. "Undoubtedly someone wants to put a development behind the building."

Jaudon accepted the heavy section of glass MJ handed down and went to lean it against the wall. "Can't. It's wetlands as far as that subdivision off Eulalia. Remember Berry had to show the environment inspector around?"

"And she foresaw no impact from the Center."

"Not unless we dump medical waste out back. Anyway, why not have a nonprofit in with the for-profits?"

"Presumably, it worked to somebody's disadvantage once upon a time."

"We're up against a wall. The egg-suckin' dawgs will pay bigger taxes than us. Against someone like that, we can't win for losing."

MJ smirked. "Oh, we'll win alright. This isn't my first rodeo with zoning. I never needed a lawyer. Never had to fight anonymous pig-headed opposition with its heels dug in. Seriously, we resolve that and the freight elevator permission, and the Center is home free."

She watched MJ's quick meticulousness compared to her own messy pile of glass chips. "Will they crab about that too?"

"I don't know why they would. There's a building height exception for elevator housing and other roof structures we'll need. Our engineer is passionate about the project—she's one of those throwaway Job Corps kids we hired when we started VONCO. Put herself through college."

"Engineers are expensive."

"She's interning with another woman engineer for the experience she needs to earn her license. Don't worry, there's a decent honorarium for her. We have to use an engineer for safety. You know what I mean—can the framework bear an elevator installation? Will it retain its structural integrity with an elevator's transits up and down? What kind of motor and how fast do we need it to be?"

"Makes me happy I had sense enough never to build any new Beverage Bays after we lost the two." Jaudon leaned backward, hands splayed behind her hips, and stretched her back. "Truth to tell, I guess it was Rouie Waver and Pops talked me out of it. New construction swallows money whole."

"I make deals where I can. The elevator and a lot of the HVAC Vaughn and I can't do, but honestly? Vaughn's and my contacts discount for us because they believe the Center is needed."

"Did you have women's health services in Washington State?" MJ's descriptions sounded so different from Florida.

"Are you kidding me? We didn't have a medical practice in my town. There was a teensy hospital a bit downriver."

"What did you do, canoe there?"

MJ laughed in her soundless way. Jaudon noticed she no longer screened her mouth with her hand as much. As a kid, had she been shut down for laughing?

"Shoot," MJ said. "The Columbia is a windy river with powerful waters. No way you'd drag me out there in a canoe, a kayak, or—remembering all the tourist accidents—a motorboat. We did have roads, for your information, and vehicles with rubber tires."

As they tromped to the dumpster, Jaudon held the paper bag of glass away from her body like it contained radium. "It's hard to believe some people think women's health isn't fit to mention in polite company. Berry has patients who still call ob-gyns *lady doctors*." She gave a braying laugh. "The Center would be safer named Lady Doctors."

Later, when the window was reinstalled, MJ asked, "Are you thinking this might be more than a zoning issue?"

"I'm inclined to disbelieve what the county tells me. I'm equally interested to know more about who this pest is that complained. We done here? I need to use the john."

Tools stored in her truck, MJ followed Jaudon inside. She talked through the wall of the stall. "I did a quick check myself, and he's not a developer, not an attorney, not a Realtor, though there are so many of those I might have missed one. We need Allison's investigation."

She called out, "You don't reckon he's from one of those holier-than-thou groups that want to ban *Huckleberry Finn* from the libraries? They seem to think women in business means bake sales."

MJ laughed. "I don't know that it will improve now we know Al Gore will run against Bush."

"You don't think he can beat that do-nothing Texan?"

"He should, but I'm not too confident he will. These Republicans are desperate to ruin President Clinton's accomplishments. In the meantime, I'm confident Berry will score a variance from the county. As you said, they never cared about this part of town before."

"You have a walloping heap of confidence for someone who grew up in a family like yours."

"You and I have grit to spare, Boss. Your mother wasn't exactly your biggest champion."

"I had Pops, and Berry shared Gran with me when Momma wasn't around to keep us apart. Momma didn't like competition, despite the fact the competition, Gran, baked treats for the family or made soups when a Vicker came down sick."

Jaudon emerged wiping her hands on a paper towel and launched it basketball style into a bin.

"Now, there's an idea," said MJ. "Why not have a bake sale? A five-dollar cake, a fifty-cent cookie, bring money in as certainly as large donors, and you might make a dent in our lawyer fees."

Jaudon pushed open the front door with her bottom and locked it behind them. "Maybe you're not as bright as I assumed you were. You want to have a bake sale outside a bakery?"

"You know what I'm saying, smart-ass. Some kind of fundraiser."

"A homegrown street carnival?"

"Think of your liability issues first." One minute outside and MJ already wiped sweat from her forehead. "We don't have to be fancy. Hopscotch, jump rope contests, a basketball hoop, a white elephant sale for the adults. You can store donated items here at the Center."

Jaudon was getting psyched up. "A couple of those sets where you stand behind a painted costume with your face showing and have a Polaroid picture taken. A popcorn machine."

"By the time you rent that stuff you might break even."

She pointed her key at MJ. "You can be a total goofball. You're the one to take a notion to put on a charity event."

"You can boil peanuts in the Center kitchenette and bring your grill here to keep them warm. I'll bet Shady knows where to borrow a basketball hoop. We can set up in the parking lot if Mrs. Lanamore allows it. Simple is free."

"Let's do it next weekend."

"Boss, you're as excited as a nine-year-old. Carnivals happen spring or summer. It'll take time to set this all up."

CHAPTER FIFTEEN

MJ Beaudry

May 2000

Not six months later, Attorney Rich Slumkey deciphered the department's own rules for the zoning administrator. Strangely, the area disallowed not-for-profits like trade and professional associations, fraternal societies, and sports clubs. The Center, in contrast, was a nonprofit organization—owned by the community, with a board of directors which held regular meeting to make decisions about budgets, mission, staffing—and was perfectly legal right where it was.

There would be no fine, but Rich's fees were an unanticipated expense not in the Center's budget.

Word of the Center's laudable plans and need for funds got around. Neighborhood kids who agreed to post or hand out flyers for the fair earned free admission. Throughout the morning, MJ and Jaudon gave each other high fives as the homespun street fair crowd surged in Mrs. Lanamore's parking lot.

Berry's Gran had signed on first thing, saying, "I can't help the dead, so I may as well try and help the living."

Gran and Leslie claimed dibs on prepping and selling fresh-squeezed lemonade and boiled peanuts. Leslie's strapping girlfriend, whose hobby was weightlifting, did the squeezing with such intense concentration MJ wondered what lighthearted Leslie saw in the woman.

As MJ helped assemble the sales table, Gran became nostalgic.

"I used to take young June, Berry's Ma, to a church fair like this near the elementary school in Plant City. That neck of the woods wasn't nearly so built-up then. I don't recall sidewalks. Houses plopped down here and there.

"The carousal organ music was recorded, but she baby-danced to it, in the floral print pinafore dress I made from a pattern. June was a cutie, with thick wavy hair and a smile made of white sugar. There was no holding her from whatever she wanted to do, be it picking posies on the roadsides or marrying her daredevil true love." Gran bent her head. "I'm well pleased June was with me at all. And I always love a fair."

At the other end of the building, Mrs. Lanamore turned her open sign to *Closed* at noon. The bakery was churning out goodies to make money for the Center. Duval, with his flair for art, had designed large poster board arrows to tack on poles and walls, directing customers toward the fair, but had not referenced the purpose of the fair itself. They didn't want to catch the attention of any cops or city officials.

Jaudon and Tad covered the borrowed tables with butcher paper. Tad wheeled his basketball hoop stand and backboard out of storage. He wouldn't hear of anyone but himself presiding over the free-throw drills and contests—he'd never made the team in high school but loved the sport.

The Senior Center activity program, of all places, loaned Benedict Hula-Hoops and jump ropes for the day. Berry enticed her work friend Laura to coordinate the Hula-Hoops for fun. Laura invited her sister, Olive Ponder—who'd been a neighborhood jump rope champ in her youth—to supervise and judge the jumpers.

Olive's lawyer son, Emmett, covered her shift at the store for the cause. He'd worked his way through college and law school at the Beverage Bays. Benedict Lam now mentored him in his own specialty, regulated industries and public utilities.

Benedict and Berry were at the makeshift gate, selling fifty-cent entrance tickets to the kids—the youngest got in free—and two-dollar tickets to the adults who were drawn to the music and danced on a green square Duval painted across the parking lot concrete. Shady invited a newly formed Latin band eager for an audience and ferried equipment on his lap to and from the taped area he called the main stage. Later, older people swung to a pickup group of gray-haired brass players, Black and white mixed. They were joined by a woman singer, big, loud, and sexy, who sang pop songs from the forties and fifties. A rap/break dance team with a monster boombox brought in the teens.

MJ slipped over to Vonnie for a one-minute rumba. They'd

practiced often on the beach for the love of the dance and moved with precision and enthusiastic hip action.

Encouraging cries of "Olé!" erupted on all sides.

Vendors of handcrafted goods gave half their sales to the Center. Candles, soaps, laser-engraved leather products, jams and jellies, books, and a psychic worked off their own tables. Perfecta Maldonado, another old feminist friend of Berry's, offered chair massages, all proceeds for the Center. Judy Fish and Mercie Lewis staffed a health information table and offered handouts explaining the Center.

Vaughn laid out basic carpentry tools on a six-foot table. He and one of his crew taught interested kids—and women—how to use each tool. His pupils practiced on scrap wood.

Donation buckets dotted the tables. Mayor Allison and Vonnie, seasoned fundraisers, worked the crowd with donation pails. Jaudon pulled her wallet from her rear pocket and seeded the buckets with five-dollar bills. Duval sold jumbo cinnamon rolls and sugar doughnuts he and Tad made early that morning. Cullie was on nights that week so wore her uniform to provide a semblance of security.

Midway through the festival, Tad hoisted himself atop a table and called for attention. "Some of you might not have heard that two days ago, May 18, 2000, both houses of the South Carolina General Assembly voted to take the Confederate flag down from their capitol dome."

The mixed-race crowd clapped and cheered.

"'Bout time we celebrated—about one hundred and fifty years too late."

People called out, "Damn right," "Praise the Lord," and "'Bout time."

He said, "Did I plan to buy one of those flags to burn? Fat chance."

He waved over a full-bodied, pretty Black woman with a loose Afro and contagious smile. "I asked this artist I know to draw that flag. This here is Laura Bathgate."

"Hi, Laura," called a patient from the ob-gyn office and a man with an easel who made and sold caricatures of people.

She and Tad unrolled a length of butcher paper that depicted a hastily drawn and colored Confederate flag.

"Okay with you if I burn this cursed flag?"

"Long as I can help," answered Laura. She called to the crowd, "Those South Carolina dudes planted a smaller Confederate flag in front of the building."

The fairgoers booed, echoed loudly by the children.

Tad held the flag while Laura flicked his red lighter to the paper. Those gathered around them fell quiet. Once it was ash, Tad and Laura sat at the edge of the table, legs swinging, talking. MJ pictured an electric current flowing between them.

The rummage sale was a hit.

Ah, the rummage sale, thought MJ. Run by the three business-women: Mrs. Lanamore, Jaudon, and herself. Each asked for an extra dollar more than any item cost as the fairgoers crowed over bargains. They made the most money from raffles. The biggest prize came compliments of a large local appliance and repair store: an old model, but brand-new refrigerator with ice cube and cold-water functions. The company had serviced the Beverage Bay refrigerated cases since day one. MJ's plumbing parts supplier offered a set of new faucets, and her locksmith came up with a generous gift certificate.

All day they sold ice cream sandwiches and Popsicles from that refrigerator.

By two p.m., the rummage sale items were down to unappealing vases, several mugs, two complete sets of encyclopedias, an avocado-green electric can opener, garish costume jewelry Mrs. Lanamore beseeched bargain hunters to buy, and a brick-red hide-a-bed that Jaudon allowed in on the condition that if it didn't sell, the donors remove it.

Once she finished judging the cutest pet event, Berry dropped to a donor's clumsily repaired cane chair. She was smiling, but tears of gratitude leaked from her eyes and she patted them with a tissue. Women stopped to thank and praise her.

MJ studied Berry. She asked Jaudon, "Am I wrong, or is your girl frailish? She's not sick, is she?"

Jaudon raised her face to the cloudless sky and lifted her arms. "I have asked her and asked her, but she'll never admit she's feeling low. She doesn't like to be a burden on other people. She's run down because she juggles too many jobs and projects, but those look like happy tears. It'll mean a lot to her that the people who'll use and, in due course, operate the Center are here to champion it."

A hot wind came up, blowing away the last of the smell of popping corn. They wanted to end the fair before the afternoon rain soaked everything. As MJ watched Berry at rest, she caught sight of a white man parking a black minivan directly in front of the entrance table. Her hopes of more buyers rose.

"What the hey," she said aloud when he went to the rear of the van and robotically passed signs to his passengers and to a string of people who'd arrived in cars. Skateboarders hovered, doing ticktacks around the van and between stony-eyed women and men, mostly white, and three people of color. The brass band lowered their instruments. The children slowly ended their games, competitions, and horsing around. Soon the jump ropes stopped their whirring, and the shouting and laughter ceased. All eyes were on the sign bearers.

Jaudon asked, "Who are those sourpusses? They look like they've been chawing on briars and can't pass 'em. Jiminy, Samantha O'Connor from Berry's old women's group is with them. She was a feminist, for crying out loud."

MJ caught Cullie's eye and told Jaudon to stay put, but Jaudon raised her eyebrows at Mrs. Lanamore, who signaled that she'd cover the rummage sale and raffle tickets by waving her away. The three butches marched to the van.

They passed Leslie, who impeded the intruders by stepping in front of them, looking daggers, not her usual unfazeable self.

"Excuse me, sir," MJ said. "This is private property."

The man with the signs never looked her way.

"Folks," Jaudon shouted, arms out to block the entrance. "The fee is two dollars per adult." They kept coming, about twenty of them, signs held high. Judy and Mercie bolted from their table and locked arms to either side of Jaudon and MJ. The newcomers split into two columns, walked around them. Their signs condemned abortion and birth control or praised abstinence. The women were in long skirts and plain long-sleeved blouses. The men wore their hair military-short and their beards untended.

Cullie stood aside, watching. Jaudon asked her if there was a way to legally kick them out.

"Nope. They're trespassing on private property, but that doesn't hold water when the fair is open to the public."

The intruders buttonholed young and old alike, spitting the words *abomination*, *abstinence*, *genocide*, *murder*, *adultery*; informing Black people that abortion was a plot to decrease their numbers.

"Who do you answer to?" they chanted at the white women, to raise the Blacks' suspicions, as if woman's health was controlled by some conspiratorial entity.

Their signs depicted fetuses and smiling white babies. A squat man proselytized Berry. She held her face in her hands, swiveled her head back and forth, repeating, "No, no, no." He turned up his lip as if seagull droppings landed on him.

MJ hesitated to interfere. If anyone, it should be Jaudon, but she was shouldering intruders into the street, Leslie's beefy girlfriend beside her, as intent as she'd been while squeezing lemons. This was an invasion. She thought, *don't these joyless people ever give up?*

Berry stood with an abruptness unlike her mild self. MJ watched as she trotted away. The guy harassing her followed, leaning over her shoulder, haranguing. Olive pursued him, tried to grab his arm.

In one startling movement, Berry swirled and kicked him hard in the knee. He yelled foul curses as he went down. Berry tore the sign he'd dropped and stomped on it. Even in his pain he tried to grab her but fell back after a shove from Olive.

His compatriots helped him up. "We're coming back for you, you lezzie baby killer. You're going to be sorrier than shit."

MJ was certain those were the most violent actions Berry and Olive had taken in their entire lives. She watched to see if the proselytizer would retaliate. He went to Cullie. "I hope you arrest those women for assault."

"And hope is a full-on banshee. How about"—Cullie rubbed her hands together—"if I arrest you for harassment and provocation. She defended herself. The other lady helped."

Berry held her own, but this invasion was going to interfere with the Center's ability to pay the lawyer. MJ jogged over to Shady.

Shady had clearly decided to drown out the protesters with Michael Jackson's "Billie Jean."

"How do we rid ourselves of these fanatics?" Berry yelled.

"They're freaking me out," said Shady. "Cullie can't arrest them for harassment?"

"I wanted to call it in, but she thinks that would cause more problems. After all, this fair is open to the public."

"You'd better believe if it was an intrusion of Black people, they'd be on us like water ants on a crumb."

Ironically, two more white adults arrived, but Jaudon greeted them with warmth. She led Attorney Rich Slumkey and his wife to the impromptu bandstand. A musician offered him the mic, and Rich turned it over to his wife.

"I'll be brief," she announced. "My name is Penny Slumkey. My husband signed on as the Center's attorney at its inception. His bills have added up, but he hasn't pressed for payment because we subscribe to the absolute necessity of medical resources like the Center. When Rich heard the community was holding a fundraiser to pay him, we made a decision. Consider his labor on the Center's behalf as a donation in kind, or pro bono. Use today's proceeds for other expenses. You owe, and will owe, Attorney Slumkey nada."

She heard translations, applause, a rise in the tone of comments. The hecklers continued their siege. Finally, nearby, a woman shouted out at a gaggle of them. "Shoo, shoo, shoo, you round-eye devils, or I'll genocide *you*."

It was Yan, the pintsized Asian American grandmother who already volunteered at the Center, setting up appointments for Berry to introduce Center resources and establish networks with local health care providers.

The woman carried a wide-brimmed sunhat and brandished it to fend off the interlopers. It didn't take long for other women in the crowd to join the attack. "Shoo, shoo, shoo," they taunted, surrounding the protestors and swiping at them with purses, hats, and wraps. "Shoo, shoo, shoo," they continued as the van filled up with the attackers, and cars left parking spaces.

The man who tried to intimidate Berry limped past, grumbling, "We won't give up."

Rich Slumkey stepped in front of him. "You do that, and I'll see the lot of you in court."

The half-dozen defenders and Yan hugged one another, gave a last chorus of *shoo, shoo, shoo*, and were applauded as some returned to the fair and others left, chattering about the experience.

"A shoo squad. Exactly what was called for," MJ said to no one, to everyone.

CHAPTER SIXTEEN

Berry Garland

September 2001

The conversion from factory floor to Women's Health Center was not accomplished overnight. The VONCO volunteers had worked long and hard on evenings and weekends for years now. Six might show up, or it might be one or none. Vaughn and MJ worked on their own when they had time. They had lives outside her dream, but Berry went daily, after work, to see the Center shape up, and now it was finished enough to work out of. She needed to have an official grand opening.

Not immediately. Not after today, September 11, 2001. Dog-tired, shaken by the barbarity she'd seen on the office TV, she went directly home and peered in on Gran, who was snoring, and wiped a thin line of drool from her face with a tissue. Poor Gran, to live long enough to see the agonizing murder of thousands more people.

She was relieved to open the fridge and find an iron skillet of veggie bean hash and a pan of string beans and taters left for them by Gran and Leslie. She teared up in gratitude. She did a lot of that these days, now that menopause had arrived at age fifty. Jaudon, whose change of life came a few months ago, had performed a private celebration with a compact fire by the pond. She'd thrown in all the tampons and pads in her supply and did a skip-step dance around the flames. She looked like a human-sized leprechaun dancing in the dark to the shrieking, crying, and screaming calls of brown-feathered limpkins plucking snails from the pond, and the bugling and peeping of hundreds of frogs.

Berry plated their meals, ready to warm in the microwave oven when Jaudon arrived. She threw some butter in the skillet to toast slices of cornbread and hoped the meal satisfied Jaudon's appetite.

She knew it was Jaudon out front because her car made such a racket bumping in and out of potholes and hitting the pea gravel. She'd tried her best to persuade Jaudon to buy a Subaru like her own if for no other reason than MJ's enthused announcement that the company advertised in a gay magazine. But Jaudon loved her first new car, heart and soul, a Buick sedan, and last year, at an age when it needed more work than the cost of a replacement, she'd refused to consider anything other than another Buick. She'd long expressed admiration for the vintage station wagon MJ lost to a hurricane. When she learned Buick had what they called Estate wagons, she bought one to haul whatever, wherever. That was her Jaudon, practical, loyal, passionate, and balky as a mule. Berry wouldn't have her any other way.

She set the table. Their portions steamed as Jaudon turned to toss her Beverage Bay vest into the laundry hopper. The ink stains from the pricing gun were the worst, but Jaudon was also expert at absorbing sour milk smells, polka dots of bleach, and all manner of grime from cleaning what part-time employees missed.

Jaudon raged. "This unhinged knucklehead drove in as I was leaving. On his radio, a newscaster talked about how hard it was to identify remains at the World Trade Center. This guy was in a patchwork gray pickup with a green hood, a cracked windshield, and bald tires. He claimed to know for a fact that the buildings were brought down with controlled demolition set up by our own government, so we'd go to war and take over the oil resources."

"He thinks we'd kill our own people to make more oil billionaires?"

"He swore he wasn't the only one who was convinced, and they plan to stop the plot."

She waited while Jaudon worked off her steam.

"As if it wasn't bad enough that terrorists attacked America? Killed thousands on collapsing dark stairways to escape burning jet fuel? I wish I had been in the plane over Pennsylvania. I'd have tossed those hijackers out at thirty-five thousand feet. See how they liked it. And this nitwit wants to start a war."

"Patients streamed into the practice all the livelong day. They didn't know what to do with their emotions about the unimaginable crashes, so they thought they were sick from burning chemicals drifting south. The doctors were run off their feet."

"Most of the customers came in, I swear, because the stores are familiar and remind them of a world that respected the United States. I told them to go home, they shouldn't be driving, but they needed things. We don't carry what they needed today, except for the liquor."

"Patients cried nonstop. Some were angry, they wanted the US to be like it was twenty-four hours ago. So do I."

They sat and faced each other, crisscrossed hands held tight over their knees, seeking reassurance in each other's eyes. When they let go, Jaudon rubbed her chin and looked puzzled.

"Was today shocking enough to interrupt hair growth?"

Berry looked at Jaudon's unusually smooth face. "Looks like it might have. This morning scared me worse than the harassment at the Center."

Jaudon slapped her hands on her knees and pushed herself up. "I haven't eaten since it happened. A hot meal will improve our outlooks." She used a napkin to wipe a tear balanced on Berry's upper lip.

Jaudon nuked Berry's plate first. Because poor Jaudon was determined to take Berry's mind off the tragedies, she choked down a bite.

"Jiminy, it doesn't get any better than this," said Jaudon in her most robust voice. "A fine hot dinner and you. I've survived on peanuts and chocolate bars and trifling amounts of you, seems like, for weeks."

Berry opened her arms. "We both have."

Before sitting, Jaudon squeezed her in a hug. "There's not a thing on earth better than coming home to you. I might have to ease off your nightie and nibble on you for a while later."

While the suggestion didn't repel her, it didn't stir her either. "I'm so tired and downhearted my hind end is dragging."

"Believe me, Georgia gal, I'm not up for anything energetic." Jaudon scooped up hash and followed it with a forkful of greens.

Berry laid her fork on the table, not intending to apologize, but to reassure. "I know we haven't made love in too long." She'd noticed that Jaudon, who always clipped her fingernails just short of the quick out of consideration for Berry's sensitive parts, had continued the practice.

"Don't be apologizing, it's both of us," said ever-understanding Jaudon. "We're busy people. Especially you, getting the Center ready to open, keeping appointments with your counseling clients, steadily working as a part-time nurse at the ob-gyn practice, Gran taking sick, the pesky zoning complaint, the protestors, your peculiar sister dropping by to set a spell. It's more than a body can take. You eat your dinner. It helps."

"I can't leave my clients in the lurch. It'll be a while before I earn an income from the Center—you agreed I'd best keep my job at minimum part-time, and anyway, Dr. Garza will donate her time until we can afford a doctor of our own. As for Gran, Leslie and Benedict have done wonders for her, but she's weak as dishwater and bears watching. I should have factored in the toll this clinic would take on Gran and you."

Jaudon was known to make snap decisions when she panicked. Most recently, she refreshed a stockpile of necessities inside a used metal shed she bought for the eventuality of Y2K toppling the world. Their friends still teased her, almost ten months later, when the supply chain held, computers kept computing, and the earth managed to stay on course.

Since then, Jaudon made an effort to take her time. After an hour or a week of pondering, her eyes would clear. She either dealt with whatever needed fixing, or she'd talk it over with Berry. Tonight, she was certain Jaudon had schemed for a while because it wasn't ten seconds before she presented her idea over bowls of peach ice cream.

"It's time to lighten your load," Jaudon announced in her business owner voice. "Attorney Slumkey made magic when the Beverage Bays almost went under. He corrected the zoning like it was of no consequence. I want you to run to him to tackle any burden that comes up, legal fees be darned. He's so slick. He unearthed that information about Encouragement Zones. If the county wanted certain highway funds, it had no choice then but to rezone this half-mile strip of Laudre Flats Boulevard from industrial/commercial to general and professional use—which makes us doubly legal."

Berry pushed uneaten food around her plate before exclaiming, "But is this health center truly what the Great Spirit means me to do? Did you hear the lies those protestors told the fairgoers? That we want to kill off the minority populations with birth control and abortion? I'm asked questions about who I answer to, as if our little Center is part of a conspiracy."

"That's hurtful." Jaudon stopped Berry from clearing the table once they finished their meal. "Go start your bath, Georgia gal. I'll clean up, take a quick shower, and meet you in bed. Don't try to stay awake on my account. I can snuggle up to you as well if you're asleep."

Between her exhaustion and Jaudon's kindness, she found herself with no will to object to Attorney Slumkey's offer of free lawyering. She wasn't comfortable taking this kind of help, but it wasn't for her; it was for the patients and clinic.

"I'll shower in the morning. Bed is calling."

"Do not pass go and do not collect two hundred kisses?"

Berry managed a weak smile.

With lovely relief she let her body find peace under the cool bedcovers.

The pleasure was short-lived. Halfway to sleep, her inviting pillow betrayed her, as her mind repeated and repeated the unwanted thoughts she'd banished. She partly rose and hit the pillow, hit it again, battered it to quiet the worries that circled round and round in her head.

Then Jaudon was behind her, drawing her fists away from the flattened bag of polyester. Jaudon pushed it off the bed and slid her own pillow under Berry's curly locks. She stretched her whole body, in her soft, worn boxer shorts, along Berry's back.

Berry welcomed the strength of Jaudon's arms and thighs. She focused on deliberate breaths to still her mind, hoping for respite from the persistent insomnia of recent nights.

"I love you," Jaudon crooned continuously until the words wreathed her mind and put Berry to sleep.

She woke as the sun sent a first gentle ray through a crack in the curtains. Her worries had congealed in her mind, her muscles, and the pit of her being. Jaudon rolled toward her and asked how she was, if she slept well. She wanted to answer Jaudon, knew simple words of reassurance, but she struggled to access them. Her vocal cords were frozen. Her brain refused the urge to speak.

What was wrong with her? It was impossible to do whatever she was supposed to do, be whoever she was supposed to be anymore. She nodded yes to Jaudon and forced her legs over the side of the bed.

Back in the kitchen for breakfast, Berry refused Jaudon's pleas to take the day off. "Oh, sweetie, leave me be, won't you?"

"Can't you talk sense to her, Gran?"

Gran said, "Don't try and shush us, pet. You've been out of kilter for a while now. Are you sick at your stomach? I can boil you up a teaspoon of saw palmetto berries—they're good for what ails you."

"I'm fatigued, is all. Will you two worrywarts stop pecking at me? I'll do what Jaudon said and call Lawyer Slumkey when I need to. Or Benedict can help and Emmett Ponder. Today, I want to curl up in the porch hammock for the rest of my life."

"That rotted out string hammock?" Jaudon said. "Don't go near it. I'll buy a new one today and set it up for you. I've meant to do that. Sometimes I'm glad those ugly big-box stores have shot up in Brandon. Makes life easier."

"While you're out, will you pick up some of that holy basil herb at the health food store?" Gran asked. "We've got ginseng right here, but it nearabout keeps me awake for a week. A cup of tulsi tea is a fine way to up my pep any time of day."

Jaudon fiddled with her new over-the-ear hearing aids. They were, thanks be, smaller and less visible than the originals. "I'll stop at the ear doctor too. This right-side gizmo gives me feedback unless I pull it halfway out."

Berry forced herself to leave the homey chat and drive to work. She rested her eyes at traffic lights and was honked to attention once.

She was too tired to make lunch before work and, instead, crossed her arms on the staff room table to serve as a pillow for her head. Dr. Garza's entrance startled her. She sat up, blinking.

"She was asleep when I got here about twenty minutes ago," said Laura Bathgate.

Dr. Garza sat down next to Berry and placed a hand on her shoulder. "You're not yourself these days. I checked your file and saw that you have quite a bit of sick time built up. I want you to use it now."

"I've saved it for a time when I'm sick."

Dr. Garza looked at Laura. Laura raised her opened hands and shrugged.

"I know you nurses think you're superhuman and impervious to health problems, but I've watched your performance suffer and you suffer."

"My performance? I'm sorrier than I can say. I'll admit to my distractedness, but I'll improve my focus."

"Your focus will return after you take some time off."

"The doc is right," Laura said. "You told me yourself you don't sleep well. Your appetite has disappeared, and you're moody, not like the Berry I know. You have so much on your mind that you're pulled every which way. That's the cause of your muscle aches and soreness."

"Laura, have you slotted anyone into that cancellation at two thirty?"

"I'm trying, Doc, but I don't have any takers yet."

"Good. We'll do a checkup and labs on Berry to be sure, but I think we'll come up with a diagnosis of exhaustion." She pinched the skin on Berry's arm. "Some dehydration. We need to help you to regain your health."

"I guess it might be true I've been about as low as a toad in a dry well for a while now, but I can't stay for a workup. I have to get together with the tile man to learn what I need to cover that concrete floor."

Laura laughed. "Don't you love it when she talks pure cracker?"

The doctor smiled with her eyes. "To be honest, I do. So do the patients. Go ahead and fit Berry into my schedule. And I want you to stay away from the health center for a couple of weeks. Let your friends complete it and your lawyer work out the legal kinks. They're knowledgeable and have your best interests at heart."

CHAPTER SEVENTEEN

Berry Garland

The next Sunday, September sixteenth, while the grueling cleanups in New York, Pennsylvania, and Washington, DC, were in full swing, and teams sifted through rubble in a desperate effort to find survivors and bodies that weren't already ash, Berry put her weeding tools, gloves, kneeling pad, and a bottle of water in the garden cart, her mood determined and avenging. In the kitchen garden she deployed keen-edged clippers to chase down the skunk vine that choked her native shrubs and plants with its quick, dense growth, wishing the vine was the September eleventh attackers and whoever was behind the Center's harassment.

Would Ma have gardened in California? Surely, she'd want to reproduce the scents and sights of Florida in its prime: fields of blueberry bushes, strawberries, and oranges, the sweetest oranges. When Berry was little, Gran took her to the library to find books about the state. She'd dreamed over full-color photographs of the great forests and exotic flowers, waiting for Ma and Pa to send her the airplane ticket.

The cut vines gave off a wet, woody scent she found invigorating.

Her mind raced despite the soothing odors and textures of this sandy land. Partly, she was in a stew to avoid thoughts about a war of vengeance, and partly, she needed to erase the image of people who fell or leaped from one certain death to another. That brave gay man on the Pennsylvania plane who led the attack to tackle the terrorists. The horror of it. Impossible to take in.

Jaudon said she was deciding whether to show up at one of the sites to help or ask the Army to enlist her fifty-year-old self—then she remembered the don't ask, don't tell business and became too discouraged to follow through. "You'd think they'd want gay people killed in battle, the way some politicians talk."

Berry's appetite to tame the garden seemed piddling next to turning a plane filled with jet fuel into a bomb. She considered surrender— Jaudon would mow the whole garden down for her. She'd start over, but the skunk vine and its allies would proliferate with their countless seeds. The birds, the breezes, a smidgen of fertile soil or sand, and soon stems would crawl along the ground, rooting and growing into woody vines that climbed trees, posts, poles up to thirty feet. More than once, she saw a tree limb fallen from its trunk under the weight of these runaway weeds. Crush a skunk vine leaf and, as Gran said, it stinks so bad it could knock a buzzard off a gut wagon.

She stopped herself. What was she thinking? She'd have to have a thumpin' gizzard for a heart to convert their garden into a battlefield.

Had Ma and Pa talked as country as Gran and Jaudon and Cullie? She didn't recall. The airplane ticket never came, but Gran knew how to mother and never raised a child the likes of Opal. Gran didn't have a mean bone in her body. She taught Berry to live and let live. By Gran's example, she knew her job on earth was to give in return, lovingly, in thanks for her life and the gifts that came with it.

The sole plus in the garden was the lack of thorns. If you got skunk vine young and pulled it before it rooted, you won. She stooped when she had to and used a hoe if she could to protect her knees and back but liked easing the roots out of the ground by hand best. Her fingernails were dark with packed sandy dirt. Sweat sprang to her scalp and soaked her hair. When she found a loose creeper on a tree trunk or slender shrub branch, she ripped the whole vine off, her thoughts of US enemies, thorny Opal, and how grateful she, Berry, ought to be for a sibling, how loving she ought to feel toward her.

The sulfury, garbagey smell of the weed tried to gag her, and she discovered, in her determination, she'd practically enveloped herself in a flowering lantana shrub. Later, she'd use an industrial cleaner on her hands, but for now, she crawled away, breathed better air, sneezed, and wiped sweat from her eyes with a clean rag from the cart. The lantana flowers were vitally pretty, the color of sherbets—lemon, raspberry, orange—but the plant was toxic to humans and other animals.

She paid too much attention to thoughts of last week's violence and her sister's insensitivity instead of what she was doing. Annoyed at herself, she jerked at patches of skunk vine, not as careful as she should be—slivers of roots and vines easily re-insinuated themselves into the soil and festered the way Opal had. Her sister learned Berry's very full schedule and way too often dropped by during the scant free time she had with Jaudon. Behind her chirpy facade, Berry sensed a negativity that pervaded Opal's thoughts and actions.

Berry had served sun tea to her sister a few weeks before.

Opal started that visit by saying, "I do adore the floral pattern on your blouse."

Berry had recently gotten home from work. Gran was in bed with her TV on. Jaudon, still a licensed CPA, had a home computer in her room. She was teaching herself QuickBooks because Rouie Waver, despite a career without the program, now used it. Berry had kept her sister in the kitchen.

"Thank you," she'd responded and aimed to look pleasantly interested but waited for the catch. She wished visits with her sister were light and filled with discovery about each other—their similarities, their differences. She wished she loved Opal. Berry remembered Ma and Pa clearly, but Opal continued to dismiss them as irresponsible hippies and made it obvious she was no longer interested in Berry's memories.

"It's a shock to me, nurses without starched white caps and dresses, white nylons and shoes. It's hard to respect a professional who dresses in pajamas."

Opal confused her. Was she insulting her? "Scrubs," Berry said. "They're called scrubs. The physicians wear scrubs, as do the CNAs and the surgical cleaning techs. They're inexpensive, functional, easy to take care of, so much more practical than starched white dresses. I don't know how nurses worked in those caps unless they glued them on."

"I'm sorry, but flowery or plain, they strike me as sloppy." Opal's smile returned to her lips—the woman would never have crinkly smile lines around her eyes. "Tell me how Gran Binyon is doing."

To follow Opal's questions and remarks was mental whiplash. "You'd hardly know Gran experienced a stroke, what is it, six, seven years ago? She's outside tending our garden or in the kitchen cooking or watching her soaps."

"Do you work her too hard?"

"Work her?" Berry snapped. She didn't care if she looked offended. "Gran does as she pleases."

"And whatever pleases you and your roommate."

"Jaudon's not my roommate, she's my life partner."

Opal paused, as if to reload a weapon. "I know Gran cares about you. Did it never occur to you that she's paying her keep with the work she does around the house?"

It hadn't. Now guilty thoughts filled her mind. It would be so Gran to think she owed Jaudon for shelter and Berry for not abandoning her to a home for the aged. Did they take her for granted? She'd never questioned Gran's motives or their own. They were a team from the start, Gran more of a mother to Jaudon than Momma Vicker ever was.

"We're a family. Each of us pitches in."

"I suppose I'd see it your way if I was in your shoes."

Had Opal wanted to undermine her confidence, and her perception of reality? Opal's visits left Berry all bollixed up, but she'd accepted her first invitation to visit her sister's house. She admitted to some curiosity about how Opal lived and longed to get to know her nieces and nephews. Nor was she disposed to give up on Opal herself, Ma and Pa's other child.

She turned to her weeds. Why wouldn't someone want to know more about her parents? She'd imagined so many lives for Ma and Pa, from cheerfully raising a family they wanted in California to spending years in prison for drug possession in the summer of love to a terrible accident along the Route 10 swamplands. She'd cried over her abandonment. Now she cried in grief at their demise.

It was a miracle, magnificent, to learn she had a sister, even a disturbing—or disturbed—sister. Equally, how very relieved she was to know peewee Berry had never been at fault for Ma and Pa's disappearance. How egotistically childlike to think she had that much power. At the same time, she was distraught at their deaths. And how was it possible Opal was disinterested in the people who'd given her life?

She yanked her hand away from a thorn. She'd kept blackberries out of the front yard for years, and here was a thorny vine smack in the middle of the bold marmalade lantana. A drop of blood formed on her finger, lifeblood given to her by Ma and Pa. She wanted to scream in protest at their loss. Instead, with her gloved hands, she ripped the bramble as far out of the ground as she could and used her sharp-edged spade to dig farther. Berry knew it helped nothing, but she was uncharacteristically furious at Ma and Pa's fate, at the careless truck driver in California, at her disapproving Garland grandparents, at her brainwashed sister. She summoned the Great Spirit to calm her and ruthlessly severed the cane of her ancient past.

In that instant she decided to hold the grand opening right before Thanksgiving, an antidote for the unfathomable tragedy of 9/11. A new medical facility—what better way to honor the victims, survivors, and everyone who came to their aid?

Chapter Eighteen

Jaudon Vicker

November 2001

Jaudon spilled the news about the grand opening as soon as she saw
Olive at the Buffalo Street store.

"But first," she added, "we need to name the Center."

Olive asked, "Will Berry name it after her grandmother?"

"Words out of my mouth, but Berry wants to honor a person of
color in the community, maybe Mrs. Lanamore. When I mentioned it,
Mrs. Lanamore said, *What are you going to call it, The Pansy Center?
That would really fuel the crackpots' fires.* She laughed herself into a
coughing fit and refused the honor."

With a sidelong glance, Olive said, "Berry herself told me Gran
was half Native American through her mother and probably some from
her father. And if you're born and raised on the ancestral land of a
people, whether they were driven out or managed to stay, you can't deny
that piece of yourself. Why, besides being a woman of color herself, Ida
Binyon raised Berry to be a healer, taught her all she remembered from
her own grandmother. We wouldn't have a Women's Health Center
without Ida."

Jaudon paused. What a dope—she'd never thought of Gran that
way. "Gran's a woman of color?"

Olive turned her eyes upward. "Child, what did they used to call
Indians?"

"Jiminy." She wouldn't even think the slur. "That's awful, and not
even true."

"The Ida—what was her maiden name?"

"Hold up. It's on the tip of my tongue."

She waited on a customer, then two more, and went to Olive, who was doing an order. "Tommie. That's her maiden name."

"There you go. And another thing, some freed and escaped Blacks joined the Seminoles and fought in the Seminole Wars. They were called Black Seminoles, and some intermarried with Seminoles."

"So it's possible you, Gran, and Berry are related?"

"Not sure there are records to prove it, but that's a nice thought."

"It is. I wish Gran knew more about her family background."

"Never mind. Shake a leg and find a wood-carver to make a lasting sign."

Berry didn't need to be sold on Olive's suggestion when Jaudon raved about it that evening. She called Olive right up to thank her.

"Gran would object, but you're right, Olive. Gran fashioned me. I may not drink dandelion root tea or weave mugwort garlands, but Gran taught me the closeness of the words *heal* and *hear*. Listening is a major part of healing. I'm pretty good at that."

She hung up and nodded to Jaudon.

"We better get cracking, then. Want me to find a sign shop?" Jaudon asked.

"That would be a big help. Let me think a minute. Olive thought we should leave my grandfather's name off?"

"Said it's too much of a mouthful to remember. You can use her married name in the brochure."

Berry's eyes went wide with panic. "Brochure? Who has time to write a brochure?"

"How about Shady? He was an English teacher. I'll ask him. Duval always liked to do artwork."

"I'll start a list: sign, brochure. You're firing on all cylinders, Jaud, what else will we need?"

Berry's enthusiasm lit a rocket of ideas. "A great big ribbon and king-size scissors."

"Maybe Allison can source those."

"We used to celebrate store openings. I surely have something we can use."

"I remember a red carpet."

"You're right as rain. It's rolled in plastic at the Buffalo Street store."

"We need to advertise. Who does listings of community events?"

"That local TV station, radio stations, the newspaper. You can ask Leslie to research more in her spare time."

"She has spare time?"

Jaudon laughed. "I've done some advertising, even a few interviews. I'll try to get that ball rolling." She reached for Berry's hands and held them high. "Excited, Georgia gal?"

"I'm a little fearful to be this excited. What if the protestors come and ruin our little ceremony?"

"Let me take care of that too. I have some ideas."

The speakers arrived first, ready for the ten a.m. ceremony: Mayor Allison, Dr. Garza, Berry's former college advisor who became the Nursing Department director before she retired. Berry advised all to keep their words short as the Center was open for afternoon appointments.

Jaudon checked the temperature—only seventy-nine, perfect after all the blood, sweat, and tears. The trees were losing their bronze leaves, but not bare yet. She was in chinos, a white shirt, and her red Beverage Bay vest, as was Olive.

Jimmy Neal and Rigo brought along a trumpet player friend. Sun glinting off his polished brass, he provided flamboyant fanfares at the introduction of each honored guest, all of whom concisely but extravagantly praised the community's support—dozens were in attendance—and thanked Berry.

To either side of the front door, Cullie and Jeff Maple stood at attention, in uniform, with two gold-fringed American flags. They'd borrowed the flags and stands from the sheriff's department.

Gran and Shady were no longer in wheelchairs—they used mobility scooters now. With all the exuberance in the air, they challenged each other to a race. Yan the *shoo* lady urged them on until Leslie had to intervene. A reporter from the *Tampa Bay Times* and another from the public radio station showed up. Under the big trees across the street, behind yellow nylon rope strung and guarded by Tad and Duval, protestors were lined up, shouting and waving offensive poster board signs.

Through a borrowed microphone, Berry spoke a few deceptively calm words of welcome and gave a brief history of the clinic. She paid homage to Pansy Lanamore, explaining she'd made it all possible by her donation of space. Her hands shook as Mrs. Lanamore lifted the red ribbon and bow for Berry to cut. The audience applauded. Then the trumpeter rolled out a complex, extended fanfare. Emmett Ponder climbed a ladder to the top of the front door and pulled the fabric away from an outsize carved wooden sign.

Berry watched Gran as she moved her lips to read. "The Ida Tommie Women's Health Center." As the supporters vigorously applauded, Gran leaned to Shady. He took her hand, smiling and nodding. Then Berry, standing proudly, smiling widely, explained the meaning of the Center's name to the assemblage. She presented Gran, healer and her inspiration, and spoke of their ancestry right here in Rainbow Gap, history few of the locals knew.

Gran was crying by the time she followed Berry inside for the tour. So many people stopped to shake hands and hug her, Gran stayed put like a one-woman welcoming committee.

At the reception area Leslie sold raffle tickets, Tommie Center T-shirts, and bumper stickers. Business cards were out for the taking, mostly the Center's, but a few stacks for VONCO.

The hallway walls were decorated with children's drawings, made in the childcare room. Only two examination rooms were fully equipped, but Vaughn and MJ bowed guests into others that stood empty. Vaughn spoke. "If anyone knows of a funding resource, come talk to us. We need to equip these rooms. We're running out of space already."

Near the back door, Laura Bathgate made appointments for new patients. The space was decorated with balloons. A long table held snacks by Pansy's Pastries with paper cups for nonalcoholic bubbly and cards for the bakery. As people left, Shady gave them flyers.

As soon as she could, Berry made her way back to Gran and opened a folding chair beside her.

"You've done yourself proud, Berry Garland. You've done us proud."

"I hope using your name was okay."

"I wasn't expecting it. Some old pals from when I worked at the farmstand ribbed me something awful. Every last person thanked me. At first, I thought to make you change that sign, but then I saw my name is not about me—it's a symbol. You've honored the Great

Spirit that dwells in this place and the ancestors who dwell in the Great Spirit. Thank you, my truly grand-daughter. I couldn't love any living being more than I love you today."

CHAPTER NINETEEN

MJ Beaudry

December 2001

In the relative cool of December, it was Vonnie who found herself
overburdened. At a barbecue in the senior Lowes' backyard one town
over from Rainbow Gap, MJ watched Vonnie absentmindedly massage
her collarbone and knew she was nervous.

Vonnie said, "I might take a leave of absence from the Housing
Authority."

Her mother said, "That's such a secure job. You were lucky to be
hired right out of college. You don't want to lose it, dear."

Above them, a lazy wind urged white clouds forward. Trifling
tufts drifted off like passengers alighting from a never-ending train.

MJ sat with Vonnie, Vaughn, and Vaughn's first girlfriend, Nisa,
on the roomy screened-in back porch where the twins had grown up.
They were invited over for the inauguration of Vonnie's dad Grady's
fancy new smoker, bought at an after-summer sale. She had a warm
affection for the Lowes' comfortable house, with its shiny hardwood
and mosaic tile floors and fireplace. The property was enclosed on
two sides by a four-foot brick wall, and on the third, orange, lemon,
avocado, and walnut trees.

Grady, a high school teacher, was out on the flagstone patio he and
Vaughn built off the porch for outdoor cooking. "See here?" he said.
He proceeded to point out to everyone the thermometer, the firebox, the
setups to smoke or to grill.

Grady groaned as he straightened up creak by creak. "Who's going to win this election, do you think?" Grady liked to talk world events with MJ. "Nobody else reads the papers anymore," he'd frequently grumbled.

Nisa grew up with the primary language of Ghana, a lightly accented English. "I have to hope it's not that dumb child of Bush."

"Al Gore's a smart man and he has the experience," MJ said.

"But as you say, nobody reads the papers anymore, especially Floridians," Nisa said.

"And that will make the difference," Grady said. "Mark my words."

Vonnie's mom, a paralegal named Lollie, wore her straight gray hair in a wavy ponytail that exposed her signature theme earrings—daisies today—which picked up the yellow in her multicolored blouse and sandals. Lollie was white, with deep laugh lines around her eyes and mouth, and happened to be Jaudon Vicker's youngest aunt on her mother's side. Lollie sat in front of a trellis covered with fuchsia blossoms. Hummingbirds gathered at the flowers and darted this way and that, their wings a constant drone of flutter, but Lollie didn't smile when she said, "Grady Lowe, listen to your daughter."

Grady, who was crouching, leaned on his heels. He was in already smudged khaki carpenter shorts and an orange Gators T-shirt. "You think that would be the best move, Vonnie? Your problem won't slink off with its tail between its legs while you're away, if that's what you hope. Who'll fight for your program with you gone?"

"I don't want to mess up what MJ and I have. I don't want to fall apart, same as poor Berry. Her dream is coming true, but between the hassles of a nonprofit launch, bureaucratic blockades, and demonstrations, the conflicts and stress take what should be jubilation out of the incredible discovery of her unknown sister. If Berry can't cope, how can I expect to?"

Lollie took Vonnie's hand. "Oh, sugar. We had no idea you were so down."

Vonnie held her other hand up, index finger and thumb almost touching. "Vergie Redfern, our conniving maintenance lead, persuaded the director to let him apply for the same program funds I did. He's setting a precedent, and I'll be left to write grant after grant Vergie will intercept. I'll look weak, a powerless girl. But if I disappear, so does any new funding. With no money from DC to pay his preferred contractors, Vergie loses his perks. The director will take his side, not mine."

Grady was a handsome, balding Black man in wire-rimmed glasses. He stood and opened his arms. "Baby girl, come to your dad."

MJ watched her normally buoyant Vonnie, in tears, melt against her father. He patted her shoulder, saying, "There, there, darling girl, you're stronger than any ten crooked maintenance men. The world is a hard, cold place. We do what we can to make it better."

Her mother sighed audibly and turned to MJ. "Yvonne has wanted to help others since she was a mite. When Grady's mother was dying, every morning and evening this three-year-old climbed into her grandmother's bed and snuggled close or pretended to fix her hair. She always asked me to pack extra in her lunchbox for the children who had none. If I forgot, she'd split whatever was hers with another child. There was no stopping her."

"Now, that's what I call direct services," Grady said with a chuckle.

MJ remembered thinking, the first time Vonnie took her home to meet her parents: Aha, so this is what a functional family is like.

Her darn glasses felt loose again. She took them off, wiped, and resettled them. Her own inadequate upbringing made her aware of how indebted she was to the Lowes for raising two exemplary people. A white-haired woman in the next yard over caught her eye. She unclipped laundry from a clothesline, filled a woven basket at her feet. The Lowes were well-liked and active in their mixed-race and mixed-income neighborhood.

Grady opened the grill, releasing a burst of charred ribs and sauce that made her mouth water.

Vaughn leaned forward, legs spread, elbows on his knees. "Too bad it would be nepotism for VONCO to contract with the Housing Authority. Hearing about this dirty trick, we'd turn down any work offered."

MJ gave Vaughn a thumbs-up.

Next to him was the landscape designer Vaughn dated for close to two years, Nisa Larbi. She came to the US from Ghana in her late teens, on a student visa. Once she received her associate's degree, she completed paperwork that allowed her to stay for another twelve months in an internship with a landscaping company. They liked Nisa so much she was offered a job, and the owner sponsored her application for citizenship. She was now a full US citizen.

MJ wrung her hands. "If you quit and need a job, Vonnie, you'd be the perfect solution to the messes Vaughn and I make in the VONCO office if you wanted to take over the admin work."

"Does our Vonnie need rest?" asked Lollie.

"I don't want to rest. I want to be useful, a tool sent to fix the miseries I see."

"Everyone has to take a break now and then," said Grady. "MJ, why don't you take some time off too? A vacation never hurt a family."

MJ grew warm all over every time Grady included her in the family. "Vaughn, can you see our way clear to comfortably juggle our projects for a couple of weeks?"

"Ah," he said, "that depends. Nisa and I, we kind of have an announcement."

Lollie's mouth made a perfect O. She motioned Grady to come sit beside her.

Grady moved onto the porch and took Lollie's hand. "Do tell."

Nisa's gaze was nothing if not worshipful as she watched Vaughn.

MJ became aware she was immersed in a divine aroma. She spotted its source, a spill of small white flowers along the brick enclosure.

Vonnie whispered, "Star jasmine."

Vaughn swallowed so hard his Adam's apple bounced. "I've asked Nisa to marry me. She said yes. We're engaged."

Vonnie was transformed. She rushed to Vaughn and embraced him so energetically he came close to toppling over. Nisa, a tall, slender woman with a lot of hair, steadied him until Vonnie enveloped her too.

"I'm so sorry to bitch and moan on your big announcement day." She pulled Nisa into the hug, then stepped out of the way for Lollie's turn and the handshake Grady gave Vaughn.

MJ raised her eyes to watch a swirl of finely sculpted clouds linger above the betrothed couple. She congratulated them, while at the same time she fumed inside: she could never give Vonnie a gift this weighty, never have a wedding at all.

"Like Berry, I have a surprise sister," Vonnie crowed.

MJ said, "You honestly won that contest."

Vonnie cocked her head in question.

Vaughn spoke under his breath. "Not the wicked sister down from Georgia?"

Lollie gave him an indulgent look and asked, "When?"

Nisa said, "Soon and quietly. No fuss. At the County Clerk of Court's office. My mother and father will be there. They love Vaughn." Nisa had brought them to the States. With her father's experience as a tropical gardener and his English language skills, he picked up jobs from the start.

Lollie's hand pressed the fleshy fold under her chin, a question in her eyes.

"It's like this, Mom," Vaughn said. "When my sister and MJ got together, I don't know if they wanted it or not, but they can't be hitched at the county or anywhere else. I have the privilege of legally and publicly promising to love and take care of Nisa, and I want to give her that, but no way either of us wants to make a big splash. I mean, that's who we are anyway—"

"Small splashers," Nisa said with a breathy laugh.

"Yo," said Vonnie. "You both deserve to celebrate and be celebrated big-time."

"Sis, that's not the route we want to take. We want to treat Nisa's parents and the six of us to a nice restaurant."

Vonnie said, "I want Berry, Jaudon, Gran and Benedict, Cullie and Allison there too. I'll pay my share."

"I guess I can ask a couple of my buddies. And, Sis, we'll plan around your time off."

"But where?" Nisa asked.

MJ suggested, "What about the ice cream parlor?"

Nisa's face went from concern to a wide-mouthed smile. "What a fun idea. Would we be able to sit together?"

"Sure. They have parties in that large room."

Vaughn was laughing. "Perfect for us. If that's what you want, Nise, that's what we'll do, have a reception at that ice cream parlor."

Lollie took Grady's hand. "What a story for the grandchildren."

"And the great-grandbabies," said Grady.

Vonnie was quietly applauding. "You two go marry tomorrow if you want. As for moi, a pep talk from Dad, comfort from Mom, and the prospect of a vacation with MJ? Watch out, Vergie Redfern."

CHAPTER TWENTY

Jaudon Vicker

May 2002

"Dadburnit," said Jaudon when she arrived home from work. Berry was on her knees in the kitchen, a sopping dish towel in hand, a soy milk carton on its side, and her lips pressed together so tightly it was obvious she was suppressing a scream of frustration and fear. Jaudon stung with a wash of overwhelming love and apprehension.

"It slipped right out of my hand. One second, I had a firm grip on it, the next…"

Jaudon lifted the used towel and squeezed it over the sink. "That's not the first time I've seen you scramble for items you dropped or lost. Let's right this minute schedule an appointment for you to let Doc Garza do that workup on you. It's been ages since you agreed to make an appointment."

"Don't have a duck fit about it. I'm tired, is all," Berry answered.

"You're never *not* tired. You think you're anemic? One of my customers is and says she's always tired. And she gets irritable the way you do, which in turn makes me cranky as all get-out. Where's my sweet Georgia gal? Did you forget the breathing exercises the doc gave you? I'd believe you're on drugs, the way you can't remember what you said or did three minutes ago and how you need to do tasks very deliberately. Or you sleepwalk, stumble, act dizzy."

"I am dizzy and lightheaded, off and on. That's because I'm so busy I forget to eat."

"You always had a healthy appetite. Now all you crave is

portobello and tomato sandwiches, and sometimes you don't bother with the bread."

"Who licked the red off your candy today?"

"I love you and I'm scared to death for you—can't you tell after all these years?" She was already at the phone. "You weaseled your way out of one appointment with Dr. Garza, but you're not dodging it again."

Laura at the office thanked Jaudon for taking the bull by the horns and scheduled Berry for what she termed the works. "You make sure she doesn't sidestep this one the way she did the last, you hear?" Laura lowered her voice. "One of our doctors suggested it's repressed anger. If so, she sure needs to let it out."

"She'll be there if I have to ask Tad to carry her."

"He's got what it takes to do it." MJ had mentioned the almost visible current between Tad and Laura, but she didn't want to pry, thanked her, and hung up.

Berry, eyes half closed, shoulders slumped, let Jaudon lead her to bed. They lay down, spoon position, her arms around a shaking Berry.

"You'll come with me to the appointment?" asked Berry.

"If you let me."

"What if it's an awful disease?"

"You're the strongest person I know, excepting Gran. She's worked her way to decent health when we might have lost her."

Berry rolled to her side. "She let Benedict persuade her to go for acupuncture, and she faithfully guzzles the ancient Chinese herbal medicines the acupuncturist advises."

"Please be careful. I refuse to watch you shrink away to nothing. The doc said you have too many plates in the air. I'll ask Benedict what medicines you should take."

"See if there's something for energy. Where has my stamina gone?"

"You expected more women to offer their time. You're doing their volunteer work."

"I've burned up my brain for ways to recruit. They want the services, but they're old and/or disabled, or work two or three jobs, or have no daycare and we have very few daycare volunteers."

"Is there somewhere you can list volunteer opportunities?"

"I've done that. In the papers, at the county and the city, newspapers paid and free. Leslie and Nisa put notices up wherever they go."

"Can we have cards made up for my customers? We can hand them out with their orders."

"You'd lose customers. We haven't asked small business owners for help for that reason. Except the natural food store on Kings Avenue."

Jaudon pulled Berry tighter, as if that would protect her as she whipped up suggestions for their quandaries. But Berry was as protected as a lightning rod.

"I'm so sorry I'm like this. I may have reached my midlife crisis."

"I don't know about that. You sure do have a snootful of other crises on your hands."

Once Berry was fully sleepy, Jaudon went to Gran's room to watch TV with the volume low. Gran was asleep but liked the TV playing. On the news, an anchor reported that an FBI agent who spied for Russia had been caught. What is wrong with people, she thought. America is the greatest nation in the world. Where is their patriotism?

"Dadburnit," she said again and left Gran's room disgruntled. Even when Leslie was around, she and Berry were hyperalert, anticipated Gran's needs, fetching this, that, and the other thing. She prowled the house now, stepped onto the porch, and sniffed the air. The sweet almond bush was flowering. Its fragrance gave her the gumption to settle at the kitchen table and assemble information Rouie Waver needed for quarterly taxes.

The house phone rang way too soon after Berry went to sleep. Jaudon leaped to quiet the ring.

It was MJ. "Vaughn was pulled over and taken to the sheriff's office on suspicion of theft."

She heard Vonnie crying.

"Our Vaughn? He's the most law-abiding guy in the county and practically a newlywed. What do you need me to do?"

"We're trying to forestall them from actually arresting and processing him. They have him in handcuffs. I mean honestly— Vaughn? We're lucky it's Friday night—there's a backlog in booking. We told them he's a legitimate businessperson, but they're not listening. Let me ask you, your lawyer Slumkey, does he do criminal cases?"

"I don't think so, but I'll call. He'll know someone. Emmett Ponder might give us an idea as well. And Allison, she has an unbeatable contact list."

"Cullie too, okay?" She hadn't heard MJ this panicky since Cullie picked her up. "Didn't Officer Friendly—Jeff—give you his home phone number? Please call him. Let me quickly tell you what happened. Vaughn went to Orlando in his own truck to pick up building materials from a teardown. It was completely aboveboard. He had a red flag for the overhanging lumber, showed his commercial driver's license, met the whole nine yards of regulations.

"The deputy pulled him over for no obvious reason and accused him of stealing the lumber, the other supplies, the truck itself. People gathered and watched the arrest. Vaughn showed him the right documents, but the cop pulled him out of the truck, kicked him to the ground, patted him down, and pushed him into the rear of the cruiser. At the needless kick, the onlookers got rowdy, and more people came out to the street."

Vonnie took the phone and said, "Vaughn did exactly right. He went all docile to avoid antagonizing them."

MJ agreed. "It was the bystanders who acted up when the cop kicked him. The cop shined his flashlight through the truck windows. The crowd was used to police searches for hidden drugs or guns, to make a bigger collar. They were angry—shouting, getting closer and closer to the deputy who turned toward them with his hand at his holster. He crab-walked to the squad car, his eyes on the people the whole time."

MJ continued, "Then a bunch more cops materialized, sirens and lights going. They don't believe a Black man is capable of telling the truth. We need to spring Vaughn out of this place before he ends up with a record. No businessman can afford that."

"Mom stayed home, paralegal or not, for fear the sight of a white woman and her Black son will inflame the situation. She tried the law office where she worked instead and left a message with the answering service."

"I'll take one of her sisters over to sit with Aunt Lollie," Jaudon said.

Vonnie said, "They're the last people she'd want around at a time like this, but what if you take Nisa to my mother? I'm calling Nisa, and I don't think she should drive right after she hears. I'll transport Nisa and assure her having a business partner stand up for Vaughn will help."

While she talked to Rich Slumkey and Allison, she scratched

out a condensed version of the night's events and left it on the kitchen table—communication central in their house—on the chance Berry or Gran woke before she came home.

"I know about the arrest from Cullie," was Allison's rapid-fire response as Jaudon cleared her throat. "She's on duty and probably assigned to crowd control. The deputy who pulled Vaughn over is a racist jerk by her account, though those two words are redundant. She said Vaughn needed help—code three. I'm calling my contacts and was going to tell you to reach out too."

"I'm on it like a duck on a june bug. Vaughn is one of the finest specimens of humanity in the whole state." She had a panicked thought. "What if they plant drugs in the truck? Code three it is."

Jaudon explained the situation to Rich Slumkey, who asked one question: "Is the deputy white?" At her answer, he said he'd see her at the jail.

Jeff Maple was already involved at the scene. She filled him in about Vaughn, and he said the chief wouldn't put up with a riot on his watch.

"You didn't hear it from me, but," he said, "there's been grumbling at the station about, as they describe it, the abortion mill out in colored crackerville and the trouble it's causing."

Jaudon was fit to be tied. "That is a *pure-tee* lie. They blame us for the trouble?"

"I wouldn't put it past them to target one of you for your association with the Center. The guy that pulled Vonnie's brother over is not long out of the Academy and high on his speck of power. This incident puts him so far out of line he needs to be canned."

"I hope they don't piddle around about it."

She restrained herself from running out to her car after all. Better to stay by the phone and coordinate. She knew no one and had no influence. More important, Berry might wake to the crunch of the Estate wagon as it left their front yard.

She waited past her regular bedtime for news. Berry must have sensed her absence and padded out to the kitchen barefoot.

"Why're you sitting by the phone?"

"Waiting on word of our predicament."

"It's not the Tommie Center again, is it?" Patients and neighborhood residents were taken with Gran's Native American maiden name, Tommie, so the Tommie Center it had become.

"Not directly." Before she related the story, she took a pitcher of sweet tea from the Frigidaire and poured some for both of them into their long-treasured polka-dot jam jars.

Berry said, "It doesn't take much to put these Southern boys in a tizzy with a cradle to coffin diet of prejudice. Have I done harm by disturbing their ant nest?"

"Hogwash. Any dummy will tell you that's not true. Hold on, this might be a report."

Berry hit the speaker button on their phone. Jaudon never used it.

"Vaughn was released," MJ said.

"Well, I'll be," said Jaudon. "That was quick."

Berry asked, "They freed him this soon? Is he alright?"

Jaudon thought, that's Berry in a nutshell: nurse first.

"He's pretty shaken up. He knows how badly it could have gone. Once the crowd was cleared, Cullie and Jeff came to the station. They escorted Vaughn, Vonnie, and their dad through a side door to Allison's car as reporters gathered at the front of the station. Oh, and, Cullie said to tell you guys that the cop who stopped Vaughn and almost started a riot? He's Shrimp's son. She said you'd remember Shrimp."

"She's right about that," said Jaudon. "I'm not surprised. Shrimp is the deputy who, years ago, wrecked my hearing when Allison and Cullie were on the run."

Berry let her head fall to Jaudon's shoulder. "Whatever you folks did, I am so very relieved and grateful."

"All we did was put word out," MJ told them. "You should have seen Allison storm the sheriff's office and give him what for. Accused him of tolerating rogue deputies and running a racist department."

"Woo-hoo!"

"Bless that woman's heart," Berry added, shaking her head and smiling.

"Meanwhile," MJ said, "Attorney Slumkey laid down the law. The snide arresting deputy made up a bogus traffic offense and added suspicion of contraband in order to take Vaughn in while the truck was impounded and searched. Of course, there was nothing to find, and Slumkey made the right noises about suing for false arrest, racial targeting, and more. I would not want to be in Shrimp Jr.'s shoes about now."

"Vaughn wasn't hurt?"

"Pretty sore ribs from the kick. But listen to this. Turns out, Vaughn's father taught two of the sheriff's wayward sons and spoke up for them at school more than once—they behaved themselves in Mr. Lowe's classes, everyone did. The sheriff agreed to see him, and Mr. Lowe went in mad as a hornet and lashed out."

"Was there any mention of the Tommie Center?" asked Berry, face taut. "I hope there's no tie between Vaughn's arrest and the hate toward the Center."

"Only in general, like I said. Sexism's been around as long as racism."

"Pat on the back, Squirrel. You done good."

"Teamwork, Boss. Thanks for rallying the troops."

But when she ended the call and looked to Berry with a smile of achievement, Berry had her arms up around herself. "Poor Vaughn. I'd be nervous as a mama quail in raccoon country. How will this harassment change him?"

CHAPTER TWENTY-ONE

Vonnie Lowe

June 2002

The new VONCO office behind the Tommie Center was done, the elevator approved and installed. Mrs. Lanamore sometimes made barely necessary trips up and down for the simple pleasure of it.

After Vaughn's traumatic experience with the police and her own negative experiences at work, Vonnie became more active within the Black community. The ongoing tensions in Cincinnati, following last year's police killing of unarmed Timothy Thomas and his killer being found not guilty of even misdemeanor charges, had everyone on edge. At the end of a day battling bureaucrats, though, she needed to put her energy into an undertaking less stressful than, say, a police oversight committee or filing a racial profiling suit against the police department. She joined the Lecoats County African American Cultural Preservation Committee.

Vonnie could not stop talking about the committee. They were home in Causeway finishing a meal of leftover honey-lime chicken MJ grilled the Sunday before and the green onion rolls Vonnie made at the same time, when Vonnie said, "I can't take this street violence and the surprise ambushes on the clinic. I have to desert my post for a while. We're going to DeLand."

"The land? What land?"

She gave MJ a playful jostle. "The cultural committee told me about an African American Museum of the Arts. That's what's in DeLand."

"Give me a hint. Are you talking Florida?"

Vonnie thought she was catching a slight excitement vibe from MJ. "On the way to Daytona Beach."

"Where I, for one, never wanted to go. You're the adventurer in this family."

"You're in luck, stick-in-the-mud. It isn't that far." She was grateful daily that they'd taken that trip to Washington State. It had many times allowed her to anticipate MJ's sarcasm, occasional touchiness, and to be cautious of her pride, be sensitive to the lasting effects of her upbringing, not to mention coming into the world butch.

MJ went to the box of maps in their home office and unfolded one.

This was a definite sign that MJ was about to be all-in. Vonnie placed her finger on their destination. "It's under three hours from here," she said. "The museum is a historic one-room building. Lots of Black history in the area."

"A day trip or an overnight?" asked MJ.

"I'll abscond with you for as long as I can."

"In that case we'd better stuff our mega backpacks. We can celebrate surviving the dot-com crash. None of my bets went under and some have improved."

"I'm past those gargantuan bags. They're too heavy. I'm into suitcases on wheels."

"Go buy a set. You want the telescopic handle too. Better still, let's go to the mall together and pick some out."

Vonnie gave MJ a long open-mouthed kiss. "That's a sample of what I have in store for you, my stock market gambler. We'll be rich soon. Until then, I'll ask for the time off."

"I don't know about rich, but certainly comfortable if these investments hold up. I'll check with Vaughn. I don't know if his mojo has come round enough to cover for me."

"I was over there yesterday. Nisa said he's extra cautious outside their house, but he laughs again, and he's more appreciative than ever of her and their home and his freedom. I'm so relieved."

They hugged under the sign they'd bought from an artist who did poker work, or wood burning, and sold it at the Ybor City Saturday Market. Their sign read *Be Kind*. Whenever either of them went off the rails, and like any other couple they both did, the other pointed to the sign. It was working for them.

MJ said, "Florida is one messy pile of contradictions. Here you have this sunny vacationland, but it's the South with baked-in customs and values that lead to bogus arrests of people of color. You've got first-class waterways hiding quick-moving gators with jaws as effective as demolition equipment. How many tourism ads have we seen about hikeable subtropical forests and swamps splendid with bright flowers and ancient trees—ads that don't mention pythons, green anacondas, and who knows what else, dropping off branches and consuming mammals larger than us. And now the churches are being exposed as financial scams. Lovely Florida."

"You, my love, need this break more than I do, from the sound of it."

"Take me deeper into the mysteries of Florida the Beautiful."

The next week they unpacked at a long-established resort on Lake Beresford.

Pleased with MJ's choice of lodging, Vonnie asked, "How do you come up with these retro finds? This place is so fifties, right down to the turquoise and orange accoutrements."

MJ raised her eyebrows. "I have my sources."

"What, your internet research?"

"Not this time, though businesses are slowly catching on to the advertising potential of the web. I mentioned to Ro—you met her, my go-to electrician—that we're staying in DeLand. She and her partner drive over to this vintage charmer twice a year to soak up the tranquility. It occurred to me we deserve some of that. Ro mentioned the area teems with wildlife."

"As long as the owner's attitude isn't vintage and the wildlife doesn't consist of Klansmen."

MJ handed her a brochure for the African American Art Museum. "I found it on display in the office."

"Thanks for spotting this. You're my hero. Always and forever."

"I picked it up and brought it to you. Not quite heroism in my book."

"Can you spell relief that this business supports a nugget of Black culture? You don't have to fight a war to be a hero."

MJ bowed her head and raised it, cracking a smile. "Glad to be of service, ma'am."

"Darn. The museum closes in an hour. Let's go look for that lake tranquility and wildlife now, so we can take our time with the exhibits tomorrow."

MJ rented a canoe. Paddling, they wandered the lake's winking wavelets and planned to explore the river tributaries, see a manatee. For a native Floridian, Vonnie thrilled as a vacationer would at sightings of

Florida wildlife. An alligator lumbered out of the water on its stumpy legs, its jaws permanently fixed in a toothy, innocent smile. Turtles sunned on the dryest, hottest rocks.

She pointed to a turtle with yellow stripes on its head. "You know what that is? That's a Florida red-bellied cooter. I've never seen one in person before. Isn't it the handsomest?"

MJ laughed at the name and bent to kiss Vonnie's slender hand.

The next morning, she was as rested as she'd ever been and champing at the bit to see the museum. They found a waffle restaurant and split orders of chicken, waffles, and country fried steak. They walked to the museum to shed some of the calories, both determined to avoid middle-age spread.

When they arrived, the docent was escorting a Black family through but left them at a showcase to welcome Vonnie and MJ, exhorting them to donate, buy from the gift shop, and sign the guest book with comments on their way out. The docent's nametag read *Vivian Gainer*. She was a proud-appearing woman in her late seventies, tall, unbent, and wearing a short dark brown wig highlighted with silver.

Ms. Gainer said, "We were looking at our banjo. Made by an enslaved person, mind you."

Vonnie lingered by the instrument in its glass case. She imagined a tired man, at work by the light of an outdoor cooking fire, carving and assembling the pieces that would allow him to make music for his uprooted companions, encourage them to dance and sing and, for a few hours, forget their homesickness for the lands they were forced to leave. Out of their shared displacement came gospel music and a lament called the blues.

Ms. Gainer said, "Gather round."

The two young sons were well behaved eleven- and twelve-year-olds in short sleeves and clip-on bow ties.

"This is a photograph of one of the upscale houses built during the Progressive Era of our country. The Yemassee Settlement was a residential neighborhood developed right here in DeLand, Florida, for African Americans. Did you ever hear of the Progressive Era before, any of you?"

The boys shook their heads along with their mother, and the father shrugged and raised his arms. Vonnie elbowed MJ, who, self-conscious about her skin color, reluctantly answered.

"In the late nineteenth and early twentieth centuries, middle class people rejected industrialization, racism, political corruption. They wanted to oust political machines and corrupt bosses. They pushed to regulate monopolies. They supported the creation of agencies—the Food and Drug Administration, for one."

"You are completely correct, miss," said Ms. Gainer. "I recommend the rest of you read more about that movement. The Yemassee Settlement had some fine residences. One landmark we haven't lost is the J. W. Wright Building, built by a Black businessman." She pointed to a picture of it. "Doesn't look like much now, but it housed a Black dentist and shops."

"Why isn't some agency renovating? Has anyone considered making a new plaza to fit right there?" asked the father.

"We have an application in to the National Trust for Historic Preservation to do that. Come along and we'll see some African and Caribbean paintings, quilts, sculptures, artifacts."

After the tour Vonnie bought an eight-by-ten print of a Black woman pouring water from a bucket into a metal washtub.

Ms. Gainer commended her support of a Black artist. "Our people possessed such talents, and look what they had us doing—white people's laundry. What we could achieve if we weren't forever embroiled in struggle. I do believe conditions are improving by degrees. Yes, I do."

MJ stuffed a fifty in the donation box.

The dilemma about being half white, Vonnie thought, was the guilt she bore. Her mother's people acknowledged no remorse for their forebears' actions or their own attitudes. Her father's family took generations to break out of poverty. Then came the double whammy of discovering she was a dyke because she never questioned her attraction to girls, then women, despite her parents' initial concern.

That first lesbian experience came at age twelve, with a white girl in her Girl Scout troop. She'd been drawn primarily to white girls since she first had playmates. What was that about? It lent her a sense of betrayal of her Black side. MJ called her the whole package: feminine, forceful, self-aware, and compassionate. She didn't seem to mind that Vonnie's child-self was a permanent fixture who emerged now and then, sometimes for better, sometimes for worse. Vonnie liked to think she knew how to keep her woman happy.

Ms. Gainer urged them to return for new exhibits and performances. Today, she sent them to wander around the Greater Union Baptist Church, which she described as late Gothic Revival, and to the Elizabeth R. Burgess Pavilion, a plain house behind the formerly white hospital. It wasn't all that long ago when Black patients weren't allowed in the big hospital any more than their physicians had been. From what she and MJ read the night before, this must be what was called the Old DeLand Colored Hospital. Vonnie pressed her hand over her heart as she studied the place.

MJ placed her fingers gently on Vonnie's arm. "You'll be okay?"

Vonnie wrapped them with her other hand. My cloak of solace, she thought, leaning into MJ's strength. Once again, the great swell of incredulous, hurting misery had risen inside her. White henchmen with torches crowded into her brain, the fetid holds of boats crammed with people her color who'd passed down to her dad what was left of their spilled blood. She was frightened of these thoughts, scars of a history she'd rather not know, but to refuse them was an onerous effort of will.

Vaughn had nightmares throughout their childhood. Because their bedrooms were side by side, she was able to quiet him before his muffled screams woke their sleeping parents. She told him about what she called her daymares, which were near duplicates of his bad dreams. They counseled each other not to go through life defined by their Blackness. As they grew older, they learned their resolution was merely a skirmish in an unending war.

Now Vaughn had lived one of his worst nightmares. What would have happened to him if it hadn't been drummed into him not to run, not to fight, no matter how terrified he was? What if there hadn't been bold onlookers to shout objections to the white cop's actions—to shout support to Vaughn? She was grateful to the shouters.

Since then, he was constantly tense, according to Nisa. Saw himself as nothing but a target. They'd planned on two, maybe three, children. Vaughn didn't want kids anymore. Feared to bring dark-skinned innocents into this white country. He was certain racism could only be regulated, never rooted out.

She'd spoken to no one of their personal struggles but MJ, who'd acknowledged she'd never fully understand, despite her own bewildered, shut-out childhood. MJ's memory of alienation, they'd agreed, afforded her an inkling of Vonnie's everyday, every minute treatment by a majority society that heedlessly dismissed the worthiness of her and her twin, or worse.

Their parents, with the best intentions, scrimped, she told MJ, to send them to a private school. The administrators pledged safety along with a progressive education. The twins never wanted to disappoint their parents so stayed mum about the digs, the insults, the occasional shoving or tripping, the social exclusion, and the too liberal teachers who publicly and humiliatingly offered them extra help or extra time, despite being privy to their exceptional IQs and above-grade-level reading and math scores.

After a few silent, mourning moments, she and MJ drifted through the grounds of the pavilion and the neighborhood beyond, arm in arm. She dwelled on her MJ, how sometimes she'd go silent and retreat to one of her ongoing home projects for an hour, two, the whole day. She watched as wrongs done long ago took hold and MJ's shoulders slowly slumped, her handsome head bowed down, and power left her speech until her voice was barely audible. MJ might be solving a knotty problem from work or having one of those days when her past—specifically the ostracism of her childhood—drew her into what she described as a dense gray cloud, a darkness filled with the slicing splinters and shards of a sorrow and turmoil not unlike her own.

MJ had told her that ever since Vonnie's insight into her career— that she was salvaging or reconstructing her childhood—she'd considered changing to something else, probably in finance, but she wouldn't bail on Vaughn, and besides, she loved construction and restoration. Instead of evading what made her MJ Beaudry, when the cloud of despair consumed her, she picked up a hammer or a wrench and worked with her hands until she regained her native strength and the cloud dissipated.

"MJ, my squirrel, I don't care to visit the other landmark Ms. Gainer mentioned today. I'm down enough as it is."

She almost saw the pall over MJ retreat into the distance, and Vonnie experienced a lightening of her own mood as they walked to the historic district. Outside a nineteenth century home, MJ bent and fingered a pale blue wildflower, one of dozens.

Vonnie said, "Twinflower."

"Why's it called—"

"I don't know, but Mom appointed it our flower, Vaughn's and mine."

MJ pointed at a yellow flower.

"Saint-John's-wort. We had it in our yard when we were kids. Dad removed it before it crowded out the other plants. And there, wild petunia, that lavender plant with the butterfly on top."

When she tried to see what bird was singing from a nearby tree, she got a glint of a rocket launch from Kennedy Space Center. She shouldered MJ and pointed.

"Are you kidding me?" MJ said, awe in her voice.

"Can't see much this far away."

"It's as close as I've ever been. There goes the first stage separation."

"Second stage ignition—those flames can probably be seen from Texas."

Vonnie barely noticed that she'd stopped imagining her life as an enslaved person. All at once she was hungry. The docent had recommended a mom-and-pop restaurant on the main drag.

Vonnie wolfed down the catfish plate she'd ordered in honor of her dad, who had taught her, along with her twin, the secrets of fishing for catfish, which liked to hide. Fresh caught, they had a slightly muddy flavor. MJ tried the pan-fried red grouper and gave it a B-plus for its mild, sweet taste.

Then they were off to the resort's recommendation for the best ice cream in Florida. They ate double cones and signed up for a guided airboat tour the next day.

That night Vonnie lay naked on their bed, patting her stomach. When MJ emerged from a cool shower, Vonnie said, "I am stuffed."

Towel around her shoulders, MJ launched herself onto the bed—and Vonnie.

"You are my greatest joy in life, my sweet squirrel."

Each minute spent with MJ reminded Vonnie of the first. MJ made her light of heart, and MJ, after her glum childhood, would always need her sunshine. MJ set a cool hand on Vonnie's flat belly. Eyebrows raised, the hand traveled downward. MJ asked, "You still hungry?"

The touch of MJ's hand never failed to rouse her, but she said no. "You hold on to that thought, my handsome swain. I've had some guilt follow me from Causeway. I should have used this vacation time to help Berry, and it never occurred to me till we were on our way. She drops everything for her friends. What if we're not there for the next attack?"

MJ petted her hand, found her towel, and finished drying off. "Tomorrow is ours to explore the backwaters of the St. Johns River. There's manatees out thar! Armadillos, gopher tortoises, and outrageously plumaged birds. Some things we do for us, some for our particular selves, and others for our friends. Our trip ticks off two of those boxes for me. We'll work on the third soon enough."

"True. You, especially, have done so much already. I know you remodeled the Tommie Center practically for free, and no surprise, I suspect you donated cash as well. What more can I do?"

MJ covered the room's desk chair with her towel and sat on it. She leaned forward, forearms resting on her thighs, hands dangling in front of her. "What you do best. Share your professional knowledge about operating a public program. It's what you studied for your master's degree, what you do daily. You and Allison are teaching Berry how to work within bureaucracies. Berry doesn't comprehend that bureaucrats are a different species. How about spending money from your Family Self-Sufficiency Program on the Center—contract with interpreters. Isn't resident health part of the Housing Authority mandate?"

"I've focused so much on my battle with Vergie Redfern, I lost track. It's true, health is recognized as a priority initiative for public housing. We're supposed to create partnerships with community health facilities. Why didn't I think of the Tommie Center? Darn it, MJ, it turns me on that your brain makes these lightning-fast connections."

"Nail down a plan on paper and grab the money. You're not powerless. You said Vergie doesn't know about this forgotten resource. Continue to defend your federal application."

Vonnie had a change of mind and beckoned to MJ. With an I-knew-you-would smirk, MJ returned, leaned over the bed, brushed lightly across her pubic triangle.

Vonnie failed to withhold a sibilant exhalation. Bent farther, MJ licked both stiff nipples. Vonnie's legs fell slowly open. "First you assuage my hunger, next you solve my problems, and now—"

"You're mine."

"Yes," Vonnie said, and MJ's fingers entered her as her nimble thumb stretched to trace circles a bit higher.

Her voice now throaty, Vonnie patted the bed and said, "Get down here, you."

CHAPTER TWENTY-TWO

Jaudon Vicker

September 2002

She was behind time to Berry's follow-up appointment with Dr. Garza and upbraided herself for it, but she pushed the Buick hard and used shortcuts she learned in the days she drove a noisy Adler 250cc bike around town.

Through one distraction after another, Berry had managed to delay her lab work for close to a year. Laura, in reception, rushed from behind the counter and led Jaudon to the correct exam room. Berry, her smile faint, sat on the exam table with her hands in her lap, teeth clenched.

Jaudon kissed her on the forehead and said, "I can't hardly wait for the promising news."

After a beat too long, Berry answered. "Oh, sweetie, will there ever be promising news now we're advancing in age?"

"We've no call to assume otherwise. The doc will whip you into shape, once you let her."

Dr. Garza entered, a look of frantic weariness on her face. She apologized for her tardiness and dropped to the wheeled swivel stool, hands over her face. She fumbled for the tissues on the counter while tears ran down her cheeks.

Berry watched her, stiff and grave.

Was Dr. Garza unhinged by bad news from these new tests?

"I'm sorry, Berry, this isn't about your results. You may remember my closest cousin is an environmental engineer. Her office was in the second tower last year?"

"You've had news of her?" asked Berry. She descended from the examining table and dragged a chair to sit with the doctor, reaching out to touch her.

"That's our Berry," said Dr. Garza. "I've seen you comfort enough patients to know you'd try to comfort me. But no, I received word today that they haven't found her so far through DNA testing. Our hopes for an answer today, as promised, were for sweet nothing. We have a widespread Greek family, and we all know one another's business—if she's alive, she'd be in touch with one of us."

"You reckon she lost her memory?" Jaudon asked.

The doctor squeezed her eyes shut, but Jaudon again saw wetness force its way out. Berry gave her a new clump of tissues and pressed the trash can pedal for the used batch.

Jaudon said, "From all I've read about last September, I can imagine all too well what she went through. Frankly, I might want to lose my memory."

The doctor took a deep breath, released it open-mouthed, patted her eyes and nose, then straightened. "But let's move on to more pleasant news, shall we?"

Berry nodded, eyes big and scared, akin to the eight-year-old Jaudon first met.

"I can't hardly wait," said Jaudon.

After a beat too long Berry said, "About me?"

"Yes, about you, and how you can whip you back into shape."

"Her tests were good?" Jaudon asked, eager for a black and white answer.

The doctor scooted to Berry. "I have a few questions about your symptoms."

Berry covered her bottom lip with the top. Jaudon, who endlessly spun her ring around her pinkie finger, knew she'd see faint tooth marks of anxiety on Berry's bottom lip.

"Yes or no to these symptoms. Do you continue to experience fatigue?"

"Till the cows come home," Berry answered.

"You're often cold?"

Jaudon said, "You'd think we had air-conditioning the way you wear that ratty sweater around the house."

"Only when dark falls."

Dr. Garza waylaid any argument when she asked if Berry's diarrhea had ever cleared up.

Berry blushed and said it hadn't.

"The one anomaly is your elevated blood cholesterol level, which is commonly associated with menopause. I'll write a scrip that will help to control it."

"Is that why she's all the time itchy, Doc? I give her rubdowns for her dry skin and her achy muscles."

"We use coconut oil and cayenne. Hot and cold packs work for my muscle aches. I'm tired, that's all, Dr. Garza."

"Can you be more explicit?"

"Tired as a plow horse put out to pasture. My thigh muscles and upper arms are tender to the touch and hard to straighten in the mornings or when I sit too long."

"I remember your recent charting errors, which surprised me."

"I may have too much on my mind, Doctor. I forget details I never used to forget."

Dr. Garza ran through the test results and explained them to Berry and Jaudon. "There's one other area of concern, but it could explain a lot. Your thyroid gland is underactive, which is, as you're aware, a condition called hypothyroidism." The doctor turned to Jaudon and explained. "Hormones affect your energy, effectively turning your metabolism up or down. Berry's is seriously low, a condition that can be caused by stress."

Jaudon said, "It doesn't kill you, does it? Berry's got stress steaming out her ears."

Berry squeezed Jaudon's hand. "I'm not going anywhere, Jaudon."

"I'd go with you."

"I'm sure the doctor will write me a scrip for, what, Synthroid? I'm grateful it's nothing worse. You can't imagine what I feared."

"Oh, but I can," said Dr. Garza as she wrote the prescription. "I'll give you the generic version—much less expensive. It will take four to six weeks before your levels look normal, so let's retest in eight weeks to be sure this is the optimal dosage. Drink six to nine large glasses of water daily for the dehydration and spend some time in an activity that doesn't stress your mind. Have some fun."

Berry looked at her watch. "I need to go over to the Center and finish writing thank-you notes to donors. The nurses I graduated with managed to raise eight thousand dollars. Do you remember Lari, who has those challenging mental health issues?"

The doctor lowered her eyes and her brow creased. Lari Hand was a painful memory for her too.

Berry laughed. "Lari spends most of her time up north gambling very successfully with money inherited from the Florida aunt she lived with. She's known as the blackjack queen. She sent the Center her winnings for the past two months, minus taxes. That was another few thousand."

Dr. Garza said, "I haven't heard you laugh in ages."

"To hear Lari has made a life for herself, however strange, and that she still wants to make a difference for women means the world to me." Berry put a hand over her heart and pledged, "This weekend I'll stay away from work, pull weeds in the garden, so we can plant Gran's tomatoes and greens. Otherwise, Gran will be out there on her hands and knees courting another stroke."

"Don't push it, Nurse Garland. Give the medicine a chance to work."

Jaudon said, "Berry loves to dig in the dirt. It's all pleasure for her. You'd think the kitchen garden was a playground."

"I'll try. Please let us know when you hear about your cousin."

"She's the kind of person we can't afford to lose. We became close in early childhood. She calls herself a peace warrior and goes— or went—on Greenpeace actions all over the world. We need fervent activists like her."

Berry covered her mouth. "I've been scared for the past year that we'll retaliate."

"I trust the military has plans."

Berry said, "Please don't go to war, Shrub."

CHAPTER TWENTY-THREE

Vonnie Lowe

December 2002

Vonnie was flustered when Berry arrived at her Housing Authority office, and reassured by a long, warm hug. She'd become a curious and admiring young girl again, fascinated by Cousin Jaudon and her always-smiling friend Berry. She grew up with the idea that the two lived in a tree house on the Vickers' land and were both her cousins. Vonnie's mom was the youngest of the four Batson girls, making Vonnie and Vaughn the youngest cousins. Despite their age differences, Jaudon and Berry were their fast friends.

Here she was now, a successful adult herself, a fact that amazed her. True, she'd *married* well. She possessed the benefits of a long-term stable relationship, which she partially attributed to the humble role model who sat on the other side of her desk waiting to hear Vonnie's proposal.

Pressing her fingers where her collarbones met, Vonnie asked, "Has the Center picked up more patients since we last talked?"

Berry took a spreadsheet printout from an uncluttered portfolio briefcase. Vonnie compared the briefcase to the chronic disarray of her own canvas and leather carryall. She was certain the trim on Berry's bag was not leather—Berry wouldn't own items made from animals.

"Okay," Berry said. "It's the start of the year. Let's see our numbers for the holiday month."

"It makes sense that a holiday would see more minor injuries. Flu season isn't over either."

"A couple of other things have upped the numbers moderately, but you can't blame women for avoiding cursing picketers and their pamphlets. When I go out there to stop the harassment of patients, I'm accused of the vilest things you can imagine. That hurts our number served."

"What are you planning to increase your numbers?"

"For one, I moved my private counseling patients to the Tommie Center. They come in the evenings, so there's no conflict. I add them as visits, they pay the Center, and one of these days, we can afford to increase Leslie's salary out of this additional income. We don't want to lose her. Her new girlfriend has a transfer request in for Milwaukee Airport."

"Who would want to live in Milwaukee?"

"Wisconsin seems to be the bodybuilding capital of the country."

"And Leslie would follow this woman?"

"She's done it before. Remember the shuttle driver who always waved at her?"

"Not the one with tattoos and nose ring? She creeps me out."

"They had a two-week fling. Leslie called me from Pride Fort Lauderdale to say she'd gone away for a day or three on impulse and was sorry for the inconvenience. The driver never notified anyone."

"What about you?" asked Vonnie. "Are you paying yourself for your work at the Center yet?"

"As I can. I work mornings at the practice, and the Beverage Bays are doing well. Jaudon and I agreed that we'd be fine if I didn't bring in more money for a couple of years."

"Tell me about Jaudon. I've known her my whole life, but what really makes her tick? She always seems happy and incredibly busy."

"The stores are her joy. I don't know if she'll ever retire, or let herself die, for that matter. She wouldn't trust many people to operate them for her."

Vonnie laughed. "Like you and the Tommie Center?"

"Far from it. Because it's not mine. I'll be happy when the community we're building it for takes it over." Berry slid another printout across the desk. "Look from how far afield we're drawing patients."

"These are great numbers given the circumstances. What magic did you work?"

"Not me—Shady."

"Shady?" Vonnie asked.

"He taught literature at the college level until he was let go for overfraternizing with his students. He believes in children, their education, their health, their potential. He put his niece through college on drug and alcohol sales."

"Legal?"

"Of course not," Berry said. They both laughed. "Don't think I have no qualms about that. On the other hand, he recently restarted the manual car wash business he and Tad operated before Tad took on Pansy's Pastries. Shady added detailing and hires kids working their way through school."

"How does he help increase our patient numbers at the Center?"

"He loads his employees up with flyers and instructs the kids to pass the flyers out, tack them up, take them to school, involve their families," Berry explained. "Shady lives in the public housing behind the Center and knows practically every resident. We need more men in Shady's mold, personal use of illegal substances or not. Now tell me about connecting the Housing Authority and the Center."

Her apprehension higher than ever, Vonnie's voice was breathy. "The Housing Authority, and especially my program, are mandated to partner with local resources to provide our residents and other Section 8 recipients with essential services. If delivery of women to a medical office isn't an essential service, I don't know what is."

She saw the interest spark in Berry's eyes. "You're saying we can actually help each other? Double up on our resources?"

"The only way to keep money for programs is to use it and use it successfully. MJ came up with the idea when we were in DeLand, and I've studied it." She arranged more materials before Berry. "In one of our initiatives, we partner with outside health and other services to make certain our people obtain the assistance they need. Our agencies have access, in general, to limited internal monies, so we also rely on external health partners to partially fund, for example, health activities."

"Are you thinking what I'm thinking?"

"I made appointments to talk with the city mayors, the county manager and the regional transit authorities, the county social services department, the fire department, ambulance and school bus companies— anyplace else you can think of. If you're interested."

"Interested? Let's quit dillydallying around and come up with a serious plan. If you can make appointments in clusters, I'll ask for time off from my job to go find partners with you."

Vonnie popped up and rounded her desk to hug Berry. "Okay," she said, "if you give me another half hour, we'll come up with a simple script that will open doors."

Berry, eyebrows raised interrogatively, suggested, "We'll sell them on flexible and accessible transportation options for low-income people who currently have no way to travel to health appointments. Assure them funds are available."

"That didn't take long. Say it again so I can write it down."

Berry did, but asked, "Should we take out the words *low-income*? They might scare off some people."

"Let's leave them. That'll screen out providers who don't want our target patients."

"Shall we include the hospitals?" Berry held folded hands to her heart.

"Why not? We have momentum today. On that note, I'm due at work in five minutes."

"I'll check in once I make the calls. If we can't interest anyone," Berry said, "we'll establish our own shuttle routes. As Jaudon says, *We'll get 'er done*."

CHAPTER TWENTY-FOUR

Jaudon Vicker

January 2003

If Jaudon was ashamed to be half Batson before, once she learned her cousins had joined in to make Mrs. Lanamore's life miserable, she wanted to hide her blood relationship to the lot of them once and for all, except Aunt Lollie and Cousin Cal. With the family knowledge that Berry was vegetarian bordering on vegan, their favorite trick was to leave roadkill at the Tommie Center's front door. They might as well drive a stake into Berry's heart, but she saw to it that each creature was buried in land where it had thrived.

It was her turn on night watch across from the Center, her Buick partially hidden by a thick oak. She was listening to the all-Elvis hour on her big brother's ancient transistor radio so she wouldn't drain the car battery. She kept the windows closed as she didn't want to draw attention to herself with the music, even to catch a cool breeze.

Duval spent his vigils on watch from inside the Center. A week before, he opened the window at the desk where he usually sat. For his troubles, a poor man's flaming mini-bomb—a Molotov cocktail—was hurled from a pickup. It took out the computer screen, ignited paper and Duval's acetate shirt, which fused into an extensive patch of his shoulder.

Tad whisked him to the ER, but a baker's arms and shoulders are constantly in motion. Duval was at work, healing more slowly and painfully than if he'd stayed home. Laura Bathgate visited some evenings and helped Tad with Duval's physical therapy. Jaudon worried one of her relatives maimed Duval. Most of the Batsons were a sorry lot, and they'd dollars to doughnuts eventually blow themselves up making a simple incendiary device.

At least Momma, for all her faults, was ambitious enough to climb out of poverty. The other smart Batson sister, Aunt Lollie, broke the mold to earn her diploma and become a paralegal.

Aunt Lessie, on the other hand, bore five boys, starting with Roy Jack, who arrived a year or so before she married and bore her maiden name. Roy Jack believed that name branded him a bastard. Was that the cause of his bullying nature and shiftlessness? Aunt Lessie denied responsibility for her out-of-hand sons.

"Born to wear prison blues," her aunt would say. Roy Jack Batson assumed leadership of three of his half brothers who followed him in and out of the criminal courts. The fourth boy was Cousin Cal, one of three worthwhile cousins on Momma's side. He served his country and returned to work any job that was needed at the Beverage Bays. She was as proud of Cal as was his mom.

Three light-skinned teens ambled past her station wagon. She was relieved that the young men were absorbed more by the girl between them than by the night watch.

And gullible, nosy Aunt Floxie, with her big sparkly cross necklace, could gossip the legs off a chair, twisting ninety percent of her facts one hundred percent of the time. She'd married late, to a widower from the church with two stuck-up twin teen girls who ignored Aunt Floxie from the get-go no matter how many times their father threatened the hickory switch. Aunt Floxie once saw them in town, during school hours, clownish in forbidden makeup, denim shorts cut high enough for bathing suit bottoms. Jaudon heard Floxie tell Aunt Lessie how she wished she had a camera, or the nerve to pull her husband out of work to see the girls.

"Which one do you think will be in the family way first?"

"Those girls are so wicked they'd choose abortion," predicted Aunt Floxie. "Mark my words."

"Let's hope they don't do like Lollie and pop out babies who don't look like our family."

Those ignorant aunts got her goat so bad she always had to say something, not that it changed anything.

Since the Tommie Center opened, Roy Jack's pack regularly swarmed into Pansy's Home Cooking, took over multiple tables for hours, and ordered coffee—it came with free refills. They showed up often enough to make the regulars, mostly Black, uncomfortable.

They'd shout to Mrs. Lanamore, "How many babies did your health center kill today?" Or, "What rituals do you use the unborn for?" Or, if she was close by, "Hey, Pansy, you ever let a white boy show you a good time?"

Mrs. Lanamore answered them by serving sludgy, watery coffee she made a day or two before and kept on hand especially for them. The microwave oven came in handy to barely warm a cup.

This state of affairs worried Jaudon half to death. The kids were brought up on bigotry. Never taught to think for themselves the way Pops did her. Where would it lead? She heard news clips on the radio at work. Antigay organizations across the country put initiatives on ballots to curtail protections for gays. As if any old body had the right to take or give rights to American citizens they don't favor. She'd heard that megachurch ministers in Four Lakes preached politics half the time.

Rigo and his partner Jimmy Neal claimed those types of Christians secretly consolidated power by raking in money to…what?

"Get rich," Jimmy Neal had said.

"It's worse than that," Rigo claimed. "The zealots want to throw out the whole concept of democracy and make the United States a Christian theocracy." He explained how that would work. Jaudon pledged to fight any such thing.

She missed Rigo and Jimmy Neal something awful, but Rigo had found his calling in teaching, and he moved north to the state university to teach psychology there. Jimmy Neal was a registered nurse and easily found work. They even bought a house, thanks to Gran.

A few years earlier Gran said, "I am fed up with Rigo's father for disowning him." Jaudon was there when Gran called the man to berate him for visiting such rejection on his son, a man she would be proud to call son. She ended the call more instructively. Her granddaughter didn't have a living father, and how fortunate Rigo was that he did. "You come on over here and we'll hash this out over a home-cooked dinner."

After several such calls, Mr. Patate instead invited Gran to dinner. One week and a new dress later, he drove her to Bern's Steak House, a place so fancy she'd never expected to enter its famed rooms. They talked about Rigo and Berry and their own lives.

"I like to fell out," Gran told Berry and Jaudon late that night. "Dessert was served by none other than Rigo and his big honey bear. The waiter supplied two more chairs—they'd planned it all out. Mr. Patate praised me to the skies for leading him to reason. Dinner was his own commemoration of reinstating Rigo into the family, and Mr. Patate's son was his only family. He shook hands with both those boys. I blubbered into my first ever *creamed brew-lay*. I noticed those rascals playing footsie under the table and had to stop myself from hee-hawing."

Rigo's father ceremoniously gifted the guys with a check to pay off their mortgage up north where they lived.

Between work and distance, Jaudon seldom saw Rigo, her oldest friend.

Her longtime store manager, Olive Ponder, was her other best friend. Olive had clued her in about how American Blacks had fought to secure basic rights since the first enslaved person stumbled ashore in chains. "Today's citizen initiatives," Olive proclaimed, "ought to protect Americans, not make target practice of minorities."

So Jaudon sat in her dark car, protecting this investment in women of every color. She smiled at the sight of a dark sedan with antennae making a U-turn. Cullie pulled up in her sheriff's cruiser, driver's side to driver's side.

Jaudon was ready for anything. "This Center has a bull's-eye on it."

"You can bet the farm on that," Cullie said.

"I'm so mad at my no a'count cousins I could spit quarters."

"Are they the ones defacing the building? Was it them who slit the tires on the bakery truck?" Cullie asked.

"They're capable of that and more."

"I frankly don't reckon it's them. Please keep it under your hat except for Berry and Allison. You might think reproductive rights are safe."

"I haven't thought about abortion for years. The Supreme Court settled that. The justices can't change their minds, can they?"

"Sure, they can. If so, the struggle"—Cullie pointed to the Center—"may be a waste of time."

"That's what I'm telling you. The people against abortion, birth control, and gay people have conspired and raised money for years. They don't care who they elect to the school board, the congress, or even the presidency as long as the candidates are camp followers. Meaning, aren't keen on us or other minorities, don't care about what women bear, don't give a hoot what they destroy, so long as they're rich enough to run with the big dogs."

Cullie's radio squawked, but it was the dispatcher responding to a motor vehicle accident. "The FBI sends us notices about this or that going on. Local law enforcement is required to keep statistics on these dumbass organizations because they commit political mayhem with donations from their churches."

"You saw someone trashed the Saturday Women's Health trailer parked behind Dr. Garza's office?"

"I went over there. Did you bother to tow it home? It's pretty tore up."

"Gran had that camper I don't remember how many years. We've fixed it up before, we can do it again. Least ways, they didn't torch the thing. We have the blocks it sat on in the pole barn. I won't bother to replace the tires."

Cullie asked, "Who has a call to take away free medical care? Will they do the same to the Tommie Center?"

"I have a suspicion it's my cousins, the Batson brothers. Roy Jack doesn't have a political bone in his body, but for an easy buck? He'd do it or put the idea in one of his brothers' pointy little heads. They might not even know it's Gran's trailer."

A muddy Jeep Wrangler with oversize tires stopped in front of the café, and two white men got out, the slamming of their doors loud against the sparse night traffic. They'd arrived from the wrong direction to spot the sheriff's cruiser.

Jaudon, hand at her heart, looked at Cullie, but Cullie had already slunk outside. She drifted after them as they walked toward the Center. Jaudon used her binoculars to read their spattered license plate, wrote the number on her hand, and called the sheriff's office to report the active incident, in hopes they'd send backup for Cullie.

One man carried a pump-action shotgun, and a younger male toted open paint cans. As soon as the first guy blew the lock from the front door and kicked the door in, he grabbed a pail. Both men rushed inside. Through the window, she saw them heave the red contents around the reception area.

Cullie was in shooting stance, service pistol raised, when the men emerged. She shouted at them to drop their gun.

A police siren yelped. "Thanks be," Jaudon said aloud. The vandals ignored Cullie and made haste to their truck. The driver performed a screeching U-turn and clipped Cullie as she attempted a leap to safety. The truck barreled west toward Tampa.

She rocketed out her door to Cullie, who'd fallen on her side, gun in hand, and talked into her handheld radio. No blood was visible, but she saw where the Jeep ripped Cullie's side holster, duty belt and a piece of her uniform slacks right off her.

"I have the plate number." She held up her hand where she'd written it.

Her friend's voice was tinny, her breathe wheezy as she relayed that information. She let the hand with the radio fall to the street. "Ambulance ETA is—now."

In minutes, a man and a woman in blue uniforms emerged from the rescue van.

Jaudon started to stand. "Before they banish me, where are you hurt other than your hip?"

"Is everywhere exact enough?"

"I need to tell Allison something."

"A bump. Got bumped by a car."

One of the paramedics dropped a duffel bag next to Cullie. "Some bump."

A deputy drew Jaudon aside. "We'll need your statement, ma'am."

She heard her own desperation. "I have to call her family."

"We'll make that happen."

Cullie motioned to the deputy, her voice wheezy. "Two white guys, Hector. A kid and an adult. Check the raving hater clubs."

CHAPTER TWENTY-FIVE

MJ Beaudry

Cullie was released from the hospital when the doctors found no internal bleeding. Her X-rays concerned them enough to refer her to an orthopedist the next day. After the appointment, Allison needed to stop by the Tommie Center for a quick meeting with MJ and Vonnie. Cullie, on crutches, followed her in. From her expression, walking had to be grueling.

A Latina mother with two restless young children, a lone, heavily wrinkled Black woman, and two Asian teenagers who looked like dykes sat in reception, watching Cullie.

One of the preschoolers asked, "Is that the lady cop who got run over to save our healthy place?"

"Shh." The mother smiled at Allison apologetically.

Allison didn't hesitate. "Yes, it is. She's a real-life hero."

Cullie managed a thin smile for the child.

Leslie pushed a donated relic of a wheelchair from behind the counter, but Cullie refused it.

"I didn't come to make a nuisance of myself. I only want to sit and wait for Allison," said Cullie.

MJ folded her finely muscled arms. "Allison's the troublemaker. She wants the city to pay for a bus shelter out front, and they're stalling. We're glad to do it, but the city needs to approve it before we can start."

"That's why we're here," Allison said in a burst of rhetoric right in front of the patients. "I am beyond enraged at the obstructions. This"— she cleared her throat and gestured to Cullie—"never had to happen. The county, the federal government, the state, these politicians want the votes of the yowling, shrieking born-agains and pander to them no matter the manifest needs of the rest of the citizenry and some of their own flock."

"Say it, sister," the old woman shouted to the ceiling. The mother nodded and grinned. Her children clapped their hands to see their mom's jubilance. The baby dykes stared, and one loudly whispered, "That's the Four Lakes mayor."

"Mayor Millar for President," said the other.

Allison turned to the patients. She spoke slowly for the little boy who was translating into Spanish for his pregnant mother. "The Tommie Center will close if the politicians don't act and act fast. Please call them, write to them, go to Democratic headquarters and ask them for help." To the young women she said, "Ask your teachers how to communicate with your representatives. You don't need to be old enough to vote to have a voice in matters that concern you. Egg on your nearest and dearest to speak up too."

Allison went to stand by Cullie. "This sheriff's deputy was injured while she defended the Center. The violence has got to stop."

The little boy said, "My mother wants to know, where did you say the Democrat's headquarters is at? We can go there today."

Leslie wrote it all down.

MJ took the seat next to Cullie. They'd first met when MJ was new in town and learning to burgle well-off homes. As a matter of fact, the first and last time she was caught breaking and entering by a cop, it was Cullie. She'd had close calls, but Cullie, who was an auxiliary officer at the time, walked right in on her. Fortunately, it was early in MJ's search for cash and rucksack-size items. She learned from that showdown to lock doors after herself.

All those years ago, Cullie twigged that MJ was a runaway baby dyke and chose to counsel, not arrest her. Of course, there was a chase involved, and handcuffs—she was, what, fifteen at the time? Jaudon had appeared to help Cullie run her down. Nothing and no one was going to send her back to her misery in Depot Landing, where she'd lived with impossible confusion about who she really was, and her own impulses.

She asked Cullie, "What's the diagnosis?"

Leslie opened a drink from the cooler and handed it to Cullie. The inner door buzzer went off. Vaughn had installed a lock on it for their safety. Leslie walked the older patient to the physician's assistant on duty.

Cullie's voice cracked as she spoke. She dug her knuckles into her eyes. They came away wet with tears. Allison gave her tissues and held her other hand.

"It's called a hip pointer," Cullie said. "Which is a big ol' bruise right here." She touched the point of the bone on the upper outside of her hip, wincing. "It can happen from a doozy of a fall or radical thump to the hip, usually by getting creamed in basketball or football. A mishmash of inside rigging attaches to it. Anyway, that's what the ortho doc told me."

Allison ticked off details with her fingers. "They did an MRI first thing, checked for internal injuries. No treatment for forty-eight hours to be sure all bleeding stops. She's got a hematoma practically the size of Stone Mountain in Atlanta, which may have to be drained. There's swelling, minute improvement in pain, tenderness to the touch, not much range of motion from the hip down—you saw her, she can barely walk even with crutches." She covered her mouth and coughed. "Sorry, my allergies. She has some bruised ribs from falling. For a while, she gets to go from home to outpatient rehab and nowhere else."

"We'll catch the critter who did this," Cullie said. "I went through mug shots while I was in the hospital. Could be a kid named Josiah Howell, in trouble since he moved to town—shoplifting, beating up kids from the public school, calling the white boys anti-Semitic names, taunting the Black kids with the usual insults. They'll bring him in for questioning. The worst news is, I can't drive."

"Just for now. Until you're off the corticosteroids and your physical therapist says you can. Meanwhile, it's rest, icing, and anti-inflammatories for up to a month."

"I'll be crazy as a bullbat if I sit around."

"Then we'll put you in inpatient care at that nursing home the Health Department cites almost monthly."

"You wouldn't do that, my sweet jujube."

"We need a Leslie Gardner to keep you in line."

Leslie lifted her arms in helplessness as she escorted the mother and children into one of the two exam rooms. "You'll have to clone me."

"I'll bet Jaudon will come over and watch *Xena: Warrior Princess* reruns on Oxygen with you."

"Count me in," said Leslie. "I heart Xena big-time."

Cullie swiftly lifted her arms to the heavens. "Xena, where were you when I needed you—youch." She bent forward in unmistakable pain and discovered that movement compounded it. She snuffled openly.

Allison looked up, pain on her face. "Squeeze hard on my hand, sugar. It's another muscle spasm. They don't last long."

"I'll drop in to see you till you're sick of me," said MJ. "Tie her to your bed if need be."

"Oh, honey pants," Cullie replied, as she wiped the sweat along her hairline, "we're not into that scene."

"Don't expect me to show you any mercy, hotshot cop."

"Please stop," Cullie said. "Laughter pains me."

Berry and her big smile came through the door full speed ahead. She wore her palm tree and pink flamingo scrubs. She stopped short at the sight of Cullie, let fall and scatter two armfuls of documents.

"Cullie," she said and squatted before her, arms out.

"Don't touch the damaged goods," warned MJ, joking but nervous for Cullie.

"Who's the nurse—you or Berry?" asked Allison.

"You've got a point."

Berry said, "I know about your hip, but why is your face swole up? That contusion along your cheekbone is almost black. Did you also hit your head?"

"Those jackasses knocked me silly—I face-planted."

Ouch, thought MJ, which reminded her of her own facial pain. She'd better make a dentist appointment and soon.

"How do you feel?"

"Like I'm two years older than dirt."

She turned to Allison, who explained, "I worried the cheekbone and eye socket might have fractured, but I forgot what a hard head she has. She was concussed, though, so the doctors told me to keep my eyes on her."

"You do what the mayor says now, Deputy Culpepper."

"Don't I always? She comes home with her management button stuck at the on position."

"That's sometimes true," Allison admitted. "We made an agreement, though. A safe word, for lack of a better term, to use when either of us steps over a line."

Cullie came alive to say, "Two Egg."

"Two Egg?"

"Our safe words. It's a backwoods crossroad not that far from the

Alabama border. We happened on it during a road trip during Long Cane Syrup Day. Hordes of people show up for the festival."

"What in the world is Long Cane Syrup Day?" Leslie asked.

Once again, Allison cleared her throat. "You call yourselves Floridians and you've never gone? The town celebrates sugar cane. Done like in the old days, except with a four-wheeled vehicle, not men or mules. They drive a long pole around and around the grinder. When the cane stalks are fed through the grinder cylinders, they emerge flat. Their juice collects in a barrel, and people haul bucketloads to the boiling shed. You can watch the whole process and buy jars of greenish cane juice."

"I like that safe word idea. Jaudon comes home in managerial mode after a day at her stores. I tell her I'm not her part-timer, but I'd rather use a nonjudgmental reminder."

"Whatever works, but Two Egg is ours. Hey, Allison? I'd love to be home in bed about now."

"Can you give her five minutes, Cullie?" Berry said. "I need Allison and MJ to eyeball what I've worked up for our meet with the Regional Transit Authority. Vonnie will be here soon."

Cullie's eyes were closed, but she murmured, "I'll be right here jawing with Leslie." Seconds later she was profoundly asleep.

Berry took her pulse. "I think the pain meds we picked up at the drugstore have finished kicking in."

Leslie stage-whispered, "I'll take her home when she wakes up and stay with her till you're done here."

"Goddess bless you, Leslie Gardner," said MJ. "I take it you think we'll be here more than five minutes."

"Oh yeah." Leslie flashed a quick smirk.

Allison squeezed her eyes shut and pursed her lips.

It was obvious Allison was making a big decision—stay and work or be with the injured Cullie.

Allison bent over Cullie and woke her with a kiss on the cheek, explaining the plan. From her bag, she pulled two sets of medications, and gave instructions to indispensable Leslie.

❖

MJ followed Allison into Berry's office. Each grabbed a hodgepodge of the paperwork Berry had dropped. Allison pulled a tissue from a box on Berry's desk.

"You're crying," MJ said.

"More like leaking. I'm so mad at this whole rigamarole. Cullie lives a charmed life—another few inches and I would have lost her. Who doesn't want women to be healthy? Do medical doctors think we're out to steal their paltry Medicaid incomes? Are the attacks linked to county government? Who has it in for us there? Is it solely the abortion crazies? My poor Cullie." Allison was hugging herself.

Allison isn't merely some mayor, decided MJ. She was the radical lesbian feminist self she'd never leave behind, no matter what compromises she was compelled to negotiate as a politician. For herself, she'd rather build a high-rise on Mt. St. Helens than do a mayor's job.

Out loud, she said, "About the crazies, you've already heard of the Southern Poverty Law Center."

The very reminder of that group seemed to calm Allison. "They are the best. They train people like us to go into our communities and make changes."

Berry cupped her left elbow with her right hand and looked interested.

Allison explained, "They fight racism and, these days, homophobia. They monitor US hate groups and sometimes destroy them with the help of the courts."

Berry asked, "Do we have a lot of hate groups in Florida? Not that I actually want to know."

MJ puffed out her cheeks and exhaled with a *puh*. "Let's simply say we're right up there with Texas and Idaho—there's tons of them, and I am dead serious."

Berry collapsed into her chair, deflated.

"Are you ready for this?" asked MJ. "Intracoastal Ministries is on the list, and they're described as advocating for general hatred."

"That can't be true."

"Sorry," said MJ.

"I'd better tell Opal what she's gotten herself involved in."

MJ sought Allison's eyes over Berry's head. Allison showed her gritted teeth. "Why don't you wait on that, Berry," advised MJ. "You don't want to kindle any family feuds. I'll look into it further, see what the ministries are, in actual fact, up to."

"Okay, but now you've got me worried."

"I'm horrified we have so many hate groups," Allison said. She slumped into another chair. "I'm helpless about the Tommie Center. The mayor of Four Lakes has no power here."

"Did I hear that right?" It was Vonnie, surging into Berry's office with her stuffed messenger bag, African silhouette earrings, and her breathless grace. "Since when does Allison Millar cede power to anyone over anything?"

"It's not mine to cede. The Center is not in the city I govern."

"Wait a minute," said Berry. "We may be starting off dicey, but this aims to be a regional health resource. We serve any woman who comes in, and we're up to two counties right now. The shuttle bus service we need will have stops in Four Lakes."

Allison tapped her fingers on her knee, forehead wrinkled in concentration. "Will you allow me to step in and help?"

Vonnie said, "I thought you'd never offer."

"How do you see my city contributing?"

"Help us pinpoint this logjam blocking access to women's health," Berry suggested.

"Any clues?" asked Allison.

MJ said, "Follow the money."

"True," Berry said. "We have grants pending from a few sources, but the big one is from the county. We haven't found the blockade yet."

"Do you think it might be one of the hate groups?" asked Allison.

"Or," said Berry, "someone connected to a hate group who's in a position to gum up the works."

"Maybe it's a clerical person," said Vonnie. "A super-religious employee able to misplace key documents. Or a higher-up who consigns certain paperwork to the shredder supposedly in error."

"What's going through your heads?" Allison said. "Speculation that a certain mayor within our region might be able to trace the jam? Unstick what's stuck? Make a bigger stink than plain folk? Is that what you're telling me?"

"Bingo," said MJ.

"Most excellent," said Allison, "because I want a part of that."

"At least we'll always have *Roe v. Wade*," said Berry to a chorus of affirmations.

The four of them, Berry, Vonnie, Allison, and MJ, worked for a while that night drafting shuttle proposals. Since the county and state offices were stonewalling, Vonnie and Berry had already identified a number of nonprofits, federal agencies, and private individuals with stakes in linking more people to medical facilities.

Vonnie said, "Let's include volunteers to raise the estimated ridership. The shuttle can transport our volunteers as easily as patients."

Berry made a note of that. She was out of ideas herself.

"That's an outstanding point." Allison fumed anew. "Where are the volunteers? Why is it so often lesbians are the ones who fix what men break—including their women? Did straight women set up the shelters around here without our help? Where are the straight women from our old consciousness-raising group now? Their kids must have grown up. Why aren't they here? So many of us were active HIV caregivers and accelerated cures. Why aren't more gay men invested in helping us? Will anyone ever honor the lesbians?"

Berry sighed. "We can worry about gay politics another time. Unless you don't want to go home tonight?"

Allison lamented. "For that matter, why are lesbians the ones behind a health center for all women?"

"There's Mrs. Lanamore," Vonnie said. "And my mom's PFLAG group held that silent auction. As well as the AME Church, the Unitarians, the Unity Church, that gospel group that gave us the profits from their concert, and NOW. Because they're not in this room doesn't mean they're not in our corner."

"Okay, okay. But you have to admit, we had to go beg them. Lesbians are the leaders."

"So," said MJ in her most sonorous voice, "in Vonnie and Berry's plan the shuttle relies in a big way on grants. After a time, there will be nominal fares and rider donations, contracts with other medical facilities like the hospitals, possible money from our county general fund, and some from entities like the school board, nonprofits—"

"National organizations," added Berry.

All were quiet except MJ, who drummed a pencil eraser on the computer keyboard. "You can guess what I see. I see a need at this point to bundle transportation in with the Center itself. Your resources are similar, and our percentages of reliance on them are practically the same."

Allison said, "You think we can bypass the logjam. Put the local government to shame."

"Get more creative with resources," Vonnie added.

Now they turned to Berry, who had the final say. "We'd leave what we've done to date in place."

MJ nodded.

"I don't know where we'd find the time to research more aid."

Allison said, "We don't have to figure out all the details tonight."

Berry said, "And write more proposals."

"They're already written, Berry." Vonnie put an arm around Berry's shoulders. "We'll tweak them where necessary to fit new partners. Heck, there have to be liberals around here with deep pockets."

"What if"—and MJ looked at each of them in turn—"the four of us spend an hour a week for a month researching who we can hit up for a health bus or two. We compose a generic letter and follow up with phone calls, set up meetings with anyone interested. Nisa Lowe has an ace typist friend at work who wants to help us. We can ask if she'll do the typing."

The collective sigh mirrored her mix of relief, weariness, and optimism.

Allison slumped in her chair, arms folded, eyes staring at the ceiling. "We need more power. I may have to run for a higher office."

They left in a group for safety's sake, because all the monetary assistance in the world wouldn't lessen their vulnerability to closed minds.

CHAPTER TWENTY-SIX

Berry Garland

Winter 2003

Early that winter of 2003, Klem Howell dropped his wife off to visit Berry in Rainbow Gap. The women planned to weed, plant, fertilize, and mulch the garden.

Jaudon couldn't bear Opal, but Berry wanted to stay in touch with her sibling. Rather than sit down to an uncomfortable meal with the Howell kids and husband Klem—a tall, fit, ginger-haired man who possessed, by Jaudon's description, as much suavity as a feral hog—working alone with her sister normally made for a mellower visit.

She hid her amusement, thinking of Klem. One day after he picked Opal up, Gran said, "That man has tall gums, like a horse. It would be a chore to kiss him."

Aloud, Berry said, "The nights are drawing in."

"I wish the heat would as well."

"Be careful. Don't kneel there on your bare knees—that's a sandspur patch."

Her sister recoiled and pointed at another scraggly plant. "I'll root that weed out for you."

"Let it be. It's coreopsis, our state wildflower. They're so pretty come spring and summer, like mixed scoops of sherbet, yellow, orange, and red. Butterflies love the blooms. Birds come for the seed heads."

A few dried leaves rasped with a breeze.

"Grammy Garland wouldn't have any truck with them. They look like weeds."

"I remember. She gardened just enough to grow flowers for church displays. Any weed in her way, she tortured the poor thing out of the ground."

She stood to behold the plenty she and, normally, Gran, tended yearly. Three furrowed patches of kale, collard greens, onions, garlic, carrots, parsnips, radishes, spinach, beets, okra, and both Florida broadleaf and Southern Giant curled mustard greens. Off to the side were the cantaloupes and watermelons, put in the ground that weekend. The herbs were planted in a circle pattern Gran recalled from her grandmother: thyme, sage, lavender, rosemary, lemon balm, basil, chamomile, and pesty chicory at times run riot. The strife contained in and among the rows was ongoing and endless: high water from the pond, tropical storms, drought years, scavenging insects, birds, rabbits, squirrels, raccoons, moles. Kind of like human life, she thought. You tried to grow nourishment and at the same time be ready for mammoth pocket gophers.

Opal showed up in her usual outfit for gardening visits, an oft-washed and mended smock with a faded design of dainty blue flowers, like an illustration on a sewing pattern from the days Gran made clothes. She guessed the smock was passed down from Grammy Garland. Otherwise, Opal was in a kelly-green skirt and a yellow-checked short-sleeved blouse, white crew socks, and polished white canvas tennis shoes. She'd arranged a bump of her lengthening hair at the top of her head and used it as an exclamation point when speaking.

"You can grow broccoli here? Neighbors in Georgia had no luck."

"Broccoli likes cool weather. Did they plant it in the cool of the year?"

Opal had a short fuse. She snapped, "You don't expect me to recall that long ago, do you? Grammy stuck with what she knew, her decorative flowers."

Now that Gran Binyon's specialist had limited her level of activity, Berry was grateful for her sister's help with the garden, but if Opal was bent on waging a grandmother war, she just might not be warned about the next sandspur patch.

Berry pulled weeds so she didn't have to see her sister. "One woman's trash is another woman's treasure. It depends on what you want around you. A lot of weeds are native plants, and critters live off them or off whatever eats them. If that tickseed spreads too far, I'll tame it, but I'll never eradicate it altogether. On the other hand, you don't want buttonwood near your flowers, native or not. This stuff reproduces by seed, root, and—to survive a freeze—by taproot." She laughed. "Which is why I need my baby sister's help."

Opal faced away from Berry. "Does your, uh, Jaudon, ever help with this?"

"She will if I ask her to, but the kitchen garden is a project Gran and I share. As for my *uh*, you can call Jaudon my life partner any old time."

"Is that how you think of that roughneck?"

She examined the mustard greens with great concentration and hid a half smile. As she evicted a cabbage looper she answered, "For your information, Jaudon is a gentle tomboy with a big heart, nothing near a roughneck."

Opal used Gran's homemade insecticidal soap on broccoli plants over by the empty potato patch. "If you don't mind me asking, what turned you off men?"

Her hackles rose. Was Opal being ignorant or trying to insult her?

"What makes you think I was ever on to men?"

Looking up, blinking in the sun, Opal resembled the Grammy Garland she remembered an awful lot. It sent a shiver along her spine to be caught in that disapproving gaze once more.

"I can't help wondering, is she all woman? I mean, does she have the right parts?"

Anger took away her ability to speak.

"I'm supposing if she was a sure-enough man, you'd be married and have a family."

"I enjoy my family the way it is. And for your information, I love Jaudon for her ambition, high spirits, stability, sensitivity, and style. She's a scrapper born and bred, quick to take offense, but smooth with her customers and grateful to them. Plus, she loves nature every bit as much as I do."

"Style? She looks like Huckleberry Finn."

"Exactly."

"I'm trying to understand it, is all. You're a pretty woman, you didn't have to settle."

"And I don't understand what possessed you to increase more than your share of the world's population when so many children are without homes and resources grow more and more scarce."

"I don't have to explain the decisions I make with my husband. That's between us and God."

She thought but didn't say, *Yet you expect me to explain mine with Jaudon?* In a pig's eye she would. She was used to scrutiny by nosy bodies, but not this nosy. Her sister was as vexing as the cabbage loopers.

"Jaudon and I were made for each other. You won't find a more trustworthy or devoted person in this whole world."

"The Bible condemns your way of living but says not a word about how a Christian woman should treat a sister who goes down the wrong path."

"I suspect the men who wrote the Bible would advise stoning me to death."

Opal stared at her, as if considering that very option.

To brighten the mood, Berry said, "I can't think of a better church than a garden." She pointed to the coreopsis again. "I worship whatever power created that golden-yellow double flower. It grows up to twenty inches high, trying to touch the sun from spring to fall."

A snake moved slowly along the newly watered earth. Opal lifted her hoe.

"That's a black swamp snake, Opal. Won't hurt you. They're kind of handsome once you get over them being snakes."

"They don't scare you?"

"Not enough to hurt them. I mostly don't mind them outdoors. It's when one invites itself inside that Gran and I turn squeamish and call Jaudon. She has a way to catch them with a broom and a lidded trash can. Once caught, she relocates them." She was pleased at the change in topic. "But you have a houseful of boys and men—plenty of snake catchers."

"Klem beheads them. It's my daughter Lutie who learned how to catch them with a snake fork, grab them by the tail, and drop them in a pillowcase. She makes me drive five miles to resettle them away from homes. That girl is so strange, she makes me wish I didn't name her after Grammy."

"A snake fork. I'll have to suggest one to Jaudon."

"Does your partner make all the decisions?"

"Of course not. Why, does yours?"

"My husband always knows best. He talked to his pastor, who told him to have five or six more to make up for the first."

"To make up for your daughter? Your firstborn?"

"She claims she's not a Christian. I've never heard such carrying-on in my entire life. She doesn't want to belong to any church except what she calls The Earth. Klem had to thrash her into attending church with the family when she was nine.

"Now that she thinks she's grown, Sundays she's off in the woods to explore nature—she claims by herself—wearing mannish boots, carrying a walking stick. Comes home grouchy about how ugly people treat the earth. It's downright pagan to my mind, and I blame that community college for putting outlandish ideas in her head. We don't let her say grace at the table anymore because she spouts her ungodly ideas. The pastor wants us to shut her out of our home before her ideas decay the other kids' souls. See how smart she is then."

The Great Spirit was alive in this child. Her father wanted to beat it out of her? Or did he want to beat his beliefs into her? That poor young woman. Should she offer to help? "We can always make room for one more if she needs to move out but stay somewhere safe."

Opal dropped her trowel. Before she bent to retrieve it, Berry caught the abhorrence on her face.

She didn't care. Someone needed to protect the child. "We'd take care of her and keep in touch with you—daily, if you wanted."

"I'd like to keep my daughter close as long as I can."

"But you must know beating on her will drive her away."

"Her daddy knows best."

Berry refused to let it go. "Physical violence is never the answer."

"If yours was a normal household, I'd see what Klem thought about the idea. As it stands, he's now afraid one of the boys inherited your...your *abnormality*. God forbid Lutie turns out like you, or worse, like your roughneck."

"You think a gene made me fall in love with Jaudon?"

She saw her sister shudder. "Is that what you call it, *love*?"

Berry took up the hose and watered the plants. Opal could ruin a two-car funeral. She was ready to wet her sister down with the hose nozzle raised to full power.

Several robins, wintering in Florida, bobbed and hastened from spot to spot. The sight of them never failed to elevate her mood.

"I call it love, Opal, because that's what it is. If you think love is sacred exclusively when men and women love one another, you have another think coming."

"I'm looking out for your immortal soul, since you won't do it yourself. You'd be better off to come live with us than stay with that... that *creature*. I don't know how Gran Binyon can allow herself to condone what you do, much less reside with the devil. I can't be around Gran because I'll lash out at her complaisance."

"How dare you pass judgment on any of us. It's well known that's your Lord's prerogative."

"I cannot stand by and watch my flesh and blood dig a path to hell." Opal slammed the garden tools into their bucket. "It's time to call Klem to come for me. The boys will be home from school and need their snacks."

"Klem can't feed them? Can't they make their own?"

"Oh, big sister, that's what mothers are for. Not that you'll know about motherhood unless your whatever-you-call-her is a complete mutant."

She wanted to rage at her sister. Instead, she told the poor indoctrinated ninny where to find the phone.

"What about moms who work?" she asked when Opal returned.

"I am a—" Opal stopped herself. A shadow flared across her face, and she stepped away from Berry.

"You have a job?"

Her haughtiness returned. "Of course I do. I volunteer at my church."

As a nurse and counselor, Berry had become proficient at sussing out deception, but her sister deceitful? Ma and Pa's child? Opal hadn't had the first-class fortune to be raised by Gran and, before that, two loving, fun, but decent parents. She held out her arms again. "Come over here, sis. I mean it."

Opal hesitated, seemed to measure Berry—or herself, and picked up the tool bucket.

Berry dropped her arms. "I guess sisters fight."

Opal bent and stabbed the ground with the fishtail weeder and brought up a plug of carpetweed. "So I've heard."

A narrow blaze of lightning caught her eye.

Opal stood quickly at a clap of thunder.

Perfect, Berry thought, relieved to end this emotional stalemate. "You better hit the road before the spigots open up."

More lightning crackled. Thunder rolled closer.

"The heavenly spigots, my sister," Opal said.

Berry pulled her overflowing garden cart toward the pole barn. Once under shelter, she watched Klem drive into the parking area and Opal hurtle herself at his car.

What did her sister hide within the barbed arrow of herself?

CHAPTER TWENTY-SEVEN

Jaudon Vicker

Gran was assiduous about attending chair yoga classes offered at the Senior Center. A big fan of Barry Manilow, she exercised at home to his music. She reduced the rich foods she so loved and had always cooked. Butter was out, oleomargarine in. Berry didn't mind; she and Jaudon tussled nonstop with creeping middle-age spread.

Over the years, every couple of months on her day off, Olive joined them for a cracker soul food dinner. It happened to be Olive's birthday this time and the four of them sat down at the Vicker house to a turnip greens stew Gran made with ham and white kidney beans, skinny cornbread on the side.

Gran clucked as she adjusted the partial in her mouth. She claimed it was the root cause of her stroke because of the fussing it required.

"You know for a fact that's not true," Berry said.

Jaudon elbowed Gran's arm. "Tell us another one, you fibber."

"I'm hoping by the time your teeth need fixing, they come up with a better chawing tool. One fellow at the Senior Center had every tooth in his mouth pulled and wears fake choppers when he eats. And gnashes his dentures about the food."

Olive was laughing. "That sounds like my oldest brother, only he wouldn't set foot in a place for seniors."

"Why in the world not?" Gran asked. "We have dances and bingo and classes and trips."

"Because he won't admit he's old. He'd rather go to a bar where there's young people too. He was firstborn in the family, nineteen years before the youngest, which is me. The important question, though, is whether Benedict would find a toothless Ida Binyon appealing?"

Jaudon snorted laughter.

"Mind your manners, Jaudon Vicker, or you won't be served second helpings," warned Gran.

Jaudon briefly tried to look contrite. When she grabbed for the ladle, Gran pretended to slap her hand away.

"What I did want to ask you girls about is my other granddaughter, Opal. Does she think I have itch mites or something?"

Berry had mentioned how she suspected Opal's continuing absence might sting Gran. "Because she never visits you?"

"Or introduced me to my great-grandchildren. I don't know their names."

"Me neither. She never used their names when she introduced me. Her oldest, Lutie, wasn't there." Berry told Gran the story of Lutie's rebellion and Opal's reactions.

"That's plain unnatural for a mother. I predict that child will be a runaway before she's done rebelling."

"Those two are not what I'd call compatible. No way," said Olive.

"And she did once mention a Josiah, who's her eldest boy."

"A Bible name." Gran laughed, but there was an undertone of hurt at not meeting him. "No surprise there."

Jaudon passed around hefty slices of cornbread browned in butter and looked at Berry. "Josiah? Joe Howell? I know that name. Where did I hear it?"

"Howell is Opal's married name."

Jaudon snapped her fingers. "It was Cullie. Remember how she looked at mug shots for the passenger in the truck that ran into her? Cullie ID'd him from his picture. She had a run-in with him another time and said he was nothing but trouble and rough talk."

"That doesn't match up with any of Opal's perfect children. On the other hand, there's Lutie, the incompatible thirteen-year-old daughter. How does that happen?" asked Berry. "Opal's strict."

"Let me tell you, too much strictness can backfire," Olive said. "I've seen it in my own family. The boys find one kind of trouble and the girls have another. It's all to quit an unhealthy home."

Jaudon nodded vehemently. "I'll bet you'd be able to help the daughter, Gran. Her other grandparents have passed."

"If I ever meet this Lutie, I'll see what's on her mind. The boy must have some wild Binyon blood in his veins. There was plenty of it around when I was a child."

"You mean your brother who died in prison?"

"He was born with one nasty disposition, I'll tell you what," said Gran. "Both my sisters went off with boyfriends. One turned out okay—married the boy and they had a family of Army brats, lived in parts of the world I never heard of till I got her postcards. The other one came home, expecting and without a husband. She never left again."

"It's a universal story," Olive said. "We best get used to it. No use fussing every time."

"You're right about that," said Gran.

Berry had urged Opal to spend time with Gran. "See? Rebellious kids are no reason not to introduce you to her family. They're your family too."

"She is a strange one, that Opal."

One night not long after their discussion, their phone rang. Jaudon reached for it, muttering, "What now?" Her new shift manager never dared make a decision without checking with her first.

Cullie was on the line, out of breath. "We caught the paint throwers."

"The ones who hurt you? I knew you would, but how?"

"They tried again. I want to tell those boys, if you walk in the pasture long enough, you're bound to step in a cow patty."

"Why are you at work anyway?"

"I'm not working, as such. This rest, ice, compression, elevation business isn't cutting the mustard. The doc hasn't released me yet and wants more studies. Meantime, I'm bored to tears. I was fired up when the sheriff called me to come in and see if the varmints look like the guys in the truck that hit me. My sergeant sent a patrol car. Berry and one of the Lanamores need to come press charges for damage. I gotta go."

"Meet you there," she called into dead air.

Berry asked, "Who's in custody?"

"Don't know. Snag your purse."

"What were they doing?"

"Tell you on the way. I'll be out in the car. Gotta clear my front seat for your cute buns."

Their laughter was tight and nervous, the night surprisingly chilly. Jaudon squinted at the thermometer on the pole barn. "Brr. Would you believe it? Fifty-seven degrees."

They waited in the Juvenile Detention Center's lobby on cold metal chairs connected in sets of three. They first asked the desk officer to let Deputy Culpepper know they'd run her home.

Berry said, "Are we done with this, finally?"

Jaudon rubbed Berry's arm to reassure her. "You are my innocent sweet swamp flower. Nobody wins or loses in this fight. Crusaders don't compromise, not our side, not their side. MJ may be right—we're pawns in some secret plan to set American against American. Where it will end, I don't know. You've won a reprieve for a while with these two out of the picture."

"I've heard MJ's theories. She says it'll come down to who's in charge. That Republicans use issues like this and gay rights to lure voters. That way, they can claim the voters gave them the power they need to squash us."

"Next they'll restrict everyone's right to vote, like they do Black and poor voters, and we'll live under a dictatorship."

Cullie limped toward them, new orthotic shoes squeaking, and sat guardedly in the third attached chair. "Those are the guys. I wasn't allowed to ask why, why, why they're out to damage the Tommie Center."

"I'd like to ask the same thing. Jiminy, I want to go barbaric with them—do something brutal for messing with my Berry."

"You don't mean that."

"Hey, Jaud," joked Cullie, "why don't you tell us how you really feel? What was it Berry said was your animal totem, the marmot? The manatee? The magpie? The maggot? Ah, the howler monkey. As long as you're not any kind of arachnid, I'm cool."

Berry paled and asked, in a tinny, upset voice, "What exactly happened?"

"Settle down, they're behind bars now. The juvenile is waiting for his father. Leslie's bodybuilder girlfriend was on watch at the Center. She saw the two guys and a woman driver and rang Tad as she followed them. Tad told his mother to call the cops, grabbed her ring of keys, raced down and through the first floor, Duval at his heels, sore shoulder and all."

"It hasn't healed?" Berry asked. "Laura told me about the infections."

"He refuses to stay off work and let the burns heal."

Cullie wiped sweat from her face and squirmed into a new position. "The devils used a short ladder propped on a window ledge, smashed the window, and climbed inside with a couple of two-gallon gasoline cans. The new girlfriend went in after them, tackled both, knocked their rotten heads together till they were senseless, and threatened to light them on fire. She had them cowering on the floor by the time Tad and Duval arrived. They locked those vermin in a supply closet. It wasn't long before a deputy peeked over the broken window, gun pointed at Tad."

"Oh no."

"He and Duval slowly raised their hands. Leslie's friend said—and I quote—*Not them, you jackass. They're the good guys.* The deputy entered the room with the gun raised anyway."

"It's scary enough to live gay, but Black and male?" Jaudon stopped her leg jiggling to beat the clock. "This encounter won't make the world seem any safer for Duval and Tad."

Berry asked, "Who else was hurt?"

"Piddling scratches on our side," Cullie said. "One of the deputies said the getaway driver was older, white, looked to be in her sixties. She screamed that she is a soldier of Christ and will press on with his work because the Jews stopped him. She fought the cuffs, had to be wrestled into the patrol car, scratched up one deputy's face, and tried to take another's eye out. The juvenile—one Josiah Howell again—laughed and egged her on, though later, when he was walked to the room where his red-haired daddy waited, I saw the kid was greener than gooey gourd guts. As for the driver, she gave her home address as—"

Anger had turned Berry's cheeks a patchy red. "You don't have to tell me. I already suspected it's Intracoastal Ministries, my sister's church. Josiah Howell is her oldest boy. This has to be the last time. I won't put the Lanamores in harm's way again."

A captain came out for Berry and let Jaudon come along.

"So, you're friends of our Deputy Culpepper," he said, as he set colored forms across his desk.

Jaudon said, "We consider her family."

"Those thugs messed her up badly. Are we after that driver? You know it."

"We appreciate the help your department has given us," Berry said. "Do you have any idea who's behind these attacks?"

"If I had to guess, miss, I'd say there are dozens of groups in our state who're rubbed the wrong way by your services. Now, that loony old witch we're trying to get rid of, howling at the moon or whatever she's up to, doesn't have a license, won't tell us her name, much less who put her up to this. But the kid, he has no record. It might do your project better to ignore his hijinks and not press charges on him."

Jaudon minded her manners, but said, "We heard the younger attacker was let go to his parents, remember? The red paint episode? He and his pal went free while the Tommie Center had to fundraise to fix the damage."

"It would help were you to get to the bottom of these attacks soon, Captain."

"I can't change an individual's mind on this subject."

Jaudon said, "It's true, you can't arrest minds, but you can punish people who commit crimes. They've cost you one deputy already."

Berry tapped his desk flat-handed. "I will not stand by while my family and friends and patients are injured and intimidated. That big bruiser of a boy tried to burn our Center as well as two other businesses to the ground."

"Yours was the one they targeted."

"Tell that to the owner of the property," Berry challenged. "If I don't press every charge you can throw at those people, she will. My taxes pay for law enforcement to investigate this violence. I demand that these criminals pay for their hate-filled actions."

The captain shrugged and picked up a pen. "If you want to press charges, we can hold these two until they make bail—if the judge sets bail—but don't say I didn't warn you."

"Warn us of what?" Jaudon asked.

He cocked an eyebrow. "How easily some of those wackos blow up."

When asked, he wasn't at liberty to say what group. Jaudon named Intracoastal Ministries, and the captain answered by handing Berry the colored forms. "I don't know what drives these people. I'm a Catholic, but you won't see me pushing my beliefs on others. Some who worship don't apply what they're taught to their actions. The department does what we can about those who go too far."

CHAPTER TWENTY-EIGHT

Jaudon Vicker

May 2003

She wasn't going to blame every dip in the road on the Tommie Center intruders, but less than six months later, on May 17, 2003, Momma died. Dementia took her, made her too vulnerable to fight off the flu and resulting pneumonia that visiting neighbors unknowingly brought into the Vickers' Sun City home.

Pops was too overwhelmed with grief to make arrangements for the funeral and reception today. Although she never loved her distant, single-minded mother any more than her brother Bat did, it fell to Jaudon and Berry to pull things together.

As he'd done when Momma was alive, Bat got away with ignoring the woman, certainly didn't fly home to Rainbow Gap. It was obvious his wife sent the flowers.

Momma and Jaudon had been like two mules perennially fighting over a lump of turnip. Before Momma lost her reason, they never had a conversation that didn't end in rancor; afterward, she accused Jaudon of the stores' troubles, but how many mommas do you get? Jaudon did what she had to do. Berry, familiar with grieving and perplexed survivors, treated her extra tenderly through this time, touched her often, put her to sleep nights by stroking her hair.

Jaudon hadn't appreciated how many people Momma knew until she laid bare her tattered address book.

Berry was able to steer Jaudon and Pops to a package deal that would take the pressure off them. Jaudon gave the funeral staff

Momma's address book to send announcements. They took take care of the details, down to mounds of flowers for the visitation service in the conference room of a nearby motel. Jaudon didn't believe her mother was worth this much fuss or that Momma would approve of the cost, but Pops did. The hotel served a hundred or so mourners who showed up at the burial and reception.

"It's a social event," Gran said, arm in arm with Benedict and MJ as they made their way under lofty, potted sabal palms and reached Jaudon, Berry at her side. "Especially for their Sun City circle."

"And a businesspersons reunion," said MJ. "These are retired county employees and old suppliers, minor politicians she donated to, paying their respects."

"You had no church service?" Opal asked. She'd butterflied around the large room to introduce herself and hand out business cards.

Pops wouldn't have a church service; he renounced religion when a preacher bilked Momma of a minor fortune and they lost two stores despite Jaudon's frenzied, risky, backbreaking efforts. If she knew nothing else, she knew how to work hard.

Olive, indignant, showed Opal's card to Jaudon and Berry.

"What in heck?" said Jaudon.

"How downright rude," Berry said. She grabbed Jaudon's forearm.

"I assumed she was handing out her personal card," said Vonnie, "but look." The words Intracoastal Ministries were blazoned across the top with Opal's title, Services Coordinator, listed below.

Olive spoke as if she was personally offended. "The woman is proselytizing at your mother's funeral. That is blatantly disrespectful."

Pops sat and accepted condolences, the fourth big white handkerchief of the day at his eyes. He was near enough to hear Olive and lifted his Santa Claus body out of his chair, beckoning to Opal. When she responded, he held out a hand. "Show me those cards."

Jaudon was awed to see Pops intimidate Opal. He seldom used his forceful side; Momma was assertive enough for the whole family put together. She was famous for her use of her oversized white straw purses as weapons.

Opal gingerly handed Pops a card.

He looked it over. "You have more in your purse? Give them here."

Opal's eyes were wary slits, but she emptied the cards from her purse. Pops slammed them on a nearby pedestal bench.

"You can take them out of here when you leave. This is my wife's funeral, not a revival meeting. Show some respect."

Opal held the back of her hand to her mouth and withdrew. She collided with Olive Ponder and, without apology, retrieved her cards and hurried from the room.

"You got that one's goat, Pops," Olive said.

"She's got the manners of a goat," muttered MJ. Olive laughed softly and butted MJ's elbow with hers.

❖

It wasn't a week afterward that the two men showed up at the Buffalo Street Beverage Bay.

"Jaudon," called Olive from the cash register.

Jaudon was snagged up in numbers and didn't want to have to redo them, but when Olive called a second time and more loudly, she left her narrow workspace behind the coolers and hurried to the front of the store.

"These gentlemen want to talk to you."

Both short, one wore a silvery pale blue suit which sagged on his thin frame, and the bald guy was in checkered brown and green. Their Kmart caliber shirts were buttoned to the neck—no ties, twin combovers.

The men looked at Jaudon, then at each other, as if to confirm they both saw the same thing.

A big tomboy her entire life, she was used to this. "Whatcha know good?" she asked in pure backwoods Southern, to rattle them further.

She gave them a minute to collect their wits, if they had any, and wished she had a piece of straw to chew on or, even better, a corncob pipe.

"You gents selling or buying? 'Cause this place is not on the market."

Checkered suit cleared his throat. "Why, we're here to make you some money, miss."

"And how do you plan to carry this out?" Olive asked. "Are you magicians?"

"Now, wait a minute," said the talker. "I was under the impression you said this, er, lady here was manager."

"I'm the manager. She's the owner."

Olive was as proud and protective of the Beverage Bays as Jaudon. Together, they'd built a team, thanks to Olive's family, accountant

Rouie Waver who was retired but for the Beverage Bays, and cousin Cal.

The talky man banged his briefcase on the counter. "What we were told, miss, was that the owner died and this mini-chain might be up for sale."

From the corner of her eye, she watched the shiny-suited visitor scrutinize the store.

"Then you didn't do your due diligence, mister. And keep your snoop away from those shelves. They're not open to the public, by health and safety regulations."

The snoop made his way to the counter again, eying all and sundry. "Tidy little business you have here."

She knew the store's worth to the penny. It was on QuickBooks, another thing she'd learned to use when Rouie Waver computerized his CPA practice. "I already know it is. Did you stop by to hand out compliments, or did some big corporation decide to wipe out our Beverage Bays?"

"No big corporations are involved, I assure you. We represent an informal group of men of faith who like to invest in the communities where we live and use our profits to spread the Word."

"I'm not certain I believe these boys, Olive. What do you think?"

Olive rang out a customer before she answered. "Ask them what their group is exactly. Take a gander at their business card."

She looked and immediately emitted a choked-up cough to hide her shock. "Do you remember the big wide-open door you came in?" she asked. "I'd like to see if you two are smart enough to find your way out."

"As I said, it's an informal group, and we're here to do our research." He looked outside the roll-up entryway. "For example, how much is rent here, off the main drag?"

"Buffalo Street's not exactly back of yonder, mister. You might look to take over someplace closer to Tampa if you want more traffic. Rent would be higher over there, not that I rent." Momma never wanted to be beholden to anyone, so she bought the land. "My family owns every square inch our businesses sit on. So don't think you and any bloodsucking landlord can make an arrangement without letting me know first."

Olive cut her eyes at her, and Jaudon knew she was advising her not to let her mouth overload her tail.

"Ma'am, it's a win-win proposition for you. You make a pile of money, and the proceeds of our store go to help people."

She folded her sinewy arms. "It's time you boys go pick on some other one-man-band. I'm not budging."

"It's your choice to look a gift horse in the mouth—or not."

The snooper took one last look at her setup.

The talker said, "This is a family enterprise? I'd like to talk to the rest of your family."

Jaudon and Olive looked at each other and laughed outright.

"You'll get far with that."

"I'll go down to the county and find them, see if they can resist the offer."

"You ought to go do that right now, before I have to chase you out of here."

The snooper lowered his brows and widened his nostrils as if ready to take her on, but the talker put his hand up and said, "We can be persuasive in more than one way."

He looked over his shoulder at the store and nodded as he and his partner made their way to an unmarked white van.

She looked at Olive. "What the heck?"

Olive handed her an empty carton to cut up. "You ask me, I'd have to say those two weren't fishing. They picked you special."

"What? My good looks?"

Olive didn't laugh. "They got word Momma died and want to take advantage of your grief."

"That doesn't make a lick of sense. Momma quit the business way back when."

"They may know that too. I wish I never called them gentlemen."

"You didn't know."

"My attention was elsewhere, to tell God's honest truth. Did you hear from Berry about my sister Laura getting engaged to marry?"

"What? To who?"

"It's taken her a while, but she's finally fallen hard for the right man."

"Tell me who?"

"Sit down."

She pulled up two stacked milk crates.

"She'll be Mrs. Tad Duval."

"Jiminy Cricket. I never saw that one coming. Tad planned not to marry."

"He never met my sister until your street fair."

"Are you okay with the match?"

"I'm tickled pink. I'm blessed to have another son along with Emmett. It's plain as day how tight Berry is with Laura, which gives Laura my seal of approval too."

"Gran didn't raise any deadbeats."

"Somebody's momma sure did. Those two men, for example."

"Makes me question what kind of person goes to a church they represent."

CHAPTER TWENTY-NINE

Jaudon Vicker

August 2003

Three months after Momma Vicker's funeral, Jaudon and Berry drove Pops to Tampa International Airport. He wanted to see his son, Bat, on his Christmas tree farm out in the Pacific Northwest. He planned to spend a month there, to meet Bat's own Mrs. Vicker and the three grandchildren for the first time.

Jaudon was slightly sick to her stomach well into the evening with qualms about airplane crashes and other what-ifs. Bat finally called to say Pops arrived safely but bushed and was already in bed for the night.

She and Berry went to bed then, but as she tried to fall asleep in the lingering heat after a scorcher of a day, the call of a barred owl in the sweetgum tree brought her wide awake and upright.

Berry stirred and saw her. "What's wrong? What is it?"

"Hoot, hoot, who-whoo," the owl sang. Its mate replied with a plaintive trill.

She'd always cried easily and spoke now through flowing tears. "With Pops out of town, this is how it will be someday without him. I'm truly the grownup now, and I don't want to be."

Berry gave her some tissues and made her lie on her stomach. She smelled the almond massage oil before she felt it. Berry massaged her back and settled her under the covers. "Haven't you guessed, my silly angel, you've always been the only grownup in your family?"

She sneezed. "Jiminy. Gran bought scented tissues again."

To her relief, Pops was true to his word, as always. He called weekly on the cellular phone Bat gave him. "You have to have one of these. Using it's as easy as falling off a log. You're not tied up to wires. Right now, I'm outside Bat's house at the end of his driveway, and that's a long stretch in these parts."

She wanted to say she'd rather have him home. She knew it was selfish of her. She'd had Pops since she was born, but he was Bat's father too. And Pops had earned his adventures. She'd promised him a life of ease and plenty when he turned the stores over to her. She'd keep her promise no matter what.

"I'll look into those phones. If an old coot like you can learn to work one, I ought to be able to."

Pops laughed as she meant him to, while aware of a clenching in her stomach. She hadn't seen Pops this lively in years.

He said he'd stay longer than planned. "It's beauteous out here. The smell of the piney woods, a big old woodstove, and a fireplace. Nights are coolest, but I'm always in this fleece jacket—Bat took me shopping. And mountains. I've never seen mountains so high." He laughed. "Bat says I've never seen *any* mountains before. We're almost a thousand feet above sea level, and we're down in the foothills. Can you imagine? The air is so clear I can breathe through my nose." With a stutter, he added, "I met a lady at a country-western two-step class. They even do a Cajun two-step."

She held herself up by the kitchen table till she sat. Pops two-step dancing? Dating? What happened to his devotion to Momma?

Pops talked quickly into her silence. "I'm sorry, Daughter. Momma was gone long before she passed. How to be a lady with a husband was one of the things she seemed to forget for a number of years before then."

Despite her shock and upheaval inside, she was able to say, "You've done your duty by Momma a hundred times over. You deserve to enjoy yourself."

"One other thing. The Christmas tree farm is going great guns. Bat and his friend John—you remember John Lau—have a place for me in their company for a while so I can earn my keep while I'm here and fill in for Bat when he's not up to working. He thinks the chemicals they handled in 'Nam got to a lot of the guys. He catches any germ his kids track home from school, his teenager acne is bad as it used to be, and he's all the time tired. My job is close to the logistics I handled at the stores. Someday they hope I'll be shipping one of their trees the thousands of miles to Rockefeller Center in New York City. What do you think of that?"

Someday. As if he'd be there a lot longer. "You can do it with your eyes closed and one hand tied behind your back, Pops."

"Is your cousin Cal meeting my standards the way I taught him?"

"And more. He always has room on the truck for partial loads, so he canvassed businesses similar to ours and is bringing in enough most months to pay the whole beer vendor's bill."

"I should have left him in charge long ago, but that's hindsight for you. You need to take a vacation and come out here, Daughter, though I was badly shocked by the wild traffic around the airport—worse than Tampa. You drive far enough, and high enough, you forget that nightmare and never want to leave the hills. Come meet your nieces and nephews. Figure out which one will take over the stores when you retire."

"I'm not retiring."

"I didn't think I would, and here I am."

"How long before you come home?"

"Another month, I'd guess. Before the snow so I can make it to the airport if my arthritis doesn't go haywire again. I might bring one of the grandkids for a visit. You think a teenage Batson girl can handle the flight to Washington by herself? We're on a lake here and the kid— Miki—found an escaped one-seater rowboat, made it lake-worthy with Bat, spends her life out on the water. That's Miki, the girl who reminds Bat and me of you around the same age, a tomboy with energy to spare. Bat's wife is part Inuit—Miki means *little one* in that language."

She'd never have guessed Pops would take to Washington State. Generations of steamy Florida blood ran in his veins. Where would he find his gator bites? MJ claimed they didn't serve sweet tea on the West Coast. Didn't it rain buckets there all the time? But he had grandkids at the farm, not a legacy she and Vonnie offered.

No matter how she tried, her imagination wasn't capable of conjuring up where Pops was. She pictured a cardboard cutout of mountains, covered with lines and lines of shivering trees. Did trees shiver from cold as they seemed to in hurricanes?

She went into a slump. Pops used to stint on time on the daily business, but jiminy, she was stricken without him to depend on for this, that, and the other. Since he left, she'd forget a longtime beer vendor's name, or how a regular wanted his coffee, or to call Duval Lanamore when she was out of an item in a store bakery, especially the breads. Hardo and coco breads had become staples for some customers. Pops used to bring oversights to her attention.

Although the Beverage Bays were her life, Jaudon skipped work for a week and left the stores in Olive's experienced hands, explaining, "I'm as vacant as a privy after a house got plumbed."

She decided to take care of longstanding projects. It might lift her spirits to complete some and would please Berry, who had Gran at the Tommie Center most afternoons, where she and Leslie kept an eye on her. Gran helped at reception, especially calming and distracting the youngsters.

The mossy, damp pole barn where they kept their vehicles and decades of odds and ends was critter- and spider-infested and rotting at the bottom of its walls. The lone reason it stayed upright was down to repairs MJ made a while ago, around when Gran had her stroke. Since then, its tin roof rusted through in spots. The whole structure should be taken down and replaced with a civilized-looking garage, but she didn't want that big a change. She had in mind a lockable lean-to to brace one side, which she might do herself. Years ago, Pops told her to get rid of the barn junk, he didn't want a thing.

For now, she was determined to drag the junk outside, staying clear of toxic snakes and spiders. She'd make a pile of useless stuff to take to the dump. Clean house, in a manner of speaking, to mark Pops's temporary departure. She told herself, "Let's git 'er done."

She called MJ at the end of the first day. "I think I have a wagonload for you." MJ had previously offered to haul the discards to the dump.

"I can't come by there tomorrow. I'll be at the dentist's and the next day at the endodontist."

"I guess that means you're finally fixing your teeth?" MJ had not received adequate dental care as a kid and suffered for it now.

"The pain interferes with work and my homelife. I can't chew on my left side. I need to make an appointment with a periodontist too, for my gums. It'll cost a serious bundle. Why don't you keep at the barn work. I'll be over the day after, come hell or high water."

MJ did materialize at the end of the third day, her face puffed up and pulled sideways.

"Did you hear the news?" asked MJ, lisping.

"News? I've been out here since the rooster crowed."

"I should wait and let Berry tell you."

She poked MJ with the wooden wheel of an ancient iron pulley. "No, you shouldn't."

"Shoot, your spirits need an uplift too." MJ stuck her thumbs behind the straps of her cement-stained overalls and rocked back on her heels. It looked as if those straps tethered her to earth. "One of the pockets Berry and Vonnie have strained to pick is the state of Florida. Remember, with Allison's help, they pinpointed a hoard of money earmarked for rural human services that somehow was never tapped into? A few months ago, the three of them went to Tallahassee and made a presentation?"

"'Course I do. Is the state giving them some help?"

"I wish. That might give me more respect for Florida, despite Governor JEB. There was a woman at the presentation from the private sector. She represented the Gordie Feiden Foundation and asked a lot of questions. She told them their model is exemplary and exactly the pattern the Foundation wants to fund. Afterward, she gave them application forms. Out of nowhere, today Berry heard from them. They earmarked enough money for the Center to pay living wage salaries and employee benefits for the next six years, to give the Center a running start. Not one nickel will depend on availability of funds and the political winds."

"Berry will be paid?"

"Decently paid. As are the bus drivers, Dr. Garza, the assistants, and nurses. And I'm serious about that. Leslie will see a bump in her hourly, and the bunch of them will have health insurance through the Feiden Foundation."

"I need to call Berry and congratulate her."

"Be my guest." MJ handed her a beguiling handheld device.

"Not you too. Bat has one of these wireless phones he taught Pops to use." MJ instructed her in the ways of cellular communication. Further excited to use the phone, she called Berry, who was on MJ's speed dial, and heard elation in her hello. "Berry says to go to your place for a celebration. They ordered pizzas and a cake."

"Jumping Jehoshaphat. I'll buy flowers on the way." MJ set aside some of the items destined for the dump. "These are treasures, Boss. I'll bet this Hamm's brewery sign is pre-Prohibition. It needs to be straightened out and hung on a wall. Look at this, a pine tar can. Does anyone use this stuff anymore? I noticed your mess of old windows—you wouldn't believe how many people paint window frames to look authentically antique. Yours aren't spongy or falling apart at all. These hasps and rusty locks, you want to recycle them. But you don't want to give away this wood crate. It'll bring in cash."

"I'll use it for laundry in my room. Berry would be pleased for me to pick up after myself, and I like its look."

"Set a timeline to clean it, or it'll never leave the barn."

"You're right, I'll never finish. Go ahead and put aside what you can use. There may be more. I'm about a third done. Can I talk to you about reinforcing this valuable pole barn? Not many of them around these days."

MJ gave her the same doubtful look Berry did when she had a stodgy fixation. "There might be a reason for that."

"You never see a cracker house with a garage. I can tell from your face that's what you'd do. If this pole barn passed muster for Pops and his father, it's more than tolerable for me."

"You are stubborn as a mule, aren't you? That attitude won't keep your stores competitive."

Jaudon lowered to the ground the box of brass, porcelain, and nickel showerheads she was ditching. MJ was a wiz at business. Until that second, Jaudon believed one of the Beverage Bays' big draws was its old-fashioned appeal. She'd have to think on that.

CHAPTER THIRTY

Vonnie Lowe

September 2003

Vonnie arrived at the Center excited and ready to spill her news. She peered out the front window for Dr. Garza and Allison Millar, who were coming to see the newly installed graffiti-proof bus shelter.

"One lone demonstrator today," said Leslie, who had retrieved Gran's pineapple upside-down cake and lightly spiked punch from the refrigerator. "He's mainly in the way of patients, lukewarm about reading his spiel from a prompt card."

"A passionate soldier of God, right?"

Leslie looked over her shoulder. A patient and her daughter waited on the shelter bench for a ride home. "Those two snubbed him like nobody's business. They live out in Mulberry. Before Allison guilt-tripped the county into loaning us a bunged-up minivan, patients from that far away did without medical care."

"What keeps them in Mulberry?"

"The daughter's husband is a warehouseman for the big furniture store out there. The pay is decent enough that they bought a double-wide manufactured home, but they can't afford a decent car."

"One of a thousand stories and reasons we do this," said Berry with one of her golden smiles. As usual, she carried an armload of folders for Leslie to file.

Leslie unhesitatingly found their spots. "Look at that big, beautiful vandal-proof bus shelter out there."

"The contractor tried to put us off for another week," said Berry.

"Thanks to Allison, he managed to squeeze us in. Our own too-big-for-his-britches mayor wouldn't lift a finger for us. I don't know how Allison keeps so many balls in the air at once, but she's brilliant at it."

"How is Jaudon? Still despondent without her pops?" Vonnie asked. "You said she returned to work."

"She did," said Berry, "but it's hard for her. Pops used to track her down at the stores to help now and then, jabber till the cows came home. He was lonely. Or she'd go over to Sun City for supper, bring a big takeout Chinese meal or fried chicken from Popeyes. Gran and I cooked up Sunday dinners and delivered them. He was Jaudon's rock. Not much business savvy, but the friendly face of the Beverage Bays when he went out in the truck or helped customers. He let Jaudon know how much he admired her and her smarts, how much he loved her. She never got enough of his hugs."

They went silent.

Vonnie rested a hand near her heart, contemplating how lucky she was to have two loving and living parents who let her be herself even when she'd chased girls as a wild lesbian teen.

Her plan was to share her marvelous news with the whole group, but, evocative of her younger self, she didn't want to wait a minute more.

"I heard from DC today."

Leslie and Berry stopped dead.

"Not only will they deliver one brand-new ADA equipped van, but based on our rural population, we qualify for two. We'll keep the used van as a spare. In addition, the bus shelter was approved. We can use donations for that elsewhere. And they'll include funds to pay a driver."

The three of them broke into a babble of self-congratulation and hugged.

"Dang, you got it all," exclaimed Leslie. "You must write ace federalese."

"Not quite ace enough. It's a good thing the Foundation came through to supplement the county's miserliness. It was only allowing Berry and the drivers the federal minimum wage. I emphasized your credentials and contacted them twice. First, they said your background didn't fit the job description—they use one list common for these programs. On the second call, they decided you're overqualified."

She watched Berry's face. The woman had run on spare fumes to keep her income at the practice, while operating the Tommie Center. The news from the county was discouraging, but the foundation had no such quibbles about her qualifications.

"I don't know if this is any comfort to you, Berry, but if the feds can't even keep track of a bazillion dollar space probe named Snoopy, how can a mere county get anything right?"

That got a laugh from Leslie and, belatedly, Berry.

Leslie said, "I don't think they named it after Snoopy the beagle, either."

"The DC dummies lose a spy satellite and it's no big deal but won't pay health workers a living wage?"

Allison and the doctor must have parked at the same time. They walked together on the street outside the windows where today's token picketer tried half-heartedly to block them with his rote speech.

Vonnie hustled to open the front door for them.

In her street clothes, with a floral green scarf knotted below her neck, Dr. Garza, gray-haired now and, Berry said, planning for a retirement which included a seat on the Center's board of directors, scolded the protestor.

Vonnie heard the whole reproach from the doorway where she stayed despite the muggy heat that made her skin sticky and the air too heavy to easily breathe.

On the sidewalk, the doctor dropped words along the lines of democracy and rights and respect. She told him she treated children who had no chance of a decent quality of life, would always be in pain, were unwanted. Who did he think he was to interfere with a woman's or parents' decisions?

The man was literally backpedaling, partly hidden behind his sign.

"Hey," he whined, sweat glistening on his whole face. "They pay me to stand out here. You wanna pay me more to stay away, I'm gone. They'll replace me with the next guy in their soup kitchen line—and I'm not just whistling Dixie."

"Someone pays you to do this?" Allison's face was suffused pink with outrage.

His tongue was pushed against his upper lip.

"Who pays you?" asked Dr. Garza.

"Nope, can't tell you that."

"Is it a government office? A private individual? A church? An organization?"

The minivan shuttle stopped at the shelter. The daughter helped her mother inside. Leslie watched through the window. The driver pulled away without her usual wave.

Vonnie wondered who broke whose heart, Leslie or the driver, if hearts were involved at all. She almost missed it when the protestor admitted his employer was a religious organization that wanted to eliminate abortion and in vitro fertilization, plus gay adoption and even gays themselves, because gays can't reproduce naturally and therefore have no sanctioned function in his employer's eyes.

"Did anyone ever notice these protestors are white people, with scarce exceptions?" Vonnie asked.

"I certainly have," Allison said. "Which makes no sense to me. They say a million racist things. You'd think they'd promote non-white abortions to rid the country of so-called welfare queens." She turned on the sign bearer. "The Center is closed for the day now. You may as well leave."

"I'll wait for my ride."

Allison turned her eyes upward. "Put that sign down then, and sit on the bench, out of the way."

"Not if I want to be paid. He might be parked up the street, watching."

"Who, darn it? Who?"

"A dude who works for them."

As if the driver heard them talking, an unmarked white transit van braked at the curb. One of the passengers stretched to roll the door open. The picketer fled from the women, dived in, and shoved his way past a few other men with signs.

A flock of raucous blue jays made their annoyance known in a line of leafless crepe myrtles across the street. Vonnie was as annoyed as the birds, and angry. She could just wring the necks of their harassers.

She joined Allison and the doctor. "Someone's paying these protestors?"

"It's not uncommon," said Dr. Garza. "I've spoken to colleagues who've encountered the same strategy."

Allison leaned on the shelter. "I may be a pacifist, but I want to shoot whoever is behind these attacks. My poor Cullie—stuck on desk duty. Not exactly the job she dreamed of since she was in grade school. She doesn't talk about it, but she can't hide her deep sadness over losing patrol."

"I guess it'll never end, this harassment for no reason at all," said Vonnie. "We talk about ways to stamp out racism, but is that realistically possible? We want women to make their own choices, but will men ever let go so that we can? It's been a couple of months since the sodomy laws were struck down by the Supremes, though you wouldn't know it from our persecutors."

"One of the things I admire about you and your friend Jaudon," said Dr. Garza, "is how unruffled you are, as if norms and mores are none of your concern. As if you've never experienced the automatic cruelties our society heaps on lesbians and gay men, though you've both said you were born gay."

Vonnie met her eyes. "What else can we do, Doctor, but live our lives? This seems to be the best we can expect of America—that we're allowed to marry in another country."

With a sad smile, the doctor said, "I hope not. I sincerely do. Progress comes hard, but remember, Four Lakes never had a female mayor before. Lecoats County now has women deputies and the Tommie Center, despite the harassment."

Allison stood in front of them and indicated the Center. "We serve hundreds of women who might otherwise do without."

From the doorway, Leslie called, "This cake and the punch plan to disappear to my place if you don't get a move on."

"Gran makes the best cakes," said Allison as she stood from the bench.

Once inside, Vonnie raised her chipped coffee mug of punch. "To progress," she said, genuinely happy with the news.

"To progress," the other women concurred. Berry cut Gran's cake with a sunny flourish.

CHAPTER THIRTY-ONE

Jaudon Vicker

January 2004

On New Year's Day, 2004, they double dated with Gran and Benedict. Leslie and her girlfriend were at Big Cypress National Preserve with Rigo, Jimmy Neal, and a gay birdwatching group. Jaudon warned that the three of them were apt to be meals for feral hogs, pythons, or a two-hundred-pound crocodile. "I'll alert the ranger station if you're not here tomorrow morning."

The Strawberry Shed in Plant City was Benedict's favorite drive-in restaurant. He read aloud enthused reviews of their Cuban sandwiches and shakes. Today, Benedict's birthday, they would treat him.

Jaudon took the shady byways through Rainbow Gap, right hand resting on Berry's thigh. She occasionally caught the honey-like scent of sweet alyssum through the open window's breeze. Winter was her favorite time of year. The humidity was lower and temperatures in the seventies and eighties lessened the heat stress.

They stopped at the Seffner branch library to return books, and she quickly borrowed the new Ellen Hart mystery, which Berry snatched from her. "Can I read it first?" asked Berry.

Jaudon especially enjoyed visiting Jaudon Road, where the Batsons, Momma's ancestors, settled so long ago. She wanted to talk about the men who had the gall to try to buy her stores, but she'd wait until they arrived at Benedict's restaurant.

"Look," Gran said, as they passed one of the manmade ponds installed in so many of these developments. "Three rosy spoonbills. Odd place for them. Need to tell Leslie, our bird expert."

The road to Plant City was filled with old buildings and businesses. Gran knew the histories of many and told their tales with savor.

"That stone church building once drew in hundreds of worshippers in season, white Baptists. Now it's an oddball Christian sect, Holy Rollers we used to call them when they had revivals."

"You spent a lot of time in Plant City," Benedict said.

"We Binyons are spread all around these parts. For a while we lived over a breakfast restaurant—used to be right up the road on the left, past the used car and salvage lots. The noise next door was terrible, but you were within sight of a lake through the trees."

Benedict asked, "And your property in Rainbow Gap?"

"That came into Binyon hands long ago. Our ancestors named the parcel Stinky Lane and harvested its pine timber. Nobody wanted to live there because of the seasonal smell. When Berry's grandfather passed, I grieved something terrible. There wasn't a place or person that didn't remind me of him. I wanted to be off the beaten track and put my single-wide on Stinky Lane for me and Berry's mother, who was close to grown by then."

Jaudon drove them past bars, a funeral home, a used furniture store, repair and welding shops, a wooden truss builder, small trailer parks restructured to mobile home parks when the heyday of restful fishing hole vacations ended.

"Pull off the road here. Quick." Gran peered out her window. "There's one. Ever see a painted bunting, Benedict? Over there, in the brush."

Benedict located them. "Why, they're rainbow birds."

"The males are the most colorful. Red, blue, and yellow. I grew up with them here."

Jaudon said, "They should be the pride mascots."

Berry twisted around to tell Benedict, "This is great fun for me. Gran's memories and these practically falling-down businesses next to big old homes with plantation style columns make my heart beat faster. Jaudon's the same. Anytime we travel the old Florida, it beats a trip around the world. I want the incomers to leave our Florida alone."

"It's our paradise, not theirs," Benedict said.

She looked at Gran. "You used to bring me downtown to McCrory's for school clothes and buy me a vanilla milkshake and a hot dog with mustard at the lunch counter."

"Those lunch counter ladies were always surprised you didn't go for the strawberry shake."

"McCrory's strawberry shake was never as delectable as Parkesdale's."

"To this day, no one makes a better one than Parkesdale," said Gran.

"Give my Strawberry Shed a chance," said Benedict.

Jaudon felt the heaviness of middle age, but jiminy, it was the new year and the day needed celebrating. She dreamed last night that the Shed was out of any flavor but black licorice.

Gran pointed. "See that plant nursery? Your grandfather Binyon worked there on weekends. It's seen some hard times and changed hands—I lost count of how often."

"It's on its last legs too," said Benedict.

"Don't let that fool you. Sometimes those are the best places to find rarities. Or they'll have a tropical plant that hasn't sold for years and grew to giant proportions, but it's exactly what a buyer wants outside the lanais of their imitation palaces—what do you call them?"

"McMansions," Berry said.

"Right on the nose. Isn't she smart, Ben?"

"And pretty and respectful," he answered. "All the right qualities in a granddaughter. My great-granddaughters, so ill-mannered. I think it's the times. They wear whatever they want to school. Makeup. Rap music. Boyfriends with sagging pants and no self-respect. They beg for money to go to Disney World. You raised Berry better."

"Oh, my, Disney World. Remember when it opened and we went that first week? Nineteen seventy-one, wasn't it? Berry, Jaudon and her pops, and me went. Your momma wouldn't leave her Beverage Bays for a day of fun. I wore my best dress, and your pops wore a shirt and his bow tie."

Jaudon struck a knee with her fist and brayed. "He did. And no one else wore a tie except Mickey Mouse."

"He took it off soon enough because of the heat, I remember that," said Berry, her smile for Jaudon.

How Berry kept that sparkly, adoring look in her eyes after all these years, with all they'd gone through together, she'd never understand.

Didn't have to. It was the same love she felt.

Gran went on. "I don't know which of us was most excited. I thought we'd stepped into a movie that never stopped. It was a different planet. We were in a cartoon in a crowd that thought it was perfectly normal."

Jaudon reminisced. "It cost three fifty for admission, and you bought a seven-ride coupon book, for—I think it was under five dollars. Our lunch didn't go over three dollars for the four of us. And now..."

"Now," said Benedict, "you'd have to cash in your investments to send the girls. They'd need over a hundred dollars. Each."

"We learned pretty quick to eat after we went on rides."

"Pops upchucked everything but the kitchen sink on the steamboat ride. He was susceptible to seasickness, but that boat was as steady as a parking lot."

"It was so hot hens would've laid hard-boiled eggs. We moved to the bottom deck in the shade," Gran said. "It was a memorable day. You girls bought me a Mickey Mouse hat. If I didn't look silly in that thing."

Berry cheerily reminded Gran that she'd kept the pictures.

"Mercy me. Whatever you do, don't show Ben." She patted her hair where the beanie must have sat.

"Me? I can't wait to see them again. When we get home, as a birthday gift to me."

"Be a love and chuck those photographs into the drink. After the boat, your pops wouldn't go on the Peter Pan ride with us, though it was on a track, not water, and was tame as a newborn kitten but for Jaudon crying out in the dark."

"It was a real spiderweb, I swear."

Gran leaned forward and poked her in the shoulder. "It was fake netting. Your elbow disturbed a piece of it."

Berry reached to gently prod Gran's knee. "You plucked a tuft of that netting and tickled Jaudon's neck with it."

"I never."

"Did too."

Gran's face was wrinkled up with a smile. She was short of breath after a hearty laugh. "You girls are so kindly to let me tag along."

"Tag along? You lead the way."

Benedict helped Gran from the car. "Ida's a troublemaker now. Are you okay, Ida?" he asked. "Your breathing is off."

Berry heard it too.

"I'm queasy from the excitement and a new kind of pain in my tummy. I'll order a salad and poach a bite of your birthday Cuban."

They gave their orders at the roadside stand and claimed a white picnic table out front.

"We'll have this space to ourselves. No one will sit here with a Chinese man, ha ha."

"You were born right here in Ybor City," said Gran as Berry felt her forehead. "And you're a wounded United States veteran. Let them act ignorant."

For the umpteenth time, Benedict joked, "Want to see my scar?" He'd served as a translator in the Air Force. His strategic transport plane was hit, and a hot fragment of fuselage gave him an unsightly scar on his back. The pilot landed safely.

"Please, Ben, we're about to eat," said Jaudon with her hee-haw laugh.

Benedict, too, had a big laugh for such a refined, well-appointed man.

While they waited, they reminisced about roadway attractions gone by. Six Gun Territory was in Ocala, Florida.

"Pops took me and Bat. We started at an old-fashioned railway station, then boarded a woodburning narrow-gauge engine. Along the way you saw gunfights, saloons, dances, a Native settlement."

Berry said, "I favored Fairyland in the Lowry Park Zoo, though Gran says the first time Ma and Pa took me to see the locked-up animals, I tried to let one out."

"Deer," said Gran. "You wanted to set them free. I don't blame you."

"Fairyland had Snow White, Humpty Dumpty, the Three Little Pigs. They weren't caged."

Gran gave a sweaty smile. "It was free. Important in those days."

"You never denied me a thing."

Gran didn't make her usual objections when Berry mentioned her generosity.

Berry rested a hand on Gran's forehead. "You're pouring sweat. Can we help Gran to some shade?"

She and Benedict supported Gran to a bench under a sizable live oak.

Afraid to take any chances, Jaudon moved the car closer. "My air-conditioning is on. Do you want to help Gran into the car?"

She and Benedict watched Berry do some monitoring.

"Her pulse is thready. Let's go to South Florida Baptist—it's three minutes from here," said Berry.

Jaudon asked Benedict, "Are you okay?"

One look told her he was paralyzed with fear. She led him to the front seat.

"Let's go. Go," he urged.

In the back seat, Berry held Gran in her arms.

The ER waiting room struck her as dim and grimy-looking under its buzzy fluorescent lighting, but that might be her doom-filled mood. She held Berry's hand. Benedict paced.

"I want to be with her, Jaudon," Berry said, her voice forlorn. "One in four stroke victims will have another. Her faithfulness to the stroke rehabilitation program has given us a heap more time with Gran. I'm greedy—I want to hear her heart tick next to me."

"We don't know it was a second stroke for certain."

"Too right. What if it's a heart attack?"

How many emergencies can Gran overcome? How many can Berry withstand? She asked, "Want me to track someone down and tell them you're Gran's personal nurse and should be with her?"

"I tried and was told this facility won't allow it. Just stay with me, okay?"

She slid closer to Berry, put an arm across her shoulders. Berry leaned into her.

"I'll stick with you like white on rice, Georgia gal."

CHAPTER THIRTY-TWO

Vonnie Lowe

Spring 2004

Vonnie originally met MJ in the midst of a rancorous confrontation. Jaudon's shiftless cousins had ganged up on her to demand a share of her moonshine business. She told them they weren't getting a penny. She only sold local-made—and very popular—spirits so she could earn enough money to save the remaining Beverage Bays after Momma almost bankrupted them. Vonnie stuck up for Jaudon.

Vonnie had been drawn to MJ's looks and style so much she entreated her for a date at the old Sweetheart Roller Rink.

Sadly, the rink had closed years ago. Now they used inline skates at local parks. This day they rollerbladed along the Hillsborough River past the live oaks and Spanish moss of Rivercrest Park.

Vonnie's memory of organ music mingled with the songs of loud, happy-sounding finches and cries of children at play. She expected skating would take MJ's mind off her mouth pain. Florida was the perfect rollerblading state because of its unmitigated flatness. The way MJ described what the dentists did to her was torture. She was impatient for her mouth to heal from a bone graft and hoped the next step would be the end of it for some time.

They skated toward an older tourist couple on a bench. The man was a classic case of heatstroke. She pulled her water bottle off her belt and held it out to him. The woman's eyes opened wide, and her hand shot out to stave off the water. Her eyes met Vonnie's; she knew the woman would let her man die before she'd allow him to drink from the same bottle as Vonnie. She couldn't help being hurt, as if she was a different species and might pass diseases to him.

MJ poured her own drinking water on her bandanna. "You might want to call an ambulance." She slung the cool cloth around the man's neck, where it dripped. She left it with them and took Vonnie's hand as they rolled away, silent, processing yet another such encounter.

To end her Debbie Downer thoughts, Vonnie asked, "Remember how Berry, Rigo, and Cullie decided they needed to chaperone us on our first date?"

"It wasn't a date. I agreed because you wouldn't let up about it."

She sped ahead of MJ, stopped, skated backward. "Ima going to be kind. Okay, maybe it was more an engagement party."

High above came the hissing of palm fronds in scarce breezes and the songs of katydids. They knew from experience the local mosquitos were overly friendly. They'd used lemon-eucalyptus repellent until they reeked of it.

MJ caught up and muttered, "Engagement party? It was only the second time we'd met."

"Think of it as an arranged marriage."

"So now it was a wedding party," MJ said with a straight face.

"Come on, you knew at first sight we were meant for each other."

"Do you have any idea how fortunate we were to have Berry and Jaudon as great-hearted examples?"

"Remember the young gays at New York Pizza? They went from breakup to breakup. If it wasn't for those two, we might have followed the wrong path."

"Don't forget Jimmy Neal and Rigo. They've lasted just as long."

She laughed. "How could I?"

MJ took her hand again, and they continued in tandem, slowing to watch a yellow-legged green heron wait for a clueless fish to glide by.

Two boy children with hair shaved almost bald darted in front of them. One asked MJ, "Are you a boy or a he-she?" They ran across the path giggling.

MJ tried to separate her hand from Vonnie's. Vonnie gripped more tightly.

"That must be humiliating."

MJ finally separated their hands. "It may humiliate them someday—when they come out or know someone who does."

"I wish to God you'd speak up. Whenever you can't deal with a situation emotionally, you turn off and shut me out."

"Alright then, it's embarrassing, demeaning, and makes me want to die on the spot. Is that emotional enough for you?"

She knew the worst thing to do was show sympathy. MJ's pride wouldn't stand for it.

"Come on, Squirrel. Let's leave these irritants, hop in the car, and stop by Jaudon and Berry's for news of Gran—unless there's a Ragers game tonight?"

MJ looked at the ground, shook her head, raised a knuckle to the bridge of her glasses, and tapped them on tightly.

Those words had been hard for MJ to say. Vonnie gave her a minute and challenged her with a way to save face. "Race ya…"

❖

At the Vicker homestead, the news was better than Vonnie hoped. Urinary tract infections were worrisome in a ninety-one-year-old, and Berry said Gran was further weakened, but it wasn't her heart.

She noticed MJ pop another pain pill. What about her and MJ? She quailed at a sudden vision of their old age, of each other failing, body and mind—and teeth. It was enough to make someone religious, though not her. She planned to enjoy her handsome, brilliant, sexy lover in the here and now.

Gran was seated on the living room couch, wan and drawn. Her ancient metal pedestal fan cranked out more cool air than both of the newer plastic fans in the room. She raised her now wispy arms to hug them both and kiss them on their cheeks—a first. She smelled of overdosed tea rose perfume, definitely an old lady scent.

Jaudon leaned forward from her chair, rotating a sweating bottle of RC Cola between her large hands. "We were about to celebrate with some peach ice cream. Want to join us?"

"Sounds peachy to me," said MJ. Vonnie gave her a droll look.

Her voice upbeat, Berry enlightened the visitors. "Not half an hour ago, the mailman delivered the legal documents that finalized the donation of Gran's development rights for Stinky Lane to a conservation trust."

Vonnie said, "Please tell me you chose Conservation Florida."

"That's the one." Jaudon swallowed a big glug of her cola.

MJ quietly applauded. "I've had occasion to steer land their way. Good people."

Gran relaxed with a smile of satisfaction. "I've fretted for years how to be certain that property belongs to the critters, their homes, and the stinky mushrooms that drive a body mad in season till they're used to it."

"It's great land, in the opinion of conservationists," said Berry, "because it feeds itself. Most gardeners pluck and toss the mushrooms, but they don't harm gardens. Stinkhorn mushrooms will turn your mulch into nutrition for plants."

Gran's face creased up with laughter. "If you're man enough to pick them."

Leslie came back from the big freezer with a large tub of peach ice cream. Jaudon dashed into the kitchen and returned with bowls and spoons. Leslie overfilled their bowls, despite protests.

"You're dressed up, Leslie. Hot date?" asked Gran. Leslie never used makeup, but she had arrived in filigree earrings and a matching necklace.

"Only a little dressy. We have tickets for a Carolyn Gage play tonight. She's family."

"*We* being you and your wrestler?"

Leslie turned her eyes upward. "Gran, you know she's a bodybuilder."

Vonnie paused her spoon halfway up from her bowl and studied Gran. "How relieved are you to know your land will have accomplished caretakers?"

"It was never my land to begin with. It belonged to Mother Nature and all creation." She looked pained. "I do wish I'd had the chance to spread June's ashes on the land. What am I saying? The Garlands probably didn't bother with cremation, or didn't believe in it." She looked to the ceiling, blinking away tears. "Oh, honey. Oh, my June. Oh, my sweet, wild girl."

They averted their eyes to give Gran time.

After a few minutes, Leslie handed her a paper napkin.

Gran seemed to force a smile through the ice cream circle around her mouth. "Look at this messy old lady keeping you from having a lively time," said Gran.

Berry slipped her arm though Jaudon's and leaned her head on her shoulder. Jaudon swiveled to catch her on laughing lips.

"Are they happy?" Gran asked MJ. "It's all that matters now."

MJ answered with an arm around Gran. The answer was obvious.

Leslie surprised them with the bouquet of balloons she'd hidden earlier. Gran looked delighted as Leslie attached them to her walker and suggested they drive to Benedict's assisted living complex to give him the news.

Once they were gone, Vonnie thought to ask Jaudon about the men who said they wanted to buy the Beverage Bays.

"Oh, Olive and I chased them off with a good riddance."

"Who were they?"

Jaudon told her the story.

"Funny," MJ said. She pressed ice to one cheek. "VONCO had a visit from two men who said they were on the lookout for small businesses that might want to sell."

"Mentioned the word *community* about twenty times?" asked Jaudon.

"Oh yeah. That's who would profit, the community. That's a laugh and a half."

Vonnie was confused. "Is it us they're after or the businesses around here in general?"

"Hard to know. The talker started in on 9/11, professed it woke him up to the need to band together and find ways to give up our selfish dreams. He specifically said 9/11 was the fault of tenderhearted humanitarians who gave the enemy their weapons and wanted to let any old body into our country. I said, *Box cutters? We gave them our box cutters?*"

"They declared the Beverage Bays wanted an upgrade. I believe old-fashioned drive-throughs are a big draw."

"They are," Vonnie said with certainty.

"The ferrety guy tried to examine our stock and equipment," MJ said, "while the other one pushed a bill of goods about capital to expand VONCO."

She took MJ's hand and gripped it tightly. "Stinky Lane is finally safe, but why do I sense evil forces closing in on us?"

No one answered.

CHAPTER THIRTY-THREE

Jaudon Vicker

July 2004

Opal let herself into the Vicker house, uninvited again, and slammed the screen door behind her. "Where's my sister?"

Berry appeared from the kitchen with a worried smile, carrying a slim volume.

Cullie arrived seconds later. "There's an ugly anvil cloud looming out there. I took it on myself to ride out the thunderstorm indoors. Oh, and Allison happened to let slip you found a butterscotch pie recipe. I haven't had butterscotch pie in a blue moon."

Berry faced the book cover out, smiling. "In other words, this isn't an entirely social call. The recipe's in *The Southern Cookbook*, 1935. Gran's mother-in-law wanted her son fed the way he was used to. Unfortunately, it's illustrated entirely with stereotypical mammies."

MJ was perched on the couch with Jaudon, clicking a red pen, drawing plans for a new foundation under the cracker home. There was none originally, and the foundation Pops put in before he carried his bride, Momma, over the threshold, showed cracks after sinking some in the past half century. They both looked up at the alarm in Berry's voice.

"What's the matter?" Berry asked.

Berry's smile died as she observed Opal's face. Opal's expression made clear she had an axe to grind.

Opal pulled a loose thread on her sleeve, snapped it off, rolled it into a tiny ball with her fingers, and threw it at the floor. She wore her bright white tennis shoes with a shapeless purple skirt and a blouse of faded flowers. "It's sinful, sinful."

Jaudon got chill bumps up her arms. "Calm down. What has you so riled up?"

"Riled up? I'm fit to be tied." Opal spat her words. "You lied to me, big sister. That is an abortion mill you run."

She saw Berry stiffen. "We offer affordable or free health care for women without means. Not everyone has insurance or the cash to see a gynecologist. Women need access to birth control as well as birthing. We need treatment for sexually transmitted diseases. We need to know our options in life."

Opal folded her arms. "Grammy Garland would disown you from her grave. You try to control natural childbirth—we're not lost dogs and cats. We won't stand for it."

"We?"

"Intracoastal Ministries has ears and eyes throughout this region. Since day one you claimed you weren't in the killing business." She rummaged in a big blue fanny pack. "What do you call these?"

Jaudon squinted to see a fistful of the Center's green-for-health referral forms in Opal's clenched hand.

Berry said, "You? You know your church has been attacking us? I believed you were a worshipper, not a misguided agitator."

Opal walked toward Berry. "Agitator? If you weren't my sister, I'd strangle you here and now. This is a project me and Klem take on for the Ministries wherever they send us. Because you're related, it was open-and-shut you're our responsibility. Klem fought hard with the zoning commission to boot you out. I've tried the only ways I know to lead you back to our Christian principles."

Dead silence filled the room until Berry said, "You're behind the Tommie Center attacks?"

Opal stood taller. "One of many. You can take that as gospel truth."

Berry's freckles darkened as she angered. "You sneak—you want to deny our patients their necessary medical care. I want to help women—no one else around here will. If they need referrals to make informed decisions, certainly we provide them. You're destroying my life's dream. We'd come so far before these assaults, before, as you say, they set you on us. Ma and Pa would be shamed by your doings."

Jaudon walked to the sisters and reached for a form. Opal snatched them away. Cullie stepped forward, intimidating in her uniform. Jaudon seized Opal's forearm and pressed her thumb into her ulnar nerve, the way Cullie had once taught her. The forms dropped to the floor. Jaudon picked them up and gave them to Berry.

"Where did you find these?"

Opal was rubbing her elbow. "Volunteers who were expecting visited your un-healthy center and didn't take kindly to what you're doing any more than me and Klem do. Every one of them walked away with a ticket to a baby killer. You call this helping?"

"These are not tickets," said MJ. "They're information. Your volunteers were spying, and stealing."

Cullie's hands were on her gun belt. "Florida has had an Economic Espionage Act since 1996 that might fit this situation. Makes you a third-degree felon."

"Enough of this." Berry waved her hands in the air. "Law or no law, I won't allow our patients to be exposed to your spiritual credulousness, your insistence on following ancient biblical verses that can't be properly interpreted or applied to today's world. The Tommie Center has one priority and that's to offer wellness to women who ask for our help."

"Yeah," Jaudon said. "Did you abstain or did you get pregnant to force Klem to marry your sourpuss self?"

"Jaudon, that's not helpful," said Berry.

Opal ignored Jaudon and took a step closer to Berry. Her eyes were slits, her eyebrows drawn together. "I know you're one of those feminists."

Berry stood her ground. "Lesbian feminist and proud of it. You need educating. Women healers existed long before male doctors took over the practice of health care and, at the instigation of insurance companies, turned it into a for-profit business where women are always afterthoughts."

"You think like a red commie."

"No, Opal. That's another fault you can't accuse me of. Here's more education—remember the massive testing for heart disease? All those subjects were male, not one female. Years later someone woke up and pointed out that women need treatments specific to us."

"You're an unnatural man-hater. That's what comes of rearing a child in a home with no father, no grandfather. Or did you have a series of uncles?"

Jaudon restrained herself from slapping this freak, but only because MJ had a hand on her forearm that grew tighter with every volley from Opal.

Berry said, "I won't listen to your deluded misbeliefs. To think we wasted sparse money on frauds. You and your squad of liars best never show your hateful faces around the Tommie Center again."

"You're the one with the lethal baby boomer lies. You think you know everything because you went to college. You know diddly-squat if you don't follow the only book you need."

"Oh, Opal, a bunch of men wrote the Bible twenty-seven thousand years ago for their own purposes. It's not relevant."

Opal's hands were in fists. "Nothing is more relevant. That's where you find the truth, not through your blasphemous secular education. And the poor babies. The children. You kill children before they can take a breath. You murder great men of the future who might have cured cancer."

She'd never seen Berry's face this pink under her freckles. Did she have Gran's susceptibility to stroke?

"I'm a graduate of Cloud Christian College. Our teachers were as Christian as you but made a point of teaching facts, not fancies. And poor babies? Poor babies are exactly why we're here. We want to help women be physically, mentally, and economically healthy so their children can be too."

Opal opened one fist long enough to indicate everyone in the room. "Well, bless your heart. I'll bet if you and your accomplices don't kill them, you'll turn them queer as you and that mess you live with."

That took Jaudon's breath away. She called out in a strained thin warble, "Would you rather my momma aborted me?"

Voice rising, Opal said to Berry, "How dare she suggest it? Our Lord loves her despite her perversions, but you don't have to."

Jaudon had never seen Berry speak through clenched teeth before. "Listen, sister-of-mine, I love Jaudon with all my heart and soul. You can stop insulting her right now. I wouldn't have an abortion any more than you, and we're not an abortion facility."

"You are."

She saw Berry drag air into her lungs in a rushed approximation of deep breathing.

"We offer well woman doctor visits, help with sexually transmitted diseases, provide menstrual supplies so poor women can go to school or work, teach family planning, do pregnancy testing, and we screen for serious conditions. That's what you want to stop?"

"Don't be a fool. You're perfectly well aware of what we want to stop. What if it was you our mother aborted?"

"Why can't you see? Ma and Pa had a choice and the means to raise a child. Please, Opal, I would have loved a sibling to cherish, but you're a sham of a sister and a religious zealot. Reason is a foreign language to you."

"A zealot? Me?" Opal's laughter was tight with hysteria. She continued to verbally pummel Berry with condemnations, personal insults, and accusations. She ended with, "You've managed to ruin the Garland name. In spite of that, my mission is to save your soul."

Berry lowered herself to the couch, eyes downcast, forehead wrinkled, and cupped her face with her hands.

"Like hell it is." Jaudon lashed out and didn't care if her language offended Berry right then. She looked toward Cullie. "Can't you arrest this battle-ax for verbal abuse?"

In a low voice, Cullie said, "If you've got repeated and frequent occurrences, say, in a domestic violence situation, maybe. But this is Florida. Not much interest in prosecuting a woman for spousal abuse, much less for making a scene."

Jaudon instructed Opal, her voice purposely even and firm, "Tell us about the vandalism at the Center. Who in government has the pull to muck up a legitimate enterprise? Is it your ministry people coming around to investigate our commercial businesses, searching for infractions while pretending to want to buy the stores?"

Opal's mouth formed a smile, but not her eyes. She pointed at Berry. "I wouldn't have that information, but I'd do what I had to if I wanted to drive out the murderers of preborn humans. Yes, you, sister and murderer."

She expected Opal would claw Berry's eyes out if she was near enough.

Opal said, "You weren't the one taken from a dead mother under a filthy noisy freeway, minutes from Love-and-Peaceville. You had eight years of a living mother and father who adored you. But that's alright, I do the work of the Lord. Without him you are of no worth."

Jaudon issued her first threat. "You will not talk to Berry that way."

Opal thrust her jaw forward so far, her lower teeth were exposed. "What do you have to do with this, my sister's make-believe man? What does she see in a skunk ape?"

Gran went right up to Opal's face. "Hush your mouth. Get out of our home before you jinx it with your negative juju."

"You dabble in voodoo on top of everything else?" Opal's laugh

A MAGNIFICENT DISTURBANCE

was embittered, but it was interrupted by a startling clap of nearby thunder. Swift lightning brightened the widows, and the afternoon deluge began.

A lifetime of put-downs made Jaudon angry, but to hear Opal badmouth the most decent woman in the world infuriated her beyond reason. She knew how this undue hostility was wrecking Berry inside, blocking her from living her life the best way she knew—how her sister was further shredding an already shaky self-esteem and making Berry crazy with bewildered pain.

The rain went on. For a long moment everyone in the room froze in a tableau of enmity.

What hadn't she been called from the earliest age? A retard, a boy-girl, a bully when she defended herself, a sissy when she cried and ran away. She was the creature from the black lagoon for years after it was filmed at Wakulla Springs near Jacksonville. Deformed, the devil, bearded lady. Momma told her she was handy as hip pockets on a hog. When a carnival came to town, schoolkids at the store asked if she was in the freak show. Her male cousins ganged up on her at family gatherings. People on the street, at the beach, in the parks looked with suspicion at her and Berry together. As Opal vilified Berry in front of her, that lifetime of attacks put her in a frenzy of rage.

She didn't hesitate. She crossed to the storage bench by the front door and seized the old pistol they kept inside, Eddie Dill's long-ago unbidden bequest to them—thanks to Berry, who, to protect herself and Gran, had stolen and hidden it from him.

Through her anger, Jaudon knew her actions were not reasonable or even safe. She made herself aim at the floor, despite her livid will to destroy—in the person of Berry's sister—the massive hordes of Opals that came at people who tried to rid the planet of its miseries. She had to raise her voice to be heard over the downpour. "How about I shut you up with a bullet? I will, unless you walk out our door right now and never bother any of us again."

"You want to hurt a protector of babies? You have no call to threaten me with a gun because we target a place of evil." Opal searched out Berry and threatened, "If your what-you-call-it so much as points that gun, be ready for several big men with a lot more firepower to come visit that godforsaken place you operate."

Berry was pressing the back of a trembling hand to her lips. Rain continued to pound on the tin roof.

"Lawd bless that Opal," said Gran. "I would have raised her better than this."

"Get away from here, Gran."

But Gran marched toward Jaudon, cane and all. "Give me that gun, Jaudon Vicker. Your father would be mortified."

"Pops is the one who taught me to shoot."

"He never used live targets. And if that ain't a fact, God's a possum."

"You oughtn't be in here at all, Gran."

MJ put an arm around Gran and eased her out of the living room.

Opal crept backward, distancing herself from the pistol. Jaudon moved with her, too furious to think.

"No, Jaudon, no," Berry called out.

That was her Berry. She'd forgive anyone practically anything.

The roar of rain lightened, then stopped dead. Through the open windows came the last gurgle of a downspout and sporadic drips from trees. The whirr of the big ceiling fan became dominant, stirring the hot air like a roiling pot of foreboding.

Opal stood behind the stout crushed velvet wing chair, the first piece of fancy furniture Momma ever bought. It was wearing out, the same as Jaudon's patience. She stalked Opal, breath shallow and swift.

Her hands raised in prayer, Opal called to Berry, "Sister, let me save your soul."

The others cautioned Jaudon to let it go.

Jaudon wanted shut of this ugly-minded shrew. "You have caused Berry enough misery," she said and pounced in front of the chair.

Was the shriek that came out of Opal's mouth a call for help or a battle cry? She thrust the wing chair at Jaudon, toppling it, and ran across the room, behind Berry, pulled her close to shield herself.

Berry was struggling to break loose, but Opal was stronger than she'd admitted to Berry when she helped in the garden.

The fan had become white noise. A great silence inflated to fill the room, and the soft *snick* when she unlocked the pistol's safety was magnified. Although Jaudon hadn't yet pointed the gun at her, Opal jerked Berry closer and stumbled, pulling Berry with her.

Smart Berry intentionally collapsed, forcing Opal to drag her.

Jaudon said, "Some kind of Christian you are, willing to sacrifice your own sister to save yourself."

Cullie was at Jaudon's side then, whispering, "Come on, Jaud, give it up. When you're behind bars, you won't see Berry except through thick glass. You'll never live here in your cracker house again. The Beverage Bays will be confiscated. Is Berry's sister worth that?"

Frustrated, fed up tears slid from Jaudon's eyes as she said, "I want to give her sister the kind of scare she's given us. See how she likes it. Look what she did to you, Cullie, and how she torments Berry."

"You can't teach a right from a wrong, 'specially not with a bullet."

"Can't you do an involuntary commitment on her, Cul?"

MJ returned without Gran and walked directly to Jaudon. She used one unyielding hand to lower Jaudon's gun arm.

"No need to stir the pot, Boss. Her husband is out front in the church van picking his teeth and bothering the neighbors with a religious station at full volume."

Opal cast Berry aside and crawled around the furniture toward the door.

Berry said, "Go be a nice church wife and leave us in peace."

Opal gulped air through twisted, silenced lips. She never took her eyes off the gun.

Opal's husband Klem rapped briskly, walked in, and stared. He rubbed his hands together in a coach's impatient let's-go manner. His red hair was sparse in front, and his arms looked as if the hairs had resettled on them. "What's taking so long, slow-pokey Opie?"

Was it her imagination or did Opal look more afraid of her husband than she did of the gun?

"Klem, get me away from here," Opal commanded, in flight to him. "My sister's pet freak is out to kill me."

She stopped herself from taking a shot.

"Damn it, Jaudon." MJ twisted the gun completely from her grasp.

Klem scanned the group in the living room and shook his head. "Get in the car, Opie." He gave his wife a shove that tipped her through the door.

He faced Berry. "It's hard for her, her own blood sinning. She thinks she can save you from going to hell, though it's common knowledge no one but God can and will do that—if you follow his Word."

Jaudon let loose then, mindless, with the fury of all her born days, tackled him, punched, kicked, went for his eyes. She became everywoman, every-dyke, gone to her limits of exasperation and daring, risking herself to punish one or all of these malignant self-appointed judges.

"Get off me, you baboon," Klem said, so off-balance he crashed to his back.

Jaudon fell to her knees on his groin area, hit and hit with the strength of the thousand barbs she had suffered. It was less than a minute before Berry and Cullie pulled her away, but she'd hit the perfect target, done him some damage.

His hand, covering his nose, dribbled blood as he hobbled out the door, a man satisfyingly wounded in body and pride.

CHAPTER THIRTY-FOUR

Berry Garland

"Jaudon, what got into you?"

They were rid of company at last. Berry had expected a deputy sheriff to come to their door and arrest Jaudon, but none did.

Jaudon hung her head. Her folded hands rested on her knees. Her eyes searched the bedroom, lighting on what all with the exception of Berry's upset face. She muttered, "The way she talked to you—I was so mad I was ready to spit nails. I never planned to hurt her. I wanted her to feel as threatened as you do."

"But pulling that pistol on Opal and mauling Klem the way a lioness protects her cubs?"

"I didn't know another way to defend you against her wickedness except to scare the words out of her mouth. Besides, there were never any bullets in that gun—don't you remember, you only let me keep it if I tossed the ammo?"

"That was so long ago. No, I was so afraid I didn't have a rational thought in my head. I'm surprised Gran didn't have another stroke right there and then, as shocked and horrified as the rest of us."

Jaudon looked up at her. "I'm sorry. I didn't think about Gran. I wanted that granddaughter of hers to quit her yapping and be as terrified as she makes you."

"She does fit in with the troubled women we see at the Center, but we knew that about her."

"We didn't know she egged on her fellow believers to attack you and your work. Wasn't this country founded on freedom of religion? Where do they get off imposing their pea-brained ideas on the rest of us?"

"But a gun?"

"It shut her up, didn't it? No worse a weapon than terrorism, which is what Opal and her church think is fine and dandy."

"Terrorism? You're not serious."

"Serious as the business end of a loaded gun. MJ and I talked about terrorism the other day. Look it up for yourself. The FBI says terrorism is violent, criminal acts people do to have their way. How does that not fit Cullie's and Duval's injuries, damage to Mrs. Lanamore's property, and the fear these fanatics brought you? How does that not merit scaring the bejesus out of her?"

"I pray they don't come looking for retribution."

"They won't dare. The ministries may not be the only evildoer, but we have enough proof of the damage they've done to put their leaders in jail."

"Remind me, where did the gun come from?"

"You didn't recognize it?" She offered it to Berry, who raised her hands to refuse. "It's the one thing you ever stole in your life, and you can't remember taking it from Eddie Dill's tumbledown shed?"

"I managed to forget about that. What'd I tell you? He'll haunt us forever. Why do we have the loathsome thing?"

"For times when we need to scare the living daylights out of a person who threatens us. You ought to keep it at the Center."

Berry's eyes widened and her hands flew to her cheeks. "Never. Please turn it in. And I don't mean take it to your stores. No way around it, firearms beget firearms. Violence invites more of the same."

Jaudon pursed her lips, furrowed her brow. "Okay, but we need to keep the shotgun. There are times in a rural area a shotgun comes in handy."

"I suppose."

"I'll take the pistol to the sheriff's, turn it in."

Berry's cheer was inching upward. "I have to say, I did kind of want to do violence to her myself." Her gaze drifted to the open window. Bees worked the hibiscus blooms right outside. She faintly heard them buzzing under the calls of cicadas. The sun had already baked away the afternoon thundershower.

"Working as a counselor, I've learned our little girl selves remain intact inside us. You've gone through the gamut from unrestrained bullying to public questioning of who and what you are: girl, boy, queer, freak of nature, and—these days—a right to exist. Every blow to our adult selves echoes the old pain and terror. Now, we have grownup selves to protect those girls—we have better tools than fistfight reactions. We need to be tender with ourselves but take charge and refuse to give in to our worst impulses."

She moved behind Jaudon and rubbed her back until she heard a clunk. They looked at each other and ran to Gran's room.

Gran had been weak, but otherwise doing well. It was a shock to see her fallen from her upended rocker, twisted glasses in one hand, polka dot glass in a pool of lemonade and ice cubes that spread beneath her curio cabinet. Berry was frightened to see her silent and unmoving.

Jaudon bent immediately to start CPR.

"Wait." She dropped to her knees, butted Jaudon aside to check for Gran's pulse.

Berry concentrated, willing a beat to sound. She checked for breathing. Said her name.

Jaudon cried, "No! I scared Gran to death. Let me—"

"Hand me a flashlight."

Jaudon scrambled for one. As Berry checked Gran's pupils, Jaudon said, "I think Gran wet herself."

"Please call 9-1-1, although it's too late this time."

"Maybe they can—"

"She didn't want resuscitation again, remember? But we need to call them."

"But—"

"It's okay, sweetheart. I know what death looks like."

"She'll sit up, laugh, and say I fooled you good this time."

"Not Gran. She'd never do that to us. Turn off her TV and call 9-1-1."

Jaudon hit her head with the heel of her hand. "What do I tell them? That I caused a scene and killed Gran?"

"That your grandmother has a history of ischemic strokes and looks to have passed on. Go on out to Eulalia Road to flag the ambulance. The police will come too, then a hearse. Tell them she's going to that funeral parlor she picked out—you remember. I'll call ahead so they expect her. And you know perfectly well Gran was laughing at your stunt, not scared, but we can talk about that later."

She heard Jaudon rush to her assignments, stub her toe, fumble the phone.

"Gran," she said, with Jaudon out of the room. Her tears came in a rush. "Gran." Love doesn't prevent death, she thought. *What should I have done to keep you with us?*

She'd always known how fortunate she was to have Gran. The forces that were Gran paraded through her mind on a balky newsreel. Gran was the well water, the sun's gardener, the moon and stars in the skies of night. She was hurricane shelter, tiller of life and soil, a seer, more than a true mother, a skein that wove her chosen family together—and most people, all animals were family. She overflowed with sense, presence, and truth. If the corn wasn't ripe, she'd toss the kernels into a stir-fry and munch on the sweet tip of the cob. Gran talked with spirits, imagined paths into being, spread kindness as sure as the sky splashes rain.

When Jaudon slammed the screen door behind herself, Berry took Gran's cooling hand and, without speaking aloud—she was barely able to think, much less talk—apologized that she hadn't been at her side.

I couldn't have let go with you there, pet, Gran answered, also silently. *And I needed to go.*

The fact of it felled her. She studied on Gran's words until she saw her death from Gran's point of view. The medical incidents, the gradual decline of her speech, memory, and mobility, the desire to sleep her days away, had taken their toll on those who loved Gran.

Abruptly, she was again without a mother. Idle as she waited for the commotion of death to begin, she was swept away with sorrow, but Gran intervened.

And don't you be calling your woman on the carpet, said Gran. *Jaudon wanted to protect you today, which is her bounden duty. Tell Jaudon not to blame herself either. My passing was waiting to happen. If you need to lay blame, tell Opal I'll never forgive her for leaving us in the dark, no matter what your other grandmother assumed about me raising her kin. That was plain selfish. News as bad as that, you check to make sure it got to a person when you don't have a response. Poor Opal, she can't help being brought up so strict and misinformed.*

"I gave Jaudon what for about that gun is all. Should I have praised her? How will I know my way without you, Gran?"

Jaudon can most always use some dressing-down with that chip the size of a hulking live oak she carries on her shoulder. You'll do fine. You don't need me, the Great Spirit is with you, in you. 'Sides, I'm intolerable weary. I thought to lift my hand from the chair arm to take a sip of the lemonade you brought me. Thought and thought for a god-awful long time about the elbow grease I'd need and next I'd have to pee. That bathroom was as far away as the moon—I hope my body didn't leave a mess for you to mop up. I enjoyed a last taste of your sweet lemonade from our tree, pet.

"I'll never forget you for one minute, Gran, and all you've done for me."

If you ever do, I'll come spook you good. You might find a spunky gator in the kitchen garden. Now, make way, pet. The sirens are growing near. Best for me to nod off through the hurly-burly.

CHAPTER THIRTY-FIVE

Jaudon Vicker

Summer 2004

Jaudon never wanted to see anyone die again. In the new emptiness of their home, she held and consoled Berry. Teary-eyed, Berry assured her pulling a gun on Opal wasn't what killed Gran. MJ had told her Gran laughed at the expression on Opal's face. "Bet she peed her pants," was what Gran said, plainly satisfied to see Opal cut down to size.

Berry never laid a bit of blame on her. Nonetheless, Jaudon was ashamed Gran died alone after the scene in the next room. It wasn't as if intimidating Opal would change anything; there were hordes of Opals in the world.

She was all nerves about the gun and turned it in at the sheriff's office first thing.

The rest of those difficult days after losing Gran scorched blank patches into her brain. She wept at any reminder of the woman who gave her the love Momma had no capacity to give. She cried more than Berry, who held herself together in order to fulfill Gran's wishes: cremation, a get-together for the sake of her loved ones, and a return to the earth on the land she'd owned—a stipulation when she transferred ownership to the conservancy. Grandpa Binyon's ashes were spread there many years ago.

She lived on Beverage Bay cheese straws and RC Cola, unable to stomach the kindly donated soups and casseroles.

Store operations would have suffered without Olive Ponder and Olive's daughter-in-law, Stacey A. Ponder. Jaudon, as well as Berry, had to be too many places at once. Olive sat her down with an oversized desk calendar and wormed her upcoming activities and appointments out of her, jotting down what had to be done at what time and where. Olive kept a copy. Jaudon put hers on a clipboard and carried it everywhere.

She was lost. No Pops, no Gran. She'd caused Gran's death. No one would disabuse her of that truth. At the same time, she knew Gran's death was about Gran and not her, so she stopped bemoaning aloud her part in it and let the rest of them mourn their way.

At the store, Olive said, "I've included in here times to clean your house. I know Gran wasn't as active these last few years, but she was a proud lady, so I'm definite as I can be she picked up what slack she was able to."

At home, she was reminded of Gran when she used the calendar on the kitchen wall. Not one to splurge, calendars were Gran's annual gift to them. Some years they depicted flowers; others, birds, cartoons, poems by Maya Angelou. Who would fill that blank space next Christmas?

Jaudon touched a milk glass vase that held a striking posy of coral bells and red pentas. "Nisa—Vaughn's wife—mothers our plantings. She may be a sought-after landscape designer, but, like Gran and Berry, she loves to dig her hands into actual dirt. You'll see her work at Gran's memorial service. Vaughn and Nisa offered their place to hold it. Their yard could be the palace grounds." She became weepy whenever she mentioned the service.

Olive added to the calendar time for Jaudon to return the rented medical equipment and do the wrenching work of culling Gran's possessions to help single out what Berry held precious. She was to pick up the death certificates and deal with the cremation company. Together, she and Berry were to write an obituary.

"We'll hang on to each other, cry at the kitchen table."

Olive repackaged the day-old pastries. She reached for Jaudon's hand. "You go on and cry. This is a big loss." Their hands stuck together. "Now look what I've done to you. We're both sticky-fingered."

Jaudon laughed and Olive joined her.

"I expect my gran to leave for heaven any time now too. She was our backup mom while my mother worked full-time for the state to support us all."

They cried until the next customer drove in.

❖

One spectacularly hot September afternoon, soon after Gran died, Rigo called to them through the porch screen door. He was the opposite of gloomy and called out, "We've brought you a Gran-tree. Ta-da." He stood aside for Jimmy Neal, whose long arms hugged a plastic-wrapped root ball that sprouted spindly twigs and shiny green baby leaves.

Pink, yellow, and gray cumulous clouds mushroomed behind them.

"You're home," Berry cried. She jumped to clutch both of them to herself. They'd already visited as soon as she called with the news. The four of them had done some hand-holding, and the men accepted trinkets of Gran's to remember her by.

"Thank you for making the long trip again so soon after the funeral," Berry said in the hushed voice of sorrow that threatened to become permanent. "Every morning, I wake flattened by Gran's loss. It's true, what Rigo told me, that waking to a new reality is always sorrowful. Somehow that helps. Is the tree to remember Gran?"

Jaudon's nose stuffed up and she pressed on her tear ducts, hoping to prevent the flow. "What kind?"

Jimmy Neal looked at Rigo with a complicit smile.

"A berry tree, of course," said Rigo.

Jimmy Neal said, "Mulberry, to be exact."

"You fellas," said Berry. She was too choked up to speak. "Did Gran tell you she always wanted a mulberry tree? She once baked a mulberry pudding for Jaudon's birthday in August. So easy—day old white bread, berries, sugar, butter, and mixed berries, mostly mulberries."

Rigo wiped his eyes now. His hair had remained thick and curly, but the red was giving way to gray. Jimmy Neal was bald on top, and his short ponytail was in a rubber band. "She gave us the recipe, but darned if we found mulberries. Now we'll have a source, so perk up and tell us where you want this beauty."

Jaudon, happy her hair remained pale yellow, went in the fading light of sundown to the pole barn for shovels. She once would have run and started to dig before the guys did, but she had no energy for that. The poor guys, here to deliver cheer, would welcome the distraction of planting that tree.

The four sprayed themselves with mosquito repellant because it was that time of day. They trooped outside. She knew Berry would silently commune with Gran in that way she had, and sure enough, Berry announced that Gran wanted the tree to greet them morning, noon, and night. They dug beyond the kitchen garden where it wouldn't cast shade over the plants—mulberries could grow to fifty feet or more.

As Rigo and Jimmy Neal dug, Rigo said, "We'll bring over tarps and shake the berries out of the tree."

Jaudon laughed for the first time since that awful day. She saw Berry stifle a smile behind her hand. "You'll be stained purple, head to toes."

Jimmy Neal put a hand on one hip. "Maybe we can do that for Pride day."

Berry took Rigo by the wrist. "Let's leave Mr. Comedian and Jaudon to dig. We need compost and mulch from the barn, or Gran's tree will never grow."

The next time she looked up, they were almost at the pole barn. Berry carried a strong flashlight, Rigo's arm around her shoulders. He was the most likely person to guide Berry through her grief. Anyway, she hoped so.

As they continued to dig, frogs announced the arrival of dusk.

CHAPTER THIRTY-SIX

Vonnie Lowe

August 2004

Vonnie asked, "What's the latest on Berry's crazy, mixed-up sister?"

Cullie and Allison were with Vonnie and MJ at a Rainbow Ragers softball game on the east side of Rainbow Gap.

Cullie grazed a fistful of popcorn and looked thoughtful. Allison nudged her.

"Haven't heard a word about Opal Howell in particular. That ministries group she belongs to, works for, whatever they are, they should be charged with domestic terrorism in my reading of the law." A Tampa player stole a base. Cullie stood and booed.

Outdoors, Allison's voice was more hoarse than usual. "Allergies," she always explained. "Planned Parenthood has a lot of trouble with Intracoastal Ministries too. Not only here—everywhere Intracoastal sets up shop. They also target gay bars, start fights, and claim queers instigated the violence. More than one innocent person has been shoved into the rear seat of a police car and spent the night, unprotected, in jail."

"Officer Friendly—Jeff—and I are close to done with a training plan about cultural differences we'll present to the sheriff. With her experience, Allison's been a big help."

Vonnie spotted Berry and Jaudon picking their way up the seven-row bleachers, arms full of hot dogs and drinks from the concession stand. The Beverage Bays and the practice where Berry worked sponsored the Rainbow Ragers. Vonnie and the rest scooted along the bleacher to make room.

"Why the nosebleed seats?" asked Jaudon, wriggling as close to Berry as decently possible.

"'Cause we're nosebleed kinda gals. Rough and tough," Cullie joked.

MJ reached across Vonnie to touch Berry's hand. "Remember we moved to lower rows when Gran had difficulty climbing?"

Gran had loved to watch the games with her kids, as she called the three couples.

Jaudon squinted into the sun at Cullie. "How'd you make it up here. Crawl?"

"Just because the department doesn't think I'm fit doesn't mean I can't climb a step or two higher than Gran. This isn't exactly The Swamp at the University of Florida in Gainesville. Go Gators!"

Allison said, "You promised to soak in the tub and take ibuprofen after the game."

Cullie pretended to sulk. "Then I hope it goes extra innings."

Berry said, "You were all so sweet and helpful to Gran."

Vonnie caught a stack of napkins threatened by a breeze. "Are you kidding? Didn't you notice we cherished Gran, and she made each of us know we're special? I don't know another soul could do that."

Berry dabbed her eyes with the back of a hand. "Gran always said she was fortunate in our friends and threatened to adopt the lot of you."

Cullie was up again, this time cheering the Ragers into a three-run homer. Jaudon spilled most of her popcorn as she jumped for the team.

Berry was subdued even when the Ragers scored in the ninth inning to clinch their win.

The three couples deposited their debris in the trash bag Jaudon invariably supplied.

Berry held a hand up to halt their exit from the bleachers. "We have more sad news."

Vonnie asked, "What's wrong?"

"Who is it?" asked Cullie.

"Nobody's sick or dying. It's Leslie. She's done it again," Berry said.

"Done what?" asked Vonnie, searching all their faces for the answer.

"Ran off into the sunset with her new girlfriend."

The proud smiles over the Ragers' win turned to perplexity.

"Without warning?"

"Our Leslie is gone?"

"She did this with no notice and left you in a bind?" Allison asked with a sour expression.

"No, she gave two weeks' notice," Berry told them. "She cried and apologized, but she wanted to grab this chance at love."

"What can we offer her to beat that?" said Jaudon.

Berry assured them, "I told her she'll always have a job here, but they loaded their cars with their essentials yesterday and struck out for Milwaukee this morning."

Cullie asked, "Why run off? Leslie charged into our hearts, and then, kaboom, she's history."

"Way to ruin a Rainbow Rager victory," MJ groused as she led them off the field and to their cars. "My interns do it too often. Construction training is portable. Some of our more experienced workers start their own companies and compete with us."

Vonnie blew up. "The housing office has a lot of turnover because we try to hire our own clients, and they're often troubled people with fragmented families. You anticipate problems. But you'd think Leslie was an irresponsible child."

"She's thirty-nine years old," Jaudon said.

She wasn't sure what was making her so angry, but Vonnie answered, "Going on twelve." Did she continue to harbor resentment after training resident after resident who pulled the same stunt?

Berry said, "I can't hold it against her."

Jaudon clasped her hands behind her head and stretched. "Berry, you'd forgive a person whose horns held up his halo."

"When we interviewed Leslie, she described herself as a wild child. I think she was here as long as she was supposed to be."

"Well, ain't that a fine howdy-do," Cullie said and resettled her newest cowboy hat on her head with a yank.

"I want to go find her and..." Jaudon hesitated, toned it down. "And bring her to Rainbow Gap where she belongs."

Berry thought the same. "That weightlifter isn't who I'd want for my daughter."

"In our lesbian family, she is a daughter," said Vonnie.

Allison shook her head. "We don't need her. You think you know someone, and in the end you don't. She was so responsible, dependable, deliberate, wanted to honor lesbians in whatever she did. Are you sure she wasn't kidnapped?"

"Who by?" Vonnie asked. "Miz Muscles?"

Allison cleared her throat. "You're right—it affects a person's forbearance. Cops, social workers, mayors, we encounter the same levels of poverty, racism, anti-Semitism, xenophobia, and homophobia day after day, year after year, and we're the lucky ones who deal with the damaged human results. You lose your tolerance."

Berry spoke with affection. "I imagine Leslie will reappear in a year or a dozen years."

"Meanwhile, how did she expect the Tommie Center to function?"

Berry pointed her index fingers at herself. "I guess I'm it. I'll recruit a nurse to replace me, and I'll do the admin work again."

"You hate admin, Berry. You want to be the RN, the counselor."

"What you can do," said MJ, squinting into the sun. Vonnie fished in her purse for MJ's sunglasses and handed them over. "How long have you worked at the Housing Authority, twenty years or so?"

"Long enough to develop GERD," Vonnie answered.

"All the more reason to investigate how to quit without loss of retirement benefits. Convert your pension into IRAs, mutual funds, whatever, and find a job you can love," MJ said. "As you know, our company offers superior benefits."

"Never happen. Me administrate my brother? Nisa can do that at home."

"Give me more credit than that."

Berry exchanged glances with MJ. She said, "It's not posted yet, but a slot has opened that would keep you in the same field, where your experience is needed. You'd run into prejudice, so that's a con, but you'd fit right in with your coworkers. Who needs Leslie? Come work where you'll be appreciated."

Vonnie felt warmth rise through her whole being. A chance to get out of the Housing Authority? And work with Berry? "Me?" she asked. Her heart somersaulted. "You think I can handle the administration of the Ida Tommie Women's Health Center?"

CHAPTER THIRTY-SEVEN

Jaudon Vicker

September 2004

"I don't know, Berry. Leslie's priority was romance. Gran's gone. Allison won the state senate seat on her second try. That will put her in Tallahassee for two months a year, and she'll be on the road for town halls and ribbon cuttings. Our family is shrinking."

They were on their couch in Rainbow Gap, half absorbed in a women's basketball game on TV. Jaudon sat upright, and Berry stretched out to rest her head on Jaudon's well-developed thigh. She ran her fingers through Berry's soft curly hair, as dark as ever. She wouldn't mind growing older, because she was with Berry.

"Even the animals are gone," Berry said in a whisper. "I miss Gran, and I miss Kajen and Puddin almost as much." Kajen left them a year or so after Puddin. "Cancer is an affliction that should never be visited on innocent animals. Kajen should be here to sniff and hunt microscopic specks on the floor. Our plump Puddin isn't on the couch where she stole the sunlight, one eye pretending she was asleep, the other watching the cat."

"Or how she covered her eyes with her paws. I got such a kick out of those two bumpkins."

"We need to make a trip to the shelter."

"How can we take care of them without Gran? We're barely home enough to take care of ourselves."

"Since I resigned from the practice, for the first time I don't spend my days at a frantic pace. I have room for animals. You're right about time, though. We need to be home to train them."

"We pretty much have our nights to ourselves, except when I'm called to the store."

"Nights are not enough. I have to admit, though, day or night, we've learned to handle traumas as they come along."

"Even the crises are routine."

"In the end, life has calmed down since you scared off my sister. I haven't heard hide nor hair of her. I want to believe she's gotten care and not the kind her ministry has on offer."

Jaudon laughed. "Therapy by empty gun, I call it. Not that the anti-women folks have scattered, but at least we dampened Intracoastal's plans to shut you down."

"It's a lot easier now we've got patients who've taken it on themselves to defend what's becoming theirs."

"I imagine Opal's gang forgot to factor in people of color when they decided you'd be an easy target."

"Now our patients thank the protestors for their save the babies pamphlets, take as many as they can, and cheerfully tear them up in front of them. We put a barrel next to the door so we can incinerate the scraps. That has to be the most effective defense we've tried. But, oh, the emotional cost of the taunts, threats, shouting, preaching, curses, and shoves when all they want is to see a doctor."

It had happened slowly, but the patients were true-blue Tommie Center and Nurse Berry fans, even more so since Vonnie, who already knew many of them through the Housing Authority, took the administrator job and freed up Berry to be their full-time RN.

The Center supporters had gotten together and created an after-hours phone tree. Once alerted to a threat, patients and locals planned to swarm the attackers and drive them off—if any vehicles were operable after the tires were deflated, locks superglued, and gas tanks filled with sugar.

Latino men accompanied their wives and kids after a day bent low over fields of strawberries. They protected their wives' clinic by waiting outside with their kids as they polished their cars, played Latin pop, drank beer by the can, and smoked.

If only one person showed up from the call list, it was enough that she or he brazenly took license plate numbers and disappeared into the nearby warren of homes.

Jaudon looked at her Timex. "Time to go."

They locked up the house and climbed in the Buick. She'd drop

Berry off to tackle next year's budget with Allison's volunteer assistance and the Center's new employee, Vonnie Lowe.

❖

When they arrived, MJ was lounging against her pickup in the Center's parking lot. "I'm kidnapping your girlfriend," she warned Berry.

Berry joked, "As long as you don't carouse all night."

"All's I want is a tasty ol' fish fry. Cullie too. We'll meet her at Mudfoot's."

She and MJ watched until Berry and Vonnie locked the door. Allison had the lights on and would be starting the computers, ready to work on the annual budget. Jaudon left the Buick in case the ladies needed it and got in MJ's truck.

Laura Bathgate pulled into the lot. She hadn't changed out of her ob-gyn office clothes. Jaudon noticed a patch of flour on one shoulder and guessed it was there when Laura said good-bye to Tad that morning. Tad, Duval, Vaughn, and MJ had constructed a roomy second story apartment above Pansy's Café. Laura Bathgate-Lowe and Duval did the interior design. Laura waved good night as she scurried through another locked door.

Jaudon's mouth watered as MJ drove to meet Cullie. Mudfoot's Fish Camp was the sole restaurant left in what passed for downtown Rainbow Gap. Mudfoot rented cabins to older guys who, widowed or divorced, never adjusted to retirement. The rent was so cheap, the guys so idle, they helped Mudfoot keep the place going.

At the restaurant, Cullie sat in the hot dining room behind a platter of scallion buttermilk hush puppies. Jaudon took a happy sniff. The smell of fry oil at work on fish, chicken, and breading was enough to knock you over. She and MJ took seats at the table and chowed down on the hush puppies while they looked at the menu. There was never anything new, but Jaudon savored reliving the taste of each dish.

Cullie had ordered the right appetizers, and the three of them wiped out baskets of fried pickles and onion rings. They discussed their entrees at length. The waitress—Mrs. Mudfoot, they called her—had Jaudon's order on her pad before Jaudon said blackened shrimp po' boy. MJ ordered her usual po' boy, also called an oyster loaf, while Cullie decided to eat dessert first and asked the waitress for a slice of Mississippi mud pie while her gator bites were prepared.

"I guess nobody at this table watches her weight," MJ said as she folded her grease-stained napkin.

Cullie patted her trifling paunch. "On butches' night out, I need a spare stomach. Carry it around in a big fanny pack." They tried to meet without their girlfriends monthly, but it was more often quarterly due to work schedules.

Jaudon sputtered in her ice water. "That's where you already packed it, Cul. Your fanny."

They'd grunted more than talked throughout the meal but now became serious.

"Don't the cops make you stay in shape?"

MJ said, "Earth to Jaudon. Have you ever looked at older police officers? Heard the doughnut jokes?"

"The county offers us passes to Laudre Flats Fitness. It's owned by some relation of the county assessor, which is how we got the deal, but it's too far for most of us after a twelve-hour shift."

"It's not a half mile from here. You drive this far for gator bites," Jaudon said.

"You live up the road—are you a member?"

"I exercise enough when I run around my stores."

"Come work construction at VONCO for a few months—we'll be lean and mean."

"I might send Berry. She's started to look a smidge like Gran, and Gran wasn't quite slim her last twenty years or so, until her stroke."

Cullie smacked her arm. "I'll tell Berry you said that." She pointed at MJ. "How long will you work at VONCO anyways? You must be richer than clabbered cream."

"Vonnie and I have talked about that. She loves her job at the Tommie Center, I love mine, yet I can picture the day one of us will wake up in the morning bone-tired. That's when we'll know. How about you?"

"Same predicament; Berry and I want to keep at our jobs. On the flip side, I see a drop in revenue with these gas stations adding bigger and bigger essentials shops. I have no interest in gas sales, but other companies see potential in adding fill-ups to a familiar local name. Rigo and Jimmy Neal tell me my stores are an institution and beg me never to close shop."

The other waitress came on duty as the restaurant filled up. "I heard you're a grandmother now," Cullie remarked to her. They'd dated in their teens.

"Twice over. The new one's the knee-baby of the family." The waitress lightly tapped her tray on Cullie's ball cap.

"As to Jimmy Neal and Rigo," said Cullie, "I hear they'll be underfoot soon."

Jaudon said, "Jimmy Neal's mother is in a bad way. He's the only one disposed or able to take care of her, so they're heading our way. Jimmy Neal promised a homecoming Mardi Gras meal. I doubt I can eat much of it. Dr. Garza says I have heartburn. No more fatty meats or fiery spices, but I draw the line at Mudfoot's po' boys, no matter what they do to me. She says food like this gives me inflammation, and I'm too young for arthritis to pop up in new places—my left knee is the latest."

Cullie looked at her. "What the hey? Heartburn? Did you try Alka-Seltzer?"

"You've always had a cast iron gut," said MJ.

Jaudon raised her hands in an *I don't know* gesture. "I inherited the arthritis from Pops. My stomach's my own fault. I was raised up on spicy foods, but I guess I overdo things."

"What about your teeth? Are they fixed?" Cullie asked.

MJ groaned. "I've spent enough to fix every mouth in Lecoats County, but no, I have months more to go. I begged the dentist to yank them all, but he says I'll be happier with implants. They don't slip, don't ever have cavities, clack, or damage the jawbone. Meanwhile, I'm committed to put his son through dental school."

Cullie winced as she stretched a leg outside the table.

"And you're still on desk duty?" MJ asked.

"As I spiral hopelessly down into addiction and madness there in the insufferable office. It's best if you remember me as I once was, a gallant crime-stopper."

Jaudon licked her fingers behind a soggy knot of napkins. "Be serious for two seconds in your life."

Cullie made a chagrined face. "The numbness and tingling haven't quit. Or the pain. Turns out the leg swelled so severely, it crushed nerves. Now my leg and my brain aren't on speaking terms."

"Can they fix that?" asked Jaudon.

"It's supposed to fix itself, but healing is slower than molasses going up an ice hill in January. They had me exercising and in physical therapy, but both aggravate my leg so bad—well, you've seen how I walk. There's a chance of surgery paralyzing my lower body."

"Will you ever be able to work again?"

"I am working. I shuffle papers in the office, dispatch the cars. Chronic pain can lead to early retirement in my business."

"What'll you do then?" asked MJ. "You're barely in your fifties."

"Most likely I'll stay on, desk job or no, till I can take full retirement. Better than be glued to the porch rocker, watching the cars go by, chewing the fat with the trash collector and the mail deliverer, slapping at skeeters.

"Meantime, I might take Rigo's beginner psych class. I'd like to learn how to counsel other cops through rough times, even as a volunteer."

"Poor Jimmy Neal and Rigo start their new jobs right away, in the middle of their move and pandering to Jimmy Neal's mulish mother."

MJ patted her chest. "COPD, right?"

"Stage three. He wants to start her in a pulmonary rehabilitation program. When he visits, she promises to go, but Jimmy Neal said that woman can come up with more excuses than a schoolkid facing an arithmetic test. His dad is long gone from cancer, so there's no one to take care of her, the way she is, anymore."

"This is a flawless professional move for Rigo," said MJ. "He may be boomeranging to teach in the same program where he earned his master's, but he was denied tenure upstate."

Cullie covered her mouth and burped. "I'll have my twenty years in soon. If I retire then, I'll see if I can help the bumpkins out by keeping company with Jimmy Neal's mother now and again."

"His mom's a pip. You'll go to entertain her, but she'll have you laughing till your socks roll up and down. She considered Rigo her son-in-law from the get-go, well before they married."

"I'll draw my pension, work security for my politician Allison until I can sign up for Social Security and Medicare. Add Allison's government pension, and we'd have a decent number of years for travel or to stay home and garden."

"Or cause ruckuses with Allison's knack for political rabble-rousing," Jaudon said.

MJ never cracked a smile as she announced, "If Allison runs for president and wins, you'd be First Lady."

Cullie slapped her knee and whispered, "Excuse me, that would be First Dyke. And you know what would be really cool? This is a whole 'nuther idea and I'm serious about it—I'm thinking of opening a pool cleaning business and hiring other people to slosh for a living."

She laughed with MJ. "I imagine you're going to run it from the White House?"

"Quit it, you guys. Remember, I am armed."

"Mudfoot will ban you if you shoot us."

"Won't even serve you takeout."

"Never mind then. I'd rather eat his vittles than Allison run for president anyway."

MJ was grinning. "I'm picturing the two of you, newly retired, wild as March hares, collecting misdemeanors at protests across the country. It makes no sense that you got together, one a radical activist, the other ready to join the police force."

"We both wanted to do right by the world in our own ways."

"And you have," said MJ. "Vonnie told me Berry's always been keen to hand over the reins of the Center to the women who use it," said MJ. "When that happens and Berry leaves, Vonnie won't be far behind."

"Before anyone retires, I need to get myself in gear to visit my wacky pops if I want to see him alive—or dead. He wants his ashes spread near Momma. Used to be, he swore he'd be buried under a brand-new Beverage Bay. I don't know who I miss more, Pops or Gran. Guess I loved one as much as the other."

"It's rough being middle-aged, people dying on you in the middle of your own midlife crises," MJ said.

"Is that what we are, middle-aged baby boomers?" Cullie asked.

They looked at one another with big scared eyes.

"'Course not," said Jaudon.

Cullie agreed. "Naw."

MJ laid a napkin over the last fried shrimp in her basket. "Where did you say that fitness place is located?"

Chapter Thirty-eight

Berry Garland

"Berry—come watch your sister be arrested on the news."

She slammed the dryer door shut and hurried to Jaudon in the living room.

"Gracious sakes," said Berry. In the video, Opal was wrangling with two hospital security guards, stabbing at them with the pointed wooden stake attached to a sign warning about the wrath of God.

Berry puffed out her lips and hissed a breath. "She's worse than a disagreeable yellow jacket in an outhouse. I seesaw between the sadness of losing Gran and anger at my sister and her religious rabble. The conflict between emotions is worse than Hurricane Charley."

Jaudon's eyes were fixed on the TV. "We lucked out when Charley veered east last month—high winds and rain, was all there was to it. Florida sure has had a time this year with hurricanes."

"Don't forget the beautiful live oak that blew over and blocked Eulalia Road for two days. They say it was over a hundred years old."

"I fault the county for messing with the land near that tree when they cleared the way for more houses. They had no call to let people build there." She pointed at the TV screen. "Will you look at that— Opal sank her teeth into the cop's hand. She's going to be tased if she doesn't give it up."

As more police officers arrived, additional protestors surged around Opal to protect her. A news helicopter covered the commotion from above.

Berry shook her head in slow motion, tsking like Gran used to. "Wait and see, my sister won't let go. She gives me the jitters."

A reporter narrated the action as the police officer gave up on dragging her away and hit and prodded Opal everywhere he found access with his collapsible baton.

Jaudon said, "She's about as useful to her cause as a drum with a hole in it."

"There's Klem, calling her off. She obeys him like she's a pet dog."

"Don't look anymore, Berry. The cop's hand is covered in blood."

Berry inhaled with shock to see a close-up of Opal's savaged face.

"Looks like hospitals won't abide batty militants like my sister. She may think her agitation is beneficial, but she's leading a crusade against women, not for. What if these deranged people and their followers take over our country?"

"That'd be putting ugly on an angel."

"Hitler did it."

"But this is America."

"Where people elect movie stars for president, no one is powerful enough to tax the rich the way they ought to be, and ministers tell their congregations how to vote."

"Like who?"

"Mike Huckabee over in Arkansas for one."

"That jerk," Jaudon said. "The store radio was broadcasting sugarcoated lies from one of those megachurches—the one over yonder. If the congregation is anything like your sister's, that's a lot of people voting with her."

Berry sat in Gran's recliner. "This is a whole lot bigger than our fledgling Tommie Center, isn't it? Should I have dreamed bigger? I don't see an end to conflict on this earth, whether it's war between nations, between religions, or our tussle with my sister's ministry. What are we going to do, Jaudon?"

"Keep moving forward, doing our bit, accepting what we can't change while you reach more patients for the Center, inspire others to follow your success, refuse to give up. If they break something, we'll fix it, if they hurt more of us and the cops do nothing, we'll sue them and make a lot of noise when we do."

The police were taking Opal away, Klem on his phone behind her, in all likelihood calling ministry lawyers.

She thought to herself, what would Gran do? She'd gently remind Berry that Opal had her own Great Spirit standing by, hoping to be called on for help. "You're right," she said to Jaudon. "It's a waste of our time engaging with these paid or deluded protestors. We can use that energy to sing our own praises. If a megachurch can buy time on local radio and TV, we can too. We'll create programs in the schools, show up at city and county meetings, give interviews to the papers."

"In your nonexistent spare time. It's a consolation we didn't bring kids into this world of upside-down priorities. Opal could be using her get-up-and-go to feed the kids we already have. That's a positive way to make a difference. How about we connect with other groups trying to broaden, not shrink, lives. We can take over the bandstand with our common songs."

"I can't think where to start."

Jaudon looked at the ceiling for a couple of minutes while Berry settled herself.

"MJ's niece Patsy Beaudry volunteered at the food bank the week after she arrived, together with training at VONCO and starting college. We need more like her."

Jaudon gave a vigorous nod. "Patsy gets things done faster than a sneeze through a screen door. Doesn't look a bit like her aunt, though."

"MJ bragged that Patsy's always declaring herself done with one mission and asking for the next."

"Just like MJ. Once Patsy's trained, what about asking her to link up the Tommie Center with women's shelters and children's advocacy groups? You wanted to get that done."

Jaudon spread her fingers and counted off. "What were the chances, in their tiny town, of MJ's first girlfriend catching on that Patsy was gay, then drafting her computer-savvy son to track MJ, then passing letters and airfare to fly Patsy here."

"MJ would put the girl through college full-time, but Patsy is more concerned about earning her keep."

"Pops promised to bring my niece Miki one of these days, but the snows always come sooner than he can get over those mountains to the airport. Bat says the arthritis pain is too bad for Pops to travel in any case. On the phone, Miki was gung-ho about finding work on the water."

Berry laughed softly. "It's like your *Star Trek* show—Patsy's the next generation. Miki too."

"She'll have to be Xena, Warrior Princess to change the world—if that's even possible."

Berry lamented, "It may not be. The Moral Majority, war after war, 9/11, none of our terrors are going away soon. They'll take different shapes."

"Despite it all, I'm taking you to bed this minute, my Georgia gal. I have a need to love you up after this talk of gloom and doom."

Jaudon insisted on showering first. She strode into Berry's room without a stitch of clothing on, just a wet towel around her neck. For the first time in their lives, they shared the house with no one. No more lights out for them either—they knew the inside and out of each other's bodies. Jaudon launched herself at her goal, and her tongue and hands took over.

"You, you," she said, swiveling on the bed to reach Jaudon with her mouth, her fingers. What mattered was her lover's pleasure, and with it came her own—once, twice, a third time with Jaudon kneeling over her, a hand filling her, a nipple between Jaudon's lips, almost a bite.

"No more," she said, catching her breath.

Not wholly recovered, but anxious to arouse her Jaudon, she teased her with her fingers.

When Jaudon said Berry's name, she knew that was always the moment to stay with Jaudon's most sensitive spot, harder, faster, side to side with a thumb, a knuckle, her fingertips. Jaudon had to work for it, silently, for a single go, but the way she gathered Berry in her arms afterward, sometimes tearily, saying *I love I love you I love you*, two beings could not be more entangled.

Jaudon pulled herself to the top of the bed using her elbows. Berry's head had settled between their two pillows, eyes closed, breathing fast. Jaudon's head came to rest on her shoulder, and she laid a tender hand on Berry's breast.

"It's always like the first time, isn't it?" Berry said.

Jaudon loosened her embrace. "We never imagined we'd be doing this at age fifty-three."

"Let's keep on for the rest of our lives."

"A slew of more lifetimes is more like it." Jaudon looked at her hand. "If this arthritis doesn't interfere."

"Those precious hands. You think we'll retire, not die on our feet?"

"We'll have our fill of hard work one of these days, Ber. Go touring out west like MJ and Vonnie did. They retraced their steps back to Rainbow Gap none the worse for wear. Pops said to use cash from the sale of his Sun City house to visit him."

Berry knew her tell-all eyes were full of excitement. Jaudon hadn't exactly deprived her of this kind of travel. She didn't want to leave the Center any more than Jaudon believed the stores could survive without her, even though she had Vonnie and Dr. Garza, and Jaudon had Olive and Stacey A. Ponder. "What about the stores? You won't leave Florida."

"I don't think about leaving Florida except when an alligator makes its way onto somebody's porch or worse." Jaudon held out a knobby knuckle and misshapen thumb from the time a case of beers fell on her hand. "We need these hands, this spine, these legs more than a stack of milk crates in a cooler does."

She changed positions and burrowed into Jaudon's arms like the young girl she'd once been, well before they understood the word sex, much less homosexual. Wriggling a hand between Jaudon's legs, she stroked her inner thigh. "What'll you do with yourself? Your whole life is work."

"I see lots to do—fixing up the place, helping you in the garden. We'll take some rides, find what's left of old Florida, take in a Florida-Georgia home football game. In season, I'll drag an old table out by the roadside here, sell fresh strawberries, pecans, cold sweet sun tea in Dixie cups. Remember grafting from MJ's pecan tree outside that first fixer-upper she bought by Little Rooster Lake? I'd like to pick the pecans now to sell to passersby on Eulalia Road. We can take cuttings from our potted plants to sell—for the fun of it, and for gifts, not the money."

She watched Jaudon. "You'd sell the stores?"

Jaudon's face twitched like it did when the heartburn pained her. "The most recent out-of-left-field offer I got was enough to keep us, Bat, and Pops not rich, but comfortable and secure."

"We didn't imagine, when we played in the tree house, what we'd accomplish. It must be tempting to sell."

"Not yet. It's not tempting yet, despite the challenges to retail food when takeovers are in full swing. The big chains swallow up the next size down, until a hedge fund with nothing to do with food buys the bloated chains and more than half the time runs them into the ground. Plus, I try to keep prices down, but my overhead keeps going up."

"I'd like to hear the other challenges, but whatever you're doing with your thigh is distracting."

She let Jaudon lay her down and sweep her fingers over Berry's soft triangle of hair. "You're mighty wet for a middle-ager."

"I did lubricate a little, but it mostly has something to do with the woman I love."

Chapter Thirty-nine

Jaudon Vicker

October 2004

It was only because Pops had done it, flown in a plane, that she let herself be persuaded and packed his old grip. In the end, the experience bored her, especially the long lines through security. The four of them might have had more fun, seen more of the country, if they'd driven, but this time away from the stores was long enough. She recognized signs that Berry worried about the Center surviving for a week without her too, but both of their staffs knew their business.

And Leslie Gardner had returned to work. Berry said she'd sat in the waiting area of the Tommie Center until the last patient left, then asked the temp on reception if Berry was available. True to herself, Berry embraced her.

"That woman swore she never took steroids," Leslie had complained to Berry, "but she lied."

In the time they lived together on the edge of Milwaukee, the girlfriend picked fights, cursed at Leslie, and on the last night, hit her. Leslie said her fist was like a sledgehammer. "She could have been killed, or lost an eye, her teeth."

Jaudon wasn't sure what to think. "So, you forgave her."

"I pulled a gel pack from the freezer and held it to bruises that hadn't even turned yellow yet. The girlfriend left Leslie cowering under their bed and went out for beers with the other powerlifters. Leslie took the money she found in the flat, her clothes, bathroom supplies, food, and drove south in her little Canary pickup truck, practicing apologies to all of us. Milwaukee was too cold for her, even in October, in too many ways after the years with her Rainbow Gap family."

It was a last bit of drama they hadn't needed, but Leslie's reappearance, as always, came in the nick of time. She was staying at their place while she looked for a rental and was their transportation to the airport today.

Jaudon hadn't quite forgiven Leslie, but knew she would. Berry explained that Leslie had been convinced the girlfriend was her last chance at love.

"Jiminy. We love her more than any ten weightlifters."

She'd already put Leslie to work as a roving trainee at the Beverage Bays while Vonnie, at Berry's insistence, sought money enough to hire Leslie as her assistant at the Tommie Center. Berry had been of the opinion that the girlfriend was too rough around the edges for Leslie and was uneasy the whole time the two younger women were together. Leslie's return was a happy relief.

For Mrs. Berry Garland-Vicker, Jaudon reminded herself. They were flying to Boston and driving from there to Provincetown to be married. A bubble of anticipation washed through her and came close to drowning the prickles of fear. They might have to pay someday because they claimed their rights today.

MJ told them she planned to take Vonnie's surname, glad to be rid of a piece of a past that was never legitimately hers. She said, according to Patsy, Bo Beaudry was right about one thing: He was not her father. She had no idea who was. Patsy was a genuine Beaudry and, as long as she hid her girlfriend, got along fine with the family. Patsy planned to get an answer about MJ's real father next time she called home. Jaudon had been there the first time they met and saw Patsy's double take at sight of her aunt. The kid was still trying to remember who MJ reminded her of in Depot Landing.

They landed at Logan with a thud. She was scared silly. She had no faith that the plane's screeching brakes would ever stop them. She stopped herself from singing out the word *hallelujah* as she set foot on solid ground—well, as solid as this huge terminal should be. They'd heard news stories about shoddy construction and corrupt politicians here in Boston.

MJ, Vonnie, and Berry laughed and chattered as they trudged a thousand miles to baggage claim. Vonnie and Berry had come through their storms happy as two possums eating sweet taters. She used the time to check in with Olive about the stores and registered a minor disappointment when there was zero for her to fix long distance.

Rigo and Jimmy Neal had invited them to their Provincetown wedding. Those two flew north in June, fitted with white suits. In the photographs they sent, both wore lavender veils. Their example was what it took to inspire the women.

"This is corny," Jaudon said.

Vonnie looked at her skeptically. "Since when is marriage corny? Nisa said it was the best day of her life."

"It's old-timey, don't you think? I mean, a piece of paper can't make Berry and me more married."

Their baggage claim carousel clanged its readiness and began circling.

"But," Berry said, "you asked me to marry you how many times?"

"A thousand?"

"Didn't you mean it?" Vonnie asked.

"You two have me snarled up."

"There's your suitcase."

She hurried to snag it and Berry's, right behind. MJ waited at the mouth of the carousel, empty-handed.

Vonnie explained that MJ was more long-suffering than Jaudon, open to put up with wedding rituals and frills, which weren't adequate to express the depth of emotions that led to marriage.

Berry confided, "Jaudon isn't someone who cares for ceremony ordinarily."

"I surely do not."

MJ found the last suitcases, and they caught a shuttle to the car rental office. MJ rented a roomy GMC Envoy to drive to Provincetown, where they'd establish residency before their big beautiful day.

The road to Cape Cod took them within sight of downtown Boston's bland whitish-blue skyline, and she surprised herself when she agreed to return—Berry confided she'd always wanted to follow the Freedom Trail.

The Mid-Cape Highway toward the tip of the Cape displayed the occasional dramatic color of early turning leaves. Nevertheless, Jaudon snoozed until they reached Route 6A in Truro and the honest to goodness New England shoreline.

Berry had already sent a thank-you note to Chief Justice Margaret Marshall, who had written the opinion legalizing gay marriage in

Massachusetts that May. She wished Gran was there to stand up for them.

One of Olive's sisters was in a quilting group. Olive bought a homemade wedding band quilt from a member of the group, and Jaudon cried with surprise and gratitude when Olive presented it to them. Berry threw her arms around Jaudon's friend.

MJ brought Hop, the childhood stuffed rabbit she was given as an infant. "Hop's our witness from home. Patsy refused to leave school and work to come with us."

Vonnie swung her hip against MJ's. "Patsy's not exactly your doppelganger, but she works as hard as you ever did."

"It's conceivable all of it was worthwhile," mused MJ, who had pulled off the road to admire the view. "Very likely I had to live through the hard knocks in order to give Patsy a kick start, a taste of acceptance, and exposure to choices she didn't have in Depot Landing."

MJ had flown Patsy to Florida. Patsy's father, who had successfully revived the Beaudry Pump business his father abandoned, was eager to pay college costs. Several years ago, MJ and Vonnie bought and rehabbed a neat white bungalow and dock on the channel in front of them. They'd been using it as a vacation rental cash cow but decided to forgo the extra income and rent it to Patsy. While Vonnie and MJ were away, Patsy guarded and tended their home.

Cottage after cottage lined the two-lane road, interrupted by motels designed to resemble the white-painted, dark-shuttered style that surrounded them. Vonnie had rented a condo, but they went directly to the town hall, a half hour before it closed. They were there to fill out Notices of Intention of Marriage, which had to be completed three days or more before the ceremonies.

The Town Clerk gave them guides and wished them a happy Women's Week and very gay weddings.

"What will we do for three days?" Jaudon asked once they'd unpacked in their rooms and were seated at a restaurant close by. "Go someplace?"

Vonnie laughed. "We *are* someplace. This is a destination site. Smell the ocean air. Briny, isn't it? Not like our coast where the smell of sun-heated sand hits you first."

"We'll rent bikes and explore the dunes," said MJ.

Berry told Jaudon she'd signed them up for a whale watching jaunt.

"I wish Cullie and Allison were here for that," Jaudon said. "Allison lecturing us on how to save the whales and Cullie up there with the captain, steering us wrong. Those two are hitched but not churched."

Eyebrows knitted in sadness, Berry said, "Cullie couldn't walk very far along the big wharf or stay upright on a boat. She's got to hurt most of the time."

"Not that she'll admit it," MJ said.

They agreed to visit the gay beach, though it was likely few people would be there this time of year.

"And there are dozens of shops to dip into," Vonnie said. "For souvenirs."

At the mention of shops, Jaudon asked, "Is there a drive-through store around here?"

"Massachusetts has drive-through package stores—liquor stores. One of our medical assistants is from here and gave me a quick lesson on the state's quirks. She didn't know of any grocery drive-throughs on Cape Cod."

"Would you settle for a walk-in convenience store?" said MJ.

Berry started a list of kitchen supplies on a scrap of paper from her purse. "We need a trip to a full-sized grocery store first."

"Why?" asked Jaudon. "This is a honeymoon. We're not cooking."

MJ agreed. "We have a week to sample the local fare. Three meals a day, three different restaurants a day."

"There are two florist shops in this guide the Town Clerk gave us," Vonnie reported. "We need to put orders in—boutonnieres for you and MJ, corsages for Berry and me."

"What colors?" asked Berry.

"It depends on what they can offer us."

Berry leaned to Jaudon and gave her a kiss on the cheek. "I never thought I'd see this day. I'm embarrassed. People devoted their lives to marriage equality and we've done…What?"

"Showed them what we're made of as model community members and professionals?" Vonnie suggested.

Jaudon's tone was defensive. "We send money to Equality Florida year in and year out."

"Still," said Berry, "once we're retired, I want to be more politically active."

MJ perused the Women's Week flyer. "There are too many

restaurants to sample in one trip—this is amazing. Is every one of these entertainers a lesbian? We have our choice of comedy shows, concerts, films."

Jaudon watched two women walk by hand in hand. "Have we landed smack-dab in Dyketown?"

"You remember how afraid you used to be to say the word *lesbian*?" MJ said, laying an arm across her shoulders. "And now you actually speak the word *dyke* out loud."

She shouted, "Dyke!" and her friends applauded. Across the street another woman raised her voice, echoing the word.

They passed the flyer around. Vonnie joked, "The whole town is here to celebrate our weddings."

"Will we have to invite them all?" she whined, grumpily self-conscious after her shout.

Berry gave her a fretful look. "Don't be silly. If we meet some nice gals, though, I wouldn't mind a couple of them as our witnesses."

They did meet women, lots of them. On the whale watching boat, they drifted into comfortable conversation with two long-term couples from Bloomingdale, New Jersey. One pair consisted of two nurses. The others owned a bookkeeping business. She was so excited to meet them she lost her peevishness and spontaneously invited the four to their weddings as witnesses. Vonnie upped their orders for corsages and boutonnieres. MJ did the same with the reservation for their wedding dinner. Both New Jersey couples claimed Ptown as their second home—they visited two weeks a year. With the wedding the next day, they played tour guides for the betrothed Floridians and joined them for dinner at a Spanish restaurant out Shank Painter Road.

Jaudon came down sick that night. She curled up on the cool bathroom floor between bouts of voiding. She had no fever, though she shook with chills.

Berry was clearly beside herself with worry and had exhausted her diagnostic skills without the tools she needed. She'd called MJ who, in turn, picked up the nurse couple. One was a retired Army medic and brought the emergency trauma kit she always carried in their car.

Based on her vitals, and except for the digestive symptoms, the nurses said Jaudon would be fine by morning, once her system finished cleaning itself out. An ingredient in the paella she'd had for dinner might not have befriended her.

"It's true she never had paella before," Berry said. "I sampled it and found it heavy on the saffron."

"I smelled that spice from the end of the table," said Vonnie. "They were very generous with it."

MJ added, "It's supposed to be the most expensive spice in the world."

"So, an intolerance to an untried spice? A bad mussel?" the ex-medic mused aloud. "Let's see if she can keep down sips of water to rehydrate."

"We've come too many years and too many miles for Jaudon to miss today. She'll rally for the weddings." Berry met the eyes of the other nurse and saw that she, too, was concerned it might be much worse.

By then, it was three a.m., and they were supposed to meet the nondenominational minister at two p.m. Jaudon was tucked into bed and kept the water down. Berry set the alarm for sips on the half hour.

Sure enough, by the time they met with the woman minister on the beach at low tide, Jaudon, pale and weak with hunger, after saltines for breakfast lest she ruin the happiest day of their lives, stood tall, unable not to smile, Berry's arm under hers. Strangers stopped to watch, with their own smiles and wishes of luck and happiness. MJ pointed out that the sky was cloudless.

Vonnie and MJ's ceremony was first. Vonnie, in a short, breezy, tunic style dress with an African-inspired pattern, called MJ resplendent. MJ wore a black faux-leather blazer over a gray cashmere turtleneck and slim white pants. MJ pulled Vonnie in close after they said their vows and announced their new legal names: Vonnie and MJ Lowe. "I'll go by MJ Lowe from now on, thank you very much. It's about time I ditched my false father's name."

Berry squeezed Jaudon's hand with the regularity of a granddaddy clock and looked misty-eyed. Jaudon's easy tears were in free fall. She honked into the bandanna from her rear pocket.

"Sorry," she said.

Berry patted her on the knee. "My heart is beating so fast."

After congratulations and hugs and a confused late delivery of a rainbow of balloons, it was their turn. Berry was in a classy periwinkle suit that showed off the mature curves and swells that turned Jaudon into a love pudding. She, in turn, was in navy blue pants, vest, a ruffled white shirt and, gifted by Cullie and Allison—Allison didn't believe in marriage for themselves—a pair of rainbow cufflinks.

She whispered to Berry, "It sure is a relief not to have anyone gunning for us here."

Lightheaded to start with, as they walked the few steps to the minister, Jaudon covered her mouth to burp and tasted acrid green-pepper fumes. Maybe it wasn't the saffron at all, she thought and inhaled with her nose, exhaled through her mouth. Was it fear of marriage? What in heck did she have to be scared of? Rogue elements making lists of married gay couples to hunt down? Up to the last minute, she had suspected someone would take their legitimacy away, keep this marvel from them.

Berry always knew when Jaudon seemed off. They went through the ceremony side by side, arms interlinked to steady Jaudon, and followed their short scripts to the letter. Once they'd kissed and been swarmed by their old and new friends, Jaudon stood alone and watched the happiness their unions engendered. She imagined herself a hummingbird, almost lighter than air, as relief replaced the menacing saffron-tainted fear that had sickened her. She put aside thoughts of mortality and loss, of mortality and the perils that awaited their own bodies and those of their friends.

At long last she and Berry were safe—weren't they? With their marriage license, they were safe from being forcefully parted, were official in legal documents, had joint ownership of their lives, their home. It didn't matter what the State of Florida or the federal government said or did—they had the choice to pack up and relocate up north till death did them part.

The minister took pictures of and with the newlyweds. MJ clasped hands with Jaudon and pranced her around in a quick, joyous two-person reel.

Jaudon hadn't expected the rip current of emotions that barreled up to her. She was elated, but it was sad Gran hadn't lived long enough to see Berry marry. It stung that Pops expressed no interest in her wedding. He said his body pained him too much to fly. She guessed men didn't think of sending cards. Not straight men. Jimmy Neal and Rigo had presented them with a no-limit gift card to the boys' favorite restaurant, Bayside Betsy's on Commercial Street, and insisted they order the warm berry crisps for dessert.

She was famished by the time they were seated, and she checked the menu right away to ensure no dishes were flavored with saffron or peppers. The thought of New England seafood made her stomach cringe. She ordered fried chicken, though she didn't hold out much hope that Yankees would do it right. Bayside Betsy herself came to their table with congratulation cards from the boys.

It was quarter to four on a sunny Sunday, the tenth of October 2004, their wedding day. She stared at an empty table, bowled over by the momentousness of the times. Her sudden illness had passed, along with her confounding fear. There was no Momma to rule her, no Gran to console her, and Pops had gone off to live a second life. Fleetingly, her unyielding sense of abandonment and ineptness vanished. People her age ran the show now, herself included. That was enough to terrify anyone. She was a fifty-three-year-old business owner, yet in marrying Berry, it seemed like from sundown last night until this minute, she'd passed into true adulthood.

Berry drew closer on the cushioned bench. They tilted their heads till they touched and held hands. Jiminy—if they weren't the eighth wonder of the world, she couldn't say what was.

About the Author

Lee Lynch was born in the Hell's Kitchen neighborhood of New York City, many years later moving to the sticks. *A Magnificent Disturbance* is the third book of her queer family saga. Bold Strokes Books has published her award-winning works *Beggar of Love*, *The Raid*, *An American Queer*, *Rainbow Gap*, and *Accidental Desperados*. Her novel *The Swashbuckler* received the inaugural Golden Crown Literary Society Lee Lynch Classic Award. Other awards include The James Duggins Mid-Career Novelist Award. She has been chronicling lesbian life since *The Ladder* magazine in the 1960s.

Books Available From Bold Strokes Books

A Conflict of Interest by Morgan Adams. Tensions rise when a one-night stand becomes a major conflict of interest between an up-and-coming senior associate and a dedicated cardiac surgeon. (978-1-63679-870-7)

A Magnificent Disturbance by Lee Lynch. These everyday dykes and their friends will stop at nothing to see the women's clinic thrive and, in the process, their ideals, their wounds, and a steadfast allegiance to one another make them heroes. (978-1-63679-031-2)

Big Corpse on Campus by Karis Walsh. When University Police Officer Cappy Flannery investigates what looks like a clear-cut suicide, she discovers that the case—and her feelings for librarian Jazz—are more complicated than she expected. (978-1-63679-852-3)

Charity Case by Jean Copeland. Bad girl Lindsay Chase came home to Connecticut for a fresh start, but an old, risky habit provides the chance to save the day for her new love, Ellie. (978-1-63679-593-5)

Moments to Treasure by Ali Vali. Levi Montbard and Yasmine Hassani have found a vast Templar treasure, but there is much more to the story—and what is left to be found. (978-1-63679-473-0)

The Stolen Girl by Cari Hunter. Detective Inspector Jo Shaw is determined to prove she's fit for work after an injury that almost killed her, but a new case brings her up against people who will do anything to preserve their own interests, putting Jo—and those closest to her—directly in the line of fire. (978-1-63679-822-6)

Discovering Gold by Sam Ledel. In 1920s Colorado, a single mother and a rowdy cowgirl must set aside their fears and initial reservations about one another if they want to find love in the mining town each of them calls home. (978-1-63679-786-1)

Dream a Little Dream by Melissa Brayden. Savanna can't believe it when Dr. Kyle Remington, the woman who left her feeling like a fool, shows up in Dreamer's Bay. Life is too complicated for second chances. Or is it? (978-1-63679-839-4)

Emma by the Sea by Sarah G. Levine. A delightful modern-day romance inspired by *Emma*, one of Jane Austen's most beloved novels. (978-1-63679-879-0)

Goodbye Hello by Heather K O'Malley. With so much time apart and the challenges of a long-distance relationship, Kelly and Teresa's second chance at love may end just as awkwardly as the first. (978-1-63679-790-8)

One Measure of Love by Annie McDonald. Vancouver's hit competitive cooking show *Recipe for Success* has begun filming its second season, and two talented young chefs are desperate for more than a winning dish. (978-1-63679-827-1)

The Smallest Day by J.M. Redmann. The first bullet missed—can Micky Knight stop the second bullet from finding its target? (978-1-63679-854-7)

To Please Her by Elena Abbott. A spilled coffee leads Sabrina into a world of erotic BDSM that may just land her the love of her life. (978-1-63679-849-3)

Two Weddings and a Funeral by Claudia Parr. Stella and Theo have spent the last thirteen years pretending they can be just friends, but surely "just friends" don't make out every chance they get. (978-1-63679-820-2)

Firecamp by Jaycie Morrison. Going their separate ways seemed inevitable for two people as different as Fallon and Nora, while meeting up again is strictly coincidental. (978-1-63679-753-3)

Coming Up Clutch by Anna Gram. College softball star Kelly "Razor" Mitchell hung up her cleats early, but when former crush, now coach Ashton Sharpe shows up on her doorstep seven years later, beautiful as ever, Razor hopes the longing in her gaze has nothing to do with softball. (978-1-63679-817-2)

Fixed Up by Aurora Rey. When electrician Jack Barrow and artist Ellie Lancaster get stuck on a job site during a blizzard, close quarters send all sorts of sparks flying. (978-1-63679-788-5)

Stranded by Ronica Black. Can Abigail and Whitley overcome their personal hang-ups and stubbornness to survive not only Alaska but a dangerous stalker as well? (978-1-63679-761-8)

Whisk Me Away by Georgia Beers. Regan's a gorgeous flake. Ava, a beautiful untouchable ice queen. When they meet again at a retreat for up-and-coming pastry chefs, the competition, and the ovens, heat up. (978-1-63679-796-0)

Across the Enchanted Border by Crin Claxton. Magic, telepathy, swordsmanship, tyranny, and tenderness abound in a tale of two lands separated by the enchanted border. (978-1-63679-804-2)

Deep Cover by Kara A. McLeod. Running from your problems by pretending to be someone else only works if the person you're pretending to be doesn't have even bigger problems. (978-1-63679-808-0)

Good Game by Suzanne Lenoir. Even though Lauren has sworn off dating gamers, it's becoming hard to resist the multifaceted Sam. An opposites attract lesbian romance. (978-1-63679-764-9)

Innocence of the Maiden by Ileandra Young. Three powerful women. Two covens at war. One horrifying murder. When mighty and powerful witches begin to butt heads, who out there is strong enough to mediate? (978-1-63679-765-6)

Protection in Paradise by Julia Underwood. When arson forces them together, the flames between chief of police Eve Maguire and librarian Shaye Hayden aren't that easy to extinguish. (978-1-63679-847-9)

Too Forward by Krystina Rivers. Just as professional basketball player Jane May's career finally starts heating up, a new relationship with her team's brand consultant could derail the success and happiness she's struggled so long to find. (978-1-63679-717-5)

Worth Waiting For by Kristin Keppler. For Peyton and Hanna, reliving the past is painful, but looking back might be the only way to move forward. (978-1-63679-773-1)

All For Her: Forbidden Romance Novellas by Gun Brooke, J.J. Hale & Aurora Rey. Explore the angst and excitement of forbidden love few would dare in this heart-stopping novella collection. (978-1-63679-713-7)

Finding Harmony by CF Frizzell. Rock star Harper Cushing has to rearrange her grandmother's future and sell the family store out from under her, but she reassesses everything because Gram's helper, Frankie, could be offering the harmony her heart has been missing. (978-1-63679-741-0)

Gaze by Kris Bryant. Love at first sight is for dreamers, but the more time Lucky and Brianna spend together, the more they realize the chemistry of a gaze can make anything possible. (978-1-63679-711-3)

Laying of Hands by Patricia Evans. The mysterious new writing instructor at camp makes Grace Waters brave enough to wonder what would happen if she dared to write her own story. (978-1-63679-782-3)

The Naked Truth by Sandy Lowe. How far are Rowan and Genevieve willing to go and how much will they risk to make their most captivating and forbidden fantasies a reality? (978-1-63679-426-6)

The Roommate by Claire Forsythe. Jess Black's boyfriend is handsome and successful. That's why it comes as a shock when she meets a woman on the train who makes her pulse race. (978-1-63679-757-1)

The Blessed by Anne Shade. Layla and Suri are brought together by fate to defeat the darkness threatening to tear their world apart. What they don't expect to discover is a love that might set them free. (978-1-63679-715-1)

Seducing the Widow by Jane Walsh. Former rival debutantes have a second chance at love after fifteen years apart when a spinster persuades her ex-lover to help save her family business. (978-1-63679-747-2)

www.ingramcontent.com/pod-product-compliance
Lightning Source LLC
Chambersburg PA
CBHW032209030726
47494CB00020B/933